Little Mink got to his feet. He was going to die.

The thought was crystal clear, shimmering in his mind. And now, all of a sudden, the terrible fear left him. So he was going to die. So was that so bad? No. When it became an established fact, you stopped fighting against it, and then all at once it wasn't so bad any more.

Not as bad as you'd thought ...

Charles Boeckman (sometimes working under the byline "Charles Beckman, Jr.") started writing in 1945 and never stopped. His stories about sad people lashing out at their dreary existance brought action and pathos to publications like ***Alfred Hitchcok's Mystery Magazine****,* ***Manhunt****, and* ***Pursuit****. He combines his interests in jazz and crime in the stories selected for this volume.*

To learn more about the author, see the "About the Author" section at the back of this book, or read the author's website: **www.charlesboeckman.com**

Rich Harvey, Design
Audrey Parente, Editor

ISBN-13: 978-1508671220
ISBN-10: 1508671222
Retail cover price $16.95

Printed and bound in the United States.
10 9 8 7 6 5 4 3 2 1

Published by Bold Venture Press
www.boldventurepress.com

Strictly Poison

and other stories

Charles Boeckman

CONTENTS

CONTENTS

For my grandsons,
Jayden And Micah

ACKNOWLEDGEMENTS

My thanks to my lovely wife, Patti, for the long hours of hard work she put into the publication of this book. I can write the stories, but it took her dedication to the task of putting this manuscript together, one story at a time, to ready it for the final layout.

Thanks to Heather for her skills and equipment to scan the printed stories into editable copy.

Strictly Poison

LITTLE Mink had not known what it would be like to be actually snake-bitten. He had dreamed about it lots of times and awakened in a tangle of bedclothes, his pointed little weasel face bathed in sweat, his popeyes staring frightenedly at the hotel room ceiling.

Next to big Joe Decasso, there was nothing Little Mink feared more than snakes. Mostly, he had put Big Joe first because Joe was concrete and present, towering over him, browbeating and ordering him around all day, making him do the menial dirty tasks. So far the snakes came to him only when he slept. But ever since he saw that one in the Chicago zoo, he had been plenty scared of the snakes, too,

And now he had actually been bitten by one. A writhing, slimy, grey diamondback rattler, as thick as his wrist. Two tiny fang punctures on his hairy pipe-stem leg just above the ankle attested to the fact.

He stared at the already swelling spot, his eyes bulging. A whimper croaked out of his pigeon breast and he sucked in a gasp. "J-Joe!" His voice went up, high-pitched and shrill like a woman's. "Joe, it bit me! That snake! Joe, I'm bit…"

"Shut up, you damn little fool!" Big Joe's face was shiny with perspiration. He was so worried he neglected for once to follow up his impatient command with a kick. "It bit me, too—first."

The big man stood swaying in the deserted, tumbled-down shack, staring through the acrid revolver smoke at the dead snake. His bullets had cut it to shreds. It had been coiled under the rusty wood stove. He'd reached down, and it had hit him on the forearm, and when he'd shaken it off, it whipped into a coil and hooked Little Mink's leg in a flash. Little Mink had danced around howling while Joe dragged out his revolver and shot it.

Little Mink whimpered again. "What—what we gonna do, Joe? Huh, Joe?"

Joe drew his left hand across his mouth, smearing the saliva that had gathered in a corner across his cheek. He put the revolver back in his shoulder holster. "Do?" He looked at Little Mink vacantly. Then slow, gathering rage narrowed his eyes. "You little rat. You ignorant, little bad-luck rat. This shack would be a good place to hide, you said?"

Mink cringed into a corner, stumbling over a broken chair, pushing back into the cobwebs. "No, Joe," he begged. "Not now. We're dyin'. Don't you know? We're gonna d—"

Joe hit him hard. He used his flat hand and slapped Mink until the little man's teeth popped. Then, spent and panting, he stopped. Something akin to the fear in Mink's eyes crept into his own.

"We gotta get outta here," he muttered. "Yeah, fast. Get to a doc in town. We can do it. We'll have to do it on foot, but we can do it."

Mink crept hopefully out of the corner. Joe told him to pick up the black satchel which held the money they'd stolen from the bank three hours ago. Then Joe stumbled outside, and Mink scurried after him, limping on his throbbing leg.

OUTSIDE, the Texas morning was still warm and beautiful. A mockingbird sang off in the mesquite clump near the creek. All around Joe and Mink the post oaks, the tangles of grapevines accented the wildness. They were in the sandhills, an untamed, unclaimed part of Texas. A part of Texas a man could get lost in, and never be found.

A good part, though, to hide in. The pursuing Highway patrol had shot the tires off their car down on the main road two hours before.

They'd skidded up a country lane, and gone on the rims a piece before the sand got too deep. Then they had run on foot. A close call, but they had gotten away.

If it hadn't been for the snake.

"You damn little rat!" Joe repeated, plowing into the underbrush. He cursed Little Mink in a steady stream.

Mink was silent, thinking about dying. It wasn't as if he'd chosen this kind of life, he thought.

He'd grown up mostly in the city slums, but he'd of gone straight if it hadn't been for big Joe Decasso. Always there had been big Joe, bossing him around, scaring him into stealing for him. First fruit off stands, then bigger things.

Always Mink had to do the dirty work, while Joe stayed where it was safe and did the thinking.

"If I'd grown up here in Texas," Mink insisted to himself, "I mighta been a farmer. I like this kinda country where the air smells nice."

It didn't occur to Little Mink that he was praying. Praying for the first time in his life. Defending himself, trying to explain to the Deity that had put him on this earth why he had not turned out right.

He went right on.

If they hadn't put big Joe Decasso in the world at the same time they put him here, he mighta turned out all right.

Up ahead of him, big Joe stumbled for the first time. He fell in the sand, and stayed there for a moment, swaying on his hands and knees. Big Joe's forearm looked like a swollen, mottled sausage. Streaks were crossing his face, and he was purple around the lips. His throttled breath came in rasping, agonized gasps.

He stared at Mink.

Little Mink wasn't much better off. Pain raked up his leg in dull throbs, and increasing fever pounded the blood in his temples. He was crying, softly, to himself, drawing his coat sleeve across his eyes, his little weasely face screwed up.

"Gotta get to town," big Joe mumbled incoherently. "Y'hear that, y'sawed-off mouse? If we get to town, there'll be a doc. He can fix us up."

Big Joe lunged to his feet and plowed into the brush again. He reeled, cursing, from tree to tree, then he fell again. Little Mink helped him to his feet. They tried once more, and this time big Joe only made a few feet. This time he didn't get up any more. After a bit, he died there beside the trail. It was the first time Little Mink had ever seen anyone die from snake-bite.

Little Mink got to his feet. He was going to die.

The thought was crystal clear, shimmering in his mind. And now, all of a sudden, the terrible fear left him. So he was going to die. So was that so bad? No. When it became an established fact, you stopped fighting against it, and then all at once it wasn't so bad any more.

Not as bad as you'd thought.

But before Mink kicked off, there was something he had to do. This black satchel with the stolen bank money—Mink wanted to leave this world, square all the way round. Maybe he was still just scared, but he had a right to the feeling. He wanted to show them that Little Mink had only been a crook because big Joe Decasso and the breaks—and being scared—had made him one.

MAYBE if his mind had stayed clear, he wouldn't have made it. But the poison and excitement made him hysterical. He didn't remember anything of the next half hour. But all at once he broke out of a fringe of undergrowth, and there was the highway before him, a grey concrete ribbon winding down into the town nestling in the dusty valley, where he and big Joe had stolen the money.

There were lots of cars speeding back and forth, stirred up over the daylight robbery. After a while, someone noticed Little Mink sprawled beside the road, clutching the black leather bag. They picked him up. Mink regained consciousness, weakly, in the county jail, staring up at the sheriff's leathery face.

"I-I wanna confess," he whispered. "Me'n big Joe Decasso robbed the bank. Hid in hills…shack. Rattlesnake bit Joe first and then me. Joe died on the way to the road." He turned his pinched, ashen face toward the brick wall miserably. "Now lemme alone. I'm goin' out, too."

The sheriff shook his head and stood up. "Wish you were," he snorted. "Save the state about five years' room and board. But you big city boys don't know much about varmints. A rattlesnake just carries enough venom in its sac to kill one person. After it strikes once, it takes a while to secrete more. If the snake bit your friend first, there was just enough poison left to give you a little fever and make you sick."

Slowly, the words seeped into Mink's brain. Slowly, he realized what they meant. Big Joe Decasso was dead, and he was still alive. Five years or so in the pen and he'd be free. Free to walk the streets and do what he wanted to. Maybe come back here and open a little cigar stand on the corner. And there wouldn't ever be a Joe Decasso making him do the dirty work. Hell, he was alive, and. . .

"Yeah, Doc," the sheriff said out in the office a few minutes later when the physician arrived, "you better get in there. Snake musta had more poison left than we figgered. That crazy little loon just confessed to a robbery that will put him in jail for five years, and now he keeps hollering over and over, 'I'm free!'"

Should a Tear Be Shed?

You used to see this kid around the joints down on Bragow Street. Sometimes when the juke box was playing he'd start dancing, and the guys would stand around and watch him. Maybe they'd throw him a dime or a quarter.

He was just a ragged kid, cloudy between the ears, but he owned a pair of feet that tapped off rhythms like two metronomes. Because of that, everybody called him "Feet."

His real name was Lawrence Terrace, Jr., if you cared to go look it up.

Until Jess Norvell came along, Feet was nobody, understand, nobody. He never would have been anybody either because ever since that truck ran over him and hurt his head, his gears didn't mesh so good. Then, out of a clear sky, this big shot, Jess Norvell, became Feet's best friend.

It sure was the making of Feet, all right. Pretty soon he was dressing sharp and people were saying "Sir" to him. But nobody could figure it out, least of all Feet.

Why, Jess Norvell thought so much of Feet, he took out an insurance policy on the kid for fifty thousand dollars. You have to admit that's real friendship.

THE night it all started, Feet was down in this Bragow street joint dancing up a storm to the loud juke box. Some of the guys left the pool tables and stood around leaning on their cues, and the fellows from the bar came over with their drinks to watch.

About that time, Jess Norvell, two of his boys, and his girl friend, Candy Dreyer, walked into the place.

Jess and his party took a booth off by themselves and for a while. Jess didn't pay much attention to the kid's dancing. Feet was making so much noise, though, slapping his shoe soles against the creaking floor that you couldn't exactly ignore him. Jess finally got up and strolled over to the small crowd.

"Who's the skinny Bojangles?" Jess asked one of the guys.

"That's Feet," he was answered. "Young fellow hangs around the neighborhood."

Jess watched the young man go through his steps. The nickelodeon was thumping out a strong beat on Back Home in Indiana. Feet sure knew what to do with that rhythm. You had to give him that.

"Kid's got brains in his feet," the guy talking with Jess said. "Sure hasn't any upstairs." He made a significant circular motion with his forefinger pointing at his temple.

"Where's he live?" Jess wanted to know.

The man shrugged. "No place in particular. Wherever he can get a room for a coupla bucks a week. He ain't got any family."

Jess went back to his booth. The rest of the time they were in the place, Jess didn't talk to his girl. He sipped his drink thoughtfully and looked at Feet.

The kid danced until he was out of breath. He liked to give the people a good show for their money, but finally he was completely winded and had to stop.

The fellows watching him went back to the pool games and the bar. Feet picked up the coins they had thrown around his feet. He saw that it was over three dollars which was good because he hadn't had much to eat today, and he was kind of light in the head.

He started to walk out of the place then, but paused when he heard his name called. He looked around and saw a well-dressed man waving at him from a booth. Feet wiped his sleeve across his perspiring face, combed his hair in place with his fingers, and walked over to the booth.

When he got closer, he saw it was Jess Norvell. Feet knew that Jess must have an awful lot of money because he drove big cars with a lot of chromium on them, wore good-looking clothes, and always had a pretty girl with him.

The one with him tonight was the prettiest Feet had seen. She had hair the color of honey and large gray eyes. She was about his age, about twenty.

"Nice dancing, kid," Jess Norvell said.

Feet bowed politely. "Thanks, Mr. Norvell." He shuffled his feet a little, wishing he knew what to say. Ever since he'd had that accident with his head several years ago it was hard to think up words to say. So he always let his feet do his talking for him. Most of the time, there wasn't anybody to talk to, anyway. The fellows in the bars laughed at him and made jokes about him that he didn't understand. He'd just grin and pretend to understand what they were laughing at him about. At night there wasn't anybody to talk with, either. He'd usually go to bed in some room he'd rented and listen to the music from the juke boxes down on Bragow Street, and then he'd go to sleep and dream about the music. He wasn't ever really lonesome as long as he had the music to dream about and dance to. It was just that he couldn't put his thoughts and dreams into words so well anymore, since the accident.

Right now he kind of wished he could think up something to say. Mr. Norvell had called him over to their table, and now they were all looking at him, and he had the feeling he ought to say something.

Finally, he said, "You want me to dance some more, Mr. Norvell?"

Jess Norvell shook his head. "I want you to meet my friends, Feet. This is Pete and Alec," he introduced, nodding at the other two men. Pete, the fat, bald-headed one, held a glass of beer in one hand and nodded at Feet, looking at him from under half-closed, heavy eyelids. The other one, Alec, was cleaning his nails with a tiny gold pocket knife. He didn't even look up. He just muttered, " 'Meetcha."

"The young lady," Jess continued, "is Miss Candida Dreyer. Candida means 'shining white,' " he added, grinning at the girl.

The girl got a stiff line around her mouth. She looked at Jess as if she didn't like for him to say that. Then she turned to Feet and held out her hand so he could shake it. "Please call me Candy," she said to Feet. There was a husky sound in her voice as if she had a little cold or something. But Feet liked the way it sounded.

"What is your real name?" she asked then.

"Feet," the kid said politely.

"No, I mean your last name and your real first name."

"Oh." Feet had to think for a moment. They had been calling him Feet so long he sometimes forgot himself what his real name was. "It's Lawrence Terrace," he told the girl. And then he added, "Junior."

"Then," she said, "I'll call you Larry."

"What's wrong with 'Feet?' " Jess asked. "He's sure got a pair of them. They look like banjo cases."

They asked Feet to sit at the booth with them then and have a drink. He didn't understand this at all. He couldn't think of any reason why Jess Norvell would want him to sit at their booth unless they were playing some kind of joke on him. If they were, he wished they'd hurry and get it over with so he could go somewhere and eat. He sure was hungry.

They didn't play a joke on him, though. They were swell to him, and after everybody had a drink, Jess invited Feet to come up to his apartment with them to listen to records and eat some steak that Candy was going to fry.

Well, that was the start of a friendship that soon had the whole town talking. After that night whenever you saw Jess Norvell, you saw Feet Terrace trailing behind. Jess, who was a bookie and fight promoter, gave Feet a job and pretty soon the kid was seen around town in a new suit. He even rented a room regularly and stopped sleeping in alleys.

Nobody could figure why a smooth cookie like Jess would want to pal around with this kid whom everyone knew had rocks in his head ever since that truck ran over him several years ago.

Jess really liked him, too; it wasn't just a gag. Feet became convinced of that the day Jess took him down to buy the insurance.

They were riding around town in Jess's big car with the top down one fine day. Out of a clear sky, Jess said, "You know, Feet, I think it's a fine thing, having a guy like you for a close buddy."

Feet was deeply touched. He didn't know exactly how to answer that.

"I guess you're the best friend I ever had, Feet. I'd be real broken up if anything ever happened to you."

They drove around some more. Feet was driving, and Jess was leaning back with his eyes half closed, looking up at the sky. Feet didn't say anything because he knew Jess was thinking.

All of a sudden, Jess snapped his fingers. "What we should do is take out insurance on you, Feet. The more I think about it, the more I think how I'd hate for anything to happen to you. Yessir, we ought to go right down and take out a big insurance policy on you so nothing will ever happen to you."

Feet was overwhelmed. Nobody in his whole life had ever been so nice to him. He guessed that Jess was about the finest guy who ever lived.

They went down that very afternoon, to a man who was a good friend of Jess's, and took out an insurance policy for Feet so nothing could happen to him.

The man asked a lot of confusing questions and Feet had a headache before it was all over. He always got a headache when he had to think hard this way. Jess helped him by answering most of the questions for him. Jess and the insurance man said things back and forth that Feet didn't understand. Stuff like "fifty thousand dollars for natural death or double indemnity in the event of accidental death." And, "beneficiary will be Jess Norvell."

Anyway, they finally got finished, and they showed Feet where to put his name. Then Jess slapped him on the back and gave him a cigar. He felt great, walking out of the office, even if his head was splitting. Now, nothing could happen to him because he was insured.

Jess sure was a wonderful guy to have for a friend.

The insurance policy was an impressive looking thing with a lot of gold borders and stamps on it. Jess let him carry a copy around in his pocket and it sure made him feel like somebody.

It was a good thing he had the policy, because a few days later, a car missed running him down by inches. He was crossing a street, and it came whizzing around a corner and headed straight for him, doing ninety miles an hour. By the skin of his teeth, he managed to jump to the safety of the curb.

He stood on the sidewalk, shaking all over, watching the car disappear down the street. It was a big, black car and a fat, bald-headed man who looked like Pete was driving it.

Feet told Jess about nearly getting run down. "It sure was good you took out the insurance on me, Jess," he said. Jess stared at him thoughtfully without answering.

A week later, Jess gave a big party and invited Feet. It was pretty exclusive; only Jess's best friends were there: Candy, Pete, and Alec.

Feet didn't know until he got there that it was Candy's birthday. Then he felt terrible because he hadn't brought her a present.

She got a beautiful diamond bracelet from Jess. It must have cost an awful lot of money, but it really looked fine, sparkling there on her wrist. It was quite a party they were having; all the guys were dressed in tuxedoes and Candy had on a strapless evening gown. The table was set really fancy, with gleaming silverware, lace table cloth, long-stemmed red candles giving off a flickering glow.

Everybody was in a gay mood except Candy who didn't say much. She had a white, sick look on her face, so Feet guessed she wasn't feeling so good.

Jess, who was in fine spirits, said, "We're going to take a little trip, Candy and me." He put his hand on the girl's bare shoulder, running his fingers over her smooth, white skin. He grinned. "Yes sir, I'm closing a little deal that'll bring us fifty G's. We're going to have a vacation in Mexico City, aren't we, honey?"

She got a funny look around the mouth. "Jess," she whispered, "don't you have any . . ."

Feet digested this news about the trip Jess said they were going to take. He looked across the table at Jess and blinked. "It sounds swell," he said slowly. "I never been down there. To Mexico."

Jess coughed behind his hand. "Well, I don't think you'll be able to go, Feet."

Feet Terrace looked down at his plate. It got kind of blurry in front of his eyes and he blinked hard. "I-I'll miss you, I guess, Jess, you and Candy."

Jess grinned at him across the table. "I don't think you'll miss us much, Feet. I really don't. Here, have some more of this tuna fish salad. We made it up specially for you." He shoved another generous helping on Feet's plate.

The blonde girl, Candy, suddenly stood up, dropping her fork with a clatter. She made a little choked sound in her throat and ran out of the room.

Feet watched her go. "What's wrong with Candy, do you suppose?" he asked.

"Aw, don't pay any attention to her. Women get that way sometimes. Screwy. Eat your tuna salad, Feet."

He chewed up a mouthful of the salad and swallowed it. "It-it tastes a little funny. It's good all right, but it tastes kinda funny."

"That's the new sauce we put in it."

Feet ate the rest of it to be polite, but he didn't like it at all. It tasted like it had been left in an open can for a week. But he guessed some of this fancy cooking was supposed to taste that way.

After they finished eating, Feet went in the room where Candy was to tell her he was sorry he hadn't brought a present for her.

She was putting on make-up. Her eyes were red. Feet decided that she must be getting a cold.

He tried to cheer her up, but he couldn't think of much to say, except, "Happy birthday, Miss Candy." Then he stood there, wiping his hands on his trousers, and blinking.

She smiled at him. "Thank you, Larry."

Times like this, he wished he could think of more to say. Maybe someday he'd get that operation the doctors told him about to get the pressure of the blood clot off his brain. Then he wouldn't have so many headaches, and he'd be able to think better. If the operation didn't cost so much he'd have had it done a long time ago. Then he would have been able to think of something nice to say to Candy to cheer her up.

She put her hand lightly on his arm, looking up at him with her wide, gray eyes. She seemed to be on the verge of saying something to him. But then she bit her lip and went out of the room.

Jess took them all out to a nightclub, then. It was the first time Feet ever saw Candy drink too much, but she sure did then. Her eyes became glazed, and she stumbled when she walked. Jess was still in a gay mood, slapping Feet on the back every once in a while and asking him how he felt. He must have asked Feet every fifteen minutes how he was feeling.

Jess sure was a swell friend.

Candy looked across the table at them once. "Frien'ship," she hiccuped. A strand of her honey colored hair fell across her eyes. She raised a glass in an unsteady hand. "Le's drink a li'l toast to frien'ship." She wiped her fingers across her eyes and pushed her hair away. "You know what my name means, Larry? My name, Candida? It means 'shining white'! How's that for a laugh!" She made a wry face and swallowed her drink.

"Shut up," Jess said. "When you get drunk you talk too much, and you're talking too much now."

All of a sudden, Feet thought of a present he could give Candy for her birthday. He would let his feet do his talking for him, the way he had always done.

He got up and walked out on the dance floor and began tapping. He didn't have to tell his feet what to do. When he wanted them to dance, like now, he just turned them loose, and they went right to town.

When he started dancing, the other couples left the floor and everybody watched. Somewhere a spot light flicked on and pinned him in its glare. He'd never danced in a spotlight before. It made him feel really important, as if he were an actor on a big stage, or something.

He stopped dancing for a minute and walked over to the microphone in front of the band stand. "Miss Candy," he said right into the microphone, "this is my birthday present for you."

Then he went on with his dance. He made it the best dance he had ever done, trying to tell her with his flashing steps what a nice girl he thought she was and that he hoped she and Jess had a wonderful time on their trip to Mexico City. Even if he was going to miss them pretty bad.

Then, all of a sudden, something went wrong. For the first time in his life, his feet stumbled.

He stopped dancing and looked around. All the lights in the place were going around and around. Once, he had ridden on a ferris wheel and gotten the same effect. The spotlight got brighter and brighter until it was boring into him, shining right against the inside of his skull.

He tried to start dancing again, but his feet would only shuffle. Somewhere in the blackness, on the other side of the blinding spotlight, somebody laughed.

He felt terrible for making such a dope out of himself in front of his friends, but he just couldn't make his feet go. The perspiration began running off him in a cold sheet. Then, wham . . .

A pain across his middle doubled him over.

He gasped, trying to get his breath. The floor came up in a sweeping rush and hit him right in the face.

Somehow, he got to his feet and staggered over to the table. He grinned apologetically. "I guess I'm gettin' sick," he said to Jess and Candy. Then he fainted.

Once, he woke up, feeling the cool night air against his sweating face. They were in the car, riding somewhere. He could hear Jess and Candy in the front seat, arguing. It sounded like she was crying. Vaguely, he remembered them stopping and Jess helping him up to his room. Then Jess left.

Never in his whole life had he been so sick. He crawled over to a window and lost everything he'd eaten for the past week. Between spells of fainting and heaving, he'd have the waves of cramping pain that brought his knees up against his chest.

He probably would have died there if the lady down the hall hadn't heard him carrying on and sent for the ambulance. As it was, he had a close call. They pumped his stomach out and had him in an oxygen tent. He was in the hospital for a week before they'd let him get out of bed.

He tottered down to Bragow Street, looking like a ghost. His clothes hung on him like drapes.

He walked around the bars on Bragow Street. Finally, in one of them, he saw Jess Norvell sitting at a table, drinking moodily.

Feet walked right over. "Hello, Jess," he said. "I been sick."

Norvell took a big swallow from his glass. "You don't say," he said sourly.

Feet sat down at the table, smiling happily. "I sure was sick," he repeated. "They came for me in an ambulance."

"So I hear," Jess grunted.

Jess didn't seem particularly happy to see him. He guessed Jess didn't realize how sick he'd really been. He tried to elaborate on his illness, but all he could think of to say was, "I sure was sick," and shake his head.

Jess ordered another drink, staring at him with that moody look on his face. Finally, he said, "You know, kid, you ought to go out in the country for a few days. Get some fresh air and sunshine. Put yourself back on your feet." He lit a cigarette, snapped his lighter closed. "I know a guy that has a hunting lodge in the hills. He'd let us use it. Maybe we ought to go hunting up there."

Feet was tickled pink. He liked to go out in the country where there were pretty flowers and birds singing. Best of all, he'd be there with his friends, Jess, Pete, Alec, and Candy.

Jess took him downtown and they bought some shotguns to hunt with. Two double barrel, twelve-gauge shotguns and Jess bought a box of buckshot for them. He let Feet carry the guns back to the car.

Feet sat in the back with Pete, Alec, and the guns. Jess drove, and Candy sat up front with him. She was wearing a halter and shorts. She had a silk bandana tied around her blonde curls and it whipped out in the wind as they drove. She didn't say a word on the whole trip out to the hunting lodge. Every once in a while, she'd take a drink from a bottle Jess had on the front seat. By the time they got to the lodge she was pretty tight again.

They reached the place early in the afternoon. It was very pretty, up in the hills where it was cool.

The lodge was made of logs, and it crouched back under giant pine trees. Behind it, a little clear stream laughed and chattered as it bubbled merrily over a rocky bed. The wind blowing through the tall pines had a lonely sound.

Feet got out of the car with the guns under his arm. "We goin' hunting now, Jess?"

Norvell opened his door. "In a little while, kid. Candy, you go up and make us some sandwiches. There's supposed to be plenty of food in the cabin. I want to take a look around this lay-out."

Candy climbed the hill to the lodge. Her slim, bare legs moved in lithe strides. Pete and Alec went up to the lodge, too, and Feet trailed after them with the guns.

Candy went into the kitchen and started on the sandwiches. Pete and Alec lit cigarettes, got themselves some liquor out of a cabinet and started a card game.

Feet watched the two guys play for a while. Then he went into the kitchen.

Candy had gotten lettuce and tomatoes out for the sandwiches, but she had forgotten all about them. She was looking through a window at a bird singing in a tree close by and a tear was trickling silently down her cheek.

"I used to live in a place like this, when I was a kid," she said when Feet came into the kitchen. "It was out in the country, and the air was clean, and my folks used to take me to church on Sundays." She put her hand over her eyes suddenly.

"It sure is pretty here," Feet agreed. "I like it out here."

She suddenly turned and touched his cheek with her fingers. She was looking up at him with her gray eyes wide open. "You're such a nice guy, Larry," she said with her soft, husky voice. "I'd forgotten there were nice guys like you around anymore." She kept looking at him with her eyes wide like that, acting a little scared.

"Listen, Larry," she whispered, then, "and try to understand what I'm saying." She spoke the words slowly and carefully. "You like Jess a lot, don't you?"

Feet could understand that all right. "Jess is my best friend," he answered.

She took her hand away and doubled it into a fist. "Larry," she said carefully, "things aren't always the way they seem. Sometimes people pretend to like you when all they want is to use you."

Feet tried to figure that one out, creasing his brow. Finally he gave it up. “Jess is my best friend,” he repeated.

She got ahold of his arm, squeezing it so hard her fingers hurt. “Do you remember that insurance policy Jess got you to sign? Do you know he’ll get fifty thousand dollars if you die? And twice that much if you get killed in an accident?”

Feet puzzled over that for a minute. He didn’t see why Candy was talking about all these crazy things. It was making his head hurt. He wished she’d stop and go back to making the sandwiches. “Jess took out the insurance so nothing would happen to me,” he explained to her patiently.

She shook his arm. “Larry, you’ve got to understand. You have to run away. Right now, before it’s too late. Go out the back door and run through the woods, back to the highway, Larry. Please, hurry.” Tears were running down her cheeks from her frightened gray eyes.

She sure was acting crazy. Feet shook her hand off his arm. “We’re going hunting,” he said. “Jess told me we were.”

Just then the front door opened, and Jess came into the cabin. Feet heard him talking to Pete and Alec in the other room. Candy turned quickly away and went back to making the sandwiches.

Jess came into the kitchen. “Come on, Feet,” he said. “We’re going to go down in the pasture and shoot us some birds.”

“Wait a minute, Jess,” the girl said. “Th—the sandwiches. I’m—not through making them yet. “

“Skip ‘em,” Jess snapped. “Let’s get this over with first.”

She looked at them with the frightened look in her wide, gray eyes.

“Come on with the guns, Feet,” Jess said and went back through the front room.

Pete looked up from his card hand with his heavily lidded eyes. “Need some help?”

“No,” Jess said. “I’ll do it myself.”

Feet gathered up the guns and followed Jess. They walked down the hill in the warm sunshine. Before they’d gotten very far, Candy caught up with them. “I’m going along,” she said.

Jess looked at her narrowly, then shrugged.

They walked along for a while. Then Jess stopped and loaded both guns from the shells he was carrying in his pocket. "You want to be careful with loaded shotguns, Feet," he warned. "Blow your head off if you aren't careful."

"I'll be careful," Feet assured him, taking the loaded guns. It sure was fun, hunting with Jess and Candy. He wondered when they were going to see some birds to shoot.

They walked some more; then they came to a barbed wire fence across the meadow.

"Now this is where you want to be careful," Jess said. "Crawling through a fence like that with loaded shot guns. A lot of hunters get killed every year, dragging a loaded gun with them through a fence. You leave the guns on this side and crawl through first, Feet. Then I'll hand them to you and crawl through afterward."

Feet was glad he was hunting with somebody like Jess who knew all about things like that.

He carefully stacked the loaded guns against a post. Then he knelt down, spread the strands of barbed wire apart, and began wriggling through.

Feet couldn't see Jess and Candy because they were behind him and he was busy inching his way between the strands of barbed wire. But he heard Candy whisper, "Jess—" with her voice all shaky and funny sounding.

Then Jess snapped at her, "Shut up!

Feet was almost through the fence.

"Jess—" the girl cried again, her voice climbing to a scream. "No!"

Then there was a loud roar. It was so close and so loud it seemed to shake the earth. Feet tumbled through the fence the rest of the way and scrambled around so he could see what had happened.

Jess was standing there with one of the double-barrel shotguns in his hands, pointed at Feet. Jess's face had a horrible, ashen look. The gun slowly dropped out of his hands and fell on the ground. Jess looked down at the left side of his shirt that was all mushy and soggy with blood, and he crumpled to his knees.

Feet looked at Candy. She was standing over by the post where the guns had been stacked. One of the shotguns was in her hand, still smoking. Her face was as white as a sheet of paper.

Feet scrambled back through the fence. "Golly," he whispered. "Golly." He knelt beside Jess Norvell.

Candy dropped the shotgun. She pushed her red-tipped fingers into her hair and began sobbing hysterically.

Feet looked up at her. "You shoulda been more careful, climb-in' through the fence with that gun, like Jess said, Miss Candy. Now look what you went and done."

Feet started crying a little, wiping the tears out of his eyes with his fingers.

Well, that's how the kid Larry "Feet" Terrace got started on his way to success. He owed it all to his good friend, Jess Norvell who got killed in the tragic hunting accident.

After the accident, Feet came back to town so broken up he nearly died with sorrow. He didn't hold it against Candy though. Nobody is to blame for an accident like that. In fact, he and Candy got to be pretty good friends after that, probably because they felt a bond in the sorrow each had in losing the person closest to them, Jess Norvell.

A few months after the accident, Candy paid for the operation that Feet had been needing so long for his head. Some people say she sold a beautiful diamond bracelet to get the money, but you never can believe everything you hear. Anyway, Feet came back to Bragow Street for a while after the operation, and he was a different guy. He could think and talk almost as good as anybody. He didn't stay on Bragow Street long, though. A booking agent caught his dance one night and pretty soon he moved uptown to the real big time night clubs. Not long after that, he and Candy got married.

You don't see Feet much any more now that he's a big success. Once in a long great while he comes down to Bragow Street, but he never stays long. You can tell he still misses Jess Norvell. You can never get him to talk about Jess.

So, that's the story of how Feet Terrace got his name up in lights. And he owed it all to Jess Norvell, the best friend a guy ever had.

Watch Him Die

JEWEL pressed her thin shoulder blades against the wall, as if trying to push herself through it. Her eyes were dark splashes of fright in a white face as she watched Nick pick little Gus Gavatos up by the neck. She watched the huge muscles in Nick's arms swell to the size of hawser ropes and that crazy, grinning look come into his face. Then she covered her eyes and screamed.

When she looked again, little Gus was dead. He was like a limp cloth doll with all the sawdust spilled out. Nick was still shaking him between his giant hands, like a terrier worrying a dead mouse. Slowly the insane light faded from Nick's eyes. A dazed expression took its place. He dropped Gus Gavatos and wiped the back of his hairy wrist across his sweat-drenched face.

Jewel stared at the dead man lying all in a heap almost at her feet. Her mouth opened as if to scream again, but only a small, frightened sob came out.

"You–you killed him," she whispered.

It was the first time she'd ever seen a man die that way, right before her eyes. It did something to her stomach. She steadied herself with a shaking hand against the wall and tried to keep from fainting.

Nick didn't look at Gus any more. He stumbled over to the table and poured a big drink into a glass and swallowed it all in one gulp. He swayed, looking around the room with the dazed expression. Then from a shelf he took down the tin box containing all the receipts from today's sponge auction. He opened it and dug his hand into the pile of greenbacks there. Something of the crazy look came back into his face.

"Look at it, Jewel," he whispered hoarsely. "Thousands. As much as I make in a year, diving for that smelly dog. And this time I don't split it with nobody. No engineer, deck hand, or captain is going to get a piece of this. I'm gonna get it all. Me, Nick Hiskro!"

Jewel watched him put the lid back on the tin box.

"Come on," he snapped at her.

She couldn't move. All she could do was stare at him. Nick had killed a man. Nick, her husband. He had taken a life. The realization spun around in her mind and sickened her.

Nick started getting mad at her. He came over and stood in front of her. "I said to come on!" His voice had a deep, hoarse rumble, like a rusty metal drum being dragged across a yawl's deck.

"But you killed him," she whispered. "You shouldn't have done that, Nick. You shouldn't have killed anybody. It's a bad thing—"

His big, hairy hand came up and slapped her face. The blow threw her against the wall and she cowered there, thin body quivering, looking at him with scared eyes.

"You keep your mouth shut," he said. "Don't you start talking to me."

She didn't say any more; she just hugged the wall, looking at him. He caught her shoulder and dragged her roughly out of Gus Gavatos' house and into the patio.

The Florida night was hot and sticky. Perspiration shone on Nick's face like a wet mask. He was very still for a moment, listening; then he whispered:

"They're comin' up the front walk, Sebastian and Sovey and the others, coming for their shares. They'll find Gus in a minute and yell for the law. Every cop in town will be lookin' for me."

The whole community knew there was bad blood between Nick and Gus. Nick had gotten drunk on the last sponge fishing cruise and Gus had fired him. There wouldn't be any question about who had killed Gus.

Nick wiped his fingers across the sticky wetness on his face. "We got to get out of here."

"You can't go anywhere," Jewel said dully. "They'll block all the roads. And you don't have a boat any more. You shouldn't have killed Gus. It was a bad thing, a sinful thing."

Nick laughed, low in his throat. It was a vicious sound. The crazy look spread across his face like a shadow. He took a step toward her, flexing his fingers. He was smiling. Whenever he got that crazy look and beat her, the little smile came to his lips; it had been there when he killed Gus.

"Don't you talk to me about sin, you rotten cheat!" he said.

Her hand went to her throat. "What do you mean?" she whispered, her mouth suddenly very dry.

"Thought I didn't know, eh?" he taunted, coming toward her slowly. "You thought big, old Nick was dumb. So dumb you could have a boy-friend and I wouldn't find out."

All the strength went out of Jewel's legs. She could only stand there, watching Nick move toward her, flexing his hands. He knew. He knew about Jim Davis. All this time, she had been so careful, and he had found out, anyway. Now, maybe he was going to kill her, too. He was still drunk and maybe he'd strangle her the way he had little Gus Gavatos, now that he knew about Jim Davis. A cold knot came up out of her stomach and lodged in her throat, cutting her breath off.

He came close to her so that his hot, garlic-tainted breath brushed her face. His thick fingers moved to the collar of her blouse, roughly yanked it aside and grabbed the tiny gold locket it had concealed. A cry broke from her lips as his clumsy fingers snapped the chain. She tried to grab the locket, but he pulled it away from her. He dangled it before her eyes. "He gave it to you. Didn't he?"

Tears filled her eyes and trickled down her cheeks. "Give it back to me," she asked, holding up her hands.

He only laughed. The delicate, hand-made trinket fell to the patio cobble stones and his big foot crushed it.

She dropped to her knees, searching through hot tears for the fragments of her treasure. She got the chain and a bit of the shell, and then he stepped on her fingers and hauled her roughly to her feet. "So you love him, you lousy little tramp!"

"Nick, you don't understand. Please don't!"

But he wasn't going to hurt her any more now, she knew. He didn't have time. The others were already in the house. They would find Gus's body, and in a few minutes the police would be looking for Nick. "Well, we'll fix this up later," Nick said. "I'll show you what Nick Hiskro does to a wife that thinks she can make that kind of a fool out of him!" He chuckled. "We'll talk about it, you and me and your Jim Davis." His hand closed about her wrist and he jerked her roughly ahead of him, out of the patio.

To the left, the lights of the small Greek sponge-fishing settlement sparkled in the night. But Nick walked in another direction, along the water's edge, keeping to the darkness there.

Jewel was forced to run along beside him, dragged along by her wrist. In her free hand, she clutched the broken locket chain, all she had left of the gift Jim Davis had given her that time in Tampa. Jim Davis had been in her life for a long time now, and she had always been careful that Nick did not find out. But he must have seen that letter Jim Davis sent her, the one that had been waiting for her yesterday when they got home from the cruise. He had said nothing about it, waiting, perhaps, until he could find a better opportunity to really torture her about it.

Nick was good at that, torturing people who were weaker than himself. He was a huge man. Sponge divers had to be big and strong like wrestlers. And he had a great contempt for people who were weaklings. "Jelly fish," he called them, sneering and flexing his big muscles.

She often thought that one reason he got so mean toward her was because she was thin and sick a lot. He often pointed to her thin, pale body and talked about the healthy women in town, with their broad hips and deep bosoms, and said scornful things about her.

SHE had gone along on this last sponge cruise to work as a helper, cleaning the sponges the divers brought up.

There was a lot of work that had to be done to the marine animals before they became commercial sponges. They had to be cleaned of their jelly-like covering, then pounded with clubs and hung in the sun to dry. After that, they were washed over and over again in pails of seawater, and every bit of the outside black skin was trimmed away with shears.

It had been hard work. Her back ached and her face blistered from the sun beating on the deck of Gus Gavatos' two-masted schooner. But, at the end of the cruise she was to receive one and a half shares of the catch, the usual pay of the cook and deck hands.

Of course she had known that Nick would take most of it away from her, but she had hoped he would let her keep at least enough to buy the material for a new dress.

The cruise had been successful. They had to stay out only twenty days to make their catch. It would have been fine if Nick hadn't drunk too much and got himself fired. A diver has to stay on a careful diet and leave liquor alone on a cruise because of the hard, dangerous work. When Nick got drunk, Gus fired him on the spot. And then, because the big diver started acting mean, Gus had Captain Sebastian chain him below decks for the remainder of the cruise. Nick was in a foul, murderous mood yesterday when they finally came back into port.

JEWEL had known there would be a letter waiting for her from Jim Davis. She'd tried to hurry home before Nick could get there and find it. But he had sent her to town after some beer, so that must have been when he read the letter. It had a smeared look around the flap, as if it had been steamed open. But he said absolutely nothing about it when she came in with the beer. He just opened a bottle and went out on the porch with it.

"There's some mail on the table," he said shortly and the screen door slammed behind him.

Jewel grabbed it up with shaking fingers. There were some circulars, an insurance company advertisement, a mail order catalogue and a plain white envelope with her name neatly written on the front:

Mrs. Jewel Hiskro
Route 3, Box 10
Clear Springs,
Florida

She folded it up without opening it and went into her room. There, she slipped out of her worn cotton frock and took a hasty bath, reflecting that she was still pleasant to look at—even after six years of marriage to Nick.

After the bath, she put on a clean cotton dress and went out of the house, letting the rusty screen door slam behind her. Nick sat on the shady side of the porch, tilted back in a chair with his feet propped against a post. He had finished the first bottle of beer and was starting on a second. By tonight, she knew, he would be very drunk and probably take out his rage against Gus Gavatos and Captain Sebastian on her. Well, it wouldn't be the first time he had gotten drunk and beaten her up.

He gazed at her as she walked off the porch. "Where you goin'?"

She said, "I–I thought I'd take a stroll down to the Point. It's so hot here."

"Well, don't spend all day loafing down there. I want a good supper tonight."

"I won't be long," she promised.

They lived in a weather-beaten gray shack that stood up on pilings, like a bird house on stilts. The yard was knee-high in weeds and littered with tar barrels, old rope, boards and empty beer bottles. Nick's diving equipment was piled on the front porch. On the money he made as a diver, five thousand a year and better, they could have had a nice house. But Nick drank it all up. And cursed her out if she said anything about moving to a better house.

She walked down a crushed-shell road. The glare from the afternoon sun dug at her eyes. It was hot this time of year. Perspiration stuck the threadbare dress to her body.

She went out to the Point. This was her favorite place. It was quiet and lonely here, shaded by pines and thick, squatty banyan trees. There was a plot of grass out on the edge of the Point, a small bluff overlooking the water. Here, she could sit and gaze out to sea. Jim Davis had often been with her here when the cool night wind came across the water and rustled the pine needles.

The last time she had met him here was right after Nick had hurt her in one of his drunken rages. Jim had held her bruised, aching body in his arms and kissed the tears from her cheeks. "I'll kill him," he'd whispered savagely. "Right now. I'll go up and—"

"No," she'd whispered frantically, stilling his angry words with her fingers against his lips. "They'd take you away to prison. I'd never see you again. Please, Jim, have patience just a little longer."

She wanted to go away with Jim, but she was too afraid of Nick. He would follow them no matter where they went. He would kill them both. She couldn't run away from Nick no matter how much she hated and feared him. It was a hopeless love.

But it was good to sit here and think about the clean, strong lines of his face. Jim always smelled of fresh soap and shaving lotion. He was never sweaty and sour with beer, the way Nick was at night. He was kind and tender. Sometimes he would say a line from a poem he knew. Jewel liked it when he did that. She wished she could take a book of poetry home to read to herself sometime, but she knew Nick would not stand for her mooning over a book. To Nick, reading such stuff was a sign of weakness, the thing he despised.

She had never had time for things like reading books. As a child, she'd grown up in a huge family, the daughter of a poor Florida cracker who ran a bait stand. At sixteen she'd gone to work waiting tables in a cafe where the male customers thought she went with the Business Men's Lunch. She'd always dreamed about somebody like Jim Davis. Instead, Nick Hiskro had come along. He had been big and good-looking in his flashy suits, and a diver, the aristocrat of the sponge industry, and she had been tired of the hot cafe and the men's hands.

Now she wished she'd waited for Jim.

When she'd reached the Point, yesterday afternoon, she'd taken out the locket Jim bought for her that time in Tampa. She would never forget that day. Nick had been away on a sponge cruise. One morning, she had suddenly decided to take a bus to Tampa. Jim had met her there.

They had a wonderful time. He took her to a fine restaurant and then to a movie. He had bought her this locket. It was the only thing he'd ever given her, although he was very rich. Really, it was only an inexpensive trinket from a dime store, but she treasured it more than anything else she owned.

Now it lay on the grass before her, sparkling in the late sun. Her trembling fingers slid under the envelope flap and she read the neatly penned lines. Especially the last, "...the day after you come back from the cruise. I'll meet you at the Point at ten o'clock that night. I'll be in my cabin cruiser. We'll take a spin around the Bay. The moon will be full and it will be beautiful. I miss you so."

He mentioned other things, the fun they'd had in Tampa that time, the locket he'd given her. She pressed the letter to her lips. Tomorrow night he would be here.

That was the letter that Nick had opened and read, then sealed up again. But she hadn't known it then.

NICK had been ugly drunk when she returned from the Point yesterday evening. This morning, he was worse. Before noon, he made Jewel go into town with him. He wanted to see if Gus sold the sponges at the auction today.

They went together down the white shell road to the little fishing community. Down at the docks, the brightly painted sponge boats, high-bowed yawls and two-masted schooners sparkled in the morning sun. Nick strode straight to Gus Gavatos' boat.

Sebastian, the captain, was on deck, sitting on a coil of rope in the shade of a cabin, his bare feet stretched out in the sun.

"I hear Gus is selling the sponges today," Nick said.

Sebastian glanced at him, then across the water. He shrugged. "What's it to you? You will get none of the shares."

Hiskro spit on the deck near Sebastian's bare feet. "I will get the divers' regular four shares."

"Well, that's between you and Gus. I don't think he'll give it to you."

Nick cursed him out in Greek. He was looking for a fight, Jewel knew. Sebastian had been the one who locked Nick in the chains below decks, but he had done so under orders from Gavatos. Jewel felt pity for Sebastian. He was a strong man, as were all the fishermen, but he was no match for a diver. Especially a brute of a diver like Nick.

Hiskro stood there, saying things to Sebastian that a man could not listen to and keep his self-respect. Sebastian got up and hit Nick in the face, hard.

The diver shook his head and grinned, the crazy gleam coming into his eyes. His big fist slammed the boat captain up against the cabin wall. Then Nick picked the half-unconscious man up and threw him overboard.

Weakly, staining the water with his blood, Sebastian swam to a nearby wharf. He did not pull himself up, but clung to the slippery green piling under it, looking up at Nick with frightened eyes.

"Weak jellyfish!" Nick stood on the boat's deck, reviling him, spitting down at him. Jewel sensed then that there was going to be serious trouble before the day was over.

Back in the village, they went down a sidewalk, past restaurants and the curio stores and shell stores where the tourists bought things. Jewel looked at the pretty trinkets in the windows they passed and wondered wistfully if Jim Davis would bring her a present tonight.

They ate in one of the restaurants. Nick swilled a whole bottle of wine with the meal. Then he wiped the back of his hand across his mouth and walked out of the place, to the Sponge Exchange Market, urging Jewel along a little ahead of him. Jewel did not know why he was making her go everywhere with him. She did not know, then, about his having read the letter from Jim Davis.

They stood in the hot sun, watching the sponges being auctioned off. The sponges were lying on the ground in the open-air patio of the Exchange. They were threaded on twine, twenty to a coil, sorted to size and quality. The buyers looked them over with experienced eyes, and made bids.

Nick stood there sullenly, listening to the price Gavatos' catch was bringing, adding it up in his mind. It came to a good figure.

It was dark when the auction finally closed. Nick hovered around in the fringes of the crowd, watching Gus Gavatos receiving the money.

The boat owner got it in cash and put it in a tin box. Then he went home.

Nick lingered in town for awhile, drinking some more, making Jewel stay with him. Then he took Jewel along to the home of Gus Gavatos.

The two men had a violent argument. Jewel stood back in a corner of the room and watched them with wide, anxious eyes.

It was the custom of the divers and the boatmen to come to the house of the boat owner after the auction and receive their shares of the profit. After the expenses were deducted the divers each got four shares, the combination engineer and lifeline tender was paid two shares, deck hands one and a half, and the captain and the owner of the boat took the remaining six shares.

Nick was demanding his four shares.

"You're a damn fool, Hiskro," Gus snorted. "You're not going to get any money. You only dived once before I fired you. Your wife is due one and a half shares for her work. Here it is. And now get out before I have you thrown in jail for drunkenness."

Nick's swarthy face grew dark with rage. "I'm the best damn diver in Florida, drunk or sober," he swore. "I could have dived that day."

"Yeah," Gus said, "and got yourself killed, and then I'd have the insurance company down on my neck for letting a man dive when he was drunk. Listen, Nick, you got yourself a bad reputation. Every boat owner in town's had trouble with you. I'm going to tell them all about this. You won't work for anybody on this coast again!"

That was when Nick's eyes had got the crazy look and the little smile had come to his lips and he had strangled Gus Gavatos to death.

Now, with the box full of money under one arm, he walked through the darkness with his hand around Jewel's wrist, hurting her. She knew now that Nick had sat on the porch all yesterday evening, planning to kill Gus Gavatos. He'd known he was through as a sponge diver in Florida; nobody would hire him any more; he'd caused trouble on too many cruises. So he'd thought how he would come here and kill Gus Gavatos and take the money and go away. But she did not yet know why he had kept quiet until now about Jim Davis's letter, or why he had made her go along with him this evening, not once letting her out of his sight.

They barely got to the outskirts of town when the alarm was out. They heard the yelling back there and saw the people in the street, most of them heading toward Gus's house.

Nick directed their course down by the water, where it was dark. He did not have a car or a boat. She couldn't understand how he planned to get away with this. He must have gone crazy altogether.

They skirted the town, went around it to their own house. There, Nick got out a .45 automatic that he'd brought home from the war. As he was loading it, a car drove up out in front of the house. The headlights shone in their window.

"Come on," Nick snapped at her.

Fists were pounding at their front door. He grabbed her arm again and dragged her out the back door. They picked their way across the littered yard to the mangrove trees.

Back at the house, men were shouting.

"Nick Hiskro! Come out! It's the law!"

"I don't think he's here."

"Well, break the door down and find out. Somebody down the street saw him and his wife run in here a few minutes ago."

Nick jammed the gun in her back, forced her through dense weeds and brush. Limbs slapped her face and tore her clothes. Vines tripped her. She didn't know where they were until they came out on the white shell road. Then she saw with surprise that they were headed to the Point.

The sub-tropical moon was up, full and bright. It shone on Nick's contorted face. He leered at her.

"Know where we're going now, my faithless wife? To see your boyfriend. We're all going to have a party together—you and me and your sweetheart, Jim Davis!" He laughed crazily, waving the gun.

She stopped walking, her face white. "No, Nick. Listen. Please—"

"Shut up," he said, giving her a hard push in the direction they were walking. "Oh, you thought I was so dumb, you and him. But you weren't so smart, either. You shouldn't have left his letter there where I could steam it open and read it." He laughed in the strange, twisted way. "I figured it all out yesterday—what I was going to do. First I wanted to kill you right away. But then I said to myself, 'No, wait, Nick. Wait until they are together. Let him see you do it to her. Enjoy the look in his eyes when you shoot her in the belly right before him. Then, kill him. That's the way to do it.'"

She was crying. The tears ran silently down her cheeks and she stumbled on the rutted shell.

Nick glanced at his wrist-watch in the light from the moon. "Ten o'clock. He'll be there now, waiting." He laughed. "Well, we won't keep him waiting long, eh?"

Now she knew why he'd kept her in his sight all day. And why he had killed Gus Gavatos with no apparent way of escaping the police. True, the roads out of town would be blocked. True, he had no motor boat. But Jim Davis had a powerful cabin cruiser. Hadn't he mentioned it in that letter to Jewel, which Nick had read? Yes, Jim had said he would be at the Point with his boat at ten o'clock tonight. And Nick planned to kill him and Jewel there and take over his boat to flee in. This was the scheme he had plotted out in his mind yesterday.

Far behind them there was the sound of approaching automobiles.

Nick hurried their pace, striking her with the gun barrel when she stumbled. They broke through the trees, to the clearing on the Point. Here the moon was doubly bright. The water glistened and sparkled below.

It was a beautiful scene—but there was no Jim Davis. No cabin cruiser. Nick cursed, looked at his watch.

He ran to the edge of the small bluff, looking out over the water, craning his neck in all directions. There was not a boat in sight. He cursed. He came over and slapped her so hard she fell down in the grass. "Where is he?" he cried. "Where?"

But she never had time to answer the question.

The police came then, breaking through the trees. The Point was lit by brilliant beams of light. Men were shouting. Nick stood there, spraddle-legged, bawling a hoarse scream. Then the gun in his hand roared wildly. He got to fire it only once before a dozen bullets thudded into him from the fringe of trees. He stood there with a crazy grin on his face. Then the pistol fell out of his hand and he turned and walked toward the trees in little tripping steps. A moment later, he fell down in a heap.

Jewel sat up, putting her hands to her throbbing face. She sat there a long time, quite, motionless. Finally, the police came over to where she was sitting. They shone their flashlights on her.

"It's his wife," somebody said.

"Yes. It's Mrs. Hiskro."

A policeman knelt beside her. "Who is Jim Davis?" the policeman asked her. "Just before he died, Nick kept mumbling something about a Jim Davis who was supposed to meet you here with a boat. Who is he?"

Jewel stood up slowly. The night wind brushed her face. "I don't know," she said.

She couldn't explain it to them. The loneliness, the fear of Nick, the dreams that had never come true. They wouldn't understand. Jim had been very real to her. She had, at times, almost forgotten about buying the locket herself, and writing the letters herself. He had become that real.

She took the broken locket from her pocket and let it fall in the sand.

She wouldn't need Jim Davis any more. Everything was going to be all right.

The G String Corpse

DETECTIVE Mercer Basous of the New Orleans police department left his car at the curb of a narrow street in the Vieux Carré. He hurried along close to the weathered brick walls of the ancient buildings, seeking shelter from the rain that drizzled down on the glistening cobblestones; a most gloomy morning to investigate a possible homicide.

He arrived at his destination, The Gables, one of the many excellent restaurants in the French Quarter. It was a favorite of Basous'. If one must look into an act of violence on such a cold, gray morning, he philosophized, at least he was able to do so among pleasant surroundings.

The restaurant was not yet open for business, so he entered a courtyard and knocked on a side door. It was opened by Anthony Pizano, owner of The Gables, a good friend of the homicide detective.

"Basous!" exclaimed Pizano. "I'm really glad to see you." He appeared nervous and disturbed.

"Good to see you, Anthony," Basous greeted, carefully wiping his shoes on a mat. Then he said, "What a miserable day!"

This side door opened into the kitchen. The stoves and ovens were cold now. Cooking utensils hung silently from racks over the tables.

Dishes were stacked. It was quiet and deserted, but in a few hours the room would be teeming with cooks and waiters scurrying around to cope with the noon business.

Basous' long, homely face softened with the memory of the many excellent meals he had enjoyed from this kitchen, but he forced himself to stop reminiscing and attend to business. "Now what is this about a possible murder, my good friend?"

Pizano took an umbrella from a rack and led the way back out through the courtyard to the curb. "I was taking some trash out this morning, and when I lifted the lid on the garbage can, I saw this . . ." He raised the lid.

Basous looked into the can. He murmured an exclamation in his mother tongue, Acadian French, reached into the can and pulled out a woman's robe. It was covered with blood.

"Do you have any idea who this robe could belong to?"

"Yes. Shelly Lyons."

"Shelly Lyons? 'Miss Nudity'? The stripper who works at the Godfather Club on Bourbon Street?"

"Yes. She lives in an apartment, in this building, above the restaurant. The tenants in the building use the garbage cans out here. Since she's the only woman living in the building, it must belong to her." Then he added, "After I saw the robe in the garbage this morning I went upstairs and knocked on her door. There was no answer. I became alarmed and phoned you."

"Well, that was the right thing to do, my friend. Let's try her door again. Maybe she's a sound sleeper."

They crossed the courtyard to a winding stairway that reached the second floor where the apartments were located. In the hallway, Pizano indicated the residence of Miss Lyons.

Basous hammered on the door, but got no reply. "You are the landlord of this building, are you not, Anthony?"

"Yes."

"Then you must have a passkey to these apartments."

"Yes, but I didn't want to use it without having the police present. A landlord can get into a lot of trouble these days over things like that."

He proceeded to unlock the door and they entered the apartment. The living room was tastefully furnished. It contained, in addition to other furnishings, a thick white carpet, an expensive console television and some sophisticated record and tape-playing equipment.

"Miss Lyons must earn a good living," Basous observed. Then his eyes fell on a large nude painting of Shelly Lyons. It was a misty, ethereal impression, executed with delicacy and sensitivity. "What an incredibly beautiful woman," Basous murmured.

Her features were flawless. Her hair was a soft, pale cloud. Her deep-blue eyes were luminescent, her skin so delicate as to be almost translucent. Her moist lips were parted. Basous almost expected her to whisper something intimate to him, so convincing was the effect.

"Yes. She has a lot of class for an exotic dancer. Smart, too." Pizano waved his hand toward a bookcase filled with books on a wide range of subjects, from biographies to the arts.

"Who did the painting?"

"Nathanial Dowling. He's one of the tenants in this building. Has a small shop on Royal Street."

"Yes, I know the place."

Basous gazed at the painting for another moment with the worshipful expression of a homely man gazing on an unattainably beautiful woman. Then he resumed his professional manner. "Let's see the rest of the apartment."

When they entered the bedroom, Basous exclaimed, "Mon Dieu!" and Pizano, a devoutly religious man, gasped and crossed himself. Blood was splattered over the floor and furniture, makeup bottles had been swept from the vanity to the floor where many had smashed, bedclothes were half-pulled from the bed, a bedside table and lamp were overturned.

They searched the rest of the apartment, but found no trace of Miss Lyons.

Using his handkerchief to pick up the phone, Basous got his partner, Lieutenant Roy D'Aquin, on the line and requested that the detective meet him here, bringing along a man from the police laboratory.

Then Basous asked Pizano, "Now, who are the other tenants in this building?"

"There are two other apartments. One is occupied by a traveling drug salesman, Harold Black. He's only here on weekends. The other tenant is the artist, Nathanial Dowling."

"Let's go see if Mr. Dowling heard anything last night."

They knocked on the artist's door, but got no reply.

"Well," said Pizano, "he sometimes spends the night in his shop. Has a cot or something in the back room. Miss Lyons might have been the only person in the building last night."

Basous thought about the bloodstains and said, "Not the only person. Well, we might as well go downstairs and wait for D'Aquin."

Down in the restaurant kitchen, Pizano made a pot of Louisiana coffee, strong and black with chicory, and served it to Basous with a platter of French pastries.

Basous' long, horselike face reflected an expression of pure ecstasy as he tasted a croissant. "Anthony, you have absolutely the best pastry cook in the city. Now then, let me ask you this: who would know Miss Lyons intimately—could give us information about her personal life?"

"Hmm. Well, I suppose you could begin with her employer, Isaac Iwanski, who owns the Godfather Club. He's been something of a parent to her since she came to the city five years ago and began dancing at his club."

"Bien!" said Basous. "Now if I could have just one more gâteau à l'abricot."

D'Aquin arrived presently with the laboratory man. Basous set the man to work on the bloodstains in Miss Lyons' apartment, instructing him to search thoroughly for fingerprints. Then the two detectives left in Basous' car.

"First," he said, "I want to pay Nathanial Dowling a visit. He lives in the same building and might have heard something last night." Basous drove carefully through the narrow, wet streets of the old city, his windshield wipers snapping busily at the steady downpour.

Nathanial Dowling, a pale, slender man in his mid-thirties, had an ascetic face with aquiline features and cold, blue eyes. He was a type still found in some regions of the South, the last of a long, decaying line of aristocrats dating back to the plantation era. His ancestors had owned slaves and fought in the War Between the States. Now Dowling, a bachelor, stocked his antique shop with the last of the family heirlooms stripped from the family's decaying mansion. He also dabbled in art. His shop was a dusty junk heap cluttered with bric-a-brac. Interspersed among the antiques were his oil paintings.

Yes, he said, he was acquainted with Miss Lyons on a professional basis. Six months ago, he'd needed a model. She had posed and he'd given her the painting as payment since he couldn't afford a model's fee. No, he was sorry, he couldn't give them any information about unusual sounds that might have come from her apartment last night, since he spent the night here. He showed them the cot in a corner of a back room which served as his painting studio. He was sorry to hear she was missing and hoped she would turn up not seriously injured. He said it without a great deal of concern.

"A haughty man, that one," D'Aquin muttered as they drove away. "He made me feel like a tradesman who should come in the back door."

"I don't think he's ever quite forgiven his grand-père for losing the Civil War," said Basous. "Let's see if Isaac Iwanski can tell us something about the beautiful Shelly Lyons."

The Godfather was one of those small, bare-skin joints on Bourbon Street that looked tired and seedy by daylight but brightened up at night with flashy neon, perspiring go-go dancers and a small but loud band.

The two detectives found the proprietor, Isaac Iwanski, in his office, a cluttered room not much larger than a closet. Iwanski was a spidery little man with a shiny bald head. He wore suspenders. When informed that his star performer was missing under circumstances that indicated foul play, he went all to pieces. "My God!" he cried. He paced around the tiny office in a state of agitation. Then he collapsed in a chair, weeping openly. "I loved that little girl like she was my own daughter. This is terrible."

"We don't know for certain what has happened to her, Mr. Iwanski," D'Aquin said. "She may be quite all right."

"Oh, no!" Iwanski cried, gazing at them with tearful, grief-stricken eyes. "She's been killed. I'm not surprised. She's been expecting it. For months that poor girl has lived in terror. It's that rotten husband of hers. He said he'd kill her. Well, now he's done it."

"She was married?" Basous asked with surprise.

"Yes. Separated for the last year, though. But he wouldn't leave her alone. Kept threatening her, hounding her. I told her it was a mistake when she married that no-goodnik. 'Papa Isaac,' she told me (she always called me 'Papa Isaac,'), 'I'm in love.' Then she told me who it was—Grove Niblo. 'Oh my poor child,' I said to her, 'you've picked yourself a life of trouble.' But she wouldn't listen. She was a woman in love."

"Grove Niblo," Basous repeated, again surprised.

"Sure. You're a policeman. You know him—a syndicate hoodlum, a man deep in organized crime. What a tragedy she should ever get mixed up with that man. He was crazy-jealous all the time. Never gave her any peace. Made her stop dancing. Mistreated her constantly. A year ago, she left him, but he swore to get her back. He vowed he'd never let another man have her alive. What a pity she didn't meet young James Turner first."

"James Turner?"

"Yes, the nice young medical student she's been dating the past two months. Those kids want to get married but that lousy gangster, Grove Niblo, won't give her a divorce. He made life hell for her. And now he's killed her." Iwanski took out a handkerchief and wiped his streaming eyes. "Five years ago she came to me, a country girl from the bayou. I taught her everything. Now she's gone."

"Mr. Iwanski, what time did she leave the club last night?"

"It was a slow night. We didn't do a second show. She left early—about eleven-thirty."

The two detectives walked out of the small Bourbon Street night-club. Basous paused on the sidewalk to look up at the giant posters of Shelly Lyons that adorned the front of the club. "A beautiful, beautiful woman," he sighed.

"Iwanski has good reason to cry," said D'Aquin. "Shelly Lyons was his drawing card. Without her, he's got just another hole in the wall."

They walked through the rain to the car. Inside, D'Aquin drummed his fingers against the steering wheel impatiently while Basous, in his slow, methodical manner, opened his notebook and carefully made his preliminary notes. When he had finished writing, Basous closed the notebook and said, "Now I suppose we should pay a visit to Mr. Grove Niblo and Mr. James Turner."

Niblo owned a restaurant in the French Quarter which was a legitimate front for his underworld operations. He was a swarthy, handsome man of mixed Italian, Spanish and French ancestry, a mixture not uncommon in this city. He wore tailor-made suits, imported shoes and diamond-studded cuff links. His demeanor was cool and guarded when the two detectives were ushered into his office. His air of cool self-containment dissolved when Basous informed him of the disappearance of Shelly Lyons.

Niblo became as agitated as Iwanski, but in a different manner. His dark eyes flamed, his face flushed. Hard ridges appeared along his jaw. He stood up, trembling. "I want that girl found," he said in a hoarse whisper. "And she'd better be alive, or somebody's going to be very dead."

He walked to a window, staring out at the falling rain. One clenched fist slowly, rhythmically beat against the glass pane.

"When did you see Shelly Lyons last?" Basous asked.

"I don't know—a week ago, I guess," Niblo choked.

"We've been told you made some threats to her."

He turned, his eyes blazing with fury. "She was my wife. It's none of your lousy business what goes on between a man and his wife. I love that woman more than anything else in the world. I wanted her out of that lousy nightclub and back with me where she belonged. I told her something like this would happen, her standing up there naked with men looking at her—" He choked with rage.

"Where were you last night?" Basous asked.

Niblo glared at him. "If you're going to start asking questions, copper, I'm calling my lawyer."

Basous' voice suddenly became firm. "When you get him on the phone, tell him, since you're unwilling to cooperate, we're taking you in on suspicion of abduction and possible murder. You were overheard threatening Miss Lyons. That makes you suspect number one."

Niblo had picked up his phone. He hesitated, then replaced it. He made a superhuman effort to gain control of himself. Finally he said, "All right. I was here last night, working on my books. I've got the I.R.S. breathing down my neck."

"Anybody here with you?"

"Sure. One of my boys, Eddie Gavatos."

Basous gave him a long, measured look. The Acadian's face was solemn and stern. He said slowly, "All right; I'm not going to book you—yet. We'll see if Miss Lyons turns up."

Niblo's gaze locked with Basous'. "She'd better turn up," he whispered. "I'm not waiting for a bunch of fumbling cops to try to find her—"

Basous warned him, "You and your hoods keep out of this, Niblo. It's a police matter. Otherwise you'll have more than the I.R.S. on your back."

When the two police officers returned to their car, D'Aquin observed, "That's not much of an alibi. Those punks who work for Niblo will swear to anything he wants them to."

"I know. Well, let's pay a visit to the other man in her life, this medical student, James Turner."

From the college registrar, they obtained the address of James Turner. He lived off-campus in an apartment. His late-model sports car was parked in front.

"Not exactly the average, poor struggling student," D'Aquin muttered.

Turner was a clean-cut young man in his mid-twenties. He appeared shocked and grief-stricken when Basous explained the circumstances of Shelly Lyons' disappearance. Yes, he readily admitted that he and Miss Lyons had a serious romance going. They planned to get married if she could get a divorce. He'd had lunch with her yesterday. No, he had not seen her last night. He was here all night, cramming for an important exam. No, he admitted, there was no way he could prove that, since he lived alone.

D'Aquin asked some questions about his background. Turner explained he was from a wealthy family in the East, which explained his expensive car and comfortable apartment. Then, as the detectives were leaving, Turner tearfully begged them to notify him the minute they found out anything about his missing fiancée.

"D'you think he's telling the truth—about studying last night?" D'Aquin wondered when they were back in their car.

"No way of telling. He doesn't have any better alibi than Niblo. But there's no apparent motive."

"Lover's quarrel, maybe?"

Basous shrugged. "That's a possibility."

They decided that the laboratory man should have completed his work by now, so they returned to Shelly Lyons' apartment to conduct a thorough search. An interesting item turned up in a desk drawer—a copy of an insurance policy in the amount of $100,000, payable to Isaac Iwanski in the event of the death of Shelly Lyons.

D'Aquin whistled softly. "Now we have another suspect with an excellent motive. Old man Iwanski might have been shedding crocodile tears. If Shelly married James Turner and stopped taking her clothes off at the Godfather, Iwanski might as well close his doors. So, he knocks her off and retires with a hundred grand."

"Another possibility," Basous agreed. "Although it's not entirely unusual for a club owner to insure a regular act that is valuable to his business."

There were no further developments of importance in the Shelly Lyons' disappearance case that day; but early the following morning, Basous' chief telephoned him. "Your missing stripper was found in a shallow bayou a few miles from the city this morning. At least part of her. Her head and hands are still missing."

Basous replaced the telephone and stared up at the ceiling, remembering the painting of that beautiful woman. His long face was sad.

Basous dressed, had breakfast, and went to the morgue. The body still wore the stripper's working clothes: pasties and a fringed G-string. "Miss Nudity," the stage name of Shelly Lyons, was embroidered on the brief garment.

The woman's torso had been found by two fishermen. A search party was sent out to drag the bayou for the missing parts.

Shelly Lyons had perhaps the best-known body in New Orleans. Thousands of men had feasted their eyes on every micrometer of her bare skin but, ironically, now it was difficult to establish positive identity from the trunk alone. It had lain partially submerged in the stagnant bayou water for some twenty-four hours. Crayfish had done their work. The three men who knew her best, Isaac Iwanski, Grove Niblo and James Turner were brought down to view the body. Iwanski fainted, Niblo flew into a hysterical rage and James Turner wept—but none could swear positively that they were looking at the mortal remains of Shelly Lyons. Basous had the painter, Nathanial Dowling, examine the body, reasoning that an artist had a special knowledge of the human figure. Dowling observed that the general build and bone structure appeared to be the same, and in his opinion this was the torso of the woman he had painted.

The bloodstains on the robe found in the garbage can and in Miss Lyons' apartment matched the corpse's blood type—AB. Added to all that, there was the matter of the G-string costume which was positively identified as belonging to Miss Lyons. So the official decision was that—pending location of the head and hands—the torso found in the bayou was that of Shelly Lyons.

The laboratory reported finding no fingerprints of value in the apartment. The killer had either worn gloves or wiped everything carefully.

An autopsy was performed that afternoon. At its conclusion, the medical examiner handed Basous a bit of surprising news. "This woman was probably dead from a drug overdose before she got chopped up. She was filled with enough heroin to finish off even a long-time user." Then he added, "There is no evidence of rape or sexual molestation."

That evening, Mercer Basous had dinner at The Gables. Basous had discovered from past experience that his mind worked best over a good meal. Since he was a bachelor and had few expenses, he could afford to indulge his chief pleasure in life: good French cooking.

He ate slowly, savoring an excellent meal that consisted of turtle soup, a main dish of baked eggplant stuffed with shrimp and crabmeat, and a dessert of crêpes suzette. The meal was concluded with Café Brûlot Diabolique. As he enjoyed the meal, his mind toyed with the many puzzling aspects of the case on which he was working. Finally, as he sipped the steaming Café Brûlot, he came to some conclusions. He paid his check, leaving a generous tip.

The next morning, he and his partner discussed the case. "Roy," he said, "I'm having serious doubts that the torso we found is that of the missing Lyons woman."

"But the blood type matches the stains in her room. And that G-string costume—"

"That's just it! The G-string. As we both know, it's not uncommon for a murderer to cut off his victim's hands and head so she can't be identified and traced to him. But in this case, why did the murderer go to all that trouble to hack her up and yet leave the identifying G-string on the torso?"

"Well, that is curious. Unless, of course, our murderer is a pathological sex nut who gets part of his kicks from dismembering his women victims. There are those kinds, you know."

"True enough. But then consider the medical examiner's autopsy report, that the woman died of an overdose of heroin. I've phoned Iwanski, Niblo and Turner, the three men who knew her best, and they all insist Shelly Lyons was not a user. Then there is the matter of the blood-stained robe put in the garbage can where it would surely be noticed, as if the killer wanted to advertise the murder."

"Hmm. Then who the devil did we find in the bayou wearing Shelly Lyons' G-string?"

"A very good question. It beats me. But something went on in that apartment that we haven't begun to guess at yet, and it very well may have involved a second woman."

"So what do we do now? If you ask me, we've run into a dead end in this case. We have a body wearing Shelly Lyons' dancing costume, who may not be Shelly Lyons. We have three suspects, all with possible motives and not very substantial alibis, but no way of linking any one of them directly with the crime—"

"Correction, mon ami, we have four suspects."

"Four?"

"Yes, we've been neglecting another party who was intimately involved with Shelly Lyons—Nathanial Dowling."

"Nathanial Dowling? But all he did was paint her picture."

"All he did, you say? Do you think a man could spend days, perhaps weeks, painting that gorgeous woman in the nude without becoming intimately, passionately involved with his subject? I tell you something, Roy, when I looked at the painting of that beautiful creature, I said to myself, 'Basous, this is a crime of passion. Here is a woman who could drive men to desperate, even insane acts.' Yes, a crime of passion. It has to be! And Dowling is one of the men who could have got caught up in that passion."

"Okay, so let's have a closer look at the gentleman."

The two homicide detectives made a trip to Royal Street. They found Dowling's shop open, but in charge of a temporary clerk, a middle-aged woman who said her name was Mrs. Harriet Preston. She explained that Nathanial Dowling sometimes spent the day at the old family place some miles from the city. When he did, he called her to come in and mind his shop. She expected him back by late that afternoon.

They then toured the neighborhood, asking discreet questions about the habits of Nathanial Dowling. They learned from a parking lot attendant that Dowling always left his car—a blue, 1968 station wagon—at this lot around the corner from his shop when he was in town.

The two police officers spent the major part of the day with other duties, but late that afternoon Basous stopped by the police laboratory where he obtained a can of luminol and a quartz lamp. When it was dark, he and D'Aquin went around to the parking lot on Royal Street. Dowling had returned from his trip to the country. His station wagon was on the lot. Basous warned the attendant to keep his mouth shut about what they were doing. Then they carefully looked over the station wagon. A preliminary flashlight examination did not reveal anything incriminating, but when Basous sprayed the rear floor area with luminol, then shone the quartz lamp with its strong ultraviolet radiation over the area, numerous spots luminesced, indicating dried blood that had been partially cleaned away.

With his pocketknife, Basous carefully trimmed off a small portion of the rubber mat which contained one of the blood spots. They then took the small mat fragment to the laboratory. Basous requested the forensic man to determine, if possible, whether the blood was of human or animal origin, and if human, the nature of the blood type.

Basous had his answer the following afternoon. The blood was of human origin. It was type AB.

"Let's go arrest the scoundrel," D'Aquin said.

They obtained a warrant and headed for Royal Street. "It's all very circumstantial," admitted Basous. "But now, if we arrest Dowling and impound his car, he may be shaken up enough to talk. His alibi about spending the night at his shop when Shelly Lyons disappeared is too weak to stand up. And with the bloodstains in his car."

Dowling was not in his shop, however. Mrs. Preston explained that Mr. Dowling had again driven out to the old family plantation. From her, Basous obtained directions to the place.

Basous and D'Aquin drove over the Huey Long Bridge and headed south, into bayou country. The afternoon grew old and the warmth of the sun died. Gray shadows of dusk began staining the silent depths of the swamps around the road. The dead arms of swamp cypress trees were bone-white and draped in funereal cloaks of dripping Spanish moss. A wraithlike mist was rising above the dark, still waters.

Following the convolutions of the winding bayous, the road at last brought the two detectives to the oak-fringed entrance of the old Dowling plantation grounds.

They proceeded down the ancient, private roadway that had once known the shuffle of chained slaves, the rumble of ox-drawn sugarcane wagons and the marching of Civil War troops.

Before them loomed the haunted ruins of bygone splendor, all that was left of the Dowling plantation home. The final rays of the sun in a dying burst of color tinged the decaying columns, galleries and wings with a soft diffusion of rose tints. Great sweeping shadows stretched over the ruined gardens behind the structure while pockets of darkness multiplied in the recesses of the galleries, doorways and windows.

Surely such a great old house where so many lives had been lived, love affairs consummated, fortunes made and lost, had to be haunted, thought Basous with a shiver. He could easily be convinced that ghostly forms of plantation belles in hooped skirts were moving behind the broken shutters to the music of the quadrille.

The architecture of the house was Louisiana Creole classic style with Greek Revival and Georgian influences, cast in the mold of its own time and location. The great Ionic columns, like the last desolate outposts of an army long since gone, stood in solemn dignity against the ravages of time and weather, but crumbling masonry, boarded-up windows, sagging galleries and broken shutters mutely admitted the decay of a century. Basous knew that inside the forty rooms the constant damp air must have coated the plastered walls with a tomblike green mold. The very air around the old house was heavy with melancholia.

A light burned in a single downstairs window.

Basous parked, and the two detectives walked through the weeds to the window. Basous looked through the dusty pane at an incredible tableau.

The beautiful Shelly Lyons sat before a massive dining room table. She was dressed in an evening gown of sorts, that left her shoulders bare. It looked like a dress from a bygone age that had been stored in an attic trunk. Her arms were securely tied behind her to the large chair upon which she sat. Her wide, terror-filled eyes followed the movements of the other occupant of the room—Nathanial Dowling.

Dowling, attired in a dinner jacket, held a glass of wine in his right hand. He raised it in a toast. Basous heard his voice faintly through the closed window: "To the new mistress of the Dowling plantation."

Shelly Lyons was crying. "Please, let me go home."

"You are home! You're going to live here with me forever. My darling, beautiful wife. We're going to restore this place. Once again it will take its rightful place among the great homes of the South." Nathanial Dowling looked around, his eyes burning feverishly. "We'll plant cotton, sugarcane. We'll entertain royalty." He gulped the wine. Then he knelt beside her, throwing his arms around her. "I'll never let you go from this place. You're mine forever. I knew when I painted your exquisite body on canvas that somehow, I had to possess you."

"Crazy," whispered D'Aquin. "He's completely wigged out."

Basous ran around to the door, pounded on it and shouted, "Open up, Dowling. It's the police."

From the window, D'Aquin shouted, "Watch out! He's got a gun!"

Basous jumped back off the gallery. The door burst open. Nathanial Dowling stood there, his face contorted, his eyes filled with madness. In each hand was an ancient dueling pistol. He fired. The ball shattered the air inches from Basous' head. The detective rolled away from the porch, going for his own pistol. Dowling's second shot and the report from Basous' Police Special rang out simultaneously. Dowling fell against the door casing. The dueling pistols slipped from his grasp. Then he crumpled to the gallery, dead.

Basous slowly arose as D'Aquin came running around the corner of the house, his gun drawn. He stopped when he saw Dowling's body. "Are you all right, Mercer?"

"Yes," Basous said, and he thought this had surely not been the first fatal duel between two men over a beautiful woman on these grounds.

When they untied Shelly Lyons, she threw herself into Basous' arms, sobbing hysterically. He thought it would probably be the only time in his life fate would arrange for him to hold such a beautiful creature, and he made the most of the moment.

When she had calmed down sufficiently, Miss Lyons told them the incredible story of what had happened in her apartment that night. "Ever since I posed for Dowling, he's looked at me in a way that gave me the chills. He never made an outright pass, but I'd catch him following me down the street, or sitting in his car, watching me leave the apartment, staring at me. I had him figured for a nut. Well, the night it happened, I was about to go to bed when I heard a knock on my door. It was a friend, Linda Butler. Linda is one of those lost souls who drift around the country these days. I'd met her a few months ago when she danced at the club for a while. She'd just gotten back into town and was looking for a place to crash for the night. I felt sorry for the girl. She has no family; just goes from one guy to the next, whoever wants her. I told her she could sleep on my couch. Then she went into the bathroom. I'm not surprised she went in there to shoot up. Like a lot of drifters, she was a user. I knew it. What could I do? She came out of the bathroom, floating. But then she keeled over. I could see she'd OD'd. It scared me, and I ran out of the apartment to get help. Nathanial Dowling was just coming up the stairs. I ran right into him. He went back to my apartment with me. By the time we got back there, Linda was already dead. I was going to call the police, but Nathanial was looking at Linda, then at me, and getting this crazy, wild expression on his face. He knew I've been having trouble with my husband, Grove, that Grove has been threatening me and I was afraid of him. He pointed out that Linda was about my size and build and that she had no family and nobody would miss her. He said he could make it look like it was me, instead of Linda, who was dead. Then I could go hide on that old plantation home of his and Grove would never bother me again, thinking I was dead. I told him he was out of his mind and I'd never do such a crazy thing. But I guess he'd made up his mind that this was a way he could kidnap me and hold me prisoner and nobody would come looking for me, if the whole world thought I was dead. He forced me into his car and brought me out here and kept me a prisoner. When he went into town, he locked me in a cell where they punished runaway slaves back in plantation days. He told me what he'd done to Linda, that he'd convinced everyone I had been murdered. Nobody would ever search for me. He was going to keep me here forever, make me his 'wife'." She choked.

Later Shelly Lyons said she couldn't bear to keep the oil painting of her done by Nathanial Dowling. It had too many bad memories. She gave it to Basous in appreciation for rescuing her. From then on, it occupied a hallowed place on Basous' apartment wall, and sometimes when he looked at it, he could understand Nathanial Dowling's madness. I could almost do something like that myself, to have such a woman, he thought with a sigh.

Prophetic the Portrait Painter

OF THE two paintings in the room, the one of the murdered man was the most striking. It was a large canvas on an easel across the room from the door and the paint was still wet and sticky, making the blood look even more realistic.

I stood in the doorway of my cheap, cluttered apartment and gazed on my handiwork. The sun, slanting through dusty old Venetian blinds, cast an aura of golden mist over the tableau, giving it a mirage-like appearance.

It was not unlike gazing into a crystal ball and seeing at once my failure-spotted past and my unhappy present circumstances brought about through the dark powers I had tampered with. They were all contained here in this room—with the girl I loved and the man I'd murdered.

I wiped my shaking hand across my eyes. My shirt was beginning to stick to my ribs in cold, clammy patches. And my stomach churned miserably.

I was afraid of something I couldn't see, something out of the shadows, unknown and dark.

Work your gris-gris, Madame Loo Loo. Burn your candles and sprinkle your potions and mumble your incantations over your lode-

stone. Call up all the voodoo powers you lay claim to, you old witch, and undo this mess.

Only the sound of my and Jo's breathing could be heard in the room. Downstairs, across the street in a bar, a nickelodeon was playing a Negro blues recorded by a band in the French Quarter. Somewhere in a room above us, a woman laughed shrilly. The heavy odor of cooking cabbage seeped through the walls from the next apartment.

I was sorriest for Jo. It had been a sad day for her when we met.

She was completely frozen in the center of the room, scared and sick. For the first time since we met, she was looking to me for help.

I made myself look at the two paintings again. One was the grand portrait of Joseph Porterfield, the gambler. Joseph, looking extremely opulent in a handsome suit, seated behind a rich mahogany desk, sporting a huge diamond ring on his left hand and a four-leaf clover diamond stickpin in his tie. He had specified the four-leaf clover.

Joseph, as rich and elegant as his fondest dreams. Joseph, the industrial magnate, the leader, the senator, man of wealth and distinction. All these qualities, I had painted onto the canvass as directed.

And then the other canvas. Silvester Griffith, the silver-haired prize fight promoter and manager of Pug McCarty. But a different story on this canvas, for Griffith was sprawled loosely on a threadbare carpet, wearing a mantle of red blood from a slit throat and a bloodstained kitchen knife was on the rug beside him.

And on the floor, at the base of the easel, as if posing for the already completed painting, was the real corpse of Silvester Griffith in just that position.

I had kept a diary of all of it. The first entry was **June 2nd**.

I met her tonight at her place in the Bayou, as she directed. It was a foul-smelling hut hidden under the gaunt naked limbs of dead trees and dripping moss. The ground was wet and marshy and the air had a dank, tomb-like odor. Bull frogs croaked dismally on the muddy banks of the bayou. And somewhere, a night bird warbled a forlorn and lonely melody.

The smoke from the fire inside the hut hung low in the heavy air. She was huddled over the embers, a fat greasy old woman who smelled of garlic and dead things. Madam Loo Loo, following in the ways of her predecessors, Maris Laveau, and the other voodoo queens.

The smoke stung my nostrils and made my eyes water. I set up the canvas on an easel to take advantage of what little light there was. Madam Loo Loo was swaying over the paints by the fire, chanting a sing-song chain of unintelligible words.

For the first time I looked at the third person in the room.

She was a young colored girl in her middle twenties, huddled in a corner of the hut, frightened almost gray. Her eyes rolled, showing large patches of white.

I felt sorry for her, sorry for her trouble that had brought her here, a trouble stronger even than her fear of Madam Loo Loo's voodoo, and this dismal hut in the bayou.

Madam Loo Loo stopped her chanting and looked over the fire at the girl. The glowing embers played over the thick, greasy outlines of her face, giving her a sardonic appearance.

"This here's pow'ful *gris-gris*, gal. More powerful than any voodoo you ever seen before. It costs lots of money to conjure up this kind of power. You got cash to pay for it?"

The girl nodded, too frightened to speak. She fumbled at the bosom of her dress and held out a wad of sweat-darkened bills. "W-will this be enough, Madam Loo Loo? It's all th' money I got. Please, M'am, I need help bad."

The old woman counted the money, her face sullen, and pouting. "T'aint enough, but I guess it'll have to do. You bring me again this much 'fore the end of the month, or I'll put a powerful fix on you."

The girl nodded. "Yessum. I'll get some more, somehow."

Loo Loo pointed to me. "Now, you tell him what's ailin' you. I've done cast my spell and he's got the power in his brush."

The girl moistened her lips. She looked at me pleadingly. "Please, sir. It's my husband. I love him terribly. And he's treating me bad. He stopped loving me. He's playing around with a bad woman. He told me he was, right to my face. And he laughed at me, 'cause I cried. I cain't leave him, I still love him. Please fix it so he'll love me again."

I looked away from her tortured eyes. I picked up my painting equipment that Loo Loo had chanted over, and began sketching.

The minutes dragged by, filled only with the murmur of Madam Loo Loo's chanting and the girl's frightened breathing. In about two hours, I arose, stiff and sore. I rubbed my smarting eyes, then turned the painting so the girl could see.

She was down on her knees beside Madam Loo Loo and she looked up at the painting and a slow light of hope began to spread over her face, incredulous at first, then growing stronger until her eyes were filled with tearful gratitude.

I had painted a picture of her husband taking her in his arms, and his face was the face of a man in love.

Afterwards, Madam Loo Loo counted out half of the girl's money in my palm.

"Made a strong impression on her, you paintin' her husband's face right out of the air like that." The fat, sloppy old charlatan laughed. "She didn't know I'd pointed him out to you in town, and brought you pictures of him." She looked at me, her small greedy eyes hooded. "We got a good thing here, Mack Towers. We got a new kind of voodoo nobody ever heard of before. Tonight was just for practice.

"You watch the people I'll bring to you. Big, important people in society. They believe in voodoo, jest as strong as that girl you saw tonight. I'll 'maze you with the people that believe in me, Towers. And when I tell 'em I got a new power, a way I can fix their future, through the spell I cast on your brush, I'll make more money for you in one night than you'd make in a year in your little two-by-four art studio down on Royal Street!"

I scarcely heard her. I was looking down at the pitifully small wad of crumpled bills. And I was thinking of the girl's sweat on them and the things she'd done to earn them, the menial, dirty tasks. And the hope that had been on her face when she left here.

I went out and got very drunk that night.

June 15th entry.

I saw Jo Coats tonight for the first time in nearly two weeks. I had been avoiding her. She found me in a little bar on Bourbon Street, where the jazz was loud and the drinks were strong.

She slipped into the booth, on the other side of my table, quietly. “Hello, Mack.”

I looked at her. It was raining outside and little beads of moisture had caught in her brown hair. She always went bareheaded, even in the rain. Her coat was open in front, and the line of her bare throat was clean and fine.

I frowned down at the absinthe. I tasted it, enjoying the strong licorice taste. Then I drank all of that glass and ordered another.

“Mack, can we talk about it?” she asked huskily.

I shrugged. “What do you mean?”

“You know, Mack. There’s something—I mean, you never did drink before. You haven’t been at your studio in days. You haven’t called me in two weeks.”

I turned the glass between my fingers. “Some girls might take that as a hint.”

She paled, then flushed. She looked down at her clenched fingers in her lap. “It-it isn’t like you to do it that way, Mack,” she whispered.

I was sorry I’d said that. I was sorry for a lot of things. I looked at Jo and ached inside the way I always did when she was near.

She lit a cigarette. Her fingers were trembling. “You don’t just walk into somebody’s life for two years, then casually walk out.” She looked at me suddenly very squarely. “Mack, I don’t know what it is. If you’re in some kind of trouble, or what. But, if I can help, you know I will.”

She stood up. The little band was playing *South Rampart Street Parade*, and the trumpet was very brassy. Layers of stale blue smoke framed Jo’s face. Her coat collar was turned up and she had her fists rammed deeply in its pockets. She held her breath for a moment, then said, “Mack, will you marry me? Tonight?”

I put the glass down. She looked very lovely to me. She seemed hazy and misty, almost unreal. Maybe it was the absinthe. I said, quietly, “No.”

She shrugged. Out of force of habit, she picked up the check as she turned to leave. But I caught her hand and took it back.

For two years she had been paying our checks.

“If there’s one thing I’ve got tonight, it’s the price of the check, “ I said flatly.

She looked down at me. A corner of her mouth moved. There was a New Orleans song we'd heard in a bar somewhere. She quoted the title. "Send for me if you need me."

Then she was gone and I was alone with the jazz and the smoke and the absinthe.

July 10th entry.

The money is rolling in. Just like the old hag said, she has quite a following. Prominent society people believe in her. Wonder what the newspapers would say if they found out about the prominent political figure who consults her regularly? Anyway, she's sold them on this prophetic portrait business. If they have a pet wish they want to come true, she casts a spell over my brush to give it the power. I paint the future the way they want it. And it's supposed to come true.

July 17th.

Saw Jo for a moment on a crowded sidewalk on Canal Street.

The river of humanity flowed by us on either side. We stood close together. She touched my cheek with her finger.

"You don't look well, Mack. You-you look old and tired, and thin." She took her hand away, bit her lip. "I-I was just shopping."

It was ironic. I would never marry her before, because I was a failure. I'd failed at everything I ever tried. I hadn't even had the price of a cheap wedding ring. I had money now. Over five hundred dollars in my pocket at the moment. But there was something else standing in our way now, a kind of sickness growing in me like a cancer.

We stood there a moment longer, then she was gone, dissolved into the flow of passing shoppers.

July 29th.

This will hand you a laugh. Some of the prophecies are coming true.

That's all I had written that night. I lay across my bed in the darkness and smoked and stared up at the ceiling. Outside, New Orleans' French Quarter was filled with music and fun. Neon signs flashed through the half closed Venetian blinds.

It was all a coincidence. Sure. I couldn't control the future. It had just happened that some of those paintings were coming true. Maybe they had given the people hope and confidence so they made them come true through their own efforts.

That was what I said over and over. But, I lay there drenched in sweat, and shivering. I didn't sleep much any more after that night.

September 3rd

I went to Madam Loo Loo's to collect my latest fee. The biggest one so far, one thousand dollars for a single painting. But, this was a little different from the others. We had guaranteed this one to come true.

Joseph Porterfield grinned as he paid me off.

"Yessir, I made a cool ten-thousand off that fight."

He was a florid-faced, loud-talking gambler. He had promised me a thousand dollars to paint a prophecy of the fighter, Pub McCarty being knocked out in the third round of his next fight, if the prophecy came true.

I had painted the picture. He'd bundled it up and sent it to McCarty. Maybe the picture unnerved McCarty, I don't know. Anyway, McCarty was knocked out in the third round, on schedule, and Porterfield was paying me off on schedule.

"Four leaf clovers, High John, the Conqueror roots, lodestones, I use 'em all. Burn candles, too. But this is the best gris-gris I ever saw. You really got something here, Madam Loo Loo."

I guess I was starting to look the part of a voodoo prophetic painter. My eyes were burned out holes in a gaunt face spotted with fever. I hadn't slept or eaten a decent meal in a month. I was scared, afraid of a power that no mortal should possess.

"Now," Porterfield said, "I want you to paint a picture of me, rich. All my life I wanted to be rich, see? Never had much. Pick up a few bucks now and then from the horses. Nothing really big-time, see?"

He grinned, showing a gold tooth.

He was the most superstitious man I ever saw. He crossed himself before he sat down, then took out a lodestone and held to it grimly, watching me half fearfully while I made the preliminary sketches.

After he left I told Madam Loo Loo, "This is going to be the last one. I'm quitting."

She stared incredulously, then her face got dark and mean. "What you talkin' about, boy?"

"I mean I'm fooling with something that's got me scared. When this started I thought we'd make a few easy bucks telling fortunes for some poor suckers who like to get fooled. But some of these crazy paintings are actually coming true. Remember the woman who wanted the fur coat so bad? Three weeks after I painted her with it, her husband died leaving her a lot of insurance. Then the man whose wife wouldn't give him a divorce. I painted him married to the other woman he wanted. Less than a month after that, they found his wife dead from an overdose of sleeping pills and he was free to marry this girl I painted him with. Now this latest thing, this Pug McCarty prize fight."

She blocked my way. She worked herself into a hysterical fury, screaming invectives at me.

"You can't leave me, now when we're startin' to make real money!" All the dark powers she claimed kin to filled her face. "I'll put a fix on you, boy," she whispered, almost strangling on the words. "You walk out on me and I'll put a fix on you, you'll never escape!"

I pushed the old hag roughly out of my way.

That night I got a telephone call from Silvester Griffith, Pug McCarty's owner. He had lost more than twenty grand on the fight in which McCarty got K-O'd. He accused me of being a key figure in a plot to unnerve his fighter. Everyone knew McCarty was just a big, dumb pug, superstitious to the point of being pathological. McCarty had heard of the power of Madam Loo Loo's new voodoo, so when he got the picture, he figured Loo Loo and I had put a fix on him and the fight was as good as lost. He went into the ring a cowering, whipped man.

Silvester Griffith wasn't like Joseph Porterfield or Pug McCarty. He wasn't a simple minded, superstition-ridden dolt. He was a cool-headed, unscrupulous business man and gambler who had been cheated out of twenty thousand dollars, and he was dangerous to the point of committing murder.

He figured I owed him twenty thousand dollars. He was coming around to see me about it the next day.

September 4th

No time to write this morning. Packing, leaving for the West Coast.

That was my last entry, this morning. I had been up all night painting. Now I threw the diary in my suitcase, jammed some shirts on top of it and closed the lock. I studied the two portraits that I had completed during the night. Then I left the apartment.

I spent the rest of the day in my studio, packing my painting supplies. It was late in the afternoon when I heard the door creak open. I whirled around.

"Mack . . ."

Jo came in, closed the door behind her. Her eyes were very large. She surveyed the room, the boxes and crates.

I sat down, lit a cigarette. "I was going to call you before I left, Jo."

She moved a step nearer. A shaft of light from a high window touched her face. She looked very lovely. "What ever happened to us, Mack?"

I didn't say anything. I hadn't had anything except cigarettes and coffee all day. I felt sick and weak. And the familiar old ache was back again, because she was here.

"We used to have so much fun, Mack. We were broke, and we had so much fun being broke. You had your dreams, and I believed in them. I still do, Mack. I still believe you'll paint something fine some day."

"That's great," I said. "A woman never knows when she's had enough. Let her half way like a guy and he's the finest in the world, even if he hasn't a thing on the ball."

She shook her head. "You let yourself get bitter, Mack. You shouldn't have done that. I didn't mind paying the checks. Couldn't you see that? You made me happy. Another guy with all the money in the world couldn't have done that."

Maybe it was not eating. Maybe it was not sleeping for a month, or the sickness inside me, or because I was scared of what Silvester Griffith and his strong-arm boys might do to me. Or maybe it was simply that I loved Jo the way a guy can only love one girl in his life.

Anyway, I bawled a little. She held me close against her bosom, maternally, murmuring softly. I told her the whole mess, from the time Madam Loo Loo had first come to me with this crazy scheme.

"I knew about the McCarty prize fight," she said. "The papers are making a big thing of it, ridiculing Griffith because he let his fighter get hoaxed like that. He can be a bad guy to have mad at you, Mack. I think we had better leave until he cools off." She was smiling through her tears. "We'll get married on the West coast, darling. You'll find a lot of things to paint and you'll get well again. Superstition can be a powerful sickness. Some people let it rule their lives and sometimes destroy them."

"I'll meet you at the bus station, " I agreed. "You better pick up my suitcase from my apartment, while I ship all this stuff on ahead." I touched her hand. "Promise me one thing. Promise not to look at the two paintings in the living room. They're part of this thing I want to leave behind."

I didn't want her to know how much of a hold Madam Loo Loo's power had gotten on me. I didn't want her to know that I, too, had begun to believe in the dark power Loo Loo had given my brush. And last night, frightened by his warning, I had gone a little crazy and painted a prophetic portrait of Silvester Griffith, in which he was dead.

Now in the daylight, with Jo Coat's healthy, normal presence, I no longer believed it. It was all a bad dream I had to leave behind me.

It was, until a half hour later when Jo phoned me hysterically from my apartment where she had just walked in and discovered the body of Silvester Griffith, murdered exactly the way I had prophesied in my painting.

I had murdered him. Just as surely as if I had held the knife in my hands. I was cursed with some kind of dark power that should have been left with witches in medieval times.

These crazy thoughts jumbled my brain as I stood in the doorway of my apartment.

Jo sobbed and rushed into my arms.

I pushed her away. The room was spinning.

"I'm going to call the police," I said thickly. I pushed open the door to the hallway leading to the bedroom phone. I stumbled into the bedroom, and Joseph Porterfield and Madam Loo Loo blocked my way!

Porterfield grinned, his gold tooth flashing. His face was more florid than ever. He was fingering a lodestone suspended from his vest with a tiny gold chain.

"Too bad you decided to stick around and phone the police, Mack. We thought you'd take her and run on out; but then we've had bad luck all the way around. Your girl came in the front door just after we finished off Griffith. No way to get out, so we hid in a closet back here. We hoped you two would leave the front way, give us a chance to get out. But if you're going to call the police and stick around, I guess we'll have to change our plans."

Madam Loo Loo had forgotten all her voodoo powers. She was just an old woman frightened half out of her wits.

"I don't want to get mixed up in no murder, Porterfield," she croaked. "Don't you get me mixed up in no murder!"

Porterfield grinned again, but his eyes were deadly. "Shut up, you old hag. You're in this as much as Mack Towers here, or me."

I was getting a grip on myself again. "You murdered Griffith," I whispered. "But why? He was after me."

"You didn't know the latest developments," Porterfield chuckled. "Pug McCarty lost his nerve and admitted the fight was fixed from the start. All that stuff about the picture you painted was a gimmick. We had it fixed with McCarty to lose the fight, but had to make it look convincing. So we hit on this scheme of sending the picture and makin' it look like it unnerved him."

"Griffith was goin' to the boxing commission after he came up here and found out from you who had hired you to paint the picture. I couldn't afford to let him find out it was me, nor can I afford to pay back the ten thousand I won on the fight. The only thing left to do was to kill Griffith and then make sure that slap-happy pug, McCarty, doesn't spill his brains to anyone else."

As he talked, he pulled a small, black automatic from his pocket. He gestured toward the living room. "Now let's go in and talk this over with your girl friend."

“That was a nice picture you did of Griffith,” Porterfield said, following me into the living room. “Gave us a perfect setting. Give the police something to think about, too. They’ll find out you were a painter mixed up in voodoo. Be kind of hard for you to explain, painting a picture like that, and then have a man murdered in the identical way in your apartment. A man who hated your guts and told a lot of people he was gunning for you for hoaxing his fighter.”

“Of course,” he admitted, “your finding us complicates matters somewhat. Now we have to put some finishing touches. Like a bullet in your girl friend, and one in your own head. Then the gun in your hand. Yes, that would look convincing. Painter goes berserk, after butcher knife murder, kills his girl friend and himself.” Porterfield chuckled and rubbed his lodestone.

The sun was slanting at a deeper angle now, etching streaks of light through the Venetian blinds, across Jo’s white, horror stricken face.

I remembered Jo’s words, spoken earlier today. “Superstition can be a powerful thing. Some people let it rule their lives and sometimes destroy them.”

And Joseph Porterfield was the most superstitious man I knew.

I moved in front of him, so my body obstructed his view of his own completed portrait. I moved the picture a few inches to the right, drew a shaking breath. Then I said, “So you liked Griffith’s portrait, Joseph? Have you seen your own? I mean have you looked at it closely, Joseph?”

Then I stepped aside.

He was looking at it. I watched the play of emotion across his face. I saw blind, unreasoning fear struggling with reason. And then I saw fear win out.

I saw his florid, puffy face sag, his mouth go slack and wet, his eyes’ pupils cover the entire iris. I heard Madam Loo Loo gasp a French exclamation, then go down on her hands and knees, sobbing and chanting. And then I heard Porterfield scream and the pistol in his hand roared at the canvas. Time and again he pulled the trigger, blasting at the portrait until the room was filled with smoke.

He was still yanking at the trigger when I smashed a book-end across his face, followed it with a hard right that drove him unconscious into a corner.

I picked up his gun, wiped my face shakily with the back of my sleeve. "Call the police, honey," I told Jo.

I was beginning to breathe normally again. An ugly sickness seemed to be slipping away. I could see Jo and myself in California, broke maybe, but believing in myself and the future again, and not too proud to let the woman who loved me make my ambitions come true. Loving and laughing the way we used to.

And looking at the unconscious Porterfield and the sniveling, frightened woman, Madam Loo Loo, I thought again of Jo's words about superstition, "Some people let it rule their lives and sometimes destroy them."

Then I looked up at the portrait of Joseph Porterfield. The bullets had cut part of it to shreds, but his face was still recognizable. And across it, because of the angle at which I had turned the canvas, dangled the shadow of the Venetian blind cord loop, cast there by the setting sun streaming through the window.

It looked exactly as if I had painted across his face, the shadow of a hangman's noose.

The Last Trumpet

"YEAH," Big Lip said, "so the Earl is dead. Well, it's gotta come to us all. Sooner or later, it's gotta come to us all. But it's a shame he couldn't have stayed on a few more years. There was a lot of music left in him."

"That's what I said," Slim Wilson agreed. "Those were my very words. That's exactly what I said to Little Joe when we were dressing for the funeral. I said it's a shame the Earl had to go before he played all the music that was in him. Here, wait a minute, Big Lip, let me buy you this next beer. You paid for the last two and I want to get a couple now. Hey, Harry, ain't you got none colder than these you sold us? You run outa ice or somethin'?"

Big Lip shivered. He took his frayed cigar out of his mouth, looked at it, then put it back and lit it. "I don't like funerals. They give a man the shivers. And this damp cellar don't help none. I swear, it's funny. Look at me here, shivering and drinking ice cold beer. Guess I ought to be havin' a toddy or something, but the sweat's running offa me."

"I know. That's the way funerals affect me. They give me the cold sweats."

"Well, I guess we laid ol' Earl out the way he'd a wanted."

"Man couldn't-a wanted no better," Slim agreed. "I mean a man like the Earl. Just like the old days in New Orleans. Lord, I wonder how many funeral parades he played for in those days?"

"I don't know. But that's where he got his training. You know, blasting out on Rampart Street when they came back and let the tailgate on the wagon down so the 'bone man could run his horn and they swung out on that old time jazz. Something like that built up a man's lip. It wasn't like these easy jobs kids got nowadays, whispering into a mike in a cocktail lounge. A man just can't get no lip that away."

"None a-tall. None a-tall. Here, lemme light your cigar, man. It's went out again. Yeah, though, like you say, we laid him out in the old tradition, funeral band taking him to the graveyard, then coming back playing jazz."

"Wasn't nobody's heart in that."

"No, but we had to do it right."

"Yeah. The Earl wouldn't have wanted it loused up any. I guess he'll get written up in all the papers."

They fell silent for a minute.

"You reckon they'll ever find who murdered him?"

Big Lip took his cigar out of his mouth. "Look at me, sweatin' again. I swear I don't know how a man can be so cold and sweat so much."

"Funerals," Slim asserted. "They affect a man that way. No, the, way I look at it, Earl had been messin' around with somebody's woman. I don't mean no disrespect, but he had a way of takin' after these young girls. And they went for him too. You know, he was a man up there on a bandstand with that gold horn of his. Even if he was in his fifties, he was a man, built powerful around the shoulders and good to look at. I think it was some kinda woman trouble, don't you reckon, Big Lip? I mean, I'm just guessin', but you knew him better than anybody else in town. You played with him since the twenties. Don't you think that's the way of it?"

"Well, yeah, I guess it coulda. When you start thinking about it, it coulda happened that way."

"You gonna want some more beer?"

"No, I got to get over and see Sally. She phoned me to come over. I guess she'll want us to keep the band going, anyway until the contract runs out."

"Poor Sally. She's takin' it hard, ain't she? Well, she'll have plenty to live on, though, off the royalties of the Earl's compositions. He's made a world of money off those compositions."

"Yeah, he thought up some awful pretty stuff. Give a man the shivers the way that cat'd sit there starin' off into space with that gold horn in his hands and pretty soon he'd lift it up, thoughful like and start playing a new melody he'd dreamed up."

"Here, I'll get those last two."

Slim lingered to collect his change while the heavy, tired old man with the grey hair and thick lips that were his trade mark, plodded up the stairs. In the late afternoon sunlight, his musician's pallor was more pronounced than usual.

Big Lip went over to the Earl's apartment to talk with Sally. She was a heavy, middle-aged woman with thickly powdered features and plump white fingers covered with diamonds. She had been a pretty girl when the Earl married her thirty years ago. He had long since tired of her, but she still adored him so he never ran her off more than once or twice and then he let her come back to him.

Big Lip sat down at the baby grand in their living room. Sally was rocking slowly, crying. She had taken the Earl's golden horn out of the case and laid it on the baby grand beside the Earl's picture. It glowed in the dusk, golden and mellow, like the notes the Earl had blown out of it.

It made Big Lip want to play Lament for Trumpet, and he did, reverently, the way he played all of the Earl's melodies.

"You don't want to keep carrying on this way, Sally," he said as he played with his round, fat fingers. "The Earl wouldn't want you to be grievin' like that. He always lived happy."

"I know, Big Lip. I know the Earl would want it that way, just like you said. But that ain't why I'm cryin' now. Like I told you on the phone, I wanted you to come up here because I had some other bad news." She wadded her handkerchief up into a little wet ball and covered her brow with her hand. She rocked back and forth with her grief, crying harder. "Oh, Big Lip, you was the Earl's best friend. You know how he done.

He cheated on me and he drank and gambled. But one thing he was true to, was his music. Now ain't that right, Big Lip? You was his best friend. Now ain't that the truth? He never would have stolen all that music and called it his own. Would he, Big Lip?"

Big Lip's fingers froze in the middle of an arpeggio. He took his frayed cigar out of his mouth and his lips turned down sourly. He got out his handkerchief and wiped at the beads of sweat that had come out on his forehead again.

He got up and lumbered over to Sally.

"What are you talking about, woman?"

"It's that Allan Gerald, the Earl's brother." She had both of her hands over her face now, sobbing. "He come up here today, not two hours after we put Earl in his grave. He had all them papers that said the songs was his. He said he wrote 'em back in the twenties when he and the Earl had a band together. He said they was all his ideas for Lament for Trumpet, The Red Woman, Handful of Stars, Black and Blue Rhapsody—all of 'em. He had papers, Big Lip. Copyright papers, proving it. He said he was going to sue the Earl's estate for all the royalties off them songs."

Big Lip stood there, speechless.

"It ain't so, is it, Big Lip? I don't care about the money. I swear I don't. But this'll make the Earl out to be a cheap four-flusher instead of a great musician. They'll all laugh at him, and him dead and not able to defend himself. They can't do that to his memory, Big Lip. He was a great musician. He never stole no tunes."

Big Lip finally put his soggy cigar back in his mouth. "Course not he didn't, Sally. You sit there now and get ahold of yourself. There can't nobody say the Earl did anything like that, even his brother. I got to go down and get the band started playing for this evening. Let me think about this. I just can't see how Allan can come around saying a thing like that. He's too much of a dog to play anything right, much less think up a melody of his own."

Sally said, "He claimed the Earl has been paying him to keep quiet all these years, but now the Earl's dead and can't pay him no more hush money, so he wants all that royalty money for hisself."

Big Lip nodded and walked out.

HE plodded over to "swing lane," Fifty-second Street, to the little basement joint where he had been playing with the Earl's new band for the past six months. He would take over the management of it for Sally for the duration of their contract. After that they would probably split up, Big Lip more than likely heading for the West Coast.

He sat down at the piano now, like a sullen, grey-haired judge. The rest of the six-piece band was already on the stand, warming up their instruments. He tapped off the beat, struck an opening chord, and the ensemble slid into their natural, easy jazz, the way the Earl had styled the band.

They had a new trumpet man to take the Earl's place, a young fellow who blew a pretty enough horn and played all the Earl's solos the way he'd played them. But the magnetism of the great Earl's personality was gone and it was just another band, like the other dozens of bands that played on swing lane.

At the first intermission a man in a brown suit and a soft felt hat pushed off his forehead came over and showed Big Lip a badge. Big Lip stayed at the piano, his fingers running softly over the keys.

"Lieutenant Davidson, Homicide. I have to ask you some questions about the Earl."

"Yes sir. I'll tell you what I can."

"You know the Earl a long time?"

The big, ugly man with the shaggy head and thick lips gazed through his piano into the distant past. He played a chromatic progression and messed around With Black and Blue Rhapsody in C sharp. " Well, I grew up with him, Lieutenant. I went with him down to that pawn shop on Iberville Street in New Orleans when he bought his first horn. He was eleven years old, then."

"Your name is Sidney Johnson?"

"Yessir. All the cats call me Big Lip."

"Where were you Tuesday night at eleven o'clock when the Earl was killed up in that hotel room?"

"Here with the band. I always run the band for the Earl when he went somewheres."

"Did he tell you where he was going?"

"No sir. About ten o'clock he came over and told me he had to go somewhere for just an hour. But he never came back."

"Did he look worried?"

"Yessir." The perspiration came out on Big Lip's forehead. He played a haunting minor chord.

"Did you know a gambler named Monte Rossi?"

Big Lip's fingers tripped over themselves. He stopped playing to take out a handkerchief and sponge the damp beads off his face. "Yessir, I think I did see him around here now and then."

"The Earl owed him a considerable amount in I.O.U.'s."

"Is that right now?"

"You know it's right. Monte has been spreading it around that you were supposed to take the money to him for the Earl the night the Earl was murdered. Now he's saying the Earl gave you the money before he got killed, but you put it in your pocket instead of taking it to Monte. Monte's sore about it. I hear it was something like ten grand."

Big Lip swallowed painfully.

"You know a woman named Melissa Scott?"

Big Lip dropped his cigar. He bent down to pick it up, changed his mind. He took out his handkerchief and dabbed at his bull neck.

"I can't say I know the chick, Lieutenant. Is she messed up in this somehow?"

"You might say that. The Earl went from here to a little hotel on Forty-Seventh Street Tuesday night. Shortly after he was killed, witnesses saw this Melissa Scott run out of his room. We checked his bank account. He has recently made out some large checks to this Melissa Scott. It looks like she was putting some kind of heat on him."

Big Lip took a fresh cigar out of his plaid sport coat pocket.

"We can't find where this Scott gal lives," the lieutenant said. "We thought you might help us."

"Oh. Well, I guess I don't know, mister. Do you think Monte Rossi might have killed him?" he asked hopefully.

"He might have. Or you might have. Ten grand is a lot of money."

Big Lip's hand shook.

"Or," the lieutenant added, "The Earl's half Brother, Allan Gerald, might have. There was bad blood between them. However, we checked on Allan Gerald. He was in a crap game, at the Recreation Parlor the time the Earl was killed. He's got witnesses."

Then the plainclothesman said, "I sure wish we could find Melissa Scott. You think anybody else on this band might know?"

"No, sir. But you go ahead and ask them."

The man stayed around for a while. After he left, Big Lip played for another half hour. Then he suddenly got up and plodded off the stand.

He went out and hailed a taxi and rode it down to Times Square. He mingled with the crowd, went down a kiosk and took a subway for a couple of blocks. When he came out of that, he walked into a hotel, wandered around the lobby and went out a back exit. He stood on a dark street corner for a while, looking behind him. Finally he hailed another taxi.

Big Lip walked up two flights of stairs of a shabby building on the east side of town. He knocked on a door. A woman's voice told him to come in. The girl was sitting on the edge of the unmade bed. Her face was shiny with perspiration. A lock of her dark hair had fallen into her eyes. She was smoking steadily, filling a saucer with butts.

"The police was around talking to me, Melissa," he said. "They think maybe you killed the Earl and they're looking for you."

She inhaled deeply, sucking in her cheeks. "I know. I know they're looking for me." Her lips curled. "I guess you told them where I was."

"I didn't tell them nothing. But they told me some folks saw you come running outa the Earl's room after he was killed Tuesday night."

"Yeah. I guess they saw that all right. "

She was in her early twenties. She would have been pretty except for the wasted shadows under her eyes and the looseness around her mouth and the hard glitter in her eyes.

Big Lip sat down heavily. "Ain't it a shame what the craving for money can do to a woman."

"Oh, don't be a damn fool. I didn't kill him. I got a telephone call Tuesday night to hurry over to that hotel room. When I got there I found him dead. Somebody killed him and tried to frame me for it. They sure succeeded."

"You expect the police to believe that?"

"No. That's why I'm scared. They're going to pin this on me. Just as sure as I'm sitting here."

"But if you got an idea who called you—"

"I got an idea," she said, stabbing out her cigarette in the saucer savagely.

"But you're not gonna say who it was?"

"I can't. And anyway, it wouldn't do any good. No good at all."

Big Lip chewed on his cigar. After a while he heaved himself out of the chair. He shuffled to the door.

She called after him, "Monte Rossi was up here."

Big Lip stopped and stared at the door jamb. A drop of sweat traced a crooked pattern down the creases in his thick neck. "He was lookin' for you. He's madder'n hell about something."

Big Lip nodded heavily. He took out his handkerchief and dabbed at his face. His hand was shaking. Then he went down and took a cab to the Recreation Parlor.

It was a musicians' hangout. There was a bunch of them down there tonight. They were standing around in little groups, talking about the sensational murder of the great trumpet player and composer, Earl Gerald.

Big Lip sat down at a booth by himself and ordered a beer. Presently one of the musicians, a thin, dark-haired man with slender, nervous hands detached himself from the others and sat down in the booth with Big Lip.

"Evening, Big Lip."

"Evening, Mannie. You not working tonight?"

"Naw. The job at the Purple Lounge folded. We're going into some kind of upholstered sewer in the Village for six weeks, starting Saturday. Say, have you heard what Allan Gerald, Earl's brother is spreading around?"

"What is Allan Gerald spreading around?" Big Lip asked, sipping the head off the glass of beer. "He says he wrote all them tunes that made the Earl famous. Says he's got copyright papers to prove it. Ain't that something—the Earl with all his diamond stick pins and big talk, nothin' but a bum?"

"Don't you say that, Mannie. Don't you go to believing all the jazz that Allan Gerald spouts off. Now you listen to me, ugly old Big Lip. The Earl ain't never stole a thing. I played with that cat when he didn't know how to finger the "C" scale on his horn. He didn't have to steal those melodies; he was born with them. He was playing them when we was in high school. He wrote 'em all down and the band director made an arrangement for them. He used to play them around in jam sessions, ten years before he ever bothered to write 'em and get a copyright. That no-good Allan Gerald is the one did the stealing. If he's got any copyright it's because he used to hear the Earl fooling around with those tunes when they had a band together and he stole 'em then from the Earl!"

"Well, I guess you ought to know, Big Lip. Better'n anybody. But you'n Sally will have a hard time proving it. And meantime, Allan Gerald is sure going around hurtin' the Earl's reputation."

Big Lip chewed his cigar sourly. "Say, Mannie, was there a dice game going on here Tuesday night?"

"Well, I think so. Just a small one upstairs. Three or four fellows. Allan Gerald was up there, I think, and Cat Biggers and some of the guys. Why?"

"Nothin'. That Cat over there?"

"Yeah. The heavy-set boy with the corn on his lip. He blows trumpet with a bop outfit on Fifty-second."

Big Lip got ponderously to his feet. He called Cat Biggers into a corner.

"You was playing dice here Tuesday night, Cat?"

"What if I was, Big Lip?"

"Nothin'. Was Allan Gerald with you?"

"Why yes, he was, if it's any business of yours."

"You wouldn't lie to me, Cat?"

Biggers looked startled. He covered it with a bluff of anger. "Listen, you ain't coming around here callin' me a liar."

"That's just what I'm doin', Cat. I'm callin' you a liar. Allan wasn't here at all, was he?"

Biggers was shaking all over. Big Lip thought for a minute that the trumpet player would take a poke at him. But he just stood there shaking and finally turned around and walked off.

Big Lip touched a flickering match to the dead end of his cigar. He threw the match on the floor and lumbered out of the place.

He stood on the corner waiting for a taxi.

He was there maybe two minutes when Monte Rossi came up beside him and said, "Good evening, Big Lip."

Big Lip gave a little jump when Monte Rossi came up from behind him that way. He looked around and said a bit shakily, "Well, hello, Mr. Rossi. It's nice to see you."

"I'll bet it is," Rossi smiled.

The gambler had a soft, slurring voice like two pieces of silk being rubbed together. He was dressed in a dark blue suit with a fine deep red pin stripe. He had a white silk shirt on and a wine necktie with a hula girl hand-painted on it. He had both his hands in his coat pocket.

"No use you waiting on a taxi, Big Lip," he said pleasantly. "My car is parked right around the corner."

"Well, that's sure nice of you, Mr. Rossi. But I sure don't want to put you out of your way. No, I'll just wait here and a taxi will be along directly and take me back on over to Fifty-second where I'm going—"

"I think you better come with me, Big Lip."

Large drops of perspiration stood out across the big man's forehead. One of them traced a wet pattern down his cheek. His shirt collar had become soggy. He looked around the street. It was deserted. Then he looked back at Monte Rossi. The dead cigar fell out of his mouth and he started moving.

Like most white musicians who played every night in smoke-filled joints and slept all day, his complexion had an unhealthy pallor. Now it looked grey.

Rossi's man drove the big sedan. They cruised slowly through dark back streets.

Rossi and the piano player sat in the back seat.

"Now, I just thought I'd pick up that money, Big Lip. I know it's a lot of cash to be carrying around with you. No use in you worrying about it. You just give it over to me now and I'll give you the Earl's IOU's and you can give them to his widow."

Big Lip worked his forefinger under his soggy shirt collar. "Money, Mr. Rossi? What's this money you're talkin' about?" Rossi chuckled. It sounded like somebody crumpling up an old newspaper.

Big Lip said, "You better tell your man he's sure going out of the way, Mr. Rossi. I got to get back to the place. Band sounds awful bad without a piano. You tell him to turn left up here and head back to Fifty-second—"

Rossi leaned forward. He told his driver to stop at the next deserted alley. Then he took his left hand out of his pocket. He was holding a sap, a leather covered pouch of lead shot with a braided thong.

Big Lip's mouth felt like somebody's lawn after a six-month's drought.

The driver stopped the car in the mouth of the alley. He got out and went around the front. He lit a cigarette and stood there, looking up and down. Rossi opened the door and pushed Big Lip into the alley.

It was dark there and smelled of garbage. A stray cat howled and scurried from under their feet. It was silent then, except for the scuffling of their shoes on the cobblestones and the muffled thud of the sap and the whispered grunts of Big Lip who was holding his hands before his face.

Big Lip was down on one knee, holding his arm over his face and trying to get his breath. It felt as if the sap had broken his ribs because every time he tried to breathe something in his chest grated and stabbed at his lung.

"Don't hit me no more, Mr. Rossi," he pleaded. "I don't have that ten thousand dollars. I swear I don't. The Earl never gave it to me that night. He said he was going to. He told me he was going to give it to me later that night and he wanted me to take it over to your place after we got through for the evening. He was going to put it in a bag for me and I was supposed to give it to you and get the IOU's. But he never gave it to me. He got this telephone call about ten and he told me he was leaving for a while. He never came back. I swear that's the way it was, Mr. Rossi."

"You're lying, you damn honky-tonk piano player. He gave you that ten thousand, all right. Then you knocked him off and put the money in your pocket. Now ain't that right?"

"No! Ow! No, I swear he didn't—Ow! Don't do that, Mr. Rossi! I can't stand no more—oh, my God—"

Then everything was black for a while.

When Big Lip came dazedly around, he was sitting propped up against a brick wall in the alley. A police prowl car was shining its headlights into the alley and the plainclothesman, Lieutenant Davidson, was kneeling beside him.

"You lost us for a while," he said. "I had a tail on you, but you lost him when you left your night club. We didn't pick you up again until you went down to the Recreation Club. It's a good thing you did. Rossi was about to beat your brains out."

"You arrest him?" Big Lip mumbled.

"Yeah. He won't be beating anybody up for a while."

"Are you gonna arrest me for anything?

"I don't know. Do you want to tell me where the Scott girl is hiding out?"

"I said, I don't know."

Davidson thumbed his felt hat back on his head. "You're letting yourself in for a lot of trouble, Big Lip. I'm going to have to arrest somebody pretty soon. If we can't find Melissa Scott, it might be you."

Big Lip nursed his bruised jaw in silence.

"Okay, have it your way." Davidson stood up. "Where you want us to take you?"

"Back to the club," Big Lip said. "I got to finish out this evenin's job."

"Good Lord, you don't look like you're in any condition to play."

"I'm all right," Big Lip said, crawling painfully to his feet. He felt around in his pocket for a cigar, found a broken one in his breast pocket, and stuck half of it in his mouth.

WHEN they took him back to Club 52, they let him out on the front sidewalk. Big Lip went into the club, walked between the tables, past the bandstand, out the back door, and got himself a taxi. He drove to an apartment building on Third Avenue. He went up to the third floor and knocked on Allan Gerald's door.

Gerald opened the door a crack and peered out. His jaw sagged.

"Big Lip. What the hell 'r you doin' here?"

Big Lip gave the door a shove and propelled his ungainly body into the room. He looked distastefully at the great Earl's half brother. Allan was a skinny little pale-faced weasel. He played some piano but the sound of it was like him—insipid, shallow, artificial. From a musical, physical or character standpoint, Allan wasn't fit to take the Earl's horn out of his case for him.

"I was talkin' to Sally," Big Lip said. "She says you got some crooked copyright papers says you wrote the Earl's tunes."

"Crooked, hell. They're legal. I'll show 'em to you."

"You don't show me nothin'. Even if I saw it wrote down with ten lawyers signing it I wouldn't believe the Earl stole any tunes. I knew him too well. I guess out of all the people in the world who knew the Earl, you and me know him the best. And we both know the Earl wrote those tunes. Don't we, Allan?"

Allan Gerald moistened his lip. There was a crafty gleam in his eyes. "Between you an' me, Big Lip, we know that. But from now on, in the eyes of the world, the Earl is going to be a bum. All our lives, he's had the good things—the fame, the glory, the money. I ain't had nothin', except what I could make him pay me to keep quiet about those copyrights. Well, now I'm stepping into the Earl's shoes. I got the copyrights to prove those tunes are mine and you and Sally can't do nothing about it. I'm going to get all those royalties and I'm going to take his band. I'm going to put you on notice for the first thing and then I'm going to take that honky-tonk jazz band and make a smooth commercial hotel band out of it and make me some money."

"You mean," Big Lip said sadly, his heavy mouth turning down at the corners, "you'll take the soul out of a great, sincere organization and make a cheap mickey band outa it."

He felt around in his pocket for a match, couldn't find one. Then he picked up Allan Gerald's cigarette lighter off a table and sucked the flame against the cold ashes on the tip of his cigar.

"I can see the picture," he went on, "and don't you think I can't. You never fooled me none. You was blackmailin' the Earl to keep quiet about the copyrights. And you was makin' Melissa collect for you. That's why the Earl's bank showed canceled checks made out to her. The cops found that out, but they ain't found out Melissa was married to you. Nor, they ain't found out that Tuesday night, the Earl finally got some kind of real proof that those tunes was his. He went up to that hotel room to meet you. He shoved that there proof right under your nose, Allan Gerald. So you couldn't go on blackmailin' him no more. And he was goin' to have you sent to jail for all the blackmailin' you done to him in the past. So you killed him. Jest as sure as the Earl ever hit high C, you killed him. You was tired of Melissa anyway, so you phoned and told her to go up to where the Duke was layin' dead, hopin' she'd get picked up for the murder. Well, she darn near did."

Gerald was backing away, his face sick and frightened. "You can't prove that," he whispered hoarsely, licking his lips. "I was in the Recreation Club, shooting craps with some guys. I got three witnesses."

"I know," Big Lip said sadly, heavily. "Cat Biggers is one of them. I talked to him. You paid them witnesses off. You paid 'em off too good. They'll never tell the truth. So the police won't ever be able to send you to the chair, for the murder of your half brother, the Earl. But I'm going to get you for this, Allan Gerald. The Earl was more to me than a brother. I worshipped the man from the first day he touched a horn to his lips. He was greater than, all of us. He played stuff that was beyond the power of mortal man to understand. And you killed him, and I'm gonna get you, Allan." The big, ugly man's voice sank to a whisper. "So help me—I'm going to get you for this."

Allan Gerald dragged a short-snouted, nasty-looking revolver out of his pocket. "You get outa here," he cried, his voice rising to a falsetto. "You got no call to come around here talkin' like that. You get outa here right now, Big Lip. You hear me? Get out—"

Big Lip lumbered out of the room, his face sad. He walked for a long time, out in the cold damp night. Finally he took a cab over to Melissa's room again.

This time she did not answer his knock on the door. He tried the knob. It was unlocked. He went into the room.

She was there on the floor where she died. The front of her blouse was stained red. The revolver was still clutched in her right hand.

Big Lip sat down, all the strength gone out of his legs. He wiped a tear out of the corner of his eyes with his big, stubby forefinger. Then he searched his pocket for a match. He found Allan Gerald's initialed lighter which he had picked up and absently dropped in a pocket back in Gerald's room. He lit his cold cigar with it. He sat there for a while, blinking sadly.

Finally he noticed Melissa's suicide note on the dresser.

It was lying on a legal document which was a copyright notice dated some years back. The note said she was going to kill herself because she was convinced the police would find her and pin the Earl's murder on her. And because her husband, Allan Gerald, no longer loved her. She still loved him, too much to want to go on living without him.

She wanted Sally, the Earl's widow, to have the copyright papers. They dated back to the Earl's high school days and they covered some compositions he had written, which the band master had arranged and had copyrighted for him then, when he was still a boy. They contained the themes of all the melodies he later made famous. They proved the originality of everything he had ever written.

This was the proof that the Earl had found which wiped out Allan Gerald's claim to the compositions. How Melissa had come by them, Big Lip could only guess. Probably she had found them among Allan's papers since Tuesday night.

Big Lip stuffed the copyright paper in his pocket. He tore up the suicide note and thoughtfully swallowed it.

Then he took the pistol out of Melissa's dead hand, put it in his pocket. With a handkerchief, he picked up her lipstick from the dresser, scrawled a name on the floor near her outstretched hand, dropped the lipstick. He wiped every place in the room he might have touched. Just before leaving, he took out Allan Gerald's initialed cigarette lighter, wiped it, and dropped it on the floor.

He walked out and closed the door softly.

Before returning to Club 52, he made a brief telephone call to police headquarters. It was a strange call. His voice sounded muffled and not at all like itself.

He had been back at the Club 52 a couple of hours when the police inspector, Lieutenant Davidson, came in with a pale-faced Allan Gerald. Most of the crowd had gone by now and the boys were jamming a bit in the late hours.

Allan Gerald came up to the stand, fairly dragging Lieutenant Davidson to whom he was handcuffed. Allan's weasel face was sweat-slick.

"Big Lip," he babbled, "these crazy policemen got a telephone call and they went and found Melissa murdered in a room on the east side. Then they come over to my place and arrested me. Look, at the time they said she died, you was over in my room talking to me. You tell 'em, Big Lip. You tell 'em I was there and I couldn't have killed her."

Big Lip was playing Lament for Trumpet tenderly with his broad, stubby fingers. "Why, Allan Gerald, how you carry on. You know I ain't seen you for days. He really kill that poor girl, Lieutenant?"'

"Yeah. We found out she was his wife. The way we figure it, she had been playing around with the Earl, getting money from him. Tuesday night she got sore at him and shot him. This guy, Allan, finds out, tracks her down and kills her tonight. But she wrote his name with her lipstick before she died. Sorry to bother you, Big Lip. He insisted on dragging us down here. Come on, Allan!"

"No! No, please! Big Lip, you tell 'em! You hear me, Big Lip? Don't you let them send me to the electric chair for killin' Melissa. You know I didn't—"

Long after they had gone, Big Lip continued to play Lament for Trumpet, softly, sadly.

He played it for the Earl because it had been his theme song.

Mr. Banjo

A murder trial brought me back to my home town, Whitaker. I would never have gone back there if a certain wealthy doctor's wife and her boyfriend had not decided to knock off the good doctor in a "hunting accident." Their clumsiness got them arrested for capital murder. They wanted, and could afford, the best criminal lawyer in the state. So they hired me, Roger Spencer. I come high, but I have a national reputation. Since they were guilty as hell, they were going to need the kind of courtroom miracles I could pull off.

Whitaker had changed little in the thirty-odd years since I left. I drove into town in my new car and turned slowly down Main Street, the setting of a thousand boyhood memories. Old Hester's pharmacy was now a chain drugstore. The front of the Bijou had been remodeled and was now the Ciné, but for the most part, the store fronts had the same depressing, slightly seedy look as when I'd grown up here. It was as if the Great Depression had settled here and never left. I had the spooky feeling that if I walked into the barber shop, the calendar on the wall would read "1936."

Then I passed the corner where the First National Bank was still located, and suddenly I could hear a banjo plunking. It was a trick of memory, of course, because that was the corner where old Mr. Banjo used to sit on his apple box and play for nickels and dimes. After all these years, I could still see him clearly, a frail old man, his sightless eyes looking nowhere, his faithful old dog Rascal curled beside his box, and his banjo strumming merrily away.

Then the memories became chilling. I shivered and speeded up to get away from there but the ghostly banjo music followed me down the street. I drove to the new motel where I had a reservation.

For the next twenty-four hours I was extremely busy, meeting with my clients and their local attorney, preparing for the first day of jury selection.

I was leaving the courthouse about four the next afternoon when a rather nondescript, gray, middle-aged man approached me. "Mr. Spencer, Roger, remember me?"

I put on my professional, public-relations smile. "Why yes, I think so. Let me see now…" (Actually, I hadn't the vaguest idea who he was.)

"Dick Frazer. I–I guess we've all changed," he said, apologizing for my not remembering him.

Again flashed a flood of memories—the banjo ringing faintly down the corridor of years—and a slight chill rippled down my spine. "Dick! Of course I remember," I said with genuine warmth, shaking hands with him. "Why, we were good friends. We hunted squirrels and rabbits after school."

"Had to," he laughed. "Food came scarce in those days. Remember the rattlesnakes we used to trap and sell?"

I shuddered. "Don't remind me! Like you said, though, money was hard to come by. So you're still living here."

"Yes. I'm running the town's newspaper—still a weekly like it always was. I took it over after my father passed away. Listen, do you have a minute for a cup of coffee? You're a celebrity now. I'd like to get a story about you for this Friday's edition."

I could do that much for my boyhood chum, Dick Frazer. He'd been the only person in this entire town I'd given a hang about. I hadn't even come back for my old man's funeral. His sister, my Aunt Cynthia, sent me a wire the night his booze-riddled liver finally gave out. The wire said, "Your father died at eleven p.m. tonight." I had a strong urge to wire back, "So what?" but I guess we're all slaves to our conscience. I wired several thousand dollars to the funeral home here, told them to plant the old man in their best casket. I made only one stipulation, that they put a quart of cheap bourbon beside the body.

Over coffee at the local cafe, Dick said, "Roger, I guess you know this story I'm going to write will have the old "local boy makes good" angle. You were the only one in our school crowd who had the sense to get out of this town and make something of yourself. Remember Kate Lowery, the prettiest girl in our class? Everybody said she'd be a Broadway star one day. Well, she's still here, running a dingy little dance studio for kids, supporting her no-good husband. Cecil Buford our football captain. Well, he's running a service station. Some of them are dead now."

I know what he was thinking: me of all people, Roger Spencer, son of the town drunk, the least likely of us all to make it big. Life has some curious twists.

We had our coffee and chat and Dick made his notes for the story he was going to write about me, the story I told him, of course. Nobody knew the real story except me and a couple of other people who have been dead for a long time. That's the one part of my life about which even my wife Ellen doesn't know.

We left the cafe together and walked to the parking lot. On the way, we passed the First National Bank corner.

"Hey, Roger, remember that old tramp that played the banjo here on the corner?" Dick asked.

"Sure," I said, hurrying a little to get to my car.

"Mr. Banjo, we used to call him. He was a fixture on that corner for years. Remember how somebody got the crazy story started that he was one of those eccentric misers who went around in ragged clothes while he was hoarding a bunch of money hidden somewhere in his shack?"

"Yeah, I remember."

"Would you believe it, for years after he disappeared, folks in this town rooted around that shack where he lived, hunting for his buried treasure. Of course, they never found anything. Poor old guy never had more than the clothes on his back. But people like to dream. I often wondered what became of that old man. One day he just disappeared."

"Not much telling. Well, I've got to get back to the motel, Dick. Have a lot of briefs to read. Sure nice talking to you again after all these years."

"Same here." He looked admiringly at my car as I slid behind the wheel. "So glad for your success, Roger. Again, congratulations."

He said it a bit wistfully. I understood. He was one of many men who suddenly look around and find that middle age has arrived, and they must face the fact that life is never going to deliver the promises it made when they were young.

"It's all in the breaks, Dick," I said, and that was true. I'd just been one of the lucky ones. We shook hands and I drove out of the parking lot. Dick and I had been close, but that was more than thirty years ago. Now we had nothing in common, and I probably would never see him again. I preferred to leave the past where it belonged.

In my motel room, the large vanity mirrored my reflection: a tanned, still handsome man, gray over the temples, but a body kept trim by the best-equipped gym in town plus regular golf at the country club. I took off my expensive suit, my imported Italian shoes and the fancy wrist-watch guaranteed not to lose over two seconds in two months. I put it on the dresser beside the picture of Ellen, my lovely wife, and Pam, our daughter. It was a photo that I always carried with me.

I mixed a drink, then stretched out on the bed in my shorts. I'd brought along my banjo. I began idly strumming some chords. Playing the banjo was a hobby going back many years. I played for kicks and for charity shows back home. I'd found it an excellent therapy for unwinding the knots of tension that go with my profession.

Now the instrument brought the memories back again, this time in sharp focus.

Those had been hard times, growing up in Whitaker back in the thirties, but we kids made our own fun. My greatest treasure was a single-shot .22 squirrel rifle. Somehow my old man managed to stay sober enough one Christmas season to give it to me. Most of the time he spent in an alcoholic fog in some bar while I roamed around town and into the country pretty much as I pleased. As Dick said, we spent a lot of time on the river bottom hunting squirrels and rabbits, and I had developed a little business trapping and selling rattlesnakes to an outfit in Florida that canned the meat. That paid for my .22 cartridges and clothes my old man never quite managed to get around to buying for me. School was a sketchy affair, but I'd inherited a high I.Q. from my mother, who died when I was four. I read a lot on my own and made good grades despite all the times I played hooky to hunt.

I picked up music from that old blind beggar we called "Mr. Banjo." I'd once heard that his last name was Jones—Banjo Jones. I don't know for sure if that was really his name. He never told me. He probably didn't know himself.

He lived in a one-room, tar-paper shack out of town a ways, between the city dump and the river. A familiar sight in our town was Mr. Banjo trudging in every morning to take his place on his apple box beside the bank. He'd be carrying his banjo and holding the leash of his dog, Rascal. Rascal wasn't one of those fancy seeing eye dogs. He was just a big old mongrel, but he sensed with some kind of canine intuition that Mr. Banjo was blind and did a pretty good job of leading him around.

Kids like Dick and myself were fascinated by Mr. Banjo. We'd stop by the bank on our way home from school to hear him whanging away on his banjo. All we had to do was drop a coin in his tin cup, and he'd start off like a jukebox. If we didn't have a nickel or penny for his cup, we'd drop a steel washer in. He didn't know the difference. He seemed to enjoy playing. He'd whang that old banjo like he was performing on a stage with a spotlight, showing his toothless gums in a grin and nodding his gray head to the time of the music.

I guess I made friends with old Banjo because we were both what you might call town outcasts. I was "that ragged Spencer kid," son of the town drunk. Most of the nice kids in town—like that snooty Kate Lowery that I had a hopeless crush on because she was so pretty—wouldn't have anything to do with me. The town just tolerated old Banjo because they felt sorry for him, I guess. In those days, every place had its town beggar. Mr. Banjo was ours.

My roaming around the countryside with my squirrel rifle sometimes took me down to the city dump and past old Banjo's shack. Sometimes on Sundays (the only day he wasn't in town), he'd be sitting in front, sunning himself, Rascal curled at his feet. I began stopping off to talk to him. He was a strange old guy. I don't guess he had a full set of brains, but I liked to listen to him. He wouldn't talk much to people in town, so everybody thought he was a half-wit. I think it was because he was suspicious of people; but he trusted me. I'd get him started and he could tell stories by the hour. According to him, he'd been all over the United States before he came to Whitaker. He talked about cities like San Francisco, New Orleans, Memphis. To a kid who'd never been out of his home county, that was exciting stuff, even if most of it was lies. I guess it was listening to Banjo tell those stories that gave me the itchy feet that wanted to shake the dust of Whitaker forever.

Old Banjo taught me what I know about music. He'd put my fingers on the strings of his beat-up old instrument, showing me the way chords were made. I guess I had a natural ear because it wasn't long before I caught on. He must have liked me pretty much by then, because he hardly ever allowed anyone else to touch his battered, old, treasured banjo.

I don't know who the idiot was that started the rumor about Banjo having a fortune hidden in his shack. I guess it was the hard times. People were so desperate for money, they liked to believe stories like that. It probably got started when somebody read about a ragged bum who died on skid row and the police found a bunch of money sewed up in his mattress. Things like that do happen all the time—misers who live in rags, with hardly enough to eat, accumulating a fortune, penny by penny, until they have hoarded a bunch of money they hide in their dwellings because they don't trust banks.

Of course it was ridiculous to think poor old Banjo had anything besides his dog and his banjo and the shack he lived in, but I heard the rumors. Guys down at the barber shop who didn't have anything better to do would speculate on how much Banjo had stashed away. It got to be a kind of game around town, guessing the amount. "See that old bum," somebody would say when Banjo shuffled into town, holding

Rascal's leash. "He collects a lot of nickels and dimes and never spends a cent except for a few cans of beans every week. He's a miser. Must have hoarded thousands of dollars. No telling how much he's got hid." Somebody added fire to the rumors by claiming they'd seen Banjo ride the bus into the county seat with a heavy tin box under his arm—and come back without the box.

It might have been a harmless game if Sheriff Buck Mayden hadn't decided to get serious about it. You saw a lot of law officers like Buck in the small towns back in those days; men short on brains, but long on muscle. Buck was a big, sullen man with a mean streak. Everybody was afraid of him. His way of keeping law and order was to pack a big six-shooter on his hip and bully people into respecting him.

Buck got to be sheriff when old Sheriff Honer died. Well, Buck hadn't been sheriff long before he started making life miserable for old Banjo. I saw him talking to Banjo in front of the bank one day. The next day, Banjo didn't show up in his usual place. That was the first time in my entire life I could remember that I didn't see Banjo with his dog, his cup and his apple box on Main Street.

I went out to his shack, expecting to find him sick, but he was sitting out front on his apple box, looking sad. "Sheriff says the city's got a law against beggars," he told me. "Sheriff says I got to buy a license. I ain't no beggar. I play music for a living," he said with a stirring of pride.

"How much does the license cost?" I asked.

"Sheriff says it's twenty-five dollars to start and ten dollars a week after that. The old sheriff never told me nothin' about a license like that when he was living."

I whistled softly. That was a big sum of money in 1936. "You goin' to pay it?"

"Where'm I goin' to get money like that? Guess I'll have to move along. Don't much feel like it, though. I'm gettin' too old to go driftin' around the country. Always figured to spend the rest of my days here."

The next several days, whenever I went down to Banjo's shack, he was sitting in the same place out front, staring straight ahead, his blind eyes looking at nothing. I figured he didn't have anything to eat, so I cooked up some rabbit stew and took it out to him.

One afternoon, when I was approaching the shack, I saw the sheriff s car parked there. Buck drove one of those black 1934 Ford V-Eights that Clyde Barrow liked.

I sneaked closer to see what was going on. Buck was standing over Banjo, yelling at him. The old man looked scared. "You got that twenty-five dollars. I know you have. That and a lot more! Now where is it?"

Banjo made some kind of frightened, pleading sound, holding up his hands as if to protect himself. He kept shaking his head vigorously when Buck asked about money.

Buck uttered a scorching swearword and stomped into the shack. I heard him throwing things around in there. It sounded as if he were tearing the place apart, board by board. I hid behind a bush. My heart was thumping. Like everyone else in the county, I was afraid of Buck Mayden. Wasn't a thing I could do but sit there and watch.

After a while, Buck came out, looking mad and frustrated. "Where is it, you old fool? Where you got that money hid?"

"Ain't got no money hid," Banjo whined.

"Th' hell you ain't! You stingy old miser. You been hoarding them nickels and dimes for years. Where you got them hid?"

Banjo just kept shaking his head. Buck suddenly grabbed him and gave him a hard shaking. It was like shaking a sackful of rattling bones.

Rascal was growling fiercely. Then, to protect his master, he charged Buck. He sank his fangs in Buck's leg. Buck let out a howl of pain and fury. He shook the dog loose, then drew his big old six-shooter and shot Rascal dead.

Poor old Banjo let out a cry of grief. He knelt on the ground beside the dog that had been his companion for so many years. Buck grabbed Banjo again and started giving him a terrible pistol whipping. He'd stop from time to time, sweating and panting, and demand to know where Banjo had his money hidden, but Banjo would only shake his bloody head and beg the sheriff to stop hitting him.

Finally Buck yelled, "Well, if you ain't got no money, then you're a vagrant and you're goin' to jail! Get in there!" and he threw Banjo into the back seat of his car.

I sat behind the bush a long time after they'd left, feeling sick. Finally I went down and dug a hole behind the shack and buried Rascal. I made the grave as nice as I could, and put a piece of broken concrete that I dragged over from the dumping grounds for a headstone and wrote "Rascal" on it with a pencil.

There wasn't much left inside the shack. Buck had ripped the mattress apart, torn up the flooring, cut Banjo's few clothes to shreds. I found the old banjo and tin cup in the wreckage and carried them home with me.

Next day, I went down to the jail. The sheriff's office with its two-cell jail was situated in a little brick building near the outskirts of town. Respectable people never went near the place. I knew where it was because my old man spent a lot of Saturday nights there, sleeping off drunks.

Buck was leaning back in his swivel chair, his boots crossed and propped on his scarred desk. He was chewing a match and reading the *Police Gazette.* When I came in, he glanced up. "What do you want, kid? I ain't got your old man in here today."

"I wonder if I could see Banjo," I said.

He went back to reading. "Can't nobody see him. He's a dangerous prisoner. Got him in solitary confinement."

I screwed up my courage to ask, "How come he's in jail?"

"Attacking an officer, resisting arrest. Vagrancy. Mostly vagrancy."

"How long's he gonna be in jail?"

"Till he can pay his fine."

"Where's he gonna get the money?"

"Oh, he's got it. He's got a lot of money hidden somewhere, but he's too tight-fisted to tell anybody. He'd rather rot in jail. Now go on, beat it, kid."

I stood on one foot, then another, thinking fast. "Well," I said, "me'n ol' Banjo's pretty good friends. I'd sure like to see him get out of jail. Maybe if I could talk to him, he'd tell me where his money is. He trusts me."

Buck slowly lowered his *Police Gazette,* gave me a thoughtful look as he sucked on his match. Finally, he spat out some frayed match pieces, got up and took the cell key out of his pocket. "You find out where he keeps his money so's he can pay his fine and we'll let him go."

"How much is his fine?"

"That depends. First you find out where his money is."

Buck unlocked the cell door. I went in. Poor old Banjo was lying on a smelly bunk. He looked real bad. The blood was dried and crusted on his face and in his gray hair. It was plain to see he'd had no medical attention. Probably nothing to eat, either.

"Hi, Banjo," I said, trying to sound cheerful. "It's me, Roger. I came to see you."

He turned his sightless face slowly, painfully in my direction. "Hello, boy," he whispered faintly.

I said, "I brought your banjo. Figured you'd like to have it. It wasn't hurt none."

For the first time he showed a little life. He reached out with shaking hands. I put the banjo in his hands and he hugged it close. Some tears rolled out of his eyes. That surprised me. I didn't know blind people could cry.

I looked around to see if Buck was listening, but he'd gone back up front to his desk. "Here's a candy bar," I whispered, sneaking it out of my pocket. He thanked me, but he put it beside him without eating it. I guess he was too sick to eat.

"Buck said he'd let you go if you'll pay a fine," I said.

He shook his head. "Ain't got no money to pay a fine." He turned his face to the wall. "I'm going to die here."

He wouldn't say anything else. I finally called Buck to let me out of the cell. I looked back once. The old man was lying there, hugging his banjo, his face turned to the wall.

"Well?" Buck demanded. "Did he tell you?"

I shook my head and Buck muttered some cuss words.

I went home, got my rifle and spent the rest of the day down on the river bottom, plinking around and checking the rocks for rattlesnakes. I was feeling pretty low. I couldn't sleep much that night, thinking about poor old Banjo. There wasn't any use talking to anybody in town about him. Nobody was going to cross Buck Mayden over a worthless old beggar. Banjo was going to die in that jail cell, just like he said.

Sometime during the night I hit on a way I could save Banjo. I sat straight up in bed, sweating and scared, my heart pounding. I tried to stop thinking about it, but I couldn't. Finally I knew I was going to do it.

The next day I skipped school and made a trip out to Banjo's shack. Then I hiked back to town. It was early afternoon when I got to the jail. Buck scowled when I walked into his office. "You back again?"

I wet my lips and swallowed hard. "Could I please see Banjo one more time? I sure want to get him out of jail. Maybe he'll tell me today about where his money's hid."

Buck was in a real mean, sullen mood. "Don't know why he'd tell you when he won't tell me. That's the stubbornest old miser I ever saw. He'd rather lay there and die than tell me where his money's hid."

"Let me try," I pleaded. "He came close to telling me yesterday."

Buck gave me a hard, suspicious look. "How do I know if he tells you, you won't run out there and dig the money up and keep it yourself?"

"Then how could I get Banjo out of jail?" I pointed out. "Please; he's gonna die if I can't get him out soon."

I guess I did a good job of convincing him. He scowled at me hard but said, "Well, it won't hurt to try. He's sure not going to tell me. But let me warn you, you're in big trouble, boy, if you try to make off with that money. I'll throw both you and your old man in jail."

He took me back to Banjo's cell and left us alone for a while. Banjo was worse than the day before. He was only partly conscious. I leaned over his bunk, whispering to him.

When Buck came to get me out of the cell, I said, "Well, he told me."

Buck's eyes lit up like the electric sign in front of the Bijou. "You tellin' the truth, kid?"

"Sure. I know where to find it."

"Well, I'm not trusting you. Come on. We'll go out there and you'll show me where it is."

Buck got his Stetson hat and buckled on his big six-shooter. We drove out of town fast in his V-Eight Ford. We went down the dirt road to Banjo's shack in a cloud of dust. When we got there, I led the way around the shack in the direction of the dump grounds. Finally I pointed to the rusting remains of a Model T. "Under there. He's got it buried there."

"Whoopee!" yelled Buck. "You stay back here, kid," he warned. Then he ran to the wrecked car and started digging wildly, throwing trash and loose dirt aside. There were dark sweat stains around the arms and neck of his shirt. Then I heard him give a panting exclamation when he came to the can. He clawed the lid off and plunged his hand down for the money.

Then he let out a bellowing scream and leaped to his feet. Dangling from his arm was the big, diamond-backed rattlesnake I'd put there earlier that day. The snake's fangs were sunk in Buck's wrist. He screamed again with pain and fright. He shook the snake off, yanked out his six-shooter and blew its head off.

I'd stood there, petrified. Now I broke into a dead run, back to Buck's car. I grabbed the keys out of the ignition and sprinted toward the woods.

Behind me I heard Buck's enraged bellow. "Come back here, you lousy kid!"

I ran all the faster, zigzagging around the trash in the dump grounds. I heard the roar of his six-shooter. The buzz of .45 slugs were around me like angry hornets. Then I reached the woods and plunged into the brush. I heard him coming after me, crashing limbs. He was sobbing and bellowing with a mixture of pain, fright and anger.

For a long time I ran through the brush along the riverbank with Buck floundering and crashing behind me. Luckily, I'd spent so much time down here I knew every trail and bush. I don't know how long Buck chased me but at last I heard a final crash in the brush behind me, then silence. I crept back to make sure it wasn't a trick. It wasn't. Buck was sprawled out on his back, staring up at the sky with glassy, scared eyes. Sweat was pouring off him. His arm was swollen up like a balloon. It was turning purple.

It took a long time for Buck to die. I sat on the ground and watched. He got delirious. He'd cuss for a while, then he'd sing. Sometimes he'd try to get up, but he'd fall back down and lie there. Finally, at sundown, he died. I waited a while, then went over and looked down at him. His bulging eyes were staring straight up at the sky like glass marbles about to pop out of the sockets. I forced myself to reach in the pockets of his sweat-soaked clothing for the jail keys. Then I ran back to his car.

It was dark when I drove up to the jail. I made sure no one was around; then I went inside, turned on a light and unlocked Banjo's cell. "It's me, Roger. Come on. I'm going to get you out of here."

Two things: I had to get us away from this town before people started looking for Buck, and I had to get Banjo to a doctor.

The old man was so weak I half-dragged him out to the car, but he wouldn't leave his banjo behind. He lay down on the back seat, still hugging his banjo while I drove out of town.

I figured it might be several days before somebody found Sheriff Buck Mayden, but I drove all night to be on the safe side, crossing the state line about dawn. The first large town I came to, I asked how to find a hospital that had a charity ward. It wasn't long before I had Banjo in the county hospital and a doctor was working on him.

I went to get some breakfast and I ditched Buck's car on the other side of town.

When I got back to the hospital, they'd cleaned Banjo up and he looked nice and peaceful in a hospital gown on a bed in the charity ward. He was sleeping. The awful look of pain was erased. A nurse told me they'd given him a shot to make him comfortable.

I hung around the hospital most of that day. I told them Banjo was my uncle and that he got all banged up when he fell off a horse. His foot was caught in the stirrup and the horse dragged him. I'd read about that happening to a guy in a pulp western story.

That night I slept on a park bench. The next morning I went to see Banjo again at the hospital, but his bed was empty.

The doctor saw me and called me aside. He explained that Banjo had died peacefully in his sleep during the night. "We did what we could for him, but he was a very old man." He asked if we had any money and I said we didn't and he said that he'd arrange for the county to bury the old man.

They gave me a small bundle, the bloodstained rags he'd been wearing when I brought him in, and his banjo. I went down to the park bench where I sat alone and cried a little.

I hit the road after that. I did what a lot of young guys were doing those depression years. I worked the C.C.C. camps and roughnecked in the oil fields.

In 1938, I was roughnecking in an oil field near Seguin, Texas. Wherever I went, I always took Banjo's beat-up old instrument with me. I was in my rented room one night, plunking some chords, trying to learn a tune that was popular that year. The head on the banjo split. I took it apart to see if I could fix it. It was easy—a blind man could do it. When I removed the head, I found pasted inside the banjo five one-thousand-dollar bills. That was a lot of money in those days—enough to take a smart kid out of the C.C.C. camps and oil fields and put him through law school.

I've liked banjo music ever since.

Mind Over Murder

"DOCTOR REED, I believe my wife is planning to murder me."

That was the opening statement made by the patient when he made his first office call.

"I see," I replied. "And why do you think she is planning such a thing?"

"Her attitude. A number of clues."

A guarded expression had crossed his face, one a trained observer such as myself notices at once. There were things he was not going to tell me on this first visit. Never mind; they would come out in time. It was not my place to push such matters but rather to listen when he was ready to get them off his chest.

I tried another tack, partly to satisfy my own curiosity. "And why, Mr. Clefton, have you decided to come to a psychiatrist rather than go to the police?"

He gave me a long, thoughtful stare. He was middle-aged and wore rather thick glasses. "All right, I'll be frank with you. I don't actually have any definite proof—I mean the kind you go to the police with. It's, well, it's more of a feeling I've had lately. Call it intuition, if you wish. You'd never think there was a thing wrong on the surface. Sylvia is a pleasant, agreeable woman. She's, well, I suppose what one would call a devoted wife. And yet I have this uneasy feeling. The way I catch her looking at me sometimes when she doesn't think I notice."

"Looking how, Mr. Clefton?"

He hesitated "Looking as if she wished I were dead."

"Hmmm," I said toying with a pencil on my desk, but observing him out of the corner of my eye.

He was beginning to perspire. He took out a handkerchief and mopped his forehead. "I tell you, it's getting scary living under the same roof with that woman. Still, I don't have any evidence that she's actually planning such a thing. I want you to tell me if I'm really in any danger or if I'm just letting my nerves get the better of me, if I'm imagining all this."

"Hmmm," I said again, my trained mind touching several bases. The man was obviously under a severe nervous strain. He could be hallucinating. I was inclined to suspect paranoia, but I never like to make snap judgments on such little evidence.

I cleared my throat. "Now, Mr. Clefton, can you tell me why you think your wife would want to murder you?"

He gave me a blank stare. "That's just it. I don't know why. She's always been so agreeable. Everyone who knows us will tell you what a fine, loyal and considerate woman she is."

"Does she have reason to suspect you of infidelity?"

"Oh, no. Nothing like that."

He looked shocked and I was inclined to believe him. I would verify this later with psychological testing but I doubted if sex were a very strong factor in Gladsel F. Clefton's life, so I passed it by.

"The other way around, then. Do you suspect her of being interested in another man? Would she want you out of the way for any reason like that?"

"Sylvia?" His eyes widened incredulously. "Absolutely not. If there were ever a faithful wife, it is she. Never once in the ten years of our marriage has she ever looked at another man. I resent your even implying such a thing."

He had become quite defensive and huffy, so I backed off quickly.

"I'm sure she is entirely faithful, Mr. Clefton, but we have to explore these things, don't we, if we are to get to the bottom of this matter? Now, how about money?"

His attitude changed quickly from displeasure with me to guarded suspicion. "What do you mean by that?"

"What I mean is, Mr. Clefton, would your wife stand to gain a great deal financially if she were suddenly to become a widow?"

"Oh." His expression became rather blank again. He shrugged. "Money wouldn't be that important to Sylvia. She always had plenty before we were married. Sure, she'd be well-fixed if something happened to me, but why kill me to get it? She has her own checking account now. She can have anything she wants."

I made a mental note to check his financial status. Then I said, "Well, we've pretty well eliminated the usual motives, haven't we?"

He nodded. "Yes, but you see, that's what makes it more terrifying. I thought about those things, too, and you know what conclusion I came to?" His gaze fixed on me. He leaned forward slightly. "I think she wants to kill me for the pure pleasure of it. That's what's so outright frightening."

He was frightened all right. He'd started perspiring again. His hand shook visibly as he patted his handkerchief against his glistening forehead.

I made an attempt to reassure him. "I don't think you are in any immediate danger, Mr. Clefton. Now, I'd like to set you up for a battery of psychological tests. Then we'll be talking to you some more. How about Mrs. Clefton? Do you think we could prevail upon her to come to the office?"

He shook his head. "No way. She thinks psychiatry is a lot of nonsense. Besides, how would it look, me asking her to come here because I have this notion she's planning to murder me?"

"Well, don't worry about it. It probably won't be necessary anyway." I consulted my appointment pad. "Could you come in tomorrow afternoon at 3:30? We can begin our tests then, if it's convenient."

He nodded. "I sure hope you can help me get this thing straightened out, Doctor. It's a nightmare to go around frightened all the time, afraid to eat anything she gives me, afraid to sleep. If it's just my imagination, I want to get over it. If she really is planning to murder me, I want to go to the police."

I assured him that we would help him regain his peace of mind in either case. Then he left after a rather damp, parting handshake.

I instructed my secretary to get a financial report on him, plus what other personal data she could uncover. When she put the information on my desk late that afternoon, I learned some interesting facts about Mr. Clefton, among them that he was a pretty wealthy man. I also was pleased to confirm my primary diagnosis.

We went through the usual testing, more or less as a matter of routine, then began a series of office visits twice a week. I set my fee at one hundred dollars per hour. Mr. Clefton was quite able to afford that.

I saw Gladsel Clefton on a regular twice-a-week basis for the next six months. I did not attempt any deep Freudian analysis. I simply allowed him to talk about whatever came to his mind to ease his tensions. Invariably, the conversation revolved around his wife. I came to know her quite well through our dialogues. She had married rather late in life, in her mid-thirties. She was not pretty—Mr. Clefton showed me her picture—but her eyes were large and deep and lent a haunting quality to her otherwise plain face. She was an only child of a stuffy, well-to-do, New England family. Apparently, there had been no romance in her life until she married Gladsel Clefton.

"There's always been something odd about her," Mr. Clefton told me. "She's so quiet, and always looking at me. At first I thought she was merely neurotic. You know, that sheltered, ingrown life she led at home. But now it's more than that. Sometimes I'll wake up at night and she's sitting up in bed wide awake and staring at me. God only knows how long she's been sitting there like that. I know what's going through her mind—how she's going to kill me."

"Oh, but that is only your own suspicion, Mr. Clefton. We know there is no concrete evidence that she's planning any such thing at all."

"She is!" he shouted. "I tell you, she is, and if you saw that look in her eyes just once, you'd believe me."

I have never had a patient so entirely in the grip of an obsession. It was beginning to tell on him visibly. He was losing weight. His hair was falling out. There were deep circles under his eyes. His hands shook constantly. The man was virtually aging before my eyes.

One night he called me at my home about midnight. "It's happened," he gasped hoarsely. "Poison. I'm so sick. Dying. She left right after supper to spend the night with her sister…left me to die here all alone."

"I'll call an ambulance," I said quickly, "and I'll contact a good doctor to meet you at the hospital."

I notified a friend, a Doctor Meredith. Meredith called me the next morning. "We pumped his stomach. There was no poison. He kept saying he'd been poisoned. Hell of a stomach spasm, though. I suspect an ulcer. We're making X-rays today to check on that, and I'm putting him on tranquilizers. The man's a nervous wreck."

"Yes, he is that," I agreed.

Clefton did a little better on the tranquilizers, but they did not remove his growing obsession that he was going to be murdered by his wife. His fears were reinforced by "accidents" that began occurring with increasing frequency. He was almost run down by a car. He heard a shot one night while he was crossing his lawn and swore a bullet just missed him.

"I know her plan now," he said. "She isn't going to do it herself. That's where I was mistaken. She's having it done. She's hired a professional killer. He missed those first times, but he'll get me sooner or later. I know now I'm not imagining anything. I have the kind of evidence the police will listen to. I appreciate the time you've spent on my case, Doctor, but I won't need to come here anymore. It's a matter for the police now." He arose to leave.

I glanced at my file on Gladsel F. Clefton. He had been coming to this office for exactly six months. I closed the file.

"I understand Mr. Clefton. I have to visit a patient at the hospital. I'll take you by the police station on the way."

"But I have my car."

"I think it would be better if you go with me. I might be able to help."

"Well, all right, then."

"If you'll wait outside for me, I'll be right with you. I have one call to make before I leave the office."

A few minutes later we were in my car, threading our way into the late afternoon traffic. It had been spring when Gladsel Clefton began visiting me six months ago. Now it was winter, a dark, chilly day dampened by a fine mist.

Mr. Clefton was slouched down beside me, chain-smoking cigarettes with trembling fingers. The strain of the past months had shrunk his body and yellowed his skin. There was a sour odor about him.

We drove for a while; then he sat up, becoming more alert. "What are we doing out here on the freeway?"

"It's all right, Mr. Clefton."

He became quite agitated. "I want you to take me to the police station. There's no police station out here. We're on the way out of town."

"Of course, Mr. Clefton. I just wanted to make a call first."

I took an exit road. We were on the rim of the city. I pulled into the winding drive of a cemetery.

"What are you doing here?" He began clawing at the door. "I don't want to come here." He looked at me with wild eyes. "Turn the car around. I don't want to come to this place."

"We have to come here now, Mr. Clefton."

I stopped the car, got out and walked around to open his door. He cowered back against the seat. "No," he whimpered. "No, I don't want to go out there."

"But you must," I insisted, grasped his wrist and half dragged him out of the car. He protested as I pulled him stumbling beside me along a graveled path. The cold winter wind blew wet leaves against us. It was nearly twilight. Then we stood before a headstone. "Look at it, Mr. Clefton."

"No!" he moaned. He tried to cover his face with his hands. His legs gave way and he sank to his knees. "No, I won't look."

I pried his hands from his face. "Look at it, Mr. Clefton. Come out of your make-believe world and look at reality."

His eyes, bugging behind thick lenses, stared at the words carved in the glistening, wet marble: *Here Lies Sylvia Clefton, Beloved Wife of Gladsel Clefton.*

"Your wife has been dead over a year, Mr. Clefton. My secretary found that out when I had her check on your background that first day you came to my office. You had begun hallucinating at that time. You believed your wife still to be alive and to be a threat to you. Why, sir? Was it because guilt had become too great a burden for your mind? The human mind can stand the pressure of just so much guilt, and then it has to escape into a world it invents. Your dead wife became a symbol of your own conscience, threatening to destroy you. Why so much guilt, Mr. Clefton? Because you murdered your wife? It's the only explanation. She died under mysterious circumstances, run down by a hit-and-run driver in front of her own home. The police never found the driver or vehicle that killed her. You were a poor man until you married Sylvia. You wanted her money, but not her. But she was a kind, gentle woman, and now your mind cannot live with what you have done."

An unearthly scream wrenched from his lips. He began babbling incoherently. Then he started running between the tombstones, a keening wail, more animal than human, coming from his lips.

"Jerry!" I called sharply.

The phone call I had made before leaving my office had been to Jerry Halsey, a husky psychiatric nurse. I had instructed him to be waiting for us here. Now he appeared out of the dark, cold mist and grabbed Gladsel Clefton, who was quite mad.

Anyone in the psychiatric field will tell you that confronting a hallucinating patient in Gladsel Clefton's condition with such a sudden shock of reality could push him over the edge of a complete psychotic break; but the only alternative would have been to allow him to go to the police, and that I did not want.

He has been in a private sanitarium for the past two years. I am continuing to see him on a regular weekly basis. A slight improvement in his condition has been noted but any real recovery is doubtful.

No, I have not informed the police, nor will I. As you know, information between a patient and his physician is privileged. Besides, how often does one get a patient who can afford a fee of one hundred dollars per hour indefinitely?

Class Reunion

THE banner across one wall in the Plaza Hotel banquet room welcomed "Jacksonville High, Class of '53." The crowd milling around in the room was on the rim of middle age. Temples were graying, bald spots were in evidence.

Tad Jarmon roamed through the crowd. At the bar, he found his old friend Lowell Oliver, whom he had not seen since graduation. "Hello, Lowell," he said.

Oliver drained his glass. "Hi, ol' buddy," he said with a loose grin. He shoved his face closer in an effort to focus his eyes. Suddenly, he became oddly sober. "Tad Jarmon."

"In the flesh."

"Well, good to see you, Tad. You haven't changed much." He held his glass toward the bartender for a refill. His hand was shaking slightly.

"We've all changed some, Lowell. It's been twenty years."

"Twenty years. Yeah, twenty years."

"Have you seen Jack and Duncan?"

"They're around here someplace," Oliver mumbled.

"We'll have to get together after the banquet and talk over old times," Tad said.

Oliver stared at him with a peculiar expression. Beads of perspiration stood out on his forehead. "Old times. Yeah, sure, Tad."

Tad Jarmon meandered back into the crowd. Soon he spotted Jack Harriman with a circle of friends in another corner of the room. Jack looked every inch the prosperous businessman. He was expensively dressed. His face was deeply tanned, but he was growing paunchy. He'd put on at least forty pounds since graduation.

"Hello, Jack."

Harriman turned. His smile became frozen. "Well, if it isn't Tad Jarmon." He reached out for a handshake. "You guys all remember Tad," he said a trifle too loudly. His hand felt damp in Tad's clasp.

One of their ex-schoolmates grinned. "I remember how you two guys and Duncan Gitterhouse and Lowell Oliver were always pulling off practical jokes on the town."

"Yeah," another added. "If something weird happened, everybody figured you four guys had a hand in it. Like the time the clock in the courthouse steeple started running backward. Took them a week to figure out how to get it to run in the right direction again. Nobody could prove anything, but we all knew you four guys did it."

The group chuckled.

"I saw Lowell over at the bar," Tad said to Harriman. "I told him we should get together after the banquet and talk over old times."

"Old times…" Harriman repeated a hollow note creeping into his voice. "Well, sure, Tad." He wiped a nervous hand across his chin. "By the way, where are you living now?"

"Still right here in Jacksonville, in the big old stuffy house on the hill. After my dad died, I just stayed on there."

Tad excused himself and went in search of Duncan Gitterhouse. He soon found him, a man turned prematurely gray, with a deeply-lined face and brooding eyes.

"Well, Duncan, I guess I should call you 'Doctor' now."

"That's just for my patients," Gitterhouse replied, his deep-set eyes resting somberly on Tad. "I was pretty sure I'd be seeing you here."

"Well, you know I couldn't pass up the opportunity of talking over old times with you and Jack and Lowell. Maybe after the banquet, the four of us can get together."

The doctor's eyes appeared to sink deeper and grow more resigned. "Yes, Tad."

The banquet was followed by speeches and introductions. Each alumnus arose and told briefly what he had done since graduation. When the master of ceremonies came to Tad, he said, "Well, I'm sure you all remember this next guy. He and his three buddies sure did liven up our school years. Remember the Halloween we found old Mrs. Gifford's wheelchair on top of the school building? And the stink bombs that went off during assembly meetings? They never could prove who did any of those things, but we all knew. How about confessing now, Tad? The statute of limitations has run out."

Tad arose amid laughter and applause. He grinned and shook his head. "I won't talk. My lips are sealed."

After the banquet, the four chums from high school days drifted outside and crossed the street to a small, quiet town-square park. Jack Harriman lit an expensive cigar.

"It hasn't changed, has it?" Duncan Gitterhouse said, looking up at the ancient, dome-shaped courthouse, at the Civil War monument, the heavy magnolia trees, the quiet streets. "It's as if everything stopped the night we graduated, and time stood still ever since."

"The night we graduated," Jack Harriman echoed. He pressed a finger against his cheek, which was beginning to twitch again. "Seems like a thousand years ago."

"Does it?" Tad said. "That's odd. Time, is relative, though. To me it's just like last night."

"We don't have any business talking about it," Duncan Gitterhouse said harshly. "I don't know why I came here for this ridiculous class reunion. It was insanity."

"Don't know why you came back, Duncan?" Tad said softly. "I think I do. You couldn't stay away. None of you could. You had to know if anyone ever suspected what we did that night. And you wanted to find out what that night did to the rest of us, how it changed our lives. We shared something so powerful it will bind us together always. I was sure you'd all come back."

"Still the amateur psychologist, Tad?" Harriman asked sourly.

Tad shrugged.

"It was your fault, what we did that night, Tad," Lowell Oliver said, beginning to blubber in a near-alcoholic crying jag. "You were always the ringleader. We followed you like sheep. Whatever crazy, sick schemes you thought up…"

"We were just kids," Gitterhouse argued angrily. "Just irresponsible kids, all of us. Nobody could be held accountable."

"Just kids? We were old enough in this state to have been tried for murder," Tad pointed out.

There was a heavy silence. Then Tad murmured slowly, "I used to go past the place on the creek where old Pete Bonner had his house-trailer. For years you could see where the fire had been. The ground was black and the rusty framework of the house-trailer was still there. It was finally cleared away when the shopping center was built, but every time I go by that place, I think about the night old Pete Bonner died there. And I think about us. A person acts; the act is over in a few minutes. But the aftermath of the act lives on in our emotions, our brains, perhaps forever. We committed an act twenty years ago. The next day, they buried what was left of old Pete. We're stuck with that for the rest of our lives."

They fell silent again, each thinking back to that night. It was true that Tad had been the ringleader of their tight little group, and the night of their graduation, it was Tad who thought of the final, monstrous prank: "Let's set Pete Bonner's trailer on fire."

"But Pete's liable to be in the trailer," one of the others had said.

"That's the whole point." Tad had grinned then explained, "After tonight, we'll be going in different directions. Duncan is going into medical school. Lowell's going into the Army. Jack's going to business college. I'll probably stay here. We need to do something so stupendous, so important, that it will weld the four of us together forever. So, we'll roast old Pete Bonner alive."

Tad had pointed out to the rest of them that Pete was the town drunk, an old wino who had no family. It would be like putting a worthless old dog out of his misery.

Because of the hypnotic-like hold Tad had on the others, they had agreed, sweating and scared, but they'd agreed.

That night after graduation exercises, Tad led them to Pete Bonner's trailer with cans of gasoline and matches. As they ran away from the blazing funeral pyre, the screams of the dying old wino followed them.

"I can still hear that old man screaming," Duncan Gitterhouse said, his hands shaking as he chain-lit another cigarette.

"Tad, you said we're stuck with what we did for the rest of our lives," Jack Harriman sighed. "It's true. I've made a pile of money, but what good is it? I can't go to sleep without pills. I eat too much. My doctor says I'm going to have a coronary in five years if I don't quit eating so much, but I can't stop. It's an emotional thing, a compulsion. Look at poor Lowell. He's spent the last five years in and out of alcoholic sanitariums."

Duncan Gitterhouse nodded. "My practice is a success. Compensation, I guess. I have the idea that if I save enough lives, I'll make up for the one we took. I do five, ten operations a day. But my private life is a shambles—my wife left me years ago; my kids are freaked out on drugs." He turned to Tad Jarmon. "I suspect you didn't get off any better than we did, Tad. You never married. You're stuck here, in the home you grew up in. I don't think you *can leave.*"

They sat in the park for a while. Then they got up and went off to their respective motel rooms, Tad to his big, old-fashioned house with white columns.

In his study, Tad took down one of his journals from a bookshelf. In his neat, precise hand, he carefully described the events of the evening, recording in detail all that Jack, Duncan and Lowell had said. Following that entry, he added his prognostication for their future. "I would estimate that Jack will be dead within ten years, probably suicide if he doesn't have a stroke first. Lowell will become a hopeless alcoholic and spend his last years in a sanitarium. Duncan will keep on with his practice, but will have to turn to drugs to keep himself going."

He sat back for a moment. Then as an afterthought, he added, "I will continue to live out my life here in this old house, on the inheritance my father left me, eventually becoming something of a recluse. Duncan was right; I can't leave. It is a psychological prison. But I am reasonably content, keeping busy with my hobby, the study of human nature, that will fill volumes when I am through."

He put the journal away. Then he turned to another bookcase. It was lined with similar neatly-bound and dated journals. He went down the line until he found one dated 1953. He flipped the pages, stopping when he came to the date of their graduation, then he started to read:

"Tonight being graduation," he had written, "I decided we must do something spectacular. A crowning achievement to top any previous prank. Early in the afternoon, I stopped by Pete Bonner's trailer. I had in mind giving him a few dollars to buy us some whiskey for the evening. Being underage, we couldn't go to the liquor store ourselves, but Pete is always ready to do anything for a small bribe. I was surprised, indeed, when I walked into Pete's trailer and found him sprawled out on the floor. He was quite dead, apparently from a heart attack. If I hadn't found him, he'd probably, have stayed there for days until someone accidentally stumbled upon him as I had done. I immediately got a brilliant idea for a colossal joke and a chance to test a theory of mine. They say time is relative. I think reality is relative. If someone believes he has committed an act, it's the same to him as if he *has committed the act. The consequences, as far as they affect him, should be the same."*

"This time the joke would be on Jack, Duncan and Lowell. They're so gullible, they'll do anything I tell them. I hurried home and swiped the wire recorder out of Dad's study. I recorded some agonized screams and put it under Pete's trailer, all hooked up so it would take only a second to turn it on. I then went over to talk to Jack, Duncan and Lowell. I convinced them it would be a great idea to burn up Pete's trailer and roast Pete alive. Of course, they had no way of knowing Pete was already dead. Tonight, after graduation, we slipped down to Pete's trailer with gasoline and matches. I went around the other side, pretending to slosh my gasoline around, and reached under the trailer and switched on the wire recorder. As soon as the flames shot up, we began hearing some very convincing screams. It will be most interesting, in future years, to see what effect tonight's act will have on the lives of Jack Harriman, Duncan Gitterhouse, and Lowell Oliver."

Tad Jarmon closed the journal and leaned back with a cold, thoughtful smile.

Blind Date

SHE was in the trunk of my car and she was dead.

I stood on the lonely stretch of country road in the middle of the night with the rain drumming down on me and splashing around my feet, and I stared at the body. My flashlight was frozen in my hand. I forgot about being wet and cold.

A sheet of lightning split the heavy black sky with a clap of thunder that shook the earth. For a second the macabre scene was lighted by an eerie, blue-white flash. The perimeter of my vision registered a water-filled ditch beside the road, a rusty barbed wire fence and muddy field beyond.

But the center of my vision was focused on the dead woman in the trunk of my car. In the flash of lightning her chalk-white features and staring eyes were in bold relief. The image lingered, ghostlike, in the retina of my eyes for moments after the lightning passed, revealing to me more detail than was illuminated by the sickly, yellow glow of my flashlight with its out-dated batteries.

She was an attractive brunette in her early thirties. She was dressed in a suit of dark material and a light top coat that had fallen open. The cause of her death was apparent. There was a bullet hole in her forehead.

My numb mind struggled to sort facts out of the nightmare. She had undoubtedly ridden with me all the way from Kingsbury. I had not stopped once, even for gasoline, since I had left there two hours ago. If highway construction had not forced me to take this detour where, in the darkness of the night, in a driving thunder storm, I'd hit a chuckhole and blown a tire, she probably would have continued to be a passenger, unknown to me, for the remainder of my trip to New Orleans.

I realized I was standing in a frozen position like a statue, my left hand clutching the edge of the trunk lid.

My first reaction following the initial shock was one of instinctive self-preservation. I wanted to drag her out of there, change my tire, and put much distance between myself and this damned spot.

But logic warned me against acting so rashly. After all, she had not crawled into the trunk by herself. Someone had placed her there. This was a situation involving other people and matters I didn't know about. Running from this thing might have disastrous repercussions.

I bent closer, directing the feeble rays of my flashlight around the trunk's interior The sickly glow touched briefly the spare tire, jack, and some odd rags stuffed in a corner, then returned to the dead woman. I noticed a dark stain on the trunk mat caused by blood from the back of her head.

I forced myself to study her features more closely. I had lived in Kingsbury for six months. It was long enough to have seen at least once every person in a town that size. But I was sure I had never laid eyes on this woman before I opened my trunk lid a few moments ago.

I noticed an object on the floor of the trunk near her feet. Her purse.

I reached for it. Then, temporarily, I closed the trunk lid and got back into the car out of the cold, driving rain. I started the engine and turned on the heater, one of the few things that operated properly on my old heap.

The warmth crept into my chilled body. I stopped shivering. I switched on the dome light, opened the woman's purse, and spread the contents out on the front seat, hoping to find some identification.

The first thing that caught my eye was a bundle of letters, about a half dozen altogether. They were held together by a rubber band.

I slipped the band off. They all were addressed to the same person, Cora Miller, 1216 Mayberry Drive, Encinal. That explained why I could not remember seeing her among the citizens of Kingsbury. Encinal was another town roughly the same size, about thirty miles from Kingsbury.

Then, as I was staring at the handwritten address, I became aware of a striking familiarity about the writing. Suddenly I felt the second shock of the evening. This was my handwriting!

Quickly, I opened one of the letters. My gaze raced down the page to the signature, "Frank." It was my first name. It was my signature.

Blood pounded at my temples. I started reading the letter. By the time I was halfway down the page I was shivering again, but this time not from being wet. This was a love letter of the highly personal, intimate type, the kind that would cause a judge to clear the courtroom before it was read aloud to the jury.

It was brief, but there was nothing vague about the message it contained. The writer, who had the same name and handwriting as myself, had committed himself on paper to being hopelessly in love with Cora Miller. References were made to clandestine meetings and to Cora's husband, Thurman Miller.

With unsteady fingers I flipped through the other envelopes. The postmarks covered the past two-month period and they had all been mailed from Kingsbury.

The most recent postmark was only two days ago. I removed the letter from that envelope. It was quite brief:

"My Dearest Cora,

"I can hardly believe that in two days you will be mine completely. No more lies and slipping around for us. I'm winding up things here. Quit my job this morning. I'll pick you up at the corner of the bus station in Encinal at eight o'clock Friday night. I have made reservations for us in New Orleans.

"Your lover, Frank"

I stared at the page, blinking slowly. The rain drummed steadily on the car top, splashed against the windshield, and leaked around the door.

Thunder rumbled and lightning flashed. I had the eerie feeling of reality slipping from my grasp, of walking through a bad dream.

I *had quit my job the morning the letter was written and mailed in Kingsbury. I was on my way to New Orleans where I had phoned ahead for reservations at a small hotel I knew.*

But I had made reservations only for myself. I had not known I would be taking along a blind date—Cora Miller.

I pawed through the objects from her purse, lipstick, bobby pins, keys, face tissues, the usual female junk. Then I found her billfold. In it was close to a hundred dollars in cash. One of the compartments contained a driver's license and a number of credit cards all bearing the name, Mrs. Thurman Miller. Plastic sleeves on a spiral binder held an assortment of small photographs. There was a wallet-size snapshot of Cora Miller, and several of her with a beefy-faced man who I assumed was her husband, Thurman. Other snapshots were relatives or friends perhaps, but all adults. Apparently the Millers had no children.

I came to the final photo in the billfold. The face on it leaped up to my startled eyes. It was a snapshot of me. Written in a corner, in my handwriting, were the words, "I love you, Cora Darling, Frank."

The human mechanism can absorb so much emotional shock, after which it becomes numb and dazed. I had reached that point.

I sat half slumped against the wheel for several minutes. The heater fan whirred. Cold drops of moisture trickled down my neck. Finally I pulled myself together. I could not spend the rest of the night in this forsaken spot. The normal processes of survival demanded that I do something.

I stuffed the objects back into the purse, and placed it on the rear seat among my suitcases and clothes.

Then I switched on my flashlight, turned up my collar, and again sloshed out into the rain. I opened the trunk lid, hoping that some miracle would have caused Cora to dissolve. But she was still very much there. I swallowed a normal human aversion to dead people and pushed her out of the way of the spare tire. When I did that I noticed, for the first time, her green overnight bag wedged in a far corner of the trunk atop one of my suitcases.

I went about the wet, muddy business of jacking up the car and changing the tire.

Then I was behind the wheel again. I turned the car around. In a few minutes I reached a small town which I had remembered was a few miles back on the main highway,

I got a handful of change from an all-night service station. In a lighted street-corner phone booth, I placed a call to the hotel in New Orleans. When the clerk answered I said, "This is Frank Judson. I want to check on a reservation I made."

"Yes, sir. Hold on just a minute, please."

He was back almost at once. "Yes, Mr. Judson. We received your phone call and later the telegram."

"Telegram?" I asked blankly.

"Yes, sir. The one asking us to change your reservation to a double because you'd have someone with you."

I stared at the water running in streams down the side of the phone booth. I suddenly found it difficult to breathe in the small enclosure.

"Did you wish to make any other changes, Mr. Judson?"

I wiped the back of my hand across my forehead where beads of perspiration were mingling with rain drops. "You might as well cancel the whole thing."

I got back in the car. Cold perspiration was oozing out all over me. For a moment, reason gave way to wild fancy. I was a victim of amnesia. I'd had an affair with this woman. For some reason I had murdered her, and the shock of what I'd done had blanked out my memory.

Then I got a grip on myself. That was pure hogwash. I was turning into a hysterical fool. Somebody had murdered Cora all right, but it hadn't been me. An elaborate plan had been rigged to make it look as if I was eloping with Cora tonight, but had murdered her for some reason, perhaps because she was trying to back out at the last minute.

No doubt the police in New Orleans would be tipped off to check my car. If I hadn't accidentally had that blowout, I would have had no reason to look in the trunk before I reached New Orleans. They would have found Cora. I would have had some impossible explaining to do.

I mentally ran over the events of the past six months, trying to find a clue to this unpleasant mess.

I had driven into Kingsbury six months ago broke, and needing a job. I'd gone to work with the Kingsbury Record, a small daily newspaper.

The town and job had been pleasant, but, as usual, after six months I had the itchy feet to move on to greener pastures. I was twenty-six, no ties or responsibilities. I'd been out of the army four years now, and had spent that time seeing different parts of the country. There was still a lot I wanted to see before I settled down.

One thing had made leaving Kingsbury difficult, Emily Phillips. Every town had pretty girls. But only Kingsbury had Emily. I knew lately that she was falling pretty hard for me. What scared me was that I was starting to feel the same about her. I could hear wedding bells in the air. So I'd taken the only sensible course open to a guy with itchy feet. I'd quit my job and kissed Emily goodbye.

I hadn't known I'd be taking Cora Miller along as an uninvited guest.

I could get rid of Cora easily enough. There were plenty of muddy ditches along the highway. And I could burn the letters and my snapshot that was in her billfold. But there were probably other letters and snapshots planted at her home. And how would I explain to the police the matter of the double reservation at the New Orleans hotel? And the blood stains in my car trunk?

It boiled down to this, that I had to find out what Cora was doing in the trunk of my car, and who had put her there. And the answer was somewhere back in Encinal or Kingsbury.

Two hours later I pulled into the city limits of the town I'd left earlier this evening, Kingsbury. By then it was almost midnight. Except for all-night service stations on the highway, the town had rolled up the sidewalks.

I drove to the home of Buddy Gardner, my best friend in Kingsbury. Buddy was a deputy in the sheriff's department. Like myself, he was an avid chess player. We'd spent many long hours drinking beer and waging battles over a chess board at Pop Lassiter's beer joint.

If anybody could give me information about Thurman and Cora Miller, it would be Buddy.

He lived with his parents in a big, old, ramshackle house on the edge of town. When I turned my mud-splattered heap into their yard, I saw a light on in Buddy's room. He was my age and a bachelor. I knew he had a habit of reading paperback novels most of the night.

There was a private entrance to his room. I knocked. His door opened and the light in the room silhouetted his heavy, six-foot frame and his bushy head. He was naturally surprised to see me. Only a few hours ago we'd bid one another a fond farewell over a last chess game and a few beers at Pop's.

"Frank! What the heck? Thought you were long gone."

Buddy talked in a slow drawl even when he was surprised.

"I was," I said. "I had to come back."

He pushed open the screen door. "Come on in here. You look soaked."

I stepped inside, dripping water on the linoleum. He had a typical bachelor room. Deer horns and other hunting trophies adorned the walls along with hunting rifles. A book shelf, extending all the way to the ceiling, was filled with paperback novels. On one cluttered table was a portable TV set. A novel he had been reading was spread open on the rumpled bed. On the bedside table was a can of beer and his pipe.

"What happened?" he asked, peering at me curiously. "Have car trouble?"

"Something like that. I want you to help me with something, Buddy."

"Sure. How about a beer? Or maybe you'd better have a shot of bourbon. You look half drowned."

"The bourbon sounds fine," I nodded. My clothes felt clammy against my shivering body.

"You ought to get out of those wet clothes," he said, taking a bottle of whisky out of a bureau drawer.

"Haven't got time. Thanks." I accepted the drink he handed me.

I took it straight. I felt the warmth of the alcohol spreading into my bloodstream.

"Buddy," I said, "you've lived around these parts all your life. You ever hear of a guy named Thurman Miller?"

The bedsprings sighed as Buddy sat on the edge of the bed and picked up his can of beer. He was looking at me curiously. "Thurman Miller?" His brow wrinkled. "Do you mean the county auditor who lives in Encinal?"

"I guess I do. There wouldn't be two Thurman Millers in Encinal, would there?"

"Not that I know of." Then he chuckled. "I swear, Frank, if you ain't one for the books. This afternoon you and I were was over at Pop's having a farewell beer together. Now here you are back at midnight, banging on my door, wanting to know about the county auditor in Encinal. What's up? You workin' on some kind of newspaper story?"

"Not exactly. Tell me about Thurman Miller."

Buddy shrugged. "What do you want to know? He's been county auditor over there a number of years. That's about all I know."

"Is he married?"

Buddy nodded. "Matter of fact, I think his wife's side of the family is from Kingsbury."

I took out one of Cora's wallet snapshots. "This Mr. and Mrs. Miller?"

Buddy studied the photo. "It looks like them," he said slowly, "though I wouldn't swear to it. I don't know them that well. The only times I see Thurman is when I run into him in the courthouse in Encinal when I'm over there."

"Do you think anybody in this town would know them?"

Buddy stared at me. "I swear you're acting mysterious. What's eating you anyway, Frank?"

"I'll tell you in a little while. The truth is, I'm in a kind of a jam. I thought maybe you could help me."

"Well, I'll sure try, Frank. I hope it ain't anything serious."

"It could be. Getting back to what I just asked you, do you think many people in Kingsbury know the Millers?"

Buddy massaged his jaw thoughtfully. "Oh, I guess quite a few people do. You know how folks in a small town are. And Mrs. Miller has relatives over here."

I swallowed the rest of the bourbon. I'd established who the Millers were, and that almost anyone in Kingsbury might know them.

But who, among my acquaintances, would be crooked enough, or crazy enough, to murder Cora Miller, and then try to make it look like I'd been having an affair with her over the past two months?

I paced around the room, trying to recall this afternoon in detail. If I could put my finger on the place where Cora's body was deposited in my car trunk I would be close to the truth.

I had packed my car late this afternoon. Cora had not been in the trunk of my car at that time because I had put a suitcase in it.

Then I'd driven to a service station to have the tank filled. But I had stood right beside the car. No one could have touched the trunk without my seeing them.

My next stop had been Pop Lassiter's, where I'd bid Buddy goodbye over our last beer together. Then I'd gotten in the car, and had driven steadily until I had the blowout.

The only time anyone could have tampered with my trunk was while I had my car parked in back of Pop's place. That being the case, Pop Lassiter, himself, was the most logical suspect. He was a mean old devil, and an ex-con, and capable of anything. Furthermore, he knew all about my plans to quit and go to New Orleans.

"Buddy, will you come with me?" I asked. "You might say it's in the line of duty."

"Well, sure," he drawled. "I wish to heck you'd tell me why, though."

"Trust me," I said. It was a ticklish situation. Buddy was a good friend, and I knew I could trust him to help me. But he was also a deputy sheriff. If I told him about having Cora in the trunk of my car, he'd be forced to act in an official capacity. I couldn't afford to be arrested at this point.

Buddy pulled on a pair of cowboy boots and took a rain slicker out of the closet. We sloshed out to my car.

"Man, this heap of yours leaks," he muttered after he'd gotten in and felt rain splash down the back of his neck.

"I need a new top," I said, turning on the switch.

"That ain't all it needs," he said, looking around.

I drove down to Pop's beer joint.

"What the heck are you doing here?" Buddy wanted to know. "You know Pop closes at midnight. It's past that now."

"I want to talk to Pop," I explained.

The old sinner lived in a room behind the beer joint. I walked around to his door and banged on it. Buddy was right behind me.

The door opened. Pop stood there in his long-handled underwear. He looked mad. "What in blazes you want? I don't sell no booze after closin' time."

He tried to slam the door, but I stuck my foot in it. "Since when did you get so legal?" I asked. I pushed it further open and walked in. "You used to bootleg the stuff, didn't you?"

Pop looked even madder at this invasion of his privacy. "What's buggin' you, Frank?"

Buddy came in after me. Pop's glare switched to him. "This some kind of raid? You got a warrant?"

Buddy laughed. "Pop, I don't know no more 'n you do. Frank said he had to see you and asked me to come along. I'm just here as an interested citizen."

"You didn't answer my question about bootlegging," I said.

Pop shrugged. "What if I did? That was back in Prohibition. Thirty years ago."

"You've done time since then," I reminded him. "Once for manslaughter, and once for peddling marijuana under the counter."

He looked mad enough to shoot me. "All right, you smart aleck, young newspaper jerk. What business you got comin' around here insulting me in the middle of the night?"

"I got a reason." I shoved the snapshot under his nose. "You know this couple?"

Grumbling and swearing, he put on a pair of gold-rimmed glasses. He glared briefly at the photo, then shoved it away. "'Course I do. That's the Millers from over at Encinal."

"How come you know them so well?"

"Hell, why shouldn't I? Cora Miller comes from this town. She's one of Ed Shelby's girls. I've known the Shelbys all my life."

I grabbed myself a fistful of his dirty underwear just under his breastbone and I twisted until his eyes bulged. "You knew I was going to New Orleans, didn't you?"

"Well, sure!" he yelled angrily. "That's all you been yappin' about the last two months every time you been in my place, about how fed up you are with this town, and how you're headin' for New Orleans. Good riddance, if you ask me."

I shoved him up against a wall and gave his underwear another yank until he was dancing on his toes. "Tell me what kind of a deal you're in to tie me up with Cora Miller?"

His gold-rimmed glasses were dangling from one ear. His adam's apple danced in his stringy throat. "Buddy!" he yelled in a high-pitched, frightened voice. "He's a' killin' me."

Buddy placed a huge paw on my arm. "Take it easy now, Frank," he drawled soothingly. "Don't you think you'd better tell me what's got you so upset?"

I released Pop. "You'll know all about it pretty soon," I said. "When I get this old coot to talk. You already heard him admit he knows the Millers, and he knew all about me fixin' to leave for New Orleans."

Buddy looked perplexed. "I can't help you if you won't tell me what's got you so steamed up. You want to prefer some kind of charges against Pop here?"

I looked at him in hopeless frustration. I'd come here, driven by desperation, with no clear plan in mind. I'd hoped that the surprise of seeing me back might shake Pop up and, when I confronted him, he might break down and admit he had a part in putting Cora in my car. I might have known that a guy like Pop, who'd lived on the fringe of the law all his life, wouldn't come unglued that easily. He hadn't even looked surprised when I walked in.

Either he was putting up a good front, and with his criminal experience he'd be trained to do that, or I was totally wrong about his being involved.

We went back to my car. I drove out of town fast, headed toward Encinal. Again, I was motivated by fear and desperation, rather than any clear-cut plan. The only other person I could think of who might shed some light on this mess was Cora's husband, Thurman. If he proved to be a blind alley like Pop Lassiter, I was going to have to admit the whole thing to Buddy and let him arrest me, and hope the police would believe my side of the story, which was a pretty dim hope.

I thought about Cora getting stiff in the trunk of my car just a few feet behind us and I shivered.

Buddy could see he wasn't going to get any conversation out of me, so he patiently smoked his pipe and waited to see what I was going to do next.

When we arrived in Encinal, I drove around until I located Mayberry Drive. Then I found the address I'd seen on Cora's letters, 1216. It was a sprawling, ranch-style house worth at least thirty thousand dollars. That puzzled me. "A county auditor doesn't make much money, does he?"

"Not a heck of a lot, I don't think," Buddy said.

"Then how come Thurman Miller lives in a house like this?"

"He's well-fixed from some oil property his folks left him. That county auditor job is just local politics and prestige."

That explained Miller's obvious affluence.

"Come on," I muttered quietly.

We walked up to the house. I saw a light inside and I punched the doorbell. Thurman Miller opened the door. I recognized him from the picture in my wallet. He stared at me through the screen door. Then his face turned pale. He uttered a cry and ran out of the house. The next thing I knew we were rolling on the ground, and he had me by the throat. He was a big guy, and might have choked me to death if Buddy hadn't dragged him off me.

We got him inside, where he sank onto a couch and burst into sobs. I sat down too, shaken and weak-kneed from his unexpected, ferocious attack.

He raised his face from his hands and started cursing me. "What have you done with Cora?" he cried.

"Do you know Frank, Mr. Miller?" Buddy asked curiously.

Miller glared at me with hate-filled eyes "I ought to. I've warned him to stay away from my wife. Tonight she eloped with him." He got up, walked heavily to a desk, took out a scrap of paper, and handed it to

Buddy. "That's the farewell note she left me."

The nightmare had started all over again. I felt the hopeless, numb sensation creep through my body.

Buddy read the note, frowning. "Is this true, Frank? Did you take off with Mrs. Miller?"

"No," I said. But I said it without much conviction. I was ready to stop being sure of anything, including my own sanity. Those letters, the snapshot and now Thurman Miller recognizing me on sight. Did it mean my mind was playing tricks on me? Insanity takes many forms.

Was it possible that I had been running around with Cora Miller? Had I really murdered her in a fit of passion? Could a thing like that have been blanked from my memory by my sick, guilt-ridden mind?

My brain did feel feverish. My head throbbed. I pressed my fingers against my temples. For God's sake, what are the symptoms of madness? Is a mentally deranged person aware of his own illusions?

Dimly, I was aware of Thurman Miller demanding to know where his wife was. Buddy was staring at me intently, waiting for an answer.

What could I tell him? That I'd reached the point where I was no longer certain of reality?

"Buddy, come out here a minute," I said in a hollow voice. I felt wet and tired and scared. I dragged myself to my feet and started outside. Miller arose to go with us. "Make him stay here," I mumbled, stopping awkwardly.

Buddy shot a glance at Miller, who stared angrily at me, then shrugged and sank back down on the sofa.

I led Buddy out to the car. I gave him the keys. "Look in the trunk," I said. I sat in the car, listening to the rain drum on the roof. I stared straight ahead at nothing. I heard the trunk lid open. In a few moments it closed again. Buddy got in the car beside me. The springs creaked under his weight. His face mirrored the shock of what he'd just seen.

Slowly he let his breath out. "This is real bad, Frank," he said gravely. "Why didn't you tell me about it right away?"

"Because you would have been forced to arrest me, and I wanted to try and get at the truth first. I hoped I could get Pop to admit he had put her in the trunk of my car. When that didn't work, I came over here thinking Miller would be of some help to me." I made a useless gesture.

"But why Pop?"

"Because the only time her body could have been put in the trunk was while my car was parked behind Pop's beer joint earlier tonight, when you and I were having our farewell beer together."

"Are you telling me you didn't put her there?"

"Buddy, I had a blowout on my way to New Orleans. I got out to change the tire. When I opened the trunk I found Cora Miller's body. I swear that is the first time I ever saw her in my life." Then I admitted, "But I don't blame you if you don't believe me. I'm not sure I believe myself any more."

"What do you mean by that?"

I turned and dug Cora's billfold and the incriminating letters out from under my suitcase on the back seat. "Look at these."

He read them all carefully with the aid of a flashlight he'd brought along. Then he took the picture of me out of Cora's wallet and studied it.

"Buddy, I haven't been running around with Cora Miller. The only girl I've had anything to do with around here is Emily Phillips. I was sure those letters were forged, that the whole thing was an elaborate scheme to frame me for her murder. But when we knocked on Miller's door and he recognized me on sight. Well, it's taken the wind out of my sails."

"He could have recognized you from a picture. Or somebody could have pointed you out to him on the street."

I looked at Buddy curiously. "You mean you think he's in on this scheme?"

"I don't think anything. I'm just saying that his recognizing you doesn't prove anything, one way or the other."

Suddenly, I felt better. I realized I must be emotionally drained, or I wouldn't be giving away to wild emotions like I had been for a few minutes.

Buddy had relit his pipe. He was puffing on it while he stared thoughtfully at my picture. "This is a close-up, front view. You must have known when it was taken."

I shook my head. "I don't know how it was done. Nobody has taken a picture of me since I've been in Kingsbury. In fact, I don't remember having my picture taken since I was in the army."

"Hmm. This looks like a recent one, too." He puffed on his pipe and mumbled to himself, the way he did when he was analyzing a chess move. "Looks like it was taken indoors by available light." He bent closer, squinting his eyes. "Pretty grainy. Could be blown up from part of a negative."

He stared at it some more, turning it different ways under the flashlight, while puffing furiously on his pipe. Then he said, "Listen, I don't want to break the news to Miller about his wife like this. I'm going to tell him I'm taking you back to Kingsbury. I'll phone him from over there after the coroner has a look at her, and we have her some place decent like a funeral home."

He got out of the car. Then he thrust his head back in. "Frank, I have to tell you this. You're under arrest now, and anything you say can be held against you."

I nodded wearily. "Okay. I understand."

He went back into the house to talk to Thurman Miller. He was in there a few minutes, then came out and got behind the wheel of my car. He drove the car back to Kingsbury, which was fine with me. I was emotionally drained and physically exhausted.

When we reached Kingsbury, I expected Frank to take me straight to jail and phone the coroner from there. I was taken by complete surprise when he pulled up in back of Pop's beer joint instead.

"What's up?" I asked.

"Got a hunch. Come on."

For the second time that night, we banged on Pop's door. The old man jerked the door open. His disposition had not improved. "Now what?" he demanded.

This time he was dressed in shirt and trousers. "Going someplace, Pop?" Buddy asked.

"What makes you think that?" the old bar owner snapped.

Buddy shrugged. "Peculiar time of night for anybody to be dressed." Then he said, "Unlock your bar," his tone authoritative.

Pop stared at him as if he'd lost his mind. "At one o'clock in the morning?"

"Let's put it this way; it's an official request. But I can go wake up the J.P. and get a search warrant, if you want to put me to the trouble."

Swearing under his breath, Pop Lassiter got his keys, walked across the rain-drenched yard and opened his beer joint. He switched on the lights. It was still warm inside. Stale cigarette smoke lingered in the air from the night's business.

"Frank, sit over here at the bar," Buddy directed. He walked to a doorway leading to a room off the side of the bar. His voice came to me out of the dark room. "Glance this way. Can you see me?"

"No."

He emerged into the light. "That picture of you that you found in Cora's billfold, it was taken from this room."

I stared at him in amazement. "How did you figure that out?"

"The negative was blown up, and the background was cropped out, so your face and shoulders filled most of the print. But whoever did the enlargement left the rim of that clock, up there, on one corner of the print. I recognized it as the one on Pop's wall. All I had to do was figure what angle the picture was taken from in order to get your face in the foreground and that clock in the background and, well, I wound up in that room. A person could take your picture from in there and you'd never know it."

I felt myself growing excited. "Wouldn't I have seen the flash?"

"No flash was used. There's enough light here for fast film, and the right kind of processing. Isn't that right, Pop?" he asked, suddenly turning to the bar owner.

For the first time tonight the old man lost his composure. His face turned a dirty gray. "I-I don't know what you're talkin' about."

Buddy said, "Frank, earlier tonight you mentioned the things for which Pop has done time. Maybe you didn't know about this, but I did; he once served a stretch for forgery."

Old Lassiter groped at the bar with a trembling hand. He licked his lips. "Now wait a minute. Foring those letters in Frank's handwriting was a snap for you, Pop," Buddy said. "So was putting Cora's body in his car tonight. You knew he and I would have one last chess game here before he left. We'd talked about it in here the night before." Buddy moved toward him. "Why did you murder Cora Miller, Pop?"

All the wind out of his sails now, Pop collapsed against the bar. He held out one trembling palm as if to ward off Buddy. "You ain't hookin' me on no murder rap!" he yelled in a quavering voice. "All right; I done the letters and the pictures. And I had a key made to fit the trunk of his car. That's all I had to do with it."

"If you didn't kill her and put her in the trunk, who did?"

The old man took out a handkerchief and shakily mopped his forehead. "Her husband, Thurman," he said hoarsely.

Surprise rooted me to the spot.

Buddy and I were staring at Pop. "It's the truth," he croaked. "He's got him some young blonde on the string. He wants to marry her. Cora won't give him a divorce. He come to me a couple of months ago, offerin' me money if I'd knock Cora off. I'm not going to get myself in that kind of big trouble. But I told him I could figure a way he could do it, and come clean himself. I knew about Frank here. He'd been comin' in my place shootin' off his mouth about gettin' fed up with the town an' wantin' to move on. I've seen 'em like him all my life. Drifters. Transients. I could see just as soon as he got a few bucks ahead he was going to scat out of town."

Pop Lassiter wiped his face with the handkerchief again.

"Thurman paid me good money to set the thing up. I wrote those letters. He caught the mail before Cora got her hands on it. We waited until I heard you say you'd quit your job, and were leaving town tonight, Frank. Then I put in a call to Thurman. He shot Cora tonight, and brought her over here. He was parked back of my place in the dark, waiting for you to drive up and play that last chess game with Buddy. Then he put her in the trunk of your car, usin' that key I'd had made."

Buddy took Pop down to the county jail, and phoned the coroner. Then, he drove over to Encinal to arrest Thurman Miller for the murder of his wife.

As for myself, I was chilled to the bone and close to nervous exhaustion. I drove back to the rooming house, woke my landlady, and got her to give me my old room. I took a hot bath, drank some more whisky, fell into bed, and slept until about noon the next day.

When I woke, I phoned Buddy down at the sheriff's office. "Everything okay?"

"Fine," he boomed cheerfully. "Thurman gave us a complete statement. You're clear, Frank. 'Course you'll have to testify at the trial."

"How about a chess game tonight?" I asked.

"Well, sure," he said, with a tone of pleased surprise. "You mean you're not takin' off for New Orleans now that this mess is cleared up?"

I didn't explain it to him then, but I wasn't taking off for anywhere. I had come to the conclusion that not only does a rolling stone gather no moss, it also does not gather friends. You have to stay in one place to do that.

I finished talking to Buddy. I had two more important calls to make. I had to phone my ex-boss at the newspaper to see if I could have my job back. And then I was going to phone Emily and see if I could have my best girl back.

The Piñata

It was hot and arid in Mexico.

"Fausta, how come it's always so hot and dry over here?" Miller asked.

Fausta Mendez shrugged. "It rains very little, *señor.*"

"Look at those mesquite trees on the side of the road. They got caliche dust an inch thick on them. Looks like talcum powder."

"Si, señor. It is very dry. I do not remember the last time it rained. A year ago, I think."

"It must be a hundred and twenty in the shade, if you could find any shade."

Fausta smiled with his lips. His dark eyes did not smile.

Miller wiped the back of his florid neck with his soggy handkerchief. He looked up and down the highway for the third time.

"How much longer will we have to wait?"

"Soon, *señor.*"

"What's keeping him?"

"One must be careful about these things."

"Listen, there isn't another car between here and Monterrey. Look for yourself. My car and yours parked here on the side of the road, that's all you can see as far as the horizon."

"He will be here, *señor,*" Fausta said patiently. He did not sweat like Miller. He leaned against the side of Miller's white sedan smoking his hand-rolled cigarette.

"Look at those buzzards up there," Miller said.

"There is something that will soon be dead, I think. They know about things like that, and they circle like that and wait, sometimes a whole day. But they wait."

"'Wait,'" Miller said, shaking his head. "That's the motto around here. 'Wait till tomorrow.' Doesn't anybody ever get something done today?"

"It is too hot to be in a hurry, *señor.*"

Fausta smoked his cigarette and looked up at the buzzards.

They waited another fifteen minutes. During that time only one car passed, on its way toward Monterrey. It whizzed by, funneling dust on the side of the road. It was a late model sedan with the windows rolled up.

Miller wiped his face and neck with his soggy handkerchief, wishing he was back in his car with the air conditioner on.

Suddenly, Fausta pinched out his cigarette and straightened. He moved slowly, conserving his energy like a lizard. "He is coming now, I think."

Miller tensed, his eyes probing the brush. "I don't see anything."

But presently a man appeared on the other side of the road. He seemed to materialize out of the white caliche dust and brittle-dry chaparral. His flopping, white pajama-like garments blended with the powdery dust. His face was dark brown under the shade of a broad-brimmed hat.

He stood for a moment on the other side of the road. Fausta made an almost imperceptible signal. The man crossed the highway. He and Fausta spoke briefly in Spanish. The man took a small, square cardboard box tied securely with twine from under his loose cotton shirt, handed it to Fausta. Then he walked away and dissolved back into the brush.

Miller took the box quickly from Fausta, his fingers eager. He untied it. Fausta stood back, his eyes dark and hidden, watching Miller's face. "It is as I promised, *señor?*"

Miller tasted caliche dust on his lips. He drew his sleeve across his mouth and nodded. The stuff in the box was top grade.

"It will be worth twenty thousand American dollars to you in the States, *señor.*"

"But it's not in the States," Miller said, his eyes becoming shrewd.

Fausta shrugged. "You will have no trouble getting it across, I think, *señor?*"

"You know better than that. One always has trouble."

Fausta did not answer. It was no longer his problem.

Miller tossed the box on the front seat of his car. He removed a thick wallet. From it, he counted a number of American bills in large denominations, placed them in Fausta's hand.

Fausta put them in his pocket. *"Vaya con Dios, señor!"*

Miller went around and got behind the wheel. He started the engine. Dry, cool air from the air conditioner ducts blew against him. His soggy shirt felt suddenly cold, stuck to him.

He backed and turned. He glanced into his rear view mirror. Fausta was still standing beside the road, smoking and looking up at the buzzards dipping and circling.

Miller drove back to Reynosa at high speed. The box of heroin lay carelessly on the seat beside him. When he approached the check point, he put the box under the seat. He was not worried about the Mexican inspectors. There would be more profit for informers to tip off the American border agents.

The Mexican officer asked him briefly where he'd been, then waved him on. He drove slowly into Reynosa.

Miller prided himself on one thing. He always thought about every possibility. That was why he was a successful man.

For example, he did not park right on the square where the big white car would attract attention. This was part of his taking every possibility into consideration. Instead, he pulled into a parking lot beside one of the downtown bars. He dropped the cardboard box into his coat pocket.

An old man, who wore a badge on his frayed shirt, appeared and opened his door for him. "Watch your car, *señor?*"

Miller nodded. He put a half dollar in the man's waiting hand.

Miller went into the bar. It was very modern inside, the plush interior contrasting with the dingy poverty in the streets. He sat in the bar almost an hour, slowly drinking two Scotches and fizz water.

He knew that by now the American customs office on the other side of the bridge was watching for a late model white sedan with the California license number, 78990. Somewhere down the line an informer would have given them the information, perhaps Fausta, perhaps the man in the white peon pajamas. As they said over here, *quien sabe?*

There were many men involved in a transaction of this nature. None could be trusted. There were many informers, so many men got caught.

He was cool now. The air conditioning and good Scotch had relaxed him. He paid for the drinks, walked out of a side door. He strolled along the crowded sidewalk toward the market place. There were many curio stores on this narrow street. He chose one that looked like an established firm, one that dealt in good jewelry and craftwork, not junk.

He shopped slowly, picking out gift items for a woman, jewelry, perfume, a fine lace scarf. As if on a whim, he also bought a *piñata.*

The clerk assembled his purchases on top of the glass counter. Miller took a large American bill out of his wallet. The clerk was apologetic. He did not have so much change in his store. If the *señor* would pardon him un ratito he would run across the street to the bank.

The clerk darted out into the bright afternoon heat, leaving Miller alone in the store. Quickly, he took out his pocket knife, made a small opening under the gay paper ruffles and streamers of the *piñata.* He removed the cardboard box from his pocket, thrust it into the piñata among the candies and small trinkets. He smoothed out the incision and arranged the paper ruffles.

The clerk returned with his change. Miller asked if the objects could be gift-wrapped and left for a lady friend who would pick them up later in the day? The clerk assured him this could be arranged.

Miller hung around the store, seeing that all the packages were properly wrapped, especially the *piñata.* The clerk gave him a receipt. If the lady would present the receipt to the clerk when she called for the gifts…

Miller walked slowly back to his car. On the way he stopped at a liquor store and bought a quart bottle of gin. Then he drove down to the International Bridge.

His guess was not wrong. The customs inspector on the American side waved him to a stop. Miller saw the man stare at his license plates, knew he'd be questioned.

"Hiya," Miller said, rolling down his window.

The man nodded, unsmiling. "Been to the interior?"

"Monterrey."

"Bringing anything back?"

"Bottle of gin." Miller held it up for the man to see.

The inspector did not look at it. He was looking at Miller. "Mind stepping out?"

Miller obeyed.

The customs agent made a routine search of the car. Then he called an assistant. They spent the better part of an hour going over every inch of the car. They searched under the hood, took out the trunk lining, put the car up on a rack and hunted around the underside of the frame.

Miller stood in the shade, smoking, wondering which one it had been? Fausta? That first contact in the bar in Monterrey?

No matter. Somewhere down the line one of them was bound to be an informer. That was how things were done around here and why less intelligent men, those who did not consider every possibility, got caught.

They finally gave up on the car. They had Miller step into a dressing room where they had him strip. While one officer searched his garments, another made a careful inspection of his suitcase, a fine morocco leather bag he'd bought in San Francisco last year.

Then they told him he could dress. The customs officer looked displeased with the fruitless outcome of the search. "All right, you can go on," he said, giving Miller a hard look. "Stop at the last shed on the way out and pay the liquor tax on that bottle of gin."

Miller did not permit himself the luxury of a smile until he was several miles down the road.

He drove through a number of small Rio Grande Valley towns and then pulled into the luxury motel where he was registered.

When he walked in, he said, "Hello, Shirley," to the young blonde woman who was in a comfortable easy chair, reading a movie magazine. She was dressed in green silk lounging pajamas. Her long legs swung over the arm of the chair. A drink of Scotch was on the floor within reach.

She put down the magazine and looked at him.

Miller tossed his coat on the bed. He loosened his tie and mixed a drink of Scotch from the bottle on the dresser.

"You look pleased with yourself," she said.

"I have a right to be."

"The deal went okay, then."

"Beautifully. I bought some fine stuff. We'll live in high style in Miami this winter."

She picked up her glass. The ice tinkled. She was giving him a long, careful look. "Do we still have to do it the way you said?"

He gave her a brief, annoyed glance. "Of course. You know how I planned this thing out. I took every possibility…"

"… into consideration," she muttered, frowning into her glass. "I just don't like it; that's all."

"I tell you it's perfectly safe."

"Yeah. For you." She drained her glass in a quick gulp.

"For you, too. Hundreds of people cross that bridge in and out of Reynosa every day. It's plain routine. They don't check ninety-nine cars out of a hundred. They couldn't possibly have the time, only the ones coming from the interior, and the ones they've been tipped off about. I've told you…"

"… at least a hundred times. 'You can't trust the ones you deal with over there. They're the informers. They're the ones who make it so tough to get past the border.'"

"You have a bad habit of interrupting."

She shrugged. She tossed the magazine aside, uncurled from the chair and poured more whiskey over the ice in her glass.

Miller took out his wallet. He gave her a slip of paper. "This is the receipt you'll need for the package in the souvenir shop. The address is on it."

"What good does that do me? I can't read Spanish."

He gave her directions for finding the store from the town's central plaza.

"Get dressed now," he said. "I'll phone the car rental agency."

The agency delivered the car, a small blue one, by the time she'd finished changing. She came out of the bathroom. "How do I look?"

Miller inspected her carefully. "I don't like those high heels. You should be wearing flats. You're supposed to be driving over to Reynosa to do some shopping, remember. And wear sunglasses. Everyone down here does. That sun is bright."

"Okay," she muttered, kicking off her high heels. "Are you sure I won't need a passport and vaccination and all that jazz?"

"Not just to cross the border into Reynosa for the day. They'll ask you at the bridge where you're going. Say, 'Just into Reynosa to shop.' They'll wave you right on. The same thing on the Mexican side. You won't have any trouble about that at all."

"And when I come back?"

"They'll ask you on the American side if you bought anything. Have those packages unwrapped and open in the back seat. The customs man will stick his head in and glance over to see if you owe any duty. That's all. They won't suspect a thing. You're in a car with a Texas license. You don't look any different from dozens of Valley people who drive over to Reynosa every day. They have no way of connecting you with me."

In spite of the air conditioning in the room she was beginning to perspire through her make-up. She had another fast drink.

"Don't drive over there and get the packages and come right back. It would look better if you spent a couple of hours in Reynosa. Go into a bar over there and kill some time."

"All right."

He glanced at his watch. "Let's allow an hour's driving time, thirty minutes both ways. Two hours in Reynosa. That should put you back here by eight o'clock."

She nodded.

"Play it cool. Don't act nervous when they check your car. Act bored."

"That's easy for you to say."

After she left he showered, changed into a clean white shirt and a dark, light-weight suit, one he'd recently had made by an expensive tailor in Los Angeles. He carefully repacked his leather bag, putting all of his personal travel items into it. He carried it out to his car along with his plastic suit bag, and drove into town where he had his car serviced, the tank filled. He then drove to the best restaurant in the town and had the most expensive steak on the menu. He ate slowly, savoring the flavor.

After the meal, he bought a cigar, then walked to his car in a leisurely manner, peeling the cellophane from the cigar. He lit it off the glowing tip of the dash lighter in his car.

He glanced at the luminous dial of his platinum wrist watch. He had managed to kill nearly three hours. The hands pointed to ten minutes of eight.

He started the engine, drove slowly through the town, made a circle of the main square, then turned in the direction of his motel cabin on the highway.

He parked across the street from it in the dark shadows of a grove of palm trees and waited.

He'd taken everything into consideration, even this last, final margin of safety for himself. If they caught Shirley she might talk and they would come here looking for him.

He was not concerned about her, or the deal, that much. There were other Shirleys and there could be other deals with men like Fausta Mendez. But ten years out of his life in a federal pen could not be replaced.

But Shirley returned, alone, as planned, and only ten minutes late.

He saw the little blue rented car pull into the motel driveway. It stopped in front of his cabin. The interior light flicked on as she opened her door. By the light he could clearly see that it was Shirley and she was alone. He saw her reach back into the car for something.

The *piñata.* She held it under one arm while she unlocked the motel door and went in.

A feeling of elation touched him. He started his engine, pulled into the drive behind the rented car. He went into the cabin.

She was standing at the bureau, pouring herself a stiff drink. The *piñata* lay on the bed.

He closed the door, still with the feeling of elation. "Everything went fine?"

She nodded, gulping her drink. Her hands were tight around the glass, her fingers white with tension. "Just like you said. I was scared half to death. But it went okay. There was no trouble at all."

He strode to the bed. He ripped open the *piñata.* A shower of candy and trinkets spilled over the bed. And in the middle of the pile, there was the cardboard box containing merchandise worth at least twenty thousand to him now. Actually, Fausta had undervalued it. Properly diluted and marketed, it would be closer to twenty-five thousand.

"Miller."

"What?"

He was too engrossed with the box to look up.

She repeated his name impatiently.

He glanced at her.

She had finished her drink. She picked up her large, bulky purse. "All the way over there and back I thought about this deal. It seems to me that the person who takes all the risk should get all the profit."

From her purse she drew a .38 revolver fitted with a silencer. She pointed it at him and pulled the trigger. She was an excellent shot.

That was the one possibility he had not taken into consideration.

I'll Make the Arrest

It hadn't been easy, the way she died. But then her life had not been easy. It had been a violent episode of raw emotion and bitter struggles, and much pain, splashed with a few bright flashes of glory. And under it all, the everlasting drive.

She had died here on her throne, her dressing table, before the mirror that had hurled her exquisite image back into her vain eyes.

It lay shattered around her, the make-up, facial creams and hundreds of dollars worth of perfume, with the broken jewel box and stained shears. And she was still beautiful, sprawled across the floor that way, with her golden hair framed about her face and shoulders and the silk robe fallen back from her lovely legs. Still beautiful, even with the purple, swollen throat. The lab boys were ending their routine. The fingerprints, the photograph flash bulbs, the measurements. Now, a chalk mark outlining her still figure to indicate the position on the floor. Then the boys with the stretcher taking her to her last stage, a cold slab in the morgue.

I bent over her for a moment, hiding from the others the things that should not show in the eyes of a police investigator. I touched her hand goodbye and something rolled out of her loosely gripped fingers. A plain, gold wedding band. I dropped it in my pocket without a second look.

"This all, lieutenant?"

I nodded. "Wind it up, Hank. Wind it up and lock the door. Go home and get some sleep. I'll make the arrest."

It would be that simple. We all knew who murdered her, of course. The people downstairs had seen him leave the building right after Pat screamed. They saw him run, described his white, sick face. A kid. A silly little punk had ended it like this.

He wouldn't run far. Pat had fought for her life. She'd struck out with the nearest thing at hand in her dying struggle, the shears from her dressing table. We'd examined the blood stains on the blades, the kid's blood.

I went down into the night and where it was dark and alone; I checked my gun because I was going to kill this boy who had strangled Pat.

I drove down to where the kid lived, down to hunky town, the smelly cluster of unpainted shacks huddled like a brood of bedraggled chickens around their mother hen, the smoke-belching iron works. I searched the houses, all drearily alike, until I found a number. Then I went up on the rickety porch and knocked on the door. An old woman's voice asked me in.

She was sitting in a chair, reading a book. I looked around. The modest room was furnished in old worn-out scraps of furniture and a threadbare carpet. But it was spotless.

She was a nice old lady, the punk's mother. She had white hair and gold-rimmed spectacles and she apologized for not getting up.

"Arthritis," she explained with her patient smile. "I haven't been able to walk for three years now. It's such a bother," She continued to smile, "But it isn't so bad, you know, not really, with Jimmy around. He's a fine boy, my son. You know Jimmy? Well of course," she chuckled softly, "you didn't come to see me." She motioned to a horsehair sofa. "Now you just sit there and be comfortable. Jimmy will be along directly. He went out about two hours ago, but he'll be home soon. We'll have tea and jelly bread when he comes in. Do you like home-made jam, Mr.-Mr.… "

"O'Shean. Mike O'Shean," I said roughly.

I asked her about Jimmy. This was easy, since he was the only thing we had in common to talk about. There were some things I had to find out about him since it was becoming apparent that he would not run back and hide here tonight.

I learned that Jimmy was all the family the old lady had. Her eyes trailed off into the distance, in the manner of an elderly person whose present is so mingled with the past that she forgets, at times, which is reality. "Jimmy has a good job now, you know," she said suddenly, brightly. "He's working for Miss Pat Taylor, you know, the actress? He's driving her car for her. She's a lovely person."

But these were not the things I wanted to know. I asked more questions. Then I learned that Jimmy had a girl. She worked nights in a cafe. I told the old lady that I didn't have time to wait any longer and I went out to hunt up the girl.

I left wondering who was going to put the nice old lady to bed tonight and all the nights after tonight, and who was going to tell her why her boy, Jimmy, wouldn't ever be home again.

In the cafe where his girl worked, I dropped a dime in a pay phone, spun the dial. In a moment, a girl's husky voice answered briskly, "Daily Herald, City desk; Brown speaking."

"Lil."

There was a split second's pause while she drew a quick, sharp breath. She always did that when I called her. I felt sorry for her. She was a nice young kid and I felt sorry that it should be that way for her.

"Hello, Mike. How's the detective business?"

"It stinks. I have a murder."

"I know," she said softly. "I'm working on the story now."

There was nothing more she would say. That was one of the things I liked about Lil Brown. She knew when to keep her mouth shut. She knew how it had been with Pat and me. So she knew now to keep her mouth shut.

I told her what I wanted her to do and I gave her Jimmy Barecky's home address.

"Thanks," she said dryly. "You always give me the sweetest little chores. How do you go about telling a nice old lady her son just strangled a woman?"

I hung up. I knew she could handle it. Lil Brown was an extremely capable young woman.

I sat at the counter and ordered a bowl of soup. There was only one waitress in the place. She was thin and tired. Otherwise she was pretty, except for the harried look in her dark eyes. They often had that look, the poor people from down here in hunky town. It, maybe, was the look of people trying to pull themselves out of a sucking quagmire.

It was seldom that they got out of this cluster of shacks around the great, smoke-belching iron works. Usually the smoke got them first, or they went to work in the factories. Pat had dragged herself out, but then she had more to bargain with than the ordinary girl, and she'd suffered no qualms about trading it for the places she'd wanted to go.

When the thin, dark-eyed girl brought the soup, I said, "Your name is Bess?"

Her lips tightened. She shoved a napkin, salt and pepper and a bottle of ketchup in front of me. "I'll save you a lot of words, mister. I don't go out with strangers."

I showed her the badge in my wallet.

"Lieutenant Mike O'Shean, homicide."

She looked frightened. They were all that way, down in this section of town. Mention cop and they got either belligerent or scared. Wearily, I stirred some crackers into the soup.

"You got a boy friend named Jimmy Barecky?"

Her fingers worried the hem of her apron into a tight ball. "Yeah. What's wrong? What's wrong with Jimmy?"

I told her bluntly he'd strangled a woman tonight.

She sat down and cried softly with her hands over her face.

I told her what I wanted her to do. I told her I wanted her to help us locate Jimmy. She knew him better than any one else next to his mother. She would most likely know where he was hiding.

She rocked back and forth on the chair, small and huddled, her face a white mask. "If only he hadn't gone to work for that woman. He started changing right away. He used to be so nice to me. He worked hard, studying his books at night. A lawyer, he was gonna be. We was proud of him, Ma Barecky and me. I-he used to tell me how he was in love with me and after he got to be a really sure enough lawyer, he'd get a nice little house somewhere and we'd get married and there'd be a room for his ma. Then he started working for *her*." Her lip curled. "All he could talk about was how beautiful she was. He stopped studying his books and he didn't come around to see me any more."

I stood up, dropped a half dollar on the counter. "He's in bad trouble, Bess. Hiding out isn't going to help him. And he's hurt, we know that; maybe bleeding to death."

She knotted the apron around her white fingers. "What should we do?"

"Find him. You know the places he might hide. Then you call headquarters. It will go easier on him if he gives himself up."

I told her that, looking her in the eye, with the heavy service revolver, the gun that was going to kill Jimmy, digging into my side.

I wrote a number for her on a paper napkin. Then I walked outside. I might have felt like a heel except that I had long ago lost the capacity to feel much of anything.

There would be a little time to wait out, now. Minutes that would crawl by like crippled beetles. I looked around and saw that I was in the neighborhood where Pat came from. The old house was around the corner, and two streets over. I walked down there. I don't know why. Maybe because I would feel closer to her there, for a minute.

It had been ten years. The house looked the same. Maybe a little more dilapidated. The porch sagged more. The yard had more junk in it. The house where Pat Kolojeck was born, only her millions of stage and television fans knew her as Pat Taylor, the sweet, clean, average American girl who had been born of nice, middle-class folks in a respectable small town. The role she played as well off the stage as on.

I pulled open the sagging screen door and went into the only room that had light.

Her old man was sitting there, beside a radio, with a glass of flat beer in his hand, staring blankly ahead of him. He hadn't changed in ten years. He still needed a shave and he still sat around in his smelly socks with his shirt off and his suspenders hanging down. He looked as grey and dirty and defeated as yesterday's newspaper blowing along a gutter.

How a beautiful creature like Pat had sprung from this old lush's loins was one of the wonders of hunky town.

He fastened bleary, vacant eyes on me. His bottom lip hung slackly open. I didn't think he would remember me and I didn't care, but he did after a minute.

"Mike O'Shean," he whispered. "Ain't it?"

I looked around, everywhere but at him, trying to find something of Pat in these smoke-dingy, unpapered walls. Trying to hear a girl's voice from the spent years.

"You ain't been back for ten years, ain't it, Mike?"

I looked at him.

"She's dead, hah, Mike?" he whispered with his loose, dirty mouth. "I heard it on the radio." His eyes roved and settled on the cheap table radio. "I heard it fifteen minutes ago."

I looked at him, wishing I hadn't come here.

"Well, she got there," he mumbled, his voice rambling. "She told me when she left. She said, 'Damn you, Pop. Damn you and hunky town. Next time you see me, I'll be riding in a big car with a chauffeur and I'll spit on you.' " He nodded. "Well, she made it. They say she got on the stage and people paid big money to come see her act. They told me she was on television every week. But I never seen her. You'd think she'd at least bought her old daddy a television set so's he could see her," he muttered. Then he laughed, half to himself. "Once I went up there where she lived in that fine building. I thought she might give her old daddy a little something. But they wouldn't let me in." He laughed, a dry, rasping sound. He shook his head, laughing to himself that way. Then he moved his clouded eyes in my direction again. He squinted, focusing them on me. "You still a cop, Mike? You ain't got no uniform."

"I'm still a cop," I said.

"You know who done it to her?"

I opened my mouth. I said, "I know."

"Why did he do it to her like that, Mike?"

"He was a crazy little kid. A punk. A kill-crazy punk."

"What are you going to do to him, Mike?"

"When I find him," I said, "I'm going to kill him."

Old man Kolojeck stared at me with his bleary, cataract-clouded eyes and his lips hanging slackly from broken tooth husks. Then he got up from his chair, spilling the glass of flat beer. "Why do you want to kill somebody on account of her?" he whispered so softly I could barely hear him. "You know what she was, Mike? She was my daughter, and you want me to tell you what she was? She was a tramp. That's what. She was a tramp."

I knocked him down. With my flat hand. It was like slapping down an empty paper bag. He fell over the table, throwing the cheap, plastic-case radio to the floor. Then he cowered there. I felt sick, down in my guts. I took out a twenty dollar bill from my wallet. I put it on the wrecked table beside the old man and I got out of there.

I wished I hadn't gone there. I was a fool to hunt for anything of Pat in dirt and despair. The emptiness and hurt were only worse.

I got in my car and drove to my room. Nearly an hour had passed since I talked with Jimmy Barecky's girl in the cafe. She would be my contact. She would be the tendril that would search through the back alleys and deserted buildings of hunky town until she touched the man who had killed Pat and then I'd have him. I sat down beside the telephone. I took out ten cigarettes. I laid them in a neat, white row on the telephone bench. Then I lit one. When I smoked it down to my finger tips, I lit the second. I promised myself before the row of ten was gone, the telephone would ring.

I was on number eight when the bell jangled. I picked it up.

"Yeah. Okay, speaking. All right, where? Wait a minute." I got a pencil. "All right, I got that. No, I'm taking it alone."

I put the scrap of paper in my pocket and I went down to where my car was parked in the night.

A police car had just pulled up at the curb. Hank leaned out of the window. "I thought you would be in bed. I was on my way home, and I saw a light in your room."

"I've been waiting for a call."

He looked at my face. "Barecky? You've located him?"

I nodded.

He looked up at me from behind the wheel of the squad car. "Don't you think I'd better..."

"No, I'll take it alone. You get some sleep."

I got in my car and pulled away and drove back to hunky town, to the cinder-covered alleys and the dark, deserted warehouses.

I followed the directions Bess had phoned in and soon I was at the building where Jimmy Barecky was hiding like an animal. It had started to drip out of the murky skies. The big drops spattered on the cinders around my feet.

I went into the building and Bess came out of the shadows. Her face was a patch of whiteness.

"You said it would be all right," she asked anxiously. "You said you wouldn't hurt him. "

"Where is he?"

"Upstairs. He's hurt. Please don't be rough with him, Mr. O'Shean."

I walked up the stairs, to the boy, Jimmy Barecky, to the pair of hands that had squeezed her life away.

I took out my gun and pushed the safety off. The girl stood behind me, staring with her big eyes. "He'-he's hurt and scared. You don't need..."

I went into the room. Jimmy Barecky was lying on a cot. His thin, fever-reddened face stared at me.

I lifted the gun. Somewhere, I heard the girl scream. The kid pushed one of his palms at me, as if to ward off the bullet. His eyes were big and black and disbelieving.

I wanted to put the bullets where they would hurt the most. I wanted to see him double over his belly, screaming and gagging, the way she must have gagged.

But I didn't press the trigger. Something the old man said got in the way. "Why did he do it to her like that, Mike?" That's what the old man said. And I hadn't an answer. "A kill-crazy punk," I had said. But that wasn't an answer. And there was something else. The wounds from the shears. They should have been around his face or chest, where a person being strangled by him would have struck. But there were no wounds that I could see, standing in front of him. And there was something in the back of my mind that stopped my finger, call it ten years' training on the force or call it intuition.

"Where are you hurt?" I whispered through my teeth. "Say it fast and say it right."

"Back," the kid gasped. "In my back." He was crying. "Bess said it would be all right if we told where I was. She said it would be better…"

The gun got too heavy to hold. "Where in the back?" I took his shoulder and wrenched him over and he yelled with pain. Twice, he'd gotten it. Twice, below the shoulder blade, between the ribs. Where a strangling person couldn't have reached, or had the strength to drive it in so deep, twice, and pull it out for another stab.

"Tell me," I said.

He was crying and trying to find the right words, because he was afraid I was going to kill him. "I drove her car. But I'd seen her before I went to work for her. I thought she was the cleanest, purest girl in the world. I used to see her in plays and then on television. You know, she was always like your kid sister, or the nice girl down the street."

We stood there in the dark, empty warehouse, the wide-eyed, thin girl and I, while the rain tapped at the window with gloved fingers and we listened to the nineteen-year-old boy's words. They came halting and painful.

"She advertised for a chauffeur and I got the job. After a while, I found out she wasn't like everybody thought. Inside, she was cold and hard and she'd do anything to get ahead in her career." His words rambled a little because of the fever burning in him. "There were men, a lot of them, but only the ones that would do her some good. A rich guy fell in love with her, head of some kind of corporation. The guy had a family and kids. He was going to divorce his wife and marry her. Then, one night, his wife got in Miss Taylor's car when we were driving away from the studio. This guy's wife begged Miss Taylor to leave him alone on account of their kids. She offered to pay a lot of money if Miss Taylor'd leave him alone. She got down on her knees there in the back of the car. It was awful."

"I heard it all, because I was driving. Miss Taylor needed money bad, big money. She wanted to produce a show of her own that would really put her on top if it went over. But she needed money to do it. So she promised this lady to leave her husband alone for a lot of money. I don't know how this lady got it, but she used to bring her all this money regularly. And Miss Taylor swore to leave her husband alone."

The boy wiped his trembling hand across his face. "I knew about all of this because they'd meet in the car when I was driving. Well, I found out yesterday that Miss Taylor, after taking the lady's money and swearing she'd leave her husband alone, went right on and got him hooked anyway. After the lady couldn't pay any more money, Miss Taylor talked the husband into getting a divorce from her. I guess he was pretty crazy about Miss Taylor."

"Then, yesterday," the kid swallowed, "I read in the paper where this lady had committed suicide. I thought about it all last night and today, how everybody thought Miss Taylor was such a good, fine lady. And how this man broke up his family and caused his wife to commit suicide on account of her. I went up to her place tonight. I told her to her face what I thought about how she acted. And I said I was going to this man and tell him how Miss Taylor had taken money from his wife to leave him alone and then I was going to tell the newspapers and everybody what kind of a person she was and some of the things that she did that I knew about. She screamed all kinds of things at me. She offered me money to keep quiet. Then she said she wouldn't let anybody wreck her career; it had cost her too much. I turned and started to walk out. Then I felt this burning pain in my back. It hurt awful. It took my breath away and knocked me down to my knees. Then she did it again. I went crazy with pain. I rolled over and I saw her coming at me again with those scissors she'd grabbed up. She was trying to get at my face. I caught ahold of her throat and held on. He covered his face with his hands. "I loved her because she was so beautiful. Even while I hated her for being so terrible, I loved her. I didn't want to hurt her. Believe me, Mister."

I put the gun back in my pocket. I was silent for a minute and then I said, "I believe you."

We called for an ambulance and while we waited, I told the girl and the boy again that it was going to be all right. He wouldn't die from the wounds and the jury would believe him, too. Even a poor kid from hunky town had the right to kill to save his life. And the few people who had known Pat, really known her, would back him up.

After the red lights from the ambulance had disappeared, I walked for a while in the dripping rain. Then I felt in my pocket and took out the little object that had fallen from Pat's dead hand into mine tonight. I wondered why she'd had it in her fingers at that precise moment? No doubt it was just one of the objects her dying grasp had dragged off the dressing table. But I was surprised she had kept it all these years.

It was the small, cheap wedding ring a young police rookie had given to her ten years ago. I had been her first step out of hunky town. She had been everything to me. But to her, that's all I was: a step. A year later, she found other, higher steps, and she left me.

I dropped the ring over the side of a small bridge. I found an all-night cafe and went into the telephone booth and dialed a number. Lil Brown's weary voice said, "City desk."

"This is Mike."

There was a quick little intake of breath. Then her voice, quite steady, "Hello, policeman. Why the hell don't you go to bed?"

"I thought I might come over to your apartment first for some scrambled eggs if you can leave that rag for a while."

"Sure, sure I can. Mike, I…?"

"There's something I want to tell you, kid. You see, everything's all right now. You understand, Lil?"

She said nothing for a long minute. Then she said, "I understand, Mike," and I hung up. I was surprised to feel myself smiling, because I hadn't been smiling for a long, long time.

Ybor City

It happened in an alley in Tampa, Florida, in the squalid Ybor City district. One minute he was a man, smoking a cigarette, waiting for me in the humid summer night. The next, he was a corpse, falling over with a knife in his back.

I never saw his killers at all, except for two blobs of shadow in the stinking blackness of the alley. One of them was a woman. She collided with me, giving me the feel of her softness and the smell of her cheap perfume. Then she was gone.

Something had spun out of her hand when she plowed into me. I groped around for it. My hands came in contact with a woman's small purse. Quickly, without looking at it, I stuffed it in my coat pocket. Then I walked down into the black maw of the alley where the dead man lay.

Stuccoed walls, crumbling with age, formed canyons around me. Outlined against the starry summer sky was filigreed iron grill work around a balcony, and the leaves of a banana tree waving above a court-yard wall.

The corpse was heavy, like an inert sack of potatoes. I shoved and wedged it into a doorway, and then I walked back to the mouth of the alley, lighting a cigarette. I was standing there, casually smoking, when the patrolman came up with his flashlight.

"Evening, officer," I said.

He shoved the blinding light across my face. When he got it out of my eyes, I could see by the glow of a streetlight that he was young and freckle-faced, built like a Notre Dame tackle.

I inhaled a lungful of smoke, let it drift away. His light whipped down the alley, crawled over garbage cans, packing crates, bundles of paper, went over the spot where the dead man had sprawled, and then made a circuit of the fire escapes and balconies.

"Something the matter?" I asked.

"I don't know. I thought I heard something. Some kind of yell. What're you doing here?"

"Just walking around. I heard it, too. In the alley. A couple of cats fighting, I think. They make the damnedest sounds. Like a woman getting raped."

He relaxed a little. "Yeah." He shoved the flash into his belt, lit a cigarette. Then he took out a handkerchief and mopped his freckled forehead, pushing his cap back. "God, it's hot tonight."

"Not a breath stirring," I agreed.

"Yeah, I guess that's what it was. Cats, I mean. We got a couple of old alley Toms in my neighborhood. Keep me awake squalling and fussing every night."

"They can raise a lot of hell, all right."

He stuffed the handkerchief back in his pocket. "You better not hang around here by yourself," he said in a friendly tone. "Lousy part of town. One of these cigar rollers might slug you."

I shrugged and moved away from the alley. I walked down the street and crossed over to a drug store. Like the rest of Ybor City, it was all Spanish. A placard in the window said, *English Spoken Here.*

For a long time, I stared at the window. Then I walked into the place and examined some magazines. After a bit, I went out on the sidewalk again. The young cop had disappeared. The street was empty and lonely. I stepped back into the store, dropped a coin in a pay phone and called a taxi. Then I walked quickly back to the alley.

The dead man was where I had left him, doubled over in the doorway. His skin felt clammy and damp to the touch. I lifted him, draped one of his arms over my shoulder and dragged him out of the alley. His head bounced and rolled and his hand flapped like a dead fish.

I stood there, holding him at the alley entrance. I was afraid to put him down because the taxi might come any minute and I was afraid if I stayed with him, the young beat cop would come by again, making his rounds.

So I stood there, sweating, my muscles aching, and cursed taxi companies. Finally, the cab turned a corner and rolled slowly down the street. I whistled and he pulled into the curb and opened a door.

I grinned and staggered, putting on a drunk act. In the darkness, the murdered man could pass for a friend who'd had more than his limit.

I got the corpse in the back of the car and slid in beside him. In a drunken voice, I mumbled at the driver to take us down to the Bay.

While he drove, I fumbled through the dead man's pockets, but found nothing. Finally, we reached a sandy strip under some waving palm trees, and the taxi driver stopped. I handed him a crumpled bill and dragged the corpse out again, thankful for the darkness here.

The driver stuck his head out. "Hey, he looks like he's in bad shape. You better get him to bed."

"Can't hold his liquor," I said thickly.

The man shoved his head out a couple more inches. "You look like you got blood on your face."

"Cut myself shaving," I said. "Beat it, friend."

He stared at me, his face a white blur in the night. Suddenly he started looking scared. He jerked his head back in like a frightened turtle, raked the cab into gear, and got out of there.

I dragged the murdered man along the beach. This was a lonely section: a few dark fishing shacks, some palmettos, and a row of boats tied up at a rotting pier, slapping and bumping softly in the wash of surf.

I carried and dragged the dead man until my shoulder sockets were almost pulled apart and the sweat was a dripping, slimy film all over my body.

Finally I got down to the little cabin cruiser that had brought me across the bay from St. Petersburg earlier this evening. I worked the dead man on board and into the cabin. Then I went over him again in the darkness. With a pocket knife, I ripped out his pockets, the lining of his coat. He was clean. Not a thing on him.

I played the beam of a small flashlight over his face. An aspect of a man, thin-boned and dissipated; pinched features with an angular design of sharp bones under tight skin.

I straightened my back and swore softly in the darkness. The muggy Florida night answered me across the licking water with mocking silence.

Then I remembered the girl's purse. I took it out of my coat pocket and emptied its contents on a bunk, and snapped on the flashlight again. It was a tiny bag, the kind women take with them in the evenings, that contain the bare essentials of makeup. This one had a compact, a balled Kleenex smeared with lipstick, a package of Camels with two cigarettes remaining, a gold lipstick case, and a book of paper matches.

The lipstick had a name engraved on it: "Lolita." The matchbook cover bore a picture of a nude blonde sitting in a champagne glass, underneath which some printing assured the reader that the food at *Sagura's was the best in Ybor City.*

I wedged the murdered man in the cruiser's toilet and locked the door. I didn't want the police finding him yet. It would louse up the whole show, because he was not the man doing the blackmail. He had only been the boy who ran errands. True, he could have given me the key to the situation. But the big shot had gotten to him first, tonight, and stuck a knife in him. I needed more time, something I wouldn't have if this dead man became police property and Grace Perring's blackmail became a newspaper scandal.

So I went back to Ybor City, the Latin quarter that extended two miles east from Nebraska Avenue and south to Ybor estuary.

I returned and hunted up Sagura's, a typical Spanish restaurant, a place that cooked chicken and rice, yellow with saffron, black-bean and garbanzo soups, steak catalana, crawfish and spaghetti served with wine. I ordered a bottle of wine and sat at a table under potted rubber plants and watched a string band play Cuban music.

I turned over one of their paper book match covers and looked at the picture of the nude blonde sitting in the champagne glass.

"Lolita been around tonight?" I asked the waitress who brought my wine.

She put the wine down and gave me a fleeting glance. *"Yo no se."* She shrugged and went away. But in a little while the manager of the place came around and sat at my table. He was a fat man with a round face that looked like a greasy coffee bean. He mopped at it with a white handkerchief.

"This is a hot one," he said, sighing.

I drank the wine, looking at him. The band was playing a rumba. A girl dressed in a spangled bra and ruffled split skirt came out on the floor and began shaking her rear.

"The waitress. She said you asked about Lolita." He looked around at the floor show, trying so hard to appear casual it was ludicrous.

I nodded and lit a cigarette.

"You are a friend of Lolita?" he asked. The sweat was coming through his seersucker coat.

"Maybe," I said. "What difference does it make?"

He made an elaborate shrugging gesture, ducking his bullet head between bulging shoulders and pushing fat, brown palms upward. "Please, Señor. I am not what you call sticking my nose in your business. Only, well, Vellutini, he's a powerful man around here..." His voice trailed off with another shrug of his fat shoulders.

I nodded. "Of course." I drank some more of the wine, and wondered who the hell Vellutini was. "It isn't important. About Lolita, I mean. I'm related to her by marriage. Knew her when she was a kid in another part of the state. Just thought I'd look her up while I was in town." I said it flatly, casually, as if the subject no longer interested me.

The cafe manager stood up. "Well," he said, "she comes around here sometimes. But I haven't seen her in several days." In parting, he added, "You might try the place she works in daytime, the Veloz-Rey cigar factory." And he walked off.

I paid for the wine and left the place.

It was past midnight now and I thought I had better not go back to the boat. So I wandered around until I found a cheap hotel on a dim street, where a man could rent a room for a dollar and a half a night. I bought another bottle of wine in the store just off the lobby and went up.

I lay there, in the hot, stinking night, with the wine bottle on the bed beside me, and, in my rig, the heavy .45 that I had brought along to kill a man.

It was close to noon the next day when I awoke. After dressing, I walked down to the Veloz-Rey cigar factory. I needed a shave and my gray suit was rumpled and the collar of my shirt had soaked itself into a shapeless rag.

Veloz-Rey was one of the many factories of its kind in this part of Tampa. Smaller than most, it was housed in a time-blackened brick building. A rickety stairway led up to the main factory room on the second floor.

Here, the cigar makers, the *tabaqueros* who rolled the cigars, worked at long tables in double rows.

One of them was the woman who had helped kill a man in an Ybor City alley last night.

I wandered among the workers, trying to attract as little attention as possible. Near the water cooler I started a conversation with one of the "strippers" who had paused for a drink. It was the stripper's job to remove the stems from leaves and pass the tobacco on to *boncheros* who made up the inside tripa or filler of the cigar.

"Lolita?" he said. Then he grinned knowingly. "Oh, *si,* that one." He nodded toward the *tabaqueros.* "The little one with the pointed *chibabbies.*" He took a frayed cigar out of his wet mouth and spit on the floor. "Somebody tell you about her?"

But I was already moving, down the long rows of double tables. Here, the men and women bent over their monotonous tasks, with slim, skillful fingers whipping the tobacco into shape. A radio was on, giving the news in Spanish.

I stopped behind the woman, Lolita. She was young, about twenty, and her skin was the color of a dusky rose. Perspiration made her forehead shiny, soaked through her blouse, and ran in tiny drops down the shadowy valley of her bosom. The straps of her brassiere cut into the soft flesh of her shoulders under the filmy blouse.

She worked with a steady, detached rhythm.

An oscillating fan revolved in my direction, carrying to my nostrils a heavy, familiar perfume. And I knew I had the right woman.

"Lolita," I said softly, and put a hand on her shoulder.

She gave a little jump, and her head twisted around. I got the full force of her huge black eyes.

She stared at me for a moment, with her wide black eyes, and then she took my hand off her shoulder. "I'll have you fired, you bastard," she told me softly.

"I don't work here. I came up to ask you for a date."

She looked me over speculatively. Her lips curled. "You wouldn't have the price of a drink."

"I thought maybe we could talk. You know, about the little game you were playing in the alley last night."

As I said that, very softly, I dropped the lipstick in her lap. No one around heard what I said, but she heard all right. Her face lost its color. A drop of sweat ran down her cheek. She spread her fingers fanwise over her thigh, covering the lipstick, and she shivered. I bent over her and put my hand back on her shoulder, rubbing the soft flesh under the blouse with my fingers. I let my fingers trail around to the front of her blouse. "You want to tell me where you live, honey?"

She stared up into my eyes as if fascinated by them. Her lips drew back in a stiff grimace, showing the gleam of even, white teeth behind them. I thought for a moment she was going to be sick right there. But she gave me the address in a husky whisper.

"I'll see you there tonight after you get off work," I said. "And I wouldn't mention it to anybody, honey. There's no telling how much trouble it might cause you." I smiled at her, and then I turned and walked out of the place.

I went down the street and found myself a bar. I sat there, drinking steadily, looking somberly at the glass and nothing else.

I sat there until dark and then I went up to Lolita's room. I hugged the gun under my left arm, feeling the good, hard outline of it.

She opened the door. Now, she had bathed and there was a flower in her dark hair. She looked fresh in a clean skirt, stockings, ankle-strap shoes and a crisp blouse with a low neck.

She was a hell of a good-looking woman, and they *were pointed.*

"Hello, honey," I said.

She looked at me.

I pushed her aside and went into the room. "I don't guess you mind if I look around." Hand on my gun, I went into the kitchen, a cubicle of a room with a pile of dirty dishes on the tile sink. One of them was a plate with yellow egg stains; the other, a half empty cup of coffee with a cigarette butt floating soggily in the cold, black liquid. I looked into her closets, the bedroom, the bath. Then I returned to the living room.

She sat on the couch and lit a cigarette nervously. Her skirt was tight across her thighs and an inch above her knees.

I helped myself to a can of beer.

Her somber eyes flicked across my face. "So you were there, in the alley last night?" she asked. "What did you see?"

"I saw a man die," I told her, sipping the beer.

Her face was like a poker player's now, stiff and pale with nothing inside showing. It might have been carved out of wax. She raised one dark, plucked eyebrow. "That was important to you? Men die all the time." She waited.

"I know," I answered her.

"This one was a friend of yours?"

"He was nothing to me."

She snubbed out her cigarette in a cracked saucer on the table. Then she moved closer to me on the couch. Her fingers touched my arm and her thighs pressed against mine. "Maybe you will forget this- this little thing you saw in the alley? Maybe," she said softly, "Lolita can make you forget?"

"Maybe you can," I said. I put the beer down.

She was suddenly breathing hard, her sharp bosom straining against the flimsy covering.

I touched her thigh, feeling the roll of her stocking top under the tight skirt. A little moan escaped her lips. "Wait, honey," she whispered. She caught the "V" collar of her blouse in each hand and opened the buttons down to her waist. Then I reached for her and felt warm, satin-smooth flesh quivering under my hands. I pressed her back against the arm of the couch. She was twisting and moaning under me, damp with perspiration.

Then, suddenly, I wrenched her over, so that I had her right hand pinned under me. I grasped for her wrist, twisted it until I heard the clatter of steel on the floor.

I jumped up and kicked the little knife under the couch.

She sat up and buried her face in her hands. Her black hair fell over her finger tips. In the struggle, her dress had been torn and shoved up to her hips. Her bare thighs gleamed whitely above the stocking rolls that dug into soft flesh.

I grabbed a handful of her hair and threw her head back. "So he told you to handle it alone," I said. "The man in the alley with you last night, you told him I'd talked to you. So he told you to get me busy on the couch and stick a knife in my back."

She looked up at me with her sweat-slick face, a pulse in her throat fluttering wildly, and said nothing.

I hit her across the face, twice, back and forth, so hard that her teeth clicked together and blood splattered on her naked breasts.

"I want his name, Lolita. You'll give it to me if you want to have any face left."

She panted with a hoarse animal sound. "Vellutini. Mike Vellutini."

The name the restaurant owner had mentioned.

"He your boy friend?"

She nodded.

"The dead man," I went on. "He was working for Vellutini, but he was just the errand boy, right? He collected the money from Grace Perring. But your Mike Vellutini is the real blackmailer. He's got the pictures that are making this Perring dame pay off. Yes?" I gave her hair another twist.

She cried out with pain. "Yes," she said. "Mike found out Joe was going to double-cross us. He was going to tell Mrs. Perring, or somebody she sent, where the negatives were and who the real blackmailer was, for a sum. We followed him to the alley and got to him first."

"And your sweetheart, Mike Vellutini? Where will I find him?"

"He has a little night club. He runs a bolita game in the back room." She told me an address.

I threw her back on the couch and started for the door, but she caught up with me.

"Wait," she said. "Wait. Don't leave me now." Her fingers clawed at me. She started crying, her mouth working. "Mike made me stand there and watch while he stuck a knife in Joe's back last night so I'd see what happens to anybody who crosses him."

She said, "I'm scared of him. God, I'm scared of him. He's a fat, stinking pig. I hate him and I'm afraid of him."

Then her arms went around me, tightly, pressing her breasts against me so hard they burned through my shirt. "You're not afraid of him," she whispered, "or you wouldn't be tracking him down like this. Please, please take me away from that fat pig before he kills me. Take me out of Ybor City. I'll do anything for you."

She raised her face and there was a mixture of stark fear and animal lust in her eyes. Then her mouth was against mine, hot and alive, like her trembling body. Her tongue darted out and her hands pulled at my clothes.

I walked through the hot night with the woman smell still clinging to my body. It had been hard to make Lolita stay back at the room, and I succeeded only when I told her I was going to Vellutini's. She wasn't kidding about being afraid of him.

As I walked, I took the gun out and checked its magazine. Then I flicked the safety off, nestled it back in the shoulder rig and went on through the narrow, sweltering streets to the jook place that Mike Vellutini ran. The place where one night a few months ago a St. Petersburg society woman had been indiscreet with one of her many boy friends. Vellutini had gotten pictures of her, drunk and in bed with the man. And now he was making her pay through the nose to keep the picture under wraps.

Clever, though, Vellutini had never let it be known that he was the blackmailer. Always, the man whom Lolita had called Joe had contacted the woman for the money. He carried prints of the pictures. That was all.

I had come across the bay from St. Petersburg as an agent for Grace

Perring to meet the man in the alley. I had brought with me a large sum of money to give him for the information that I now had for nothing.

I went into Mike Vellutini's, a place of thick smoke, dark shadows, hot Latin piano, and cheap liquor. An evil hole on a back street where men and women from across the bay could come and hide their sins in sweltering private rooms that Vellutini rented for a high price.

I walked across the floor and somewhere above me, in the layers of yellow smoke, a ceiling fan turned apathetically, casting a shadow, helpless in the muggy heat.

Nobody stopped me as I wandered through the place, into the back room, a closed den, rancid with the odors of stale smoke, beer, and the sweat from men's bodies. The men sat around under a single light, suspended from the ceiling by a drop cord and covered with a green shade, mostly Negroes from the docks and Latin cigar workers, playing bolita. The room held its breath while the little balls, consecutively numbered and tied in a bag, were tossed from one person to another. The players sat, dripping sweat, their teeth clamped on cigars, staring at the sack. They smoked, spit on the floor, and cursed while they waited to see if the ball clutched through the cloth would bear their winning number.

I didn't know the face of the man I was looking for, so I drifted through the crowd, seeking a clue to the owner of the place.

I moved down a hallway toward the men's room. A door opened and a man came out into the hall. He was fat and greasy and dirty. I could smell him from ten feet away. He was dressed in an undershirt, a limp grey rag, soggy and stained with sweat, and he had a towel around his neck to soak up the sweat that ran down the thick, red creases of flesh. Besides the undershirt, he was wearing baggy seersucker trousers and tennis shoes.

His eyes were buried deep in soft pads of flesh, two glittering black marbles that studied me carefully. "You want someone?" he asked.

"I'm looking for Mike Vellutini," I said, and felt the weight of the gun under my left shoulder.

"Yeah?" He moved his cigar from one corner of his heavy, wet lips to the other. "About what?"

"Business, you might say."

His voice sounded like a flat tire rumbling over hollow pavement. "Come in here." He turned his back on me and lumbered into the office room.

I followed. It was a small, hot place like the other rooms. A French door opened out onto a courtyard where banana trees stood motionless in the still night.

The heavy man sat down behind his desk on a creaking swivel chair. He picked up a palmetto leaf and fanned himself while he looked at me through the cigar smoke with his shiny marble eyes.

"Go ahead," he rumbled. "I'm Mike Vellutini."

I sat on a chair, keeping my coat loose so the gun would come out fast. I went right to the point. "Several months ago," I said, "a woman, Grace Perring, came over from St. Pete with a man who was not her husband. During the night they were in a number of places in Ybor City. She was too drunk to remember any of them. But in one of the places, she and this man were in bed and somebody took their picture. A week later, a thin little man came to call on her with prints of this picture. He represented another man who wanted a large sum of money not to show the picture to her children and friends. He kept coming back for money until it was more than she could pay. I came over to find the real blackmailer."

Vellutini sat behind the desk with an amused look on his face. "So now you find him. Me, Vellutini." He laughed, and sucked hungrily at the cigar. "Yes, that was a good picture. She sure was enjoying it, that blonde bitch. What a wrestle she was giving him!" He laughed some more, with his flabby lips around the cigar. "So why you risk your neck, you dumb flatfoot? Money? Or did that blonde bitch offer to pay you off the way she's been payin' off all those other guys in St. Petersburg?"

I shrugged. "Let's say she has some nice kids. Three of them." I reached for my gun, feeling a little tired.

Vellutini might have looked fat and lazy but he wasn't dumb. While he flicked the palmetto leaf with his right hand, his left had crept below the level of the desk to an open drawer. Now it sprang out and there was a very heavy revolver in it, pointed at me.

We both fired the first shot together. Mine didn't miss. I followed it with a second.

A pair of red roses blossomed out on Vellutini's soggy undershirt, then dissolved and ran down over his fat belly. He grunted, staring at me stupidly, his slobbery lips hanging open. Slowly, he rose to his feet, knocking the chair over behind him. He stood there for a second, swaying, staring at me. Then he fell across the desk with a crash.

Quickly, I dragged out the desk and file drawers, pawing through them while voices murmured in the hall and fists beat against the door.

In the bottom of one drawer I found what I wanted, a snapshot negative. Even in the undeveloped negative I could recognize Grace Perring, and see the drunken, animal pleasure on her face as the man with her fondled her.

I stuffed it into a pocket and went through the French doors, through the courtyard and out into the dark streets.

I walked down through the stinking alleys of Ybor City toward the boat. I still had a body to bury out in the bay on my way back to St. Petersburg, and I still had to phone Lolita and warn her to say she knew nothing if the police questioned her.

Inside, I felt tired, dirty, and defeated. It would be nice, I thought, to stick around this Ybor City and the hot-blooded Lolita, who was mine for the asking.

But I had to get home to the quiet hell I lived in, across the bay.

I had to go on protecting, the best I knew how, the lives and happiness of three wonderful children whose mother was Grace Perring, my wife.

In Memoriam

EVERYONE in Hesterton knew that Wilber Minetree was dying. In a town of five thousand souls, a thing like that gets around.

It was the main topic of conversation at the post office, one of the early morning meeting spots of the downtown business set.

The nature of Wilber's illness was analyzed; the fact that this one and that one saw Wilber only a few weeks ago "looking the picture of health" was noted with a shocked clicking of tongues and shaking of heads.

Then it was unanimously agreed that Wilber had been a fine, upstanding citizen during his tenure of life, that he had promptly discharged his debts, paid his taxes, voted the straight Republican ticket, made a success of his job, and belonged to the Elks lodge.

"Of course he owed it all to Hortensia."

This statement was also seconded and accepted with no dissenting vote.

"Why, I knew Wilber back in grade school," one of the main-street business men offered. "He was tardy every day of the year. Never got to a class on time in his life."

This little human flaw in Wilber's character was agreed upon fondly by other friends of the now almost deceased.

"Fact is," the spokesman ventured further, "I guess if he hadn't married Hortensia, Wilber would have turned out to have been a bum."

Now this was going a bit too far. Even though it was probably true, it showed remarkable lack of tact. There was a disapproving clearing of throats, shifting of feet, and a few dark looks.

Mort Fowler, owner of the Serve-U grocery store, who had made the faux pas, looked embarrassed and drew back into the crowd.

There was a moment of silence. Then one of Wilber's colleagues at the Farmer's First National Bank said, "Well, you do have to give Hortensia credit, though. She's been the making of Wilber Minetree."

There was a general agreement to this observation.

The fact was that most of them had known Wilber since childhood and they knew that Mort Fowler had been right. Without Hortensia, Wilber would indeed have turned out to be a bum. Though, it was in pretty bad taste to point this out with the poor man on his death bed.

Before Wilber got married, he'd never been anywhere on time in his life. He blissfully overslept every morning, was fired off innumerable jobs. Alarm clocks were totally ineffectual with Wilber. At the time he met Hortensia, he had been reduced to racking up pool balls at the Downtown Recreation Hall and Domino Parlor.

It was a matter of record that a startling metamorphosis had taken place in Wilber after his marriage. Fortunately, Hortensia was a strong willed woman, a fifth grade school teacher who was a few years Wilber's senior. She had a matronly bosom, a slightly brassy voice, and the hint of a mustache. But she was just what Wilber needed. She spoke to Alex Craine, president of the Farmer's First National Bank about a job for Wilber. It was in keeping with her nature that she would want her husband to have a position of dignity in the community. Needless to say, working for the Farmer's First National Bank carried more status than racking up pool balls.

It was with considerable trepidation that Alex Craine put Wilber on at the bank. Please don't misunderstand. Alex did not dislike Wilber. Nobody in Hesterton actually disliked Wilber. He was one of those happy-go-lucky, affable slobs whom everyone liked. It's just that you didn't want him working in your place of business.

But Hortensia was extremely persuasive and to escape the frontal assault of her personality, Alex had agreed to give Wilber a job in the bookkeeping department at ninety dollars a month on a trial basis. He felt justified in lowering the bank's personnel standards in this manner on the grounds that, with a clear conscience, he'd probably be able to fire Wilber after the first week.

He was extremely surprised to find Wilber reporting for work the next morning precisely on the stroke of eight. "Shocked" would perhaps be a more exact description of his reaction. To the best of his knowledge, it was the first time in Wilber's life that he had ever appeared anywhere on time. Not only that, but Wilber's shoes were shined, his suit pressed, and his shirt starched. "Good morning, Mr. Craine," Wilber smiled affably.

This was the start of a satisfactory relationship between Wilber Minetree and the Farmer's First National Bank that continued for thirty years. And not once during that period of service—let us repeat—not once, was Wilber Minetree ever tardy, nor did he miss a single day of work. There were times, it is true, when bets were laid among the employees of the bank with rather startling odds. The time Wilber dragged himself down more dead than alive with influenza, and the morning after the Elks Christmas dance when Wilber had been more lit up than the thirty foot Christmas tree down on the square.

But he always greeted Alex Craine on the bank steps at eight A.M., with his "Good morning, Mr. Craine," even though somewhat weakly on the two occasions mentioned above.

Of course, no one knew, but everyone guessed what struggles, cajoling, threats, and tears Hortensia Minetree went through in order to keep Wilber punctual. There was some rumor as to the use of force, but this was probably malicious gossip.

It was, however, public knowledge that all the clocks in the Minetree home were set a half hour ahead, that a strident and somewhat brassy voice was often heard in the early mornings issuing from the Minetree house and carrying the length of the block, and that on many occasions, Hortensia, herself drove Wilber to the bank and literally led him up to the bank steps by the arm.

But through her untiring efforts ("relentless," while being, perhaps the more exact nuance, is somewhat unkind), Wilber had escaped his destiny as the affable town bum. He held a respectable position for thirty years with the bank, advancing to the post of first teller. He and Hortensia bought and paid for a comfortable though not pretentious home. They raised two children, a boy and a girl who were now both married and had children of their own. And Wilber had even once been elected water commissioner of the city.

Hortensia had indeed succeeded alone. So she phoned Mrs. Schien, canceling her services for the evening, and when Miss Redding left, Hortensia settled herself alone in Wilber's room beside his bed, to await the end.

Wilber's breathing became more and more shallow. The quiet hours of the night ticked slowly away. Hortensia glanced at the bedside clock from time to time, remembering with a fond and tearful smile that it was still set a half hour ahead. At times she dozed, her head nodding forward.

It was during one of these catnaps that Wilber yawned and sat up.

Hortensia came awake with a startled jump.

"Hello, Hortensia," Wilber smiled affably. "Where am I?"

Hortensia's mouth opened and worked, but for the first time in her life nothing came out.

Wilber looked around, bright-eyed, but slightly befuddled. "Oh, I remember. I've been sick, haven't I?"

Hortensia was still too stunned to utter a sound. Wilber had been in a coma for three days. He hadn't spoken rationally for a week. Now he was sitting up clear-eyed and in full possession of his faculties.

"H-how do you feel, Wilber?" she finally gasped.

"Me? Oh, I feel fine. Only I'm awful hungry. You got something in the house to eat, Hortensia?"

She groped her way to her feet, clutching at the chair for support.

"Some cold roast beef maybe," he said, "or a drumstick. And a bottle of beer."

She stumbled out of the room toward the kitchen.

"See if you have any of those good homemade pickles of yours in the refrigerator," he called after her.

She fumbled blindly at the refrigerator. Wilber had rallied. The doctor said that, on rare occasions, patients in Wilber's condition did rally, though he hadn't thought it possible in Wilber's case. Hortensia remembered when Leona McPhail's husband had been in that coma last year and not expected to live the day out; he'd rallied unexpectedly and hung on for a whole month. And old man Marreth who fell down with that stroke on Main Street. The doctor said he wouldn't live until they got him to the hospital. Well, that was two years ago and the old geezer wasn't any more dead than the doctor.

Hortensia was too upset to pay any attention to what she was doing. She automatically got some food on the tray and started back to Wilber's room. But her mind was swimming with the monstrous inconvenience that this unexpected turn of events had caused. Everything had been so well organized and timed. Now Wilber had thrown a monkey wrench into the plans, throwing everything into a hopeless snarl.

It was too late to stop the relatives. By now they were on trains and airplanes converging on Hesterton. By tomorrow night the house would be swarming with relatives. Why, they might have to hang around for a week or more now, waiting for the funeral. They'd eat up a fortune in food, and her son would lose important time from his job in South America, and her daughter's husband might not have that much emergency leave from his army post in Germany. The florist had already wired for a huge order of flowers due to arrive tomorrow. They'd be completely wilted and ruined. And the obituary in the Advocate. Good heavens, she'd forgotten about that! Mr. Seelingson was starting to print the paper tonight. It would be too late to take that out now.

Completely distraught, she brought the tray into Wilber's room and put it beside his bed. He smiled at her good-naturedly. "I sure am hungry, Hortensia."

"Lay back down, Wilber," she said distractedly. "You'll tax your strength."

Obediently, he settled back against his pillow. She picked up another pillow, clapped it down firmly over his face, smothering him.

He struggled weakly. "Lie still, Wilber!" she panted. "For heaven's sake, if it weren't for me, you'd be late to your own funeral!"

Dixieland Dirge

HE stood on a corner of Basin Street, a stooped figure in a baggy suit with a dead cigar in his mouth and dead memories in his eyes. He stood there for a while and then he shifted the weight of the battered trumpet case under his left arm and shuffled away.

Moving out from the corner, he got directly in the path of the traffic. There was a squealing of brakes and a blaring of angry horns. A white-faced driver shook a fist at him. With a dark scowl, the traffic officer on the corner strode over to the muddle.

"What's the matter?" he thundered. "Jay-walkin' that way."

"I'm sorry, officer," old Mizz Milner apologized, taking his shapeless felt hat off close-cropped gray hair. His eyes wandered around with the shadowy memories in them. "I was, you know, sort of sight-seein'. Been a long time since I was back to this old town. I was lookin' for Lulu Williams' place. Used to be hereabouts somewhere." His tired face got a far-away smile. "We used to have some sessions there. Old Jelly-Roll Morton, Satchmo, and…" He shook his head. "But, it's all changed now. All changed. "

The policeman stared at him.

Mizz apologized again and moved off the street, the weariness that was always a part of him now a leaden weight in his legs.

He walked along Basin, turned down Canal, past Rampart Street, and then headed down the narrow side streets into the Quarter. Here, the old buildings looked as tired and dissipated as he did. He shuffled along, hugging the instrument case close to his side. Once, he stopped to fumble a scrap of paper out of his pocket and consult the penciled scrawl on it for the address he was seeking. These days, he didn't keep things like that in his mind so well.

At last he came to the place, a dingy old building on St. Louis Street. He stood there for a moment, looking up at the rusty iron filigree work around the balcony, the green shutter that hung from a single hinge. Then he sighed and plodded up a dark stairway.

The apartment number was on the second floor. In front of the door, he paused to take a silk handkerchief out of his coat pocket and pat his damp face. After doing that, he wedged the trumpet case more securely in the crook of his left arm and rapped timidly.

For a long time there was no answer. He looked around at the thick mantle of dust that covered everything like the fuzz of old memories. He half turned, deciding to leave the place, when the door opened.

Turning back to it, he squinted his eyes against the gloom, looking at the woman framed in the doorway. A large woman with a magnificent bosom, she still bore the traces of beauty in her face like the lingering scent of a rare perfume. They stood in the dim hallway, staring at each other across the years and then a tear formed in the corner of her eye and trickled down her cheek.

"Mizz," she said softly. "You've come back."

He smiled a little foolishly, feeling awkward with this woman who was a stranger and yet not a stranger at all.

"Yeah," he mumbled. "I always said I'd come back, Sally. You remember? I always thought about it, coming back. The years kind of got away from me, but I kept it in my mind. And finally, I said to myself, 'Well, old Mizz, you better be gettin' back to that woman if you're ever goin' to!'"

She laughed gently and put a soft hand on his arm. "You come in here, Mizz and tell me 'bout all the places you been and what's happened to you."

He shuffled into the apartment that he knew would be neat as a pin. The old mahogany sideboard was polished to a rich sheen. Carefully mended, the velvet drapes with the little balled tassels gave an air of quiet elegance to the room. It was much like an aristocratic woman growing old with pride and dignity.

Sally went to the sideboard and took down a bottle of fine purple wine and poured them each a glass. Then she made Mizz comfortable in a platform rocker and sat down on a straight-back chair beside him. He kept the trumpet case under his arm while he sat there and she was wise enough not to ask him for it.

"It's all changed," he said. He drank some of the wine and then rocked a little. "I was down on Basin Street." He shook his head. "There wasn't nothing there I could recognize."

She nodded. "Storyville's been gone for many years, Mizz. They're playing down on Bourbon Street, mostly, these days."

She studied his face, seeing the ravages that the years of liquor, loss of sleep, irregular meals and frustration had put there. There was pride and humility and waste in the deep-etched lines.

He talked softly as the evening shadows grew thicker around them. He spoke of the early days in Chicago, then the tours to Europe and the bands on New York's Fifty-Second Street, and in the Village.

She nodded while he talked. "I got all the records you made." She pointed to a stack of them on a table. "And the clippings." They were in a scrap book that she showed him.

He drank some more of the wine and rocked, his eyes remote and unsatisfied. "It's there, but it ain't there. Something, I never could quite get it. It was in me, I know. For years, I kept trying." He shook his head. "They said I never did amount to much. I guess because I couldn't get out what was inside me, way inside me."

She rested a plump, dimpled hand on his arm. "You were a fine musician, Mizz. They wrote about you in that book."

He shook his head stubbornly. "Only because I been around so long. Because I played with so many good ones. Not because I was good myself." He took the silk handkerchief out and dabbed at his moist face.

"Now the doctor says I got to quit playing." He touched his chest. "Heart gone bad. Doctor said if I ever blow one more note it's liable to stop just like that." He snapped his fingers.

She leaned back so that her face was in the shadows. For a moment she did not speak, then she said, "So you've come back to me and to your son, because he's in trouble."

Mizz Milner put the empty wine glass carefully on a marble-top table. His hand trembled a little. "I-I always wondered. I was going to write you about that."

"He's your son," she said firmly. "Jim's your son, Mizz." Then her face came out of the shadows and she was smiling. "Don't feel bad, honey. I was proud to have your son. It was something of you to remember through the years."

They were both silent then for a while, remembering.

"Jim doesn't know about you," Sally murmured. "But he's your son, Mizz. Look at him and you'll see he's yours."

"I know," the old trumpet player nodded. "I saw his picture in the trade papers. I heard his records. He's my boy, all right. He plays the horn the good way that I never could. It makes me feel good to know that."

She looked at him. "That's why you really came back, ain't it, Mizz? You heard about his trouble and you came back on account of that."

Milner avoided her eyes. "I–I don't know, Sally. There's a time in a man's life when he sits down and looks back. Then he either feels satisfied inside or he feels scared and empty because none of it meant anything. That last way is how I feel. Like all the years were nothin' but a joke and a waste. It scares a man to feel that way. I don't know. I guess I sort of come back hopin' I could do somethin' worthwhile to help him. Somethin' to make the years count for something."

She put her hand over his, squeezed his fingers. "I'm glad for you to say that, Mizz, honey. I'm an old woman with a lot of good memories stored up. You couldn't do anything for me. It's him. Say something to him, Mizz. Talk to him. You're a musician and maybe he'll listen to you. He's gone crazy, drinking himself to death. They say he's carryin' a gun. I'm afraid of what he might do."

Mizz nodded. They sat there, saying no more while the dark velvet stole into the room.

Finally, out of the darkness, she whispered, "They'll be start-in' down on Bourbon Street now. You'll find him at the Down Beat Bar.

Mizz walked down the dark, narrow streets to the crooked alley of jazz where every neon-framed doorway was a bar and the music floated out of each one, mingling like swirling eddies of smoke on the sidewalks.

He shuffled along on his weary feet, studying the signs until he found one he wanted. He went up to the bar with his trumpet case under his left arm and ordered a drink and listened to the band for a while. Then he looked around the place and saw the man he was looking for at a table by himself.

The young man was Jim Williams, Mizz's son. He was alone, brooding sullenly over a bottle. Although the evening had barely started, he was already half drunk.

Mizz paid for his drink and went over to that table. He stood there for a while, shifting his weight from one foot to the other. Then he cleared his throat and spoke up.

"Excuse me," he said, "But ain't your name Jim Williams? I've seen your picture a lot in the trade sheets and I thought I recognized you."

The young man lifted swollen, bleary eyes. For a moment he stared at Mizz, then he mumbled, "Beat it."

Mizz sat down at the table beside him. "I was over in Baton Rouge," he said. "It ain't far and I wanted to hear you play. I heard you on records a lot."

"Read *Down Beat* again," the young man said thickly. "I quit the business. No band any more, no nothing.'"

The young man poured himself a drink. He didn't offer Mizz any.

"Yeah," Mizz said. "I guess I read that all right. But I thought I might hear you play anyway." He took out his white silk handkerchief and dabbed at his face. "I guess you don't know me. My name's Mizz Milner."

The fact struggled through the boy's liquor-deadened brain. When it finally registered, he looked up blearily. "Well, I'll be damned," he said, staring at Mizz.

"Yeah," Mizz said, "Ol' Mizz Milner, himself, son. Played in this town long before you was born. Played the kind of music you play, only not so good."

The boy laughed sourly, twisting his lips.

Mizz shook his head. "She ain't worth that, boy. Ain't no woman on earth worth throwin' away what you got. Maybe a thousand men lift a horn to their lips and among them only one's got what you have."

The boy cursed under his breath and poured another drink. "Look, you don't know the story, Pops. Maybe you better go back to Baton Rouge, huh?"

"I heard the story. She still ain't worth it."

"She killed my boy," Jim Williams said through the liquor. "His own mother killed him. He was sick and he needed attention while I was down here blowing my brains out to pay for the doctor. And I was sick too, worryin' about him. All my wife had to do was sit with him to watch when he started chokin'. You know where she was when he started chokin'? In Perry Baehr's room. Drunk, in Perry Baehr's room while her son was chokin' himself to death all by himself."

Jim Williams gulped the raw liquor savagely.

Mizz sat there, his face troubled, not knowing what to say. "This won't bring the boy back," he finally said clumsily. "Drinkin' yourself to death, losin' your band, your music. It won't bring him back, or pay her back."

The young musician smiled. A lock of his black hair fell across his sweating forehead. He took a small revolver out of a pocket and laid it in his lap. "No," he whispered, "but this will pay her back. With interest. A bullet for every time she's shacked up with Baehr. I'm going to wait until I can catch them together and then I'm going to shoot her in the belly. You understand? I'm going to empty this gun in her belly and then load it again and keep shooting her, while Baehr is standing there watching and puking all over himself."

Mizz Milner began shaking. He got out the silk handkerchief and patted his forehead with his hand shaking that way. "That's an evil thing to say. You don't know what you're saying. You'll ruin yourself over a woman that ain't worth spittin' on. They'll put you away in a jail where you can never play your horn again. Maybe even the electric chair."

Jim Williams started at him with the kill madness in his face. "Shut up," he whispered, thick cords in his neck standing out. "Shut up, you lousy tin horn musician. You corny, worthless old has-been. I heard your records. You can't blow your nose. You never could. Take your lousy jazz out of here. Get out of here and leave me alone. When I want your advice I'll ask."

Mizz was shaking all over. The dull ache in his left chest and arm started up with constricting bands that closed around his lungs.

He looked into Jim Williams' face, seeing the madness there and he knew it wouldn't go away until it spent itself in violence. That look, he'd seen it before on the face of men who had killed in Chicago speakeasies years ago, and he'd seen it since then. Words, pleas, reason would be useless against the kind of dangerous sickness festering inside of Jim Williams. The boy was crazed. Insane with grief over the death of his son and the faithlessness of a tramp wife.

Mizz Milner had heard the gossip. Talk traveled fast among musicians. The rising young trumpet player, Jim Williams, was becoming a big name all over the country. Then, a few days ago, in Baton Rouge, Mizz caught up with the talk about Williams' family trouble, his drinking and the band he'd lost.

Now, Mizz stood up, looking sadly down at the boy. His words had not hurt Mizz so much as the knowledge that here, in his son, was all the music he had never played. And it was going to be thrown away because of a craziness that would not end until this woman lay dead under the gun in his hands.

Mizz walked out of the place, holding the trumpet tightly under his arm, breathing against the pain in his chest. Blinking at the mist in his eyes, he went around the places on Bourbon Street, a shuffling, stooped man with a shabby trumpet case under his arm, asking questions of bartenders and old musicians who remembered him. Then he stopped at a pawn shop and made a purchase.

Later, he walked through the dark alleys of New Orleans' French Quarter, toward an address that he had learned from the men he had talked with.

He found the place and walked up the stairs. The door, he discovered, was not locked.

All of this was bad for his illness. It made the bands in his chest tighter and caused his breath to come in shallow gasps.

He walked into the room. It was untidy and it smelled of stale smoke and liquor mingled with a woman's perfume. Magazines were carelessly tossed around on the floor. Ash trays were heaped with lipstick-stained cigarette butts. Empty and half-empty liquor glasses decorated the ringed top of a coffee table.

Mizz followed the light that spilled into another room. It was a bedroom and it was dark except for the path of light that lay in a yellow swath across the floor and the foot of the bed. Clumsily, Mizz shuffled against a chair in the gloom.

The bedsprings creaked.

"That you, Perry?" a woman's voice asked thickly.

Mizz did not answer. The sweat was a thick, greasy mantle across his face. Some of it ran down into his eyes, stinging them. He took out the soggy handkerchief and wiped at his face with it.

The bedsprings creaked again. "Perry, honey? Why don't you say somethin'," the woman's voice asked petulantly.

There was the soft padding of her bare feet on the linoleum. Then she came into the triangle of light.

She was wearing a diaphanous nightgown. Coppery hair tumbled loosely over green eyes and brushed white shoulders. She was a beautiful woman, this tramp who had married his Jim, then betrayed him and killed their son, Mizz's grandson, through neglect.

Mizz took out the thing he had purchased from the pawn shop. The heavy black gun. It was clumsy and awkward in his hands. Never before in his life had he held a gun in his hands.

She stood there, groggy with liquor and sleep, staring at him. With his back to the living room light, he knew he looked like a black shadow without face or form, framed in the doorway. Some of the blackness of his shadow fell over her arm.

Suddenly, she shivered. Then her throat corded and her red mouth opened around a scream.

"I'm truly sorry, ma'm," Mizz whispered, and squeezed the gun's trigger three times.

The sound filled the room. The girl jerked with the impact of each bullet, like a grotesque puppet doing a dance on the end of a string. She fell loosely across the space between them, into his arms, getting blood or his coat. She clawed at him, trying to hold onto his coat, but slipping down until at last she lay on the floor at his feet.

The heavy gun toppled from his nerveless fingers. "May the Lord forgive my soul," he whispered, his face gray. Then he turned and walked blindly out of the room. Doors were bursting open up and down the hall. People were rushing past him, bumping him, staring at him with their white, shocked faces, then going into the room he'd just left. He heard a woman scream and a man curse. Then he was downstairs in the cool night.

He walked along, holding tightly to the trumpet case under one arm, until he found himself on Bourbon Street again. He looked around through a kind of haze until he found the Down Beat Bar.

It was crowded now with the evening trade, men and women sitting at tables and at the bar, drinking and tapping their hands and feet to the beat of the band up on the dais behind the bar. Jim Williams, Mizz's son, was still sitting at the table by himself, brooding over his liquor. But Mizz did not look at him now. Instead, he pushed his way around the bar and went up the steps to the band dais.

It was a good band, playing with a hard, driving beat.

Mizz knew the piano player, who was also the leader. An old-time musician, he and Mizz had once worked together in Kansas City.

"Well, I'll be damned," the piano player grinned, flashing a gold tooth. "If it ain't old man trumpet, himself!" His fingers raced over the keys in a brilliant modulation, then picked up the beat again.

"How 'bout sittin' in for just one number?" Mizz asked.

"Just name the tune and the key, Mizz. That's all you got to do any time, in my band."

Mizz laid the battered old instrument case on top of the piano and opened the catches. Lovingly, he took out the horn that gleamed with a soft, mellow shine.

He patted the mouthpiece into place, touched it to his lips and blew softly to see if he was in tune.

"Remember that old blues I wrote once, long time ago, Red? I called it *Sally's Blues.* We used to play it in A-flat. Remember?"

He took out his silk handkerchief, laid it in his left palm, and held the trumpet with it. Then he lifted the instrument, pointed it at the ceiling. He closed his eyes and started blowing. He blew the notes high and clear. And after a while, they seemed to carry him with them, out of the smoke-filled room, and make him a part of them. And he knew that he was at last playing the things that had been locked up deep inside him all of his life.

A Hot Lick for Doc

THIS is a story about a certain street on Saturday night. Its moral is: "Never steal hotel towels if you want to get away with murder."

It is a tale about three lives that came together for a few hours on a certain street on a certain Saturday night, and when the evening was over, three of them were dead. It was an unusually quiet Saturday night for this street.

The six people involved:

Jim "Doc" DeFord, a skid-row bum. There was some rumor along the street that he had once been a big-time musician, but you can't believe everything you hear.

Sally Garcia, a beautiful girl who was ready to sell anything for what she needed, anything.

Ramon, the wonderful kid, the genius in loud sports coats, the poet of the clarinet.

Freddie, the big ex-wrestler who owned the joint where Ramon blew his wild, crazy music.

Mama Lopez. She sold chili in the front of her shop and tea in the back, and not the kind of tea you sipped at five in the afternoon.

And the corpse.

You could tell it was Saturday night by the sounds and smells that came up from the street. Loud jazz drifted out of beer joints and tangled with even louder mambos and sambas coming from the other side of the street. There was the corn-shuck smell of tamales, and the odor of cheap tequila.

It came through the hotel window on a breeze that stirred a curtain faintly. The curtain brushed the nose of Doc Jim DeFord and woke him from a sodden, alcoholic sleep. He groaned and sat up, then grabbed at the bed post as his head swam off his shoulders and floated across the room.

He closed his eyes and tried to think back. He could remember up to about four o'clock this morning. Then it all dissolved into a confusion of noise and thick, ropy layers of cigarette smoke and Ramon blowing some wild, crazy stuff on his clarinet and Sally Garcia laughing with her white, even teeth. And then nothing.

His head floated around for a while, then came back to rest painfully on his shoulders. He sat there a while and then got, which consisted of putting on his shoes since he'd slept in his shirt and trousers.

In the shirt pocket he discovered a limp sack of Bull Durham and rolled his first cigarette of the day. He inhaled deeply and gazed with bleary eyes through the window, down on Agnes Street, which was one of the main streets of the Latin American quarter of Corpus Christi, Texas. This part of Corpus Christi looked very much like a Mexican border town.

But at night, like a blowsy old tramp who puts on her mascara and rhinestones, the street comes alive with neon. Then there are lights, music, and tequila. Then there is much laughter and women with soft, restless hips, and sometimes a knife sinking into a man's belly in a dark alley.

Doc sucked on the limp cigarette again and tried to keep his hands from shaking off his wrists.

Behind him, he heard a yawn. He turned and watched pretty Sally Garcia wake up languorously, like a sleepy kitten. She was a lovely girl, blessed with a flawless complexion and luminous dark eyes that many debutantes would have hocked papa's bankroll to possess.

She smiled sleepily, yawned, and dug her hand into her hair. "Hi."

"Hi."

"Got a cigarette, Doc?"

He held up the sack of makings.

She made a wry face. "Lord, no. There are some ready-rolls in my purse on the bureau."

He got them for her. She wiped the back of her hand across her damp forehead. "Boy, it's hot tonight."

She was maybe twenty-five, maybe nineteen. It was hard to say about a girl like Sally. There was a story about her just as there was behind everyone on Agnes Street. She'd been down in the Latin American quarter for about three years now, working as waitress, B-girl, and part-time V-girl. But you couldn't hold that against her too much. She'd had some rough breaks and she hit the weed heavily.

You couldn't buy that much gauge on a waitress's salary; besides lately she'd gone in for the bigger kicks and heroin cost more than marijuana. Sally was Anglo but she'd married a Mexican musician named Garcia in Monterrey a few years back. After he and his rich family kicked her out, she'd never been worth much by social standards anymore. It seems there had been a baby boy, but the Mexican family was influential and Sally had no money or relatives. When they took the kid away from her, she stopped caring about things in general.

It was not for Doc DeFord, a skid-row bum, to pry into or worry about. For some strange reason, she liked him and it was nice to be liked by somebody, even a girl like Sally Garcia. So he just let it go at that.

"Got a drink around, Sally?" he asked, trying not to let his teeth chatter.

"Ummm," she murmured sleepily. "In the kitchen, Doc."

He found a pint of gin in a cupboard and broke a finger nail in his haste to get the cap off.

"You're starting early, Doc," Sally called from the other room. Sally worried about him.

He rejoined her, grinning. "Hair of the dog, *ma chère.*"

She laughed, low in her throat. "You sure talk crazy, using all those foreign words like that. I don't figure you at all, Doc. You look like a floater, but you got class underneath. I guess that's why I like you."

He put the drink on a chair and sat beside her. He leaned over to kiss her.

"Hey." She kissed him back. "Honest, honey, you ought to slow down on that gin. Ramon and Freddie had to carry you out of the joint this morning. I told them to bring you here because it was closer than Ramon's place."

That was Sally, worrying about him drinking a little too much gin when everybody knew she had troubles to spare.

Doc tried to kiss her again, but she wriggled away. "Don't be gettin' ideas this early." She got to her feet, stretched. "Look, hon, while I'm taking my shower why don't you go to Mama Lorenz's and get us a couple of bowls of hot chili? There's some money in my purse."

"No," DeFord quickly exclaimed, mentally adding up the loose change in his pocket. "Tonight it's my treat. We'll have a feast. A loaf of bread, a jug of wine, and thou, sitting beside me."

She looked at him, wide-eyed. "I like it when you talk crazy like that," she said softly.

He made a sweeping bow and walked a little unsteadily out into the hall and down the stairs.

He was in his middle thirties, but the past two years' steady diet of gin made him appear older. Not the most healthful diet in the world, but it had a numbing effect on the memory.

He wished he could go to a doctor and have the memory part of his mind cut out altogether. After that he would never have to recall that his name had once been Buddy Turner and he'd been a big name to anyone who knew anything about jazz and he'd been married to beautiful Donna.

That was the part he especially wanted to cut out of his mind. Donna, his wife. If he could just stop remembering the way she had felt in his arms at night and the way his heart used to go faster just seeing her walking toward him. Most important, if he could no longer remember the night he'd found her in the tourist cabin with his arranger, Bill Cook.

Maybe it was a mistake to ever let yourself be that gone on a dame.

Your playing goes to pot. You drink too much. Pretty soon you lose your band and nobody even wants to hire you as a sideman any more. You've had it. You're washed up.

For the past two years, he had been drifting through the better skid-row districts of Chicago, St. Louis, and Houston. He'd hocked his clarinet long ago. Then one night he had wound up in a doorway on Agnes Street in Corpus Christi. While sitting there, he heard this crazy, wonderful, God-blessed kid, Ramon, blowing his clarinet over in Freddie Garza's place, and Doc knew he'd come home. Only a musician who had once been as great as Doc could appreciate what this kid was doing.

Ramon's playing and gin. That's what Doc lived on, now. He hadn't touched a horn in two years, probably never would again. But the hunger for music was still in him and Ramon fed that hunger like no one he'd ever before heard. He loved the kid. And for an unexplainable reason, as with Sally Garcia, Ramon liked him. Agnes Street was a place of deep friendships and violent hatreds.

Now he crossed the street into Mama Lopez's chili stand. It was very warm in the little cafe. The air was greasy with the smell of corn shucks and chili. Mama Lopez was sitting near the cash register with her plump, brown arms folded on the counter before her, supporting her weight.

"Hi, Doc." She grinned cheerfully. "You look like hell. Damn, you and Ramon were tearing down Freddie's joint last night. That boy was playing like crazy and you were living it up before you passed out." She lowered her voice and leaned toward him. "You need a couple of sticks of tea for tonight, Doc?"

Everyone along Agnes Street knew that her chili stand was just a front. Her main business was selling marijuana in the back room. Here, only a hundred miles from the Mexican border, was one of the chief ports-of-entry for marijuana. There was plenty of it floating around Agnes Street.

She went on: "I got something special tonight, Doc. My son-in-law, Guadeloupe Hernandez, is in town with some choice stuff he brought across the river. Really top grade. He's going to start bringing it over regularly. And he's selling it for half of what Freddie Garza charges for that junk he handles."

Doc had been on Agnes Street long enough to know that Freddie Garza was the chief wholesaler of the stuff to retail peddlers like Mama Lopez. Until now he'd had something of a monopoly on the wholesale end. Most of it was poor stuff, but all the retailers could buy.

"Have you got this new stuff yet?" Doc asked curiously.

Mama Lopez shook her head. "Guadeloupe got in town this afternoon but he's afraid to bring the stuff down here to me. You know how they're watching wetbacks."

Suddenly she snapped her fingers. "Hey, I just got an idea. Wait here a minute, Doc."

She went into a back room. He heard her pick up the telephone, dial, then carry on a low conversation in Spanish. In a moment, she bustled back. "Hey, Doc, how would you like to run an errand for me?"

"What do you mean?"

"All afternoon I been sitting here wondering who I could send to get the stuff from Guadeloupe. I can't go myself because every damned cop in town knows me."

A film of perspiration suddenly appeared on Doc's forehead. "Now wait a minute—"

"Look, I'll make it worth your while. A week's supply for yourself, and twenty-five bucks. How's that sound, eh?"

It sounded damn good. Fifteen dollars a week, which he earned for sweeping out Freddie Garza's place, didn't go far.

He thought, *one more step down the ladder for you, Buddy Turner. From skid-row bum to narcotics traffic.* But he was thinking that maybe he could get something nice for Sally.

Mama Lopez gave him taxi money and the address of a hotel a few blocks away.

The hotel was one step above being a flop-house. When Doc walked into the lobby, the sleepy clerk glanced at him once without interest and went back to his comic book.

Doc walked up the first flight of stairs and along a dirty, moth-eaten carpet. He knocked on Guadeloupe's door. It wasn't locked. In fact, the latch hadn't even caught because it swung inward a few inches, just from the pressure of his knuckles.

It didn't open far, but enough for him to see Guadeloupe Hernandez.

Guadeloupe was sitting in a chair, looking directly at him. For a second, Doc didn't move. He became acutely conscious of minute sounds in the building, a fly buzzing in the room, a radio playing faintly down the hall, a woman laughing. Without thinking clearly, he moved into the room and closed the door behind him.

Guadeloupe didn't say a word. He just sat there, glassy-eyed, his mouth hanging open a bit, his hands resting loosely on his thighs, palms up. He didn't seem in the least concerned about the flies buzzing around the blood which soaked his shirt front.

Doc touched Guadeloupe's wrist. It was warm, but there was no pulse. It didn't take a doctor to see that he was dead.

He stood looking at the murdered man for a full thirty seconds, as if he couldn't quite believe it. Then he glanced around the room. The closet door was open. A suitcase, a cheap cardboard thing, had been yanked open and clothes strewn about.

Softly, Doc pulled dresser drawers open, found them empty. He stood on tip-toes and felt the top shelf of the closet. Then he knelt and peered under the bed. It was there all right, a large cardboard box wrapped in newspaper and tied with pieces of string, and wedged between two slats to hold it up off the floor.

He dragged it out, put it under one arm and walked out of the room, down the stairs, and through the lobby. He kept his eyes straight ahead and did not glance toward the desk where the clerk was sitting.

He was trying to figure out just what on earth had possessed him to carry the box of marijuana out of that room.

He walked for nearly an hour without coming up with an answer to that one. Finally, he sat on a curb on a deserted street corner and put the box down. Maybe, he decided, he was worrying too much about the whole thing. He was just a nondescript drifter in a good-sized city. Nobody knew him; he didn't even have a regular room.

Mama Lopez sure as hell wouldn't open her mouth or she'd expose herself to a marijuana rap. And the clerk back at the hotel wouldn't remember him from dozens of vacant-eyed, unkempt, shadowy figures that drifted in and out of hotels of that sort every day.

He found a safe place to hide the box under a rock, but first he stuffed a handful of the weed in a pocket. On his way back to Freddie's, he rolled a cigarette with it. He lit it and puffed on it, loose-lipped, sucking a quantity of air in with the bitter-sweet smoke.

Time began to shift gears. He became suspended in a floating sensation. Things began happening in slow motion. It took at least twelve hours to walk that last block to *Freddie's*.

THE music was fine. Zack, the piano player was in the groove and rocking, with the drummer laying it on right behind him. And Ramon, the poet, lifted his clarinet and said beautiful things with it.

Doc, still floating, leaned on his broom and listened to them play, *What Is This Thing Called Love?*

It was only nine o'clock, but already the place was filled. The rattle of trays and glasses almost drowned the music.

Freddie Garza came over and stood near Doc at the end of the bar. An ex-wrestler, he was a huge man with a cropped crew-cut, a jagged white scar down his left cheek. Tonight he was happy because it was Saturday night and he was selling a lot of beer. This always made him happy, though it was really peanuts compared to his wholesale marijuana business.

He raised his right hand, which had a patch of adhesive tape across it, and removed a soggy cigar from between his teeth. "You all through sweeping, Doc?"

"Yeah, all through, Freddie."

"You sweep in the back, too?"

"I swept out the back room and straightened the beer cases and I changed all the table cloths, the way you told me."

"How about the bathroom. You clean out the bathroom?"

He was sorry that Freddie remembered about the bathroom. He hated to have to clean that out.

"I forgot about that," he mumbled.

"Well, you clean that and then come around and I'll pay you, Doc. Clean it out good."

Doc went in the back and got the mop. Fifteen minutes later he returned to the bar. He was walking very slowly and carefully and the palms of his hands were sweating because now he knew who had murdered Guadeloupe Hernandez up in the Palms Hotel room.

"Get it cleaned out good, Doc?" Freddie asked, grinning.

Doc swallowed hard. "Yeah, Freddie."

Freddie put his cigar back in his mouth and went to the cash register and punched the "No Sale" button. He took out fifteen one-dollar bills and counted them twice, carefully, then he handed them to DeFord.

Doc stuffed the money in his pocket and walked around to the bandstand in slow, floating steps. His hands were getting the shakes pretty bad and there was a patch of sweat on his forehead.

The music was sharp and clear to him. Each note was a separate, gleaming jewel that he could examine, fondle, and taste before going on to the next one.

Ramon, blowing the clarinet, opened his eyes and winked at him. Tonight, Ramon was wearing one of his loudest sport coats and he'd already sweated through it. His rich, curly black hair was glued to his damp forehead. He was a handsome, wonderful boy. His laughter was like his music and he laughed at everything. If you had told him that he was a genius, he would have laughed at you. Playing was as simple as breathing to him and he never gave it a thought beyond the sport coats and women it would buy him.

Doc DeFord took out his handkerchief and wiped the patch of sweat off his forehead. He felt the sudden, crazy desire to blow a horn again. Maybe because of the sick, tight feeling inside him. He had to relieve the tension somehow, or he'd flip.

"Ramon, lemme try and blow your clary," he said, stepping up on the bandstand.

Ramon looked at him as if he'd gone off his rocker, then laughed. It struck him funnier than hell. "Hey, you are tight, Doc!" Ramon didn't even know that Doc had once been a musician. It was something Doc never told anybody. Ramon had heard Buddy Turner's records years ago, but he'd been pretty young then, and he never even dreamed of a connection between the great Buddy Turner and a skid-row bum.

Grinning good-naturedly, Ramon handed the stick to Doc, then winked at the piano player. The rhythm began to flow around Doc like a surging river, sweeping him beyond conscious thought. He lifted Ramon's horn, and started playing. It had been a hell of a long time. His lip was gone and his fingers were stiff. But it was a thing a guy never loses entirely if he'd once been as great as Buddy Turner. Some of the rich, mellow tone, the old drive, was still there. Playing untied some of the knots in him.

Ramon and the others were staring at him open-mouthed. Then out of the corner of his eye he saw Sally Garcia pushing her way past the crowded tables toward him. There was a frantic look on her face.

She came up to him and put her icy hand on his arm, pulling at him. "Doc! Doc!"

He handed the clarinet back to a bewildered Ramon, and he went with the girl out into the back alley and stood near a garbage can.

"Listen, Doc," Sally said, her words running all together, "it don't make any difference to me if you killed Mama Lopez's son-in-law. It ain't any of my business. But…"

The sweat crawled out on his forehead again. "They found him?"

"Over an hour ago. Then they came and got Mama Lopez and took her down for questioning. I'm afraid she's going to spill about you going to Guadeloupe's room when they get to working on her, Doc. She's mad at you anyway for doing it to the kid."

"Listen, shut up for a minute, will you? I didn't do anything to anybody."

Sally had stopped talking with an intake of her breath. After a second, she let it out with a relieved sigh. "I didn't really believe you'd done it. I didn't think a guy like you could, Doc."

"How did you know about me going over there?"

"I kept waiting for you to come back with the chili. When you didn't show, I finally went over to Mama Lopez's to see what happened to you. She told me you'd gone to get a bundle of hay from that crazy Hernandez kid her daughter married. Honest, Doc, you oughtn't fool around with stuff like that."

"You're a fine one to talk."

She let that go by. "Well, anyway, a few minutes ago, news began going up and down Agnes Street about them finding the kid dead in his hotel room and the cops taking Mama Lopez down for questioning."

"Wait a minute. I tell you we don't have to worry about anything. The kid was dead when I got up there."

"They say the clerk in the lobby of the hotel saw you go upstairs and come down a minute later with a bundle under your arm. He recognized you. He's seen you hanging around Freddie's this past month. Now they got prowl cars out combing this part of town. They'll be down on Freddie's like flies in a minute."

She pulled his arm again. "You got to get off the streets. I want you to go up to my room, Doc. There's some other clothes for you there. I bought them at the second-hand store. They'll make you look a little different. You got to stay in my room while I go downtown and buy a bus ticket for you."

"Wait a minute, Sally," he said. "Why are you knocking yourself out like this for me?"

The pale blur of her face turned away. "Well, I don't know. Because I like to hear you talk, I guess."

"That's a hell of a reason," he said gently.

IN Sally's room he pulled down all the shades. He peeled off his clothes, wrapped them in a bundle and put a newspaper around them. Then he dressed in the second-hand gray suit that Sally had bought. The sleeves were short but it was a passable fit. She'd thought to get a white shirt and a blue tie to go with it.

The complete outfit must have cost Sally twenty bucks. And twenty bucks was a lot of money to Sally. Somehow, he'd get it back to her.

Before he put the tie and coat on, he went into the bathroom and scraped the crust of blond beard off his cheeks. He was surprised at how thin and pale his face was underneath.

Dressed, he lay across Sally's bed with his hands over his eyes, concentrating on staying there until she returned. It wasn't easy to do because when he lay down, he began thinking. And when he let himself think, his fingers began trembling and the patch of sweat came out on his forehead again. Finally, he got up, found the bottle of gin in Sally's kitchen, and finished it.

Maybe if he hadn't started thinking he wouldn't have killed the rest of that gin. And maybe if he hadn't swallowed the rest of that gin he wouldn't have found the courage to go back to Freddie's that night.

But he did go back.

Maybe it was because he'd known, ever since he cleaned out Freddie's bathroom, who really killed Guadeloupe Hernandez. Maybe he didn't like the idea of using Sally's money so he could go sneaking out of town just because somebody else had stuck a knife in somebody else. Maybe it was the only smart thing to do, because he figured the cops would get to him eventually no matter where he ran, if he didn't straighten it out now.

Anyway, the more he lay there drinking the gin and thinking about it, the more he didn't like it. So he got up and went back to Freddie Garza's place.

Freddie was standing in the back alley near the garbage can smoking a cigar when Doc came down the alley. Freddie sometimes came back here during the evening to cool off and get some fresh air.

Doc walked up to him and said, "Hello, Freddie."

"Huh?" He took his cigar out of his mouth. "Oh, Doc. Where the hell did you disappear to little while ago?" In the dim light the white patch of adhesive across the back of his right hand stood out like a neon sign.

Doc DeFord looked at it and the patch of sweat on his forehead got thicker and a drop of it trickled down past his eye. "Guadeloupe Hernandez had a knife too, didn't he, Freddie? He got in a little cutting of his own before you finished him."

Freddie's cigar stopped halfway up to his mouth and hovered a moment, then went back down. Freddie dropped his left hand into his coat pocket. It was too dark to see his face.

Doc couldn't keep the words from coming out. He was almost babbling, "I saw a lot of blood on the floor around him in the hotel room. I thought it was all his until I cleaned out the rest room in your bar tonight, Freddie. You know what I found in the waste can? A blood-soaked hotel towel. It had *Palms Hotel on it in two inch letters. I guess you wrapped your hand in it until you could get back here."*

The moral of that is, Doc thought idiotically, don't swipe hotel towels.

"You damn, crazy lush," Freddie said softly. His left hand came out of his coat pocket and there was the soft, metallic whisper of a seven-inch spring blade jumping out.

There was more than one drop of sweat coming down Doc's face now. He took a step backward, feeling sick at the stomach. His befuddled mind hadn't planned a clear course of action except to run for the cops now. "You didn't like the idea of a foreigner bringing in higher quality gauge and underselling you, did you, Freddie?"

Freddie started coming toward him, but somebody else stepped between them. Ramon had been standing just inside the back screen door, listening. Then he had pushed the door open and came between them. In the vague light, Doc saw the flash of his teeth and the plaid stripes of his coat. Ramon said amiably:

"Take it easy, Freddie. Doc's our friend."

"He's no friend," Freddie grunted. "The gin-soaked bum is making sounds like 'cops.'" The big ex-wrestler started after Doc again. The light glinted on the sharp blade in his left fist. There was a crazy look in his eyes.

"He won't tell the cops," Ramon argued, walking toward Freddie. "Doc's my friend. He won't tell them. Not if he knows I'm the one that did it to Guadeloupe."

Doc stopped dead in his tracks.

For a moment, everything stopped.

Doc said, "You did it, Ramon?"

"Sure." He laughed softly and touched his right side. "The *cabron* nicked me when I stuck him. I put the towel there so it wouldn't show until I got back. That cut on Freddie's hand, he got it opening a bottle."

Tears came into Doc's eyes. "Ramon—"

But Freddie kept moving nearer, his eyes looking crazier by the second. "I ain't takin' any chances on a tea-headed lush. If he talks, they'll send me up too because I paid you to do it."

Then his left hand made a quick jab. Doc jumped back, lost his footing and sprawled. He saw Ramon's hand dart out of a pocket. There was another flash of steel. Ramon grabbed Freddie and whirled the big guy around. Those boys were fast with a blade. It was over before Doc could blink twice. A couple of grunts, the scrape of shoe leather and then Freddie was sprawled on his back with a switch-blade knife handle protruding from his chest.

Ramon was leaning against the building. He put his hand against his stomach. He was laughing, the way he laughed at everything. "I never did like that fat tub of pig fat, anyway." His knees buckled.

"Ramon!" Doc got over to him, fast.

"He gave me a hundred bucks to do it to Guadeloupe, Doc," Ramon whispered. "For a hundred bucks, I coulda bought two new sport coats."

Doc was tearing at Ramon's shirt, feeling with trembling fingers the big, deep gash in his gut. He was crying a little and he wanted to tell the crazy kid that a hundred dollars was nothing, that didn't he understand he was a genius and he could have had the world at his feet and a new sport coat every day? It was some kind of terrible, grotesque joke. Throwing it away for a lousy hundred bucks, this thing the kid had that happened maybe once in a hundred million.

Ramon was still laughing. "You're my friend, Doc. I couldn't let Freddie stick you…"

Somewhere in there, an artery was sending huge spurts of warm blood over Doc's hand. Ramon's voice was growing weaker. "Hey, that was fine, what you played tonight, Doc. Why didn't you tell me you know how to blow? Play that way again for me sometime, will you, Doc?"

Footsteps hurried toward them. A girl's voice cried, "Doc. Doc!"

"Down here. Light a match. Hurry, dammit!"

Sally Garcia came out of the darkness, panting, and sank down beside him. "I been goin' nuts lookin' for you. Somebody on the street said they saw you comin' this way. Why did you leave the room, Doc? Why," her voice died as she stared at Ramon.

"The match. The *match!*" He wiped the tears away from his eyes.

Sally fumbled in her purse. A safety match flared. He was still groping with his handkerchief, trying to stop the hemorrhage when the match died out.

"Light another one. Quick!"

She didn't move. "It's no use," she whispered. "Look at his face, Doc. Ramon is dead."

Sally was pulling at him, trying to get him to leave. But he stood up and went back into the bar and got Ramon's clarinet, having to almost drag Sally to get there. But with the clary hugged under one arm, he let her lead him stumbling back out of the alley.

She had bought two tickets to L.A. The bus didn't leave for a couple of hours so she'd taken a room in a downtown hotel where they could wait. She called a taxi and they went down there. She kept trying to make Doc throw away the clarinet, but he took it apart and kept it under his coat.

In the hotel room, she made him sit in a big chair near a window and she helped him take off his coat. She pressed her cool hand against his forehead. "What you told me about Freddie and Ramon might change things with the cops. The bloody towel and all."

He stared at the window into the dead, hot night. He didn't say anything. A juke box was playing jazz somewhere.

She turned the lights out, and eased into his lap. "Doc honey," she whispered, "I know how you felt about that kid. But you got to get over it."

Then she suddenly whispered, "Doc, I been tryin' the big kick lately. I only tried it a few times, but it's great, a thousand times bigger than smokin' gauge. You forget everythin' and you feel great. I got a needle in my suitcase. I'll fix us both a jolt."

She went into the bathroom. He sat there, listening to the music from the juke box. Suddenly, he put Ramon's clarinet together again and blew into it softly. It had been so long, and he'd forgotten so much. He closed his eyes and tried to play out the feeling that was inside him.

He opened his eyes and looked up. Sally was standing beside the chair with a hypodermic syringe in one hand, staring at him, wide-eyed He laid the clarinet down, took the needle from her, laid it on the arm of his chair, then pulled her down on his lap.

The stuff in the syringe was dynamite, he knew. She was just st ing the stuff, but a few more jolts and there'd be no turning back. S be hooked for good.

"Sally," he murmured in her soft hair, "I keep having the craziest thought. I keep wondering, if we go to L.A. together, maybe we could make another try at, well, at everything. There's a lot of music Ramon never got around to playing. I got the crazy feeling that I'm responsible to play it for him. And I think maybe I could, now. Would you want to try it, Sally? A new start?"

She stared at him, tearfully. "Not with me, Doc," she said in a choked voice. "You wouldn't want to. Not with a girl like me."

"With a girl like you, Sally. Now, before we go any further down the ladder."

Her body was tense and trembling when he started kissing her. But after a moment, she began to relax in his arms and he had the crazy feeling that maybe there was still a chance for both of them. His hand brushed the hypodermic syringe, and it shattered on the floor with a tiny crash.

How to Kill a Corpse

OVER in Brownsville, on the Texas side of the river, they were having a gay time of it. You know, *fiesta*. Charro Days. Everyone wearing a three months' growth of beard, big sombreros, gay *vestidos*. Everyone carrying a load. And over on the other side, in Matamores, up in a filthy little hotel room, a beautiful girl was dying with a bullet in her brain.

You'd think they'd feel it. They all knew her. Everyone in America knew her. You'd think a hush would settle over the crowd, and they'd stop their laughing and guitar playing and parades and bull fights.

But no, they kept right on. Raising dust and sweating. It was winter. But down here in Brownsville in the tropical Rio Grande Valley, it was warm. So everybody kept laughing and carrying on and sweating.

If they'd known about Kit dying, their laughter would fade away. They'd get tears in their eyes. Even the men. Because everyone loved Kit. Everybody in America, in Mexico. Everyone who ever saw her.

That's what they said about Kit, everyone who ever saw her loved her.

But they didn't know about Kit at ten o'clock that morning. We were still looking for her. Russel Pierce, the private detective the studio had hired. Funny little Max Liebswich, her director. Me, Sam Jeffry. We'd flown down here together, during the night, and we were looking for her on both sides of the river.

By ten o'clock that morning, my bum ticker was slowing me down, and I had to leave the searching up to Max and Pierce. I walked through the crowd back to our hotel. They stared at me. The *Charros*. They looked at the stooped man with the young-old face, gray and lined, the wrinkled, slept-in suit, the deathly tired eyes. And they wondered what a creep like that was doing at *Charro* Days. You were supposed to be gay, happy. You know, *felicidad.*

But I walked on, and I didn't look at them. I bumped shoulders blindly. I went up to my hotel room and took a pill and lay across the bed, waiting for the tight pain in my chest to go away. I stared up at the ceiling and listened to the yelling voices down in the street. I lay there a long time until finally the phone rang.

I didn't want to pick it up. I had a feeling about what it was going to be, and I didn't want to hear it. I kept staring up at the ceiling, listening to the phone ring. And finally I rolled over and picked it up.

I held it to my ear, there on the bed, and I stared up at the ceiling fan. I said, "Yeah?"

It was Max. He was crying. Like a baby. "Sam," he choked, "Sam…"

So I kept staring up at the ceiling fan, and I knew what he was going to say. Max loved her too. Maybe more than you'd think. He wouldn't be crying like that unless it was bad.

"Sam, we found her," he whispered. "We found her, Sam. Over here in Mexico. In Matamores, Sam." His voice went up, and he kind of giggled. "In a rotten little adobe hotel with cockroaches on the floor and flies on the wall. In a place like that, we found her, Sam." His mouth sounded as if it had got filled with rags. He was trying hard to get hold of himself. Poor, funny little Max with his roly-poly paunch, his pink, quivering jowls and his baby blue eyes. Good, kind-hearted Max. He said, "You shouldn't excite yourself, Sam. You take a pill, like the doctor gave you. You come over here, slow. To the *Cantina Blanca.* But slow, Sam. And not excited."

Yeah, I shouldn't excite myself. They'd found Kit. But I shouldn't excite myself.

I got off the bed like a guy who'd lived for a million years with insomnia. I took another pill and I walked downstairs and went across the bridge, into Mexico, where they'd found Kit, at last.

LIKE Max said, it was a dirty little place with white-washed, fly-specked walls and a dirt floor. A combination desk clerk and bartender stared at me as I went upstairs. The smell of baking tortillas and corn shucks seemed soaked into the very walls.

And then Kit's room upstairs where she'd played her most dramatic role: her own death scene.

The fat *señora* maid was rocking back and forth on a chair in a corner of the room wailing hysterically to herself, making the sign of the cross over and over. Max was standing at the foot of the bed with his baby blue eyes wide and his cheeks wet, knotting up a white silk handkerchief in his fat, shaking fingers. Russel Pierce, the Studio's detective, was prowling around the room.

And there was Kit. Kit Langford. Looking like a tired little girl who'd stretched out for a nap. Her left hand had fallen beside her cheek, and her fingers curled gently. She seemed to be smiling, like a bewildered child, patiently waiting for someone to explain this strange thing that had happened to her. Her black hair had fallen loosely like a mist around her face, and the left side of it was matted and sticky from the round, red hole in her left temple.

The room? It was a strange place for Kit Langford to die. Her suitcase was on the floor beside the bed, open. Three of her dresses hung behind a greasy curtain in a corner of the room. There was an ugly, brown, soap-stained table with a chipped enamel wash basin under a wavy mirror with a cracked corner. A little mahogany cross hung on the wall over the head of the bed.

A plain, severe room. Like a monastery. A nice twist for the publicity hacks. Kit Langford dies as she lived. Plain and simple and idealistically.

"We haven't notified anyone yet," Pierce said. "We've kept the maid in here. We thought we'd wait for you. Now I have to let the Mexican authorities know and the sheriff in Brownsville."

They stared at me. At Sam Jeffry. At the person who, it was said, loved Kit Langford the most. Sam Jeffry, the guy who made Kit Langford. Took her from the bottom, molded her out of nothing with his bare hands, into something even more than a great actress, into a symbol.

They stared at me and wondered why I didn't bawl. Why I didn't beat on the wall or grab Kit up in my arms.

They wondered why I just stood there with my face stiff and set and my eyes dry.

I whispered, "Gonzales Muntyan."

Then I hurried downstairs and out of the place. They yelled after me, but I got away from them. I walked down the dusty streets of the old Mexican village, searching for him. I knew I'd find him. I knew if Kit were here, he'd be here too. Not far away.

The dust curled around my shoes, and the tight pain came back in my chest so that I had trouble breathing. I found Muntyan in a dark little *cantina* in a squalid part of town.

The greasy, rat-faced little man was sitting at a table by himself, nursing a brandy. His face was twitching, and it had the color of a dirty lemon.

When he looked up and saw me, he spilled the brandy all over himself, and he stood up, tipping his chair over. He drew the back of his hand across his slack lips. "Jeffry, you…"

I was smiling a little. I picked up a heavy beer bottle from the bar by its neck and smashed the end of it. Then I moved toward him, holding the ghastly weapon.

He stared at it with his eyes bulging, his bloodless lips twitching. He knew he was looking at death. He backed away until a wall stopped him, and he kept staring with hypnotized eyes.

He tried. Even a cornered rat will try. He reached under his coat and came out with a knife that slashed at my throat. I caught it, twisted it away. Then I jabbed with my other hand. The one with the jagged bottle.

It wasn't pretty, but it had to be done. When they found me, I was standing over him, panting. My clothes were bloody and torn, and the pain in my chest had almost stopped my breathing. But Gonzales Muntyan was dead. At my feet. In a bloody little puddle.

The Mexican officer caught my arms and pulled me away. Max Liebswich was standing there with his fat, good-natured face befuddled and unhappy. And Russel Pierce, the private detective, looking as if he hated his job.

"I had to call the cops, Sam," he told me quietly. He shrugged. "Maybe you could explain away Gonzales Muntyan. You could say you killed him in self-defense. But," he said sadly, "not Kit. You found her first, this morning. You killed her, Sam. Then went back to your hotel."

"I found this under her bed." He held up a set of my private keys. "You must have dropped them this morning. You found her and killed her in a jealous rage, Sam. She'd come down here to marry Muntyan, and you couldn't stand that. If we go to your hotel room, we'll find the gun, won't we, Sam?"

They stood looking at me.

Max was blubbering. "How could you, Sammie? That sweet, good girl. Everyone in America will hate you, Sam!"

Everyone in America will hate you.

I thought about me and Kit. About the things they didn't know about Kit. Nobody knew. I wondered what they'd say if I told them the truth. That Kit Langford had really died in a tiny New York apartment one Christmas night, twelve years ago.

I had held her hand while she was dying, the real Kit Langford. It was pneumonia, and the doctor had told me she had only a few more hours. But she wouldn't give up to it. She held onto my hand tightly, and her eyes burned with a light I've never seen before. "I'm going to get over this, Sam," she whispered. "You mustn't worry. I'll start the show, just the way it's scheduled. And I'll be a great actress. I promise, Sam."

She looked out the window. As if she could see her name up in lights over the little theater on Broadway. It was there, all right. "Kit Langford," bright and shining through the falling snow, just as we'd always planned.

But it would have to be taken down in the morning. Because in the morning, she'd be dead.

The radio was playing Christmas carols softly, and the snow was drifting against the window pane. And Kit died that way, without a murmur, holding onto my hand.

I walked through the snow later that night. Kit was still beside me. She'd always be. One of us couldn't die without part of the other dying too. And one of us couldn't stay alive without keeping a part of the other alive.

I thought about Kit and about what a funny little girl she'd been and what a funny reason she'd had for wanting to act.

Ask a girl why she wants to be on Broadway or go to Hollywood. Ask any of them. They'll tell you. Money, fame, excitement, success. With all of them it was the same.

But not with Kit.

Maybe because of the way we grew up. You learn a lot about despair and hopelessness, growing up in big city slums. You see kids with the spark of idealism and dreams that seem to come with you when you're born. And you see them old, even before they're out of their teens, with the spark stamped out, their eyes dead.

Kit saw them. Even more than I did. She saw them every day. And one night she saw them when they came out of the movies.

"I think it would be wonderful to be an actress, Sam," she'd said, her eyes all warm and shiny. "Did you see their faces? For a few hours, they weren't afraid or lonely or bitter."

"I think it would be wonderful to be an actress so you could make people forget about being afraid and remind them of their dreams. But you'd have to be a good actress. A sort of-of symbol. You know, the kind of person they really wanted to be, and didn't quite manage."

Yeah, all right. She was a crazy kid.

I'll give you that. I thought so, too. I wanted to be a big shot as much as Kit. But with me it was money and decent living. I wanted to eat good food and dress in something other than second-hand clothes, and I wanted to drive a big car and yell at the dirty little kids playing in the streets, the way guys in big cars used to yell at me.

I'm not throwing any roses at me, Sam Jeffry.

Maybe it was because Kit was a dreamer, and I was materialistic. Maybe it was fate. Anyway, I got to the top first. After five years of starving, I hit Broadway with a play. Then another.

Kit was getting walk-on parts in plays occasionally and singing six nights a week in a basement joint in the Village so she could eat. But she was good. I knew all she needed was a break. When I wrote my third play, there was a part in it for Kit. They loved her in it. In the next one, she got the lead and her name up in lights.

Just the way she'd always dreamed.

But she didn't make it. She died of pneumonia a week before it opened, on Christmas night. And I walked through the snow and wondered why they ever built this world in the first place.

I guess I got drunk that night, in a cold, numb sort of way. I made enough bars. I felt scared and alone with Kit gone, and I wanted people around me.

And then I saw Kit. She wasn't dead at all! She was warm and alive and singing in her sweet, husky voice with the catch in it. I didn't know where I was or what time it was. Near dawn, I suppose. I saw her through a wavy haze, and she looked perfectly beautiful.

I kind of sobbed in my throat, and I pushed through the smoke and the crowd, a hatless guy with snow melting in his hair, his soggy overcoat unbuttoned. I went up to her and tried to take her in my arms. I was crying like a kid. "I knew you couldn't be dead, Kit. I knew they wouldn't let anyone like you be dead."

I was stirring up a commotion. Somebody grabbed my arm and tried to drag me off the floor. Kit was staring at me as if she'd never seen me before. I didn't understand it at all. I couldn't see why they wouldn't let me hold Kit. Why she looked at me that way, as if I were a stranger.

And then I got it.

It took a while to make them believe I wasn't just another drunk on the make. After I spilled enough words around and shoved a few ten-dollar bills into the right hands, they let me go back to the girl's dressing room.

Maybe I was a little crazy, but I wasn't drunk any more. I kept thinking about what Kit had wanted more than anything in the world and how she'd said, with that strange light in her eyes, *"I won't die, Sam. I'll be a great actress, just the way we planned. I promise, Sam."*

So I talked with this girl. I can't even remember her real name, Louise something, because, from that night onward, for the past twelve years, she has been Kit Langford.

IT WAS one of those things that happens once in a million. She was Kit's perfect double, an identical twin. Kit wasn't well known yet, and so I knew we could get away with it. I'd hush up Kit's death. And the play would go right on with this girl in Kit's part.

Day and night I coached her. I molded her into the person Kit wanted to be. Not inside really, you couldn't change her there, but outside, for the world to see and love. Inside, she was as different from Kit as she was like her in appearance.

I can't remember all the jams I got her out of. Like the time I dragged her out of a guy's apartment two jumps ahead of the cops. The man's wife had taken poison because of Kit, this new Kit, and the police were investigating.

That scared her. She'd tasted fame and money, and she liked it. She got down on her knees and begged for another chance.

"This is the way it's going to be," I told her. "We're going to Hollywood. I have a part for you in a picture. But you're going to play a part off the screen, too. No yachting parties, no drinking, no dope. While the rest of them are making headlines with their divorces, you'll be helping out some new charity. The sweet sincere girl who didn't let success go to her head, that's you," I told her through my teeth.

It was a struggle. Mess after mess I hushed up. Kit Langford became the most-loved girl on the screen. And I worked twenty-four hours a day to keep up the illusion. Worked until the doctor told me my heart was going to stop ticking one day soon if I didn't take a complete rest.

But I turned her into the real Kit, on the surface. It hurt me to look at her, she was so much like my dead Kit. At times, even I forgot it was just a game we were playing. A serious, deadly game.

The columnists said I would marry Kit soon. Then she began seeing this Gonzales Muntyan. She denied any romantic connection, but they were together a great deal, and she had a strained, tense look.

Then, one night, three days ago, Kit Langford disappeared. She walked off the set one night and vanished. Gonzales Muntyan disappeared too. We traced her down here to Brownsville. That was the whole story.

Well, almost the whole story.

We were standing in the little dirt-floor Matamoros *cantina* now, beside the body of Gonzales Muntyan. They were all looking at me in that unhappy way. Max Liebswich's blue eyes were incredulous, horror-stricken, and he kept mumbling to himself, "How could anyone harm a hair on that sweet girl's head?" Even the hard-boiled private detective, Russel Pierce, was looking at me as if I were disgusting.

Everyone in America will hate you.

That's what Max had said a moment before. He was right. They'd hate the man who killed Kit Langford.

I nodded slowly, wearily. I felt a million years old. "Yes, Pierce. I found her. Early this morning. Like you say, the gun is up in my hotel room. I killed her."

So we walked out of the place and that was the story that made the headlines in every newspaper in the country, from big New York dailies down to Oklahoma country weeklies. And, as Max prophesied, they hated me.

But it was better that way. Better for them than to know the truth.

Because if they had known how Kit Langford really died, the symbol I had built her into would have become a mockery. Cynics would have pointed to her with a bitter smile and said, "See?" And the hopes and dreams she'd stirred would have died with her.

Kit wasn't murdered. She committed suicide. She'd gotten herself into an ugly dope racket the year before. Through her, dope had been peddled to the very high school kids who went to see her pictures. Gonzales Muntyan had known about the deal. Later, he'd come to Hollywood for blackmail. He'd threatened to expose her whole ugly part in the racket unless she paid off. He bled her white. He'd come down here to Brownsville, then had wired her for more money. But she couldn't raise it. She'd come here to plead with him. But you don't make a bargain with a rat like Muntyan. She knew everything was folding up around her. Because of the way we'd built her personality, her career would be destroyed. She couldn't bear the thought of poverty and a prison term. So she killed herself.

I found her that morning. I planted my keys in the room, took the gun with me. But I had to silence Muntyan. He would have been questioned when they found Kit, and I knew the little rat would talk his head off.

That's the real story of Kit Langford. And, like I say, it's better for them to hate Sam Jeffry and love the memory of Kit Langford.

Sam Jeffry isn't anybody.

My ticker isn't going to hold out long enough for them to bring me to trial. But that's the way I want it. Because then I'll be with the real Kit Langford, the greatest actress who never lived!

Run, Cat, Run

JOHNNY NICKLE went about the business of packing as fast as he could. He dumped his shirts into an already bulging suitcase, closed it and kneeled on it to snap the lock. He unplugged his tiny radio, wound the aerial wire around it, laid it on the bed beside his suitcase and trumpet case.

He stood in the center of the room for a moment, running shaking fingers through his hair. A tall, skinny guy with a haggard face. He listened to the whisper of the surf down on the beach and wondered how long a guy could keep running.

Hurry it up, Johnny, the voice within him urged. This isn't a pleasure trip. Unless you count living a pleasure.

He stopped at the bureau long enough to pick up his key and slug down the last of a tumbler of bourbon. But before he got it all down, there came a tap at his door. He jumped, the drink spilled down his shirt-front and the glass tinkled into little pieces at his feet.

He looked at the door as if it were about to pounce at him. He moistened his lips. "Yeah?"

A girl's muffled voice filtered through the oak panel. "Johnny? Let me in."

The only girl he knew in this town was the red-headed singer at the Buccaneer Cove. He couldn't think of any reason for her coming down here to the beach.

She hadn't. The girl standing in the darkness outside his auto-court cottage was a brunette. The light spilled around him through the open door and showed him that she was slender and still at the age when she didn't have to take reducing pills to keep it that way. Her high-heeled shoes with ankle straps hugging her slim bare ankles didn't quite go with her chenille beach robe and dripping two-piece bathing suit. Her eyes were very large and dark in her white face.

"Hello, Johnny Nickle," she said softly.

Both her hands were thrust in the deep pockets of her beach robe. She took her left one out and there was a soggy, crumpled cigarette in it. She started to put it in her mouth, changed her mind and dropped it. Her gaze drifted past his shoulder, then returned to his eyes. "Aren't you going to ask me in, Johnny?"

Before he had an answer for that one, she brushed in past him. She turned slowly, giving the place a sweeping, wide-eyed look. Then she faced him again. She was plucking at the cotton tufts on her robe with her long finger nails. "You were leaving, Johnny."

Get rid of her, the voice hammered inside him. Maybe she's part of it. Get rid of her fast and then scram yourself. The minutes are ticking by.

"Look," he said. "Look, honey, this is nice. I'll give you that. Hepburn couldn't have made a better entrance. But I don't know you and I don't know what this buildup is leading to. I don't think I'd better stick around for the third act to find out."

She made her lips into a smile. "But, Johnny..."

He nodded at the door. "A gentleman wouldn't use force. In case you hadn't heard, I ain't one."

"But..."

He dropped a hand on her shoulder and shoved. She took a half-dozen tripping steps to the door, then teetered to a halt on her high heels. A lock of her black hair tumbled into her eyes. She was standing that way at the door with her back to him and she said, "Johnny..."

She pivoted very slowly. She wasn't smiling any more. Her left fist was knotted up and white at her side. Her right hand had come out of her beach robe pocket and it was filled with a .38-caliber automatic, which she carefully aimed at the third button on his shirt.

"Let's go together, huh, Johnny?"

He swallowed. The slight anesthesia the liquor had brought to his nerves vanished. He was shaking all over from the backwash of endless sleepless nights, of always looking behind him, of running, running. He pulled trembling fingers across his face, smearing the sweat that had popped out in tiny beads.

She kept standing there, balanced on her high heels, holding the gun steadily. The strand of her dark hair was still dangling over her left eye. Her lips were drawn back, almost baring her teeth. Salt water from the wet bathing suit trickled down her ankles and dripped on the floor, forming puddles.

He picked up his plaid sport coat. He felt very old and tired.

She waved the gun toward the bed. "The trumpet, too, Johnny. That's important, you see."

He didn't get that. Not at all. But he didn't argue. He just wondered numbly why she didn't shoot him here and get it over with. It was as good a place as any.

He picked up the trumpet case by its handle and walked through the door. The surf down on the beach was whispering restlessly. A full moon peeped between scudding clouds.

It was dark in the court of the stucco cottages. A yellow convertible was parked on the graveled drive in front of Nickle's cabin. "That's the car, Johnny," she said huskily, a few feet behind him. "Get in it."

She made him drive so she could keep him covered with the gun. They followed the curve of Corpus Christi Bay, along Ocean Drive. They pulled up finally, at her direction, before a large, dark apartment building hiding behind a row of tall palm trees. It was a Spanish-style job of pastel stucco, built around a patio.

Up in her apartment, she snapped the light on and locked the door behind them. She bit her lip as if trying to decide something. Then she rummaged in the beach bag with one hand and came up with a key. She smiled at him. "I'm sorry, Johnny, but a girl can't very well get dressed while she's got one hand busy pointing a gun at a fellow." She motioned with the automatic toward an open closet.

"Listen," he said. "Listen, what is this? If you're going to kill me, why don't you get it over with? Why the buildup?"

Her eyes got wide and she shook her head. "I just want to make sure you show up for your job at the Buccaneer Cove tonight, Johnny. You keep running all the time. For three years you've been running. And tonight's perfect. You have to play tonight, Johnny. Then after tonight you won't have to run any more." She nodded at the closet. "Now get in, huh? It'll just take me a jiffy."

He stood in the cramped, stuffy closet and listened to the key turn in the outside lock. Minutes ticked by while he could hear only an occasional drawer open and close and the hurried tap of her heels between rugs. Then something else. Music. A radio—no, a phonograph, throbbing with the steady, two-beat rhythm of a Dixieland jazz tune.

Recognize it, Johnny? He began sweating again and his knees lost their strength. His fingernails gnawed into his palms. What's she trying to do, the voice inside him asked? Run you nuts? Is that maybe what she's trying to do? Instead of just putting a bullet in you?

The key twisted in the lock. She swung the door open and smiled at him. "Sorry if I took long. Was it getting stuffy?"

She'd brushed her blue-black hair into an upsweep coiffure. The lines of her body flowed smoothly under a cool, strapless cocktail dress. She was still wearing the ankle-strap shoes, but her legs were sheathed in nude-shade nylons. Her fingernails were glistening with a fresh lacquer job and her lips wore a violent shade of lipstick, strikingly crimson against her sable hair and milky complexion.

But he wasn't looking at her. He was staring across the room, at the radio-phonograph combination and the shiny, revolving record.

She followed his gaze. "*Jazz Date,* Johnny. The greatest jazz record ever made. Hear that, Johnny? It's your trumpet chorus. Like Biederbeck and Armstrong and Oliver all rolled up in one. That was when you could play really good. Nobody could touch you. You were great then, Johnny, really great."

He weaved out of the closet as if he were drunk and ripped the record off the turntable and smashed it on the floor.

"It doesn't matter Johnny," she told him quietly. "I have a dozen like it. And there are thousands like it all over the country. You can't keep them from playing *Jazz Date*. Miff and Eddie and Link, they're dead. But they keep right on playing on the record. You're the only one left alive, Johnny Nickle. You and the clarinet player. And they say the clarinet player wasn't real anyway; he was Tizzy Mole come back to earth that one night to help you all make the greatest record ever cut."

Nickle sank on the sofa and dug his trembling fingers in his hair. The girl was looking at him and her eyes were strange, compassionate. "You're tired, Johnny," she said softly. "You're thin and there are circles under your eyes. Your hair's thinning on top. You can't keep running forever."

"Look," he snapped. "What do you want? Did you bring me up here to talk over old times? Or maybe you want my autograph? Johnny Nickle, the guy who made *Jazz Date*. That ought to be a collector's item!"

She shook her head. "I want to help you, Johnny. Because what's happened to Miff and Eddie and Link, and you, maybe it's partly my fault. Maybe I want to make it all right again. You were a wonderful musician once, Johnny. You played stuff that was good and right out of the skies. They don't come along often, guys that play like you used to. Only, now you've been scared so long. You've been running for three years and you drink too much, Johnny. You don't concentrate on what you're playing any more."

He swore at her. "You brought me up here to tell me that? Maybe you're a music critic?"

It was like she said. He wasn't any good any more. But who could play, with Death fingering the valves of his horn? The night he made *Jazz Date* he'd signed his life away.

It was great stuff for the publicity guys. They ate it up. They played up the superstition angle until they had even themselves believing it. They didn't have to make Johnny believe it. He knew!

For months the record made ordinary sales. Then somebody found out about the coincidence. How Zack Turner, the guy who wrote the stomp tune, *Jazz Date*, on the back of a menu in a smoke-filled tavern, dropped dead at the bar of that same tavern two hours later while Johnny and the boys were in the recording studio making the master disk. How, a few months later, the drummer, Miff Smith, was killed by a hit-and-run driver. How the piano player, Eddie Howard, got pushed off a bridge, and how Link Rayl, the guitarist, went nuts and shot himself. And there was the business about the unknown clarinet player whom Johnny and the boys had picked up that night and who played so much like the greatest clarinetist of all times, Tizzy Mole, who'd died in a Chicago auto wreck five years before.

The ghost record, they'd called it. The last of the great jazzmen cut their greatest record of all times. Then bow out. Oh, it made wonderful copy. A publicity gag that soared the record's sales to the sky.

Only it wasn't a gag. Not to Johnny Nickle. All over the country, the cats were making pools on how long it would be before he followed Miff and Link and the others.

For three years, he'd kept running, staying one jump ahead of it. In St. Louis, that time, it had been food poisoning. In California, a speeding car on the wrong side of the road. In New Orleans, a shot out of a dark alley, grazing his cheek.

Whenever he stayed in one place long. He couldn't hide because the only way he could make a dime was with his horn. And when Johnny Nickle picked up his trumpet, it was news, even if he didn't play so good any more.

Now it was coming to him here. He couldn't explain it, but tonight he had felt he must leave this place at once.

He looked up at the girl. "You know all about it. You think you can do something about it?"

She shook her head. "You've got to go on and play tonight. That's all I can tell you. If you run this time, it will be too late, Johnny."

Now that he looked at her more closely, here in the light of the room, she wasn't so young. There were tired lines around her lips, and the same haunted shadows that Johnny carried in his eyes. She was putting up a terrific front. But she was tired and alone, too, if you peeled back the surface.

"Please, Johnny. I'm awfully tired of aiming this gun at you!"

They rode to the club in the canary-colored convertible. She wasn't pointing the gun at him any more. She didn't have to. As she said, he'd been running too long. He didn't know what was behind this girl. Or if she could really do something about what was going to happen to him. He told himself he didn't care. If she wanted him to play tonight, he'd play. He was so tired inside he really didn't care much any more, one way or the other. A guy could keep running only so long.

"I've been watching you every minute since you've been in Corpus Christi," she said. "I've been at the Buccaneer Cove every night you played. In the afternoon I swam down on the beach so I could keep an eye on your cabin. Tonight, the auto court manager told me you were leaving. I couldn't let that happen."

She looked at him carefully. "Johnny, tell me about that night. When you made the record. What happened, Johnny?"

He pulled into the shell drive that wound under palm trees to the beach. The night club was built to resemble a wrecked pirate's ship. A tattered skull-and-cross-bones flag carried the name "Buccaneer Cove," and under it a huge banner lit by a spotlight advertised the great trumpet player who made *Jazz Date,* Johnny Nickle.

He drove into a parking space on the crunching shell. His jaws were tight and he stared straight ahead.

"Please, Johnny."

It was hard to get started, but it was better, talking about it.

There wasn't much to tell. One night they were drinking beer in New York. Johnny and Zack Turner. Miff and Eddie had joined them. They'd just got in from the West Coast. As musicians will do, they got mellow over a few beers, about the old days and the jazz they'd played in Chicago in the twenties. Then Zack mentioned the contract Johnny had to make a record and said why didn't they get the old bunch together and cut a real jazz record again? Show the people how music ought to sound.

After so many beers, it sounded like a good idea. They rounded up Link Rayl. The only one from the old crowd who was missing was

Tizzy Mole, who'd hit his last lick one winter night in Chicago five years before on an icy street with a skidding sedan.

But they picked up a clarinet player right there in the tavern while Zack scribbled his idea for the tune on the back of a menu. Johnny couldn't remember much about the guy. A quiet, moon-faced fellow he'd never seen around. The guy spoke up and said he played clarinet and would like to play with them. They figured him as some jerk and tried to brush him off. But he kept insisting and finally somebody brought him a stick and he ran off a few licks to show them he knew what he was talking about. He did, too.

He bowled them over. The stuff he played was terrific. When he got through, there were tears running down his cheeks, he was that good. He made the record with them and everybody agreed that Tizzy Mole himself couldn't have done it better.

Well, that was how it was, Johnny told her. Afterwards, somebody phoned them about Zack keeling over in the tavern while they were cutting the record. They drifted apart again. It was the last time they played together, the last time they saw each other. He never saw the clarinet player again, couldn't even recall his name.

She covered his hand with her cool palm. She was crying. She wasn't making any fuss about it, but her cheeks were wet. "I'm sorry, Johnny," she said. "Sorry." Her eyes had a screwy look in them.

THEY went into the place together, Johnny Nickle looking kind of beat and shabby in his old, baggy clothes, holding his battered trumpet case under his arm. He could use a new suit. A new horn. A lot of things. But he had the crazy feeling that he wasn't going to need them after tonight. This is the night, Johnny, the voice inside him said, laughing a little sadly. I warned you. No more ride choruses, no more hot licks. He wondered if they'd let him and Miff and Eddie and Link and Tizzy Mole have a jam session together where he was going.

But there wasn't any use running anymore. It was bound to catch up with him some time. This was as good as any.

He stopped at the bar for a drink because his fingers were shaking so. The girl squeezed his arm. "I'm going to get a table near the bandstand,

Johnny. By the way, I forgot to tell you, didn't I? My name's Nona."

Then she was gone, fading into the crowd and smoke and clinking glasses and he had nothing to hold onto but his drink.

He swallowed it and got another and then he shouldered his way up to the bandstand.

The kids up on the bandstand eyed him with their usual awe when he got up there with them and took his horn out of its case. They were good kids. They tried and they played all right. But something was lacking. They didn't have what Johnny and the others had had back in the twenties.

He settled in his chair and lit a cigarette and nodded at the leader. The leader nodded back. He always looked relieved when Johnny showed up for the job. You never could tell about Johnny Nickle.

Things went slow at first. But about eleven o'clock, Johnny began getting a boot out of the rhythm and they let him take over the show. That's what the crowd had come for. They forgot about dancing and crowded up around the bandstand and listened to Johnny Nickle play his trumpet. He played *Riverboat Shuffle* nice and easy, right around the melody, with a big tone like Biederbeck. His eyes were closed and his face was screwed up.

When he finished the tune, one of the waiters handed him a folded slip of paper. The penciled words on it said, "Play *Jazz Date.* Nona."

He squinted through the layers of cigarette smoke and saw her near the wall at a table by herself. Her face was a white blur and her clenched fists rested on the edge of the table. Her eyes told him, "This is it, Johnny. Play this tune and I think you'll have the answer to a lot of things."

Little cold patches of sweat broke out all over Johnny. He hadn't played it since they made the record in New York. He told the leader, "Let's play *Jazz Date* for the people."

The kid almost swallowed his baton. They'd had a thousand requests for the tune. Everywhere Johnny went, the crowd begged him to play it. But he'd always refused to have anything to do with it.

Gleefully, the emcee announced on the public address mike, "Folks, a really special treat. Johnny Nickle playing *Jazz Date.* Just the way he recorded it."

They dimmed the lights and a glaring spot formed a white circle for Johnny and the four other musicians. Johnny tapped out the beat and they caught up the rhythm. Piano, drums, guitar, clarinet, and Johnny's trumpet. Halfway through his chorus, he glanced down at the crowd. And he saw him. Just a face among a lot of other faces. But Johnny knew he hadn't made a mistake.

He stopped playing and then he was shoving through the crowd. He heard voices. Hands plucking at him.

Suddenly the girl Nona was at his side. Her icy fingers touched his hand. "Johnny?"

"I saw him. I'm sure of it. The guy that made *Jazz Date* with us that night in New York. The clarinet player." He caught the girl's shoulders and shook her roughly. "Is that what you knew? Tell me!"

He was shaking her so hard her teeth were clicking. "Johnny, w-wait. I don't know. You see, I never was sure what he looked like. That's why I had to depend on you."

They got out of the crowd. They were in the dim hallway back of the bandstand, stumbling toward the back entrance that led to the beach.

The man stepped out of a darkened doorway and put a gun in Johnny's ribs. "In here, Johnny. It's quiet in here."

HE closed the door and thumbed a light switch. They were in a storeroom filled with old tables, chairs, papers, broken slot machines, all filmed with cobwebs. Water lapped beneath them, under the building.

The yellow glow from the dust-encrusted, dim ceiling-light globe fell over the little round-faced man holding the odd-shaped pistol. It formed tiny half-moons on his puffy cheeks under his bifocal glass lenses.

"Harry Jones," the girl whispered.

"Yeah," Johnny said. "I remember. That's the name he gave us!" He looked at the girl. "You knew him."

She shook her head. She was staring at the little man's pistol with hypnotized eyes. "I only knew his name. For three years he's just been a name."

The little man spoke up. "So it turns out to be you, Johnny. By process of elimination. With the others dead, it leaves only you." He frowned at the girl. "But I don't know how you got mixed up in this. Now I have two people to kill."

Johnny said excitedly, "Wait! You mean it wasn't accidental?"

"No, Johnny," the girl whispered and her voice sounded a million years old. "None of it was an accident. And Link Rayl didn't commit suicide. Somebody, Jones here, put a gun in his hand afterwards. The only real thing was Zack's heart failure. That wasn't part of it."

"Jones," she continued. "Well, you know him better by another name, Johnny. By his real name. Tizzy Mole!"

Everything stopped for Johnny. Like a phonograph record halted. He heard dimly through the rushing, pounding surge of blood in his head. It was as if time had ceased and they were frozen and then gradually, they began moving and talking again.

"You're nuts," he gasped. "Tizzy Mole didn't…"

"He didn't look like this man. No he didn't, Johnny. Not back in Chicago, eight years ago. He had a different face then."

The round-faced man's eyes narrowed. "So it's been you. And I thought it was one of them."

Johnny was remembering a lot of things. The way this round-faced guy played a clarinet. So much like Tizzy Mole that they said it was Tizzy's ghost come back to earth.

The girl went on, "Remember how Tizzy Mole was supposed to have died, Johnny? There was an ugly mess. He'd been in a fight with a young drummer, Bob Alexander, over Bob's pretty young wife. Bob was found dead in his room, shot by Tizzy's gun. Tizzy raced off in a sedan that was later found wrecked and burning in another part of town. There wasn't much left of the body they took out of the car. They identified it by a ring and other belongings. They said it was Tizzy Mole and they buried him."

"He might have stayed buried if he could have gotten music out of his system. But you can't do that, you know, Johnny. Not if you ever played the way Tizzy once played."

"I don't know who was riding with Tizzy that night. Whose body he planted his ring and things on. But he walked away from the wreck alive and had a plastic surgeon give him a new face. He tried to start a new life. But he couldn't forget about music. It was a drug in his veins, eating at him. Every musician plays with a style all his own. Tizzy had a very distinctive style. He knew if he ever blew a clarinet again, musicians would recognize his way of playing and maybe somebody'd get wise."

"So he hung around other musicians. Listening to them play. Talking with them. He was in that tavern in New York the night you planned *Jazz Date.* It was more than he could stand. Here was a chance to make the greatest jazz record of all times with the best guys in the business. He had to take the chance or blow his top, Johnny."

"How did I know? I didn't, really. But I've listened to *Jazz Date* for hours. Listened to that clarinet chorus and wondered how it would be possible for anyone to play so much like Tizzy Mole. And then it struck me that perhaps it wasn't just somebody playing like Tizzy. Perhaps it was Tizzy.

"I phoned the recording studio. Got the name and address of the clarinet player on Jazz Date. I wrote him a note. It said, 'I have positive proof that you are Tizzy Mole. Leave five hundred dollars at a certain place tomorrow night or I'll tell the police about it.' I signed it, 'One of the cats who recorded *Jazz Date* with you.' I knew if Harry Jones wasn't Tizzy Mole, he'd ignore the note as coming from a crank. If he really was Tizzy Mole, he'd be scared witless. He'd leave the money."

"It was there. Just like I'd ordered in the note. I knew then he was Tizzy Mole." Her voice choked and she began crying "But I didn't know it would turn out like this. I didn't know he would kill the fellows who made *Jazz Date*, one by one, to make himself safe again. I couldn't go to the police or anyone. Who'd believe me? I had no real proof. The clarinet player, Harry Jones, had disappeared. And the deaths were all 'accidents.'"

"All I could do was follow you, Johnny. I ran a personal in today's paper addressed to Tizzy Mole, saying the *Jazz Date* cat needed more money, to get in touch with him immediately. I knew if he'd followed you here, he'd make some sort of move tonight."

Tizzy Mole, his round, manufactured face shiny with perspiration, swung the gun toward her. "That was clever, Nona. I sure hate to have to kill you, too. This gun has a silencer. It won't make much noise."

She began walking toward him, step by step. Her eyes looked glazed, hypnotized. "There's something wrong with me, Johnny. I make people die. And I don't mean to. I made my husband, Bob Alexander, die back in Chicago that time. And I didn't mean to. I loved him."

She was walking straight into Tizzy Mole's gun. And Johnny got what she was trying to tell him. He screamed at her. But she kept right on walking. Mole's face was the color of bread dough. He pulled the trigger of his gun twice. Nona seemed to stumble. She coughed and lifted the back of her left hand to her lips. Her other hand came out of her purse and raised her automatic very slowly as if it were amazingly heavy. It roared much louder than Tizzy's because it didn't have a silencer. The whole room shook with the roar. And Tizzy's gun tumbled out of his hand and he slid down the wall with his glasses hanging from one ear.

She kept standing there with the smoke around her and she whispered. "His fingerprints, Johnny. He couldn't change them. Tell the police." and she collapsed.

IT was nearly a week before they'd let him see her. She looked awfully thin and white on the hospital bed. "Hello, Johnny Nickle," she whispered. "So I didn't die. I should have."

"Don't talk that way." Johnny put his battered hat from one hand to the other because he didn't know exactly what to say.

"It's funny," she said wearily. "All of a sudden I don't have anything to live for. For three years, all I could think of was that the man who'd killed my husband was still alive and I had to do something about it. Well, now I have. And there isn't anything else." She looked up at him, her eyes wide. "A person ought to have some reason for living, oughtn't they, Johnny?"

"Yeah. Well, that was what I wanted to talk to you about. When you're feeling better."

Her eyes opened wider. "Why, Johnny Nickle. Are you flirting with me? Johnny!"

There was a moment's silence. Then she was smiling softly. "Is that the best you can do? Come back here. I'm not that sick, Johnny."

You read about Johnny Nickle all the time now in *Down Beat.* Something has happened to him, they say. He plays like he used to back in the old days, again. He plays great. As if maybe he had something to play for now.

Blackmail is a Boomerang

THE hotel was very quiet, asleep too, beaten down by the day's heat. A stair creaked under my foot. The gun in my hand felt heavy. In a few minutes it would destroy the stillness, and death would settle over the hotel like a fog.

Somewhere a typewriter clicked. Busy little machine, clicking off the minutes. The FBI agent, Gordon Knaves, typing a report that would never be finished.

I stood before his door. Light crept under it, a hopeful finger of life probing the black darkness of the hall. Somewhere a mouse scurried. In a room down the hall, a woman laughed.

Max, are you watching? You have a ringside seat, you know, right across the street. Front row, center aisle. Curtain going up. First and last performance. Play named Murder.

I stood before the door. My hands dripped sweat and the gun became slippery and hard to hold. I thought, standing there, that once a man becomes enslaved to evil there is no depths to which it cannot drag him. The devil was my master and had commanded me to do murder. And I did dare not disobey.

I turned the knob, stepped into the room. It was careless of the man to leave the door unlocked.

He glanced up from his desk. His fingers were hovering over the keys. Dead fingers, still alive. The report in his machine. The paper that wouldn't be finished. Stopped in the middle of a sentence.

He looked up at me, the slim, dark young man. Gordon Knaves, agent of the Federal Bureau of Investigation. Did he have a family, I wondered? A wife? Was she waiting for him somewhere miles away, like Donie was for me? Was his little boy saying a prayer?

The gun in my hand made a terrible racket. I didn't know there was that much noise in the world. It seemed to split the hotel apart, shaking windows on every floor. Three times it blasted that way, and my body shuddered and my teeth clicked with every report.

The man, Gordon Knaves, half rose. He kept staring at me. He fell forward, over the little table, knocking to the floor the portable typewriter and the report that wouldn't be finished tonight.

THE hotel sucked in its breath. Then it screamed. Down the hall, the woman who had laughed, screamed shrilly. The mouse vanished, frightened back into hiding by the strange carryings-on. Footsteps pounded. The elevator creaked. Men's voices yelled hoarsely.

I shook myself into motion. I ran down to the end of the hall. The woman was standing in her doorway in a loose negligee, clawing at her throat, her mouth wide open and screaming.

I yanked the window up. My shoes scraped on the rusty iron fire escape. The alley, then. Stumbling over a barrel of trash. A frightened cat squalling. Lights flashing on everywhere. A world full of lights splitting the darkness.

The car, Max. Please, the car. You promised.

There it was, now. Pulling away from the curb across the street. A black sedan. Swerving toward me, tires howling. I hit the running board fast. A door opened and I fell inside and the car leaped away with a jet burst of speed.

In the dark corner of the back seat, Max's cigar tip glowed. It danced around in the dark and his face pressed toward me, a round moon face, smiling, pleased.

"Nice, Tommy. Nice all the way through. We watched it all from the room across the street. We could practically see the surprised look on Knave's face."

"Shut up," I whispered, my face dripping sweat. My voice crawled up an octave and my stomach turned over. "For Lord's sake, shut up!"

I was remembering when I had received my orders, and learned I had to kill.

No, maybe it wasn't you, Tommy, Max had said. But it was somebody in the organization. There's a leak somewhere. I must be sure, Tommy. I want the kind of insurance that can't fail. If you don't do it, well, you might get off with fifteen years, Tommy, if you're lucky.

You didn't just quit Max Behelman. He knew so much about you. Things in your past. Things that could send you to prison for a long time. And you couldn't afford to go to prison and leave Donie behind with no one to take care of her.

Someone had told Gordon Knaves things that were putting him dangerously close to the inner core of Behelman's organization. Max was efficient. The solution was to eliminate the FBI man and make double sure about the pawns in his organization.

The chuckle was deep and satisfied. "The gun now, Tommy. The gun."

He reached forward and took it away from me carefully, with a handkerchief covering his hand. He folded it into an inner pocket. "My insurance, Tommy," he said.

If Tommy Lane ever got fancy ideas, the insurance was always there.

THE field under my shoes was soft and moist. The trees in the orchard were black smudges in the night. The nights were warm in this lush, semi-tropical country. The Rio Grande Valley of Texas. Once a desert, it had been crisscrossed by irrigation canals from the Rio Grande River, and a thousand citrus ranches had blossomed on the once-barren land. Now it was a paradise. Giant palm trees lined the roads. In the little cities, busy packing sheds near railroads sent countless bushels of giant oranges, lemons, and grapefruit to all parts of the country.

The air was heavy with the scent of flowers, the musk of decaying vegetation and the humid night's moisture. The house down in the middle of the orchard was full of lights. The house where Donie waited.

She was in the living room, beside the radio. She was very lovely and young, and on her face there was look of great patience. She looked up and smiled, hearing my footsteps.

The lights were for my benefit. Her turning her face in my direction was for my benefit. Because Donie couldn't see the lights and she couldn't see me, no matter how hard she looked. Donie was blind.

I kissed her very gently, cupping my hands around the sweet oval of her face.

The room was small like the house. Bare, knotty-pine walls. A bright red Mexican serape over the fire place. Flowers on the table. Donie knew I liked flowers.

She was frowning. Her hands covered mine. "They're cold, Tommy. What's the matter?"

"Nothing baby."

"Yes. You've been out with those men again, Tommy?"

DONIE with her blind eyes. With her swift, sure instinct. Knowing evilness and Max Behelman were one, that knowledge had engulfed me.

"Donie, listen. Would you want very much to see again?"

Her hands went into little white knots. "Please don't joke about that, Tommy."

"But if we had the money?"

"Yes. A cornea transplantation, the specialist in St. Louis said. But so much money, Tommy. So very much."

What was it like? I wondered. Three years of blackness.

"But," I said, "if something went wrong, you could wait?"

Her lips trembled. "Tommy. What is it? Please, you must tell me."

"I can't, Donie. I'm not sure yet. I have to go away, Donie. For a day or two. When I come back, I'll know."

If I come back, Donie. If.

"I want you to visit your sister in San Antonio, Donie. Tonight. I want to put you on the bus. Will you do it?"

She said with sudden fright, "It's those men. It's something to do with those men. I don't want to see that badly, Tommy. I'd rather stay this way."

The words were ashes in my mouth. "No, Donie," I whispered. "It isn't anything like that. It's a...kind of business deal."

It was the first time I had ever lied to her.

"You're going to sell the ranch!" she guessed wildly. "Tommy, why won't you tell me? Why?"

"Donie," I said patiently, "you must do what I say. I can't tell you because I don't know yet. It, well, it may not turn out the way I hope."

Her face was stiff and white. "I'll go, if you want, Tommy."

Her voice was cold and bleak. She knew about the shadows behind me. She could not see them, but she knew and she was afraid. And yet, there was nothing she could do.

The midnight sky was dark. Scudding clouds hid the moon at intervals. The house was a great hulking monster drawn far back into the shadows. Overhead, the palm tree fronds rustled in the strong gulf breeze. The surf washed on the beach below the cliff with a steady, sullen rhythm.

I moved through the French windows. There was a light in the library. I could hear the rumble of men's voices. My shoes whispered on the carpet. The library door opened, spilling light into the hall. Eddie came out. He was whistling a tuneless song. He passed me in the darkness, so close his sleeve brushed me.

I brought the heavy wrench handle down hard. He sighed and slid down the wall into a loose heap. I found an automatic in his shoulder rig. I slipped it out and walked into the library.

Max was working over a pile of papers on his desk. The desk lamp cast planes of shadows over the heavy lines of his face. He looked like a fat Buddha squatting over a priceless treasure. Cigar smoke hung over the desk in blue layers.

"Max," I said softly. "Max."

He looked up. He saw the gun in my hand. Slowly, he took the soggy cigar from his lips. A diamond ring on his little finger glittered.

"Tommy, you fool." He said it heavily, sadly.

"The gun I used on Knaves," I told him. "I want it."

Max shrugged. "Of course. Of course, Tommy."

He got up and moved heavily to a wall safe. He spun the dials, his diamond ring glittering. He handed it to me, butt first.

"A gesture, Tommy. It won't do you any good. The FBI man, what's his name?" he shrugged. "There are so many other things I can tell them about, Tommy. Chicago. Would you like me to tell them about that?"

He laughed and his deep chuckle was soggy. "You could have been so safe working for me, Tommy. If you'd only stayed on the level."

"You don't understand, Max," I whispered through my teeth. "Not yet. But you will. Tomorrow."

I swung the gun up and struck his temple. His face seemed to sag, like a bloated balloon that had been punctured. He pitched over sideways like a sack of grain knocking a lamp to the floor with a crash.

I knelt beside him, folded his thick, fat hand around the pistol that had blasted at the FBI man. I had wiped my own prints off it. Now there were only the prints of Max Behelman.

I wrapped it carefully in my handkerchief, and then I put it in my pocket.

THE drugstore was very small and hot.

A small boy sat on a wire-legged stood before the marble-top fountain and made sucking noises with a straw in a glass. In front, a bus was loading. Mexican fruit pickers were piling in with their bundles of clothing and battered suitcases.

I had been looking at the picture in the magazine for fifteen minutes. I didn't know what it was yet. I folded the magazine back into the stand. I wiped my face with a handkerchief, sponged my damp palms. Then I pushed into a phone booth, dropped a nickel in, gave a number to the operator.

The telephone booth was a foul-smelling cubicle. I drew my hands along my trouser legs to keep them dried.

It took a long time for them to make the connection.

I waited and I thought, *It's been five years, Donie.* I had come down here five years ago, with Chicago behind me. I was going to stay there. I married her and we were happy the first two years. Then came the accident and she couldn't see any more. But even that wasn't so bad until, a few months ago, Max had come to our place one morning. Max, who had been in Chicago, too, five years ago.

His voice was in my ear, thick, heavy.

"This is Tommy, Max," I said.

"Tommy," he said quietly, "I'm going to kill you."

"Maybe," I admitted. "But that isn't why I called. I wondered if you might like to buy something from me."

"What are you talking about?"

"The gun, Max. It has your finger prints on it now. You begin to understand?"

He was silent for so long I would have thought he had hung up except that I could hear his labored breathing.

"All right. What's the deal?"

"It won't be bad, Max. Ten thousand. You can afford that easy."

"When and where?"

"Tonight. Ten o'clock. Across the river. Yes, I think that would be best. You know that lane that cuts off to the right from the Monterrey highway just out of the pueblo? There's a bridge, two or three miles from the main road. A small wooden bridge over a dry arroyo. You put the money in a cigar box and toss it off the bridge at ten o'clock. Then turn the car around and drive back to the main road."

"The gun?"

"You'll get it by parcel post in the morning."

"You're crazy, Tommy! Do you think…"

"You haven't any choice, Max. You have to trust me. I'm going to mail the gun. It's just a question what address I'll put on the package. Yours or the FBI's."

I hung up softly. I looked down at my palms. They were wet again.

Please don't cry, Donie, if it doesn't work out. There are so many better guys in the world.

It was dark again. Darker than the night before. I lay on my stomach behind a mesquite tree, and waited. My eyes burned and my neck was stiff. I hadn't closed my eyes now in over twenty-four hours. My body felt like bruised hamburger.

The car came over the hill with a sweep of headlights. It stopped on the bridge, and I heard a small tinny rattle in the arroyo bed. Then the car rattled the rest of the way across the bridge, scraped gears getting turned around, and headed back swiftly.

I waited. Five, ten, fifteen, twenty minutes.

Then I stood up. A hot, dry wind swept across the barren Mexican countryside, stirring up dust. Off in the hills, a coyote howled. The sound echoed lonesomely through the night.

The wind struck at my face. I shuddered. Then I walked down to the creek. I skinned my hands and knees crawling down the steep bank. On the graveled creek bed, I found it. The tin box crammed with money. I jammed it under one arm, made my way back up the bank.

From behind me, a voice said. "Just stay still, Tommy. I'd like awfully well to pay you back for last night."

IT was Eddie. Max's trigger boy.

He came out of the darkness behind me with something small and deadly glinting in his hand. He ran a hand over my coat, took my automatic out, stuffed it in his own pocket. Then he took the tin box away from me.

He snicked on a pocket flashlight, waved its beam. Soon I heard the whirr of an automobile starter. The car came over the hill again, stopped near us. The rear door opened and Max smiled at me.

"Well, Tommy. It's nice running into you this way."

I felt nothing. No fear now. Only a weariness that had no bottom.

I leaned back against the cushions between Max and Eddie and closed my eyes, listening to the drum of the heavy sedan wheels. Soon we were on the main highway. I saw the flash of headlights behind us. Other automobiles. I closed my eyes and didn't look any more. There was no use looking any more. Less use caring.

We drove for an hour. When we stopped, we were still in Mexico. We had driven into the courtyard of a small hacienda. The moon came out from behind the clouds, spilled soft light over an adobe hut, a dirt-wall corral, a well. Somewhere a horse nickered and stomped nervously. A pack of thin-ribbed hounds came from under a chicken house, barking and howling at us.

I knew the place. Ybarbo's ranch. One of Max's points of operations inside Mexico. Some thought it was here Max raised his marijuana. No one knew for sure. No one but Max and the men he bought it from.

That was the thing the FBI could never uncover. The source. They caught plenty of it coming across the river. But they couldn't find the source. And they couldn't tie it up with Max. He just sat back like a fat, all-knowing Buddha and laughed at them.

Ybarbo came out of the hut, holding a lantern over his head. A thin-shanked little peon dressed in rags. There was a livid scar across his face, drawing up his lip in a perpetual grin. Max had given him that scar. Now he was afraid of Max, like the rest of them. Afraid to keep working for him, but even more afraid to try to get away.

Max turned to me. He patted my knee. "Now, Tommy, do you want to tell us where you have the gun? It'll save so much unpleasantness, boy."

I laughed but it sounded like a cackle. "That gun's my lease on life, Max. You think I'm nuts?"

"Oh, but there are so many more unpleasant thing than just dying, Tommy. You see now why you mustn't be stubborn?"

Sure, Max, sure.

He smiled. "All right, Tommy."

We went into the dirt-floor hut. Max snapped an order at Ybarbo in Spanish. The little man scuttled out, returned shortly with strips of rawhide. Eddie tied me on the floor. The strips cut into my wrists and ankles.

Max lit a fresh cigar. He sat on a hide-bottom chair, tilted it against the bare adobe wall.

"Tommy, I've read the most interesting books since I've been living in this part of the country. I find the old Indians who once inhabited this land were most ingenious. They thought up such unusual—games, shall we say? We're going to play one of them now, Tommy. I've wanted to experiment with it ever since I read about it. I want to see if it works, you understand?"

He spoke again to the Mexican. Ybarbo's face blanched. The peon whispered something under his breath, crossed himself and scuttled out on his bare feet.

"I've sent Ybarbo after a little playmate of his. I had him catch it this afternoon. I had an idea we could use it tonight." He rubbed his hands together. His eyes burned. "I'm really glad you decided to be stubborn, Tommy."

I waited without thinking.

YBARBO came in slowly. He held a long, heavy, forked stick. A loop was fastened in the fork and held tight by a leather throng reaching back to Ybarbo's wrist. In the fork, caught by the loop, was a huge, threshing diamond rattlesnake, hissing and writhing, its powerful four-foot body whipping at the trap that held it.

Eddie's face turned green. A cigarette tumbled from his slack lips and he slid around to the door, crowding the wall, his eyes wide, hypnotized.

Max laughed. "Don't be nervous, Eddie. Ybarbo knows how to handle these babies."

My tongue stuck to the roof of my mouth.

"You see, Tommy, it works on the principle that rawhide stretches when it gets wet. The victim is tied securely so he can't move. Then the snake, maddened and striking, is held to a stake with a length of rawhide. He can strike to within an inch or so of the victim's face, but he can't quite reach him. Then water is dripped on the rawhide. It stretches a fraction of an inch. The snake's fangs get closer, Tommy. You can almost feel them graze your cheek. Each strike is a fraction closer. The Indians found that their victims often lost their minds before the snake finally reached them."

His laugh was high-pitched, like a woman's giggle.

I closed my eyes. *Now, Tommy,* I said. *Now, or it will be too late forever.*

"You're smart, Max," I whispered. "The marijuana. You raise it here on Ybarbo's place, don't you?"

He grinned, shaking his head. "I'm smarter than that, Tommy. I don't raise it in Mexico at all. The FBI boys and the Mexican government agents are running themselves ragged, chasing all over Mexico, trying to find it. I let them catch small quantities of it coming across the border now and then so as to keep them guessing."

"They can't ever catch up with me, because I raise it right in Texas. On citrus ranches, Tommy, in weed patches. I have a list of the fields in my desk. They'll never find where it comes from or through which channels it goes. The nerve center of the whole organization is here." He tapped his temple.

"That FBI man I had to have you kill, Tommy, Gordon Knaves. He was the only one who was getting close. Someone in the organization, maybe you, told him about its being raised in Texas. If I'd let him go on living, he might have found some of the fields and traced the stuff eventually to me. At any rate, he was getting too close for comfort. He had to be eliminated."

Eddie was making strange sucking noises with his lips. He wasn't staring at the snake any longer. He was looking at the doorway.

His face had turned the color of the gray dirt wall. He was trying to get his gun out but his hand seemed paralyzed. When he did finally fumble it out, Knaves, the FBI man, stepped through the doorway and shot him before he could use it.

Max pitched out of his chair. He didn't stop to think about it. He moved instinctively, hurling the thin Mexican, Ybarbo, in the line of Gordon Knaves' gunfire as he snatched his own revolver. Ybarbo stumbled and the forked stick fell from his grasp.

It was all blurred. One moment the snake was a gray coil, like a spring on the floor. The next, the snake was hanging from one of Max's fat cheeks.

Knaves sprawled to duck Max's hail of bullets. Then Max was running, sobbing and screaming, out of the door. I heard his car start off in a scream of clashing gears.

Knaves got up slowly. He brushed his hand across his eyes and shot the snake. Then he cut the rawhide throngs from my wrists and ankles.

We drove back to town in Gordon Knave's coupe.

"You did a good job, Tommy," he said. "It was the only way we could ever have stopped Behelman. We didn't have a shred of evidence. It took something fantastic and desperate like a fake murder."

I looked out at the night. The stars were like Donie's smile. I said, "Do you think I'll be away up the river long, Gordon?"

He kept his eyes on the road. "For the things you did back in Chicago, Tommy? That's been a long time ago. You've straightened out pretty well the last five years. And the government won't forget you came to me with information and help that put an end to Max Behelman. I don't think it will be long, Tommy."

"And if it will make you feel better, there's a substantial reward for the person who gives information that leads to the breaking up of this narcotics ring."

That will be for Donie. The years she had to wait won't seem so long if she can see while she's waiting.

"How about Behelman? Hadn't we better try and catch up with him?"

"I don't think it's necessary to hurry. A snake bite in the head works fast, Tommy. And it is over an hour's drive to a doctor in town."

He was right. A few miles down the road, we came to a black sedan piled up in the ditch. We both got out and looked at the man who had crawled out and died on the road.

Speak of the Dead

HE was a hawk-faced man with a leathery face deeply etched by weather. His hands, curled around the "Model A" Ford steering wheel, were calloused; his fingernails were dark-ringed from field work.

He drove out of the night mist, into a side street of the tiny village nestling in the Virginia hills and parked before a dimly lit tavern. He got out of the pick-up with slow, stiff movements and walked into the joint. The air drifted around him, a thick, muggy pea soup of stale smoke, cheap perfume, and flat beer. He sat at a stool before the counter.

The lights hurt his eyes. The noise of the television and the shrill laughter of a woman sitting next to him hurt his head. He wished the noise would stop.

The woman beside him turned, her knee brushing his. She glanced at him. She kept staring at him; her face turned sick, then she screamed. She pushed her fingers shakily up along her cheeks and screamed a high-pitched, sustained note like an ambulance siren.

The bartender put a bottle down and turned around. He looked at the hawk-faced man; a glass fell out of his hand, splintered on the floor.

The man sighed and stood up. His head throbbed. He ought to do something about his head, he thought. The image in the mirror on the other side of the bar stared back at him, a stooped figure dressed in a faded blue denim shirt and overalls. His face was dark-shadowed, eyes deeply sunken in black sockets. There was a tiny round blue bullet hole in the front part of his right temple and another on the left side where the bullet had come out. A thin trickle of blood had dried on his cheek.

The hawk-faced man with the bullet hole in his head turned and shuffled out of the bar. He walked down the street and the night fog swirled around him and enveloped him like a shroud.

FAR up on the side of a hill in the Blue Ridge Mountains, Samuel Lincoln rolled over in his sour-smelling bunk and stared out his cabin window at the setting sun.

"A pretty sight," he croaked. "A sight to stir the souls of men." His lips twisted as if they'd tasted something unpleasant. He struggled out of the bed, heavy and sick with a hangover, and went about the business of cleaning himself up. He had a revival meeting to conduct down in Millsborough tonight.

Done with the task of shaving, he went to the cabin door, sloshed the soapy water out of his pan.

He gazed down the clearing, at the red clay soil broken and waiting for the seeds he hadn't gotten around to planting. There were a lot of things he hadn't gotten around to these last four years. They were empty, barren years and the taste of them was bitter in his mouth. *The Lord giveth and the Lord take'th away, said the Good Book.* Sometimes, though, it didn't make sense, even to a preacher. Especially when the thing taken away left a man empty of everything inside, including faith.

He suddenly became aware of someone stirring down at the fringe of the tall pines. A figure came running out of the twilight shadows, stumbling over the clods in the field.

Samuel made out that it was a woman. A slender, fair-skinned woman with hair as black as the coming night. He dropped the tin pan, ran down to her.

She had fallen again. She was on her knees, sobbing his name when he reached her. Her thin cotton dress had been torn half off by the brush in the woods. Her face and hands were scratched bloody. Cold perspiration beaded her face and glued strands of her hair to her forehead. Her eyes, turned up to his, were wide and black as a trapped animal's.

"Pray for me, Sam," she whispered. "Ask God to help me." Then she fell against him in a faint.

The Lord giveth. . .

Samuel took her up in his arms and carried her to the cabin and the warmth of her body against him tore open a wound that reached to the depths of his soul.

He paused in the cabin doorway, looked across the spread of hills to the setting sun. The shadows were in his eyes. "For four years," he mumbled, "I been prayin' in Your name and it's been a lie. If You brought her back to me just to cause me more hurt, I'll turn the lie into a curse."

He choked; then he took her into the cabin his grandfather had hewn out of pine and chinked with red clay. He put her gently on a bunk, lit a kerosene lamp, then bathed her wrists and face with cool water from the spring.

Her eyes fluttered open. She began crying. She pressed the heel of her hand against her forehead and frightened sobs shook her.

Samuel looked down at the bruises on her arms and shoulders and the shadows in his eyes turned black. It was true, the tales he'd heard about Elijah Matthew's treatment of her. They said Elijah had gone insane, and was taking his madness out on his young wife.

A mixture of feelings stirred in him, compassion for her, hatred for Elijah and a kind of joy at her suffering because of the hurt she'd done him.

"They're sayin' I killed him, Samuel," she whispered through stiff lips. "They came to get me, but I ran away."

A chill touched him.

He gripped her arms with his big, bony hands. "Say it slow, Martha. Tell me what's the matter."

She drew a shuddering breath. "They found Elijah this afternoon, out in the barn, shot through the head. They said I done it with his twenty-two rifle." She choked and clung to him. "God knows I hated him, Samuel. I paid a thousand times for the sin of marrying him. But I didn't kill him; I swear it! You got to hide me."

She was crossing the thin border into hysteria. Samuel held her down and washed her face with wet cloths until she was quiet. "I won't let 'em do you any hurt, Martha. You're safe here."

"But they'll come after me! Elijah's brother Tom's got the whole town stirred up against me. He's sayin' terrible things. That I was carryin' on with other men, that's why Elijah beat me." She shook her head. "None of it's true. Elijah had lost his mind; he kept saying somebody was after him; then he'd whip me. He hasn't gotten me a dress in over a year. Sometimes I didn't have enough to eat. I was afraid of him, Samuel, afraid of the terrible things in his crazy eyes."

He patted her, stood up. "You'll be all right here until morning. Martha. I'll go down to the village and see what can be done to help you."

He put on his black preaching coat and took down the worn, leather-bound Bible that he carried with him to his revival meetings. He did it without thinking, as his grandfather must have unconsciously taken down his long-barreled rifle before going into the woods.

He was a tall, gaunt man with bony joints. Folks said he looked a lot like another man named "Lincoln," Abraham, without the beard. He had a slow, persuasive way of talking that hypnotized a crowd and swayed them to the rhythm of his words.

He often thought he must be a good evangelist to make folks believe a thing he doubted himself.

He started up his battered old car and drove along a dirt lane that wound down the hill past thick woods and plow-furrowed clearings and other cabins like his own, spiraling thin streamers of smoke into the twilight air from their stone chimneys.

As he drove, he thought of Martha's slender, white body, bruised and mistreated under Elijah Matthew's crazed hands. A hard ridge bulged around his jaw.

An hour later he had twisted and bumped down the side of the mountain to Williamsborough, the sleepy village nestling in the valley where Elijah Matthews had his acres of rich farm land.

But tonight the town was not sleepy; there was a chill in the air more penetrating than twilight coolness. Tension had fallen over the frame buildings and dusty streets like a blanket of evil.

A crowd had gathered at the square. Up on the steps of the old Confederate monument, a man was yelling at them in a hoarse voice, stirring them into a milling, angry mob. From the crowd, Samuel heard the deep growl of bloodhounds. A heavy sickness lay in his stomach like a lump of wet clay. He rubbed damp palms on his coat.

He braked the flivver into a parking place, leaped out and shouldered his way through the crowd. It was Elijah's brother, Tom, up on the granite monument steps, stirring the crowd into a lynching mood.

"Elijah took that Jezebel into his home, give her more than she ever had in her whole life. And how did she thank him? By faithlessness and murder! My brother, Elijah Matthews, was a hard working, God-fearing man. Tonight he's lyin' in Tompson's funeral parlor and the woman that killed him is in the hills, getting further away every minute we stand here!"

A sullen roar swept up from the mob.

Samuel struggled through the last of the crowd, up to the steps. His voice rang above the noise of the mob.

"Tom Matthews, you're sinning in the face of the Lord!"

A momentary hush fell over the people. "It's th' Reverend Samuel Lincoln!" somebody whispered.

Samuel turned toward them. *"Vengeance is mine saith the Lord,"* he quoted solemnly. He lifted a large, bony hand. "Don't you people realize you're settin' out to commit a sin as bad as murder? You're going to sit in judgment and execute a human being. That's the work of the state and its laws. *Render unto Caesar that which is Caesar's!"*

An angry murmur rippled through the crowd. A big farmer shook his fist at Samuel. "Fine lot th' law is doin'. Sheriff Tewely and two deputies are out ridin' around the country in a jeep, as if they expect her to be settin' on the side of the road!"

Samuel pleaded with them, but he felt the tide sweeping him under.

"We know why you're stickin' up for her," Tom Matthews sneered. "You was courtin' her when she married my brother; you been in love with her all these years. Probably, you was one of the men sneakin' around to the back door when Elijah was out sweatin' in the fields."

Samuel leaped at the fat, sneering man. He felt satisfaction as the bones of his fist smashed Tom Matthews' curling lips. The farmer might have been fat, but he wasn't soft; he stumbled back against the monument, shook his head like a stunned pig. Then, with a bellow of rage, he came at the evangelist, his arms swinging like pistons.

Samuel hadn't gotten the kind of training at revival meetings that Tom Matthews had in dancehall brawls. He went down under the crushing fists. Matthews kicked him once, stepped over him. Then the tide swept down the street, a sullen, rumbling tide like dark water following the eager baying of blood hounds.

Samuel lay sprawled in his own blood in the dust of the street. In a few minutes, he struggled to his knees and swayed there.

The night had closed around him. In the east, there was a bloody tinge above the pine topped mountain crests, all that remained of a dying day.

The hills had given him life and now they were taking it away from him. In those hills he had roamed as a boy, trudged behind his father's plow and first felt the call of his work. And it was the hills he had come back to after his schooling, to meet Martha and know a fire so deep and consuming that it wrecked him.

She was a lovely girl with milky skin and a body that would drive a man out of his mind, wanting her. But there was a woman's knowledge in her eyes. "No, Samuel, all my life I've known what it is to be poor. We've lived in a shack and scratched a bare living out of the side of a hill." Her lips whispered under his, "I won't be a poor preacher's wife. Elijah Matthews has asked me to marry him. He's a rich man with a big farm; he can give me what I want."

She'd struggled out of his arms that night, shaking, because she was young and wanted him, too. Then she'd gone away to marry Elijah.

Now he was on his knees in the dusty road and the mob was following the blood hounds that would lead them straight to his cabin. And they wouldn't stop until they'd lynched her.

FROM force of habit, his head bowed and his lips moved. He had seen miracles. Cynic though he was, he couldn't blind his eyes to the crippled Parkerson boy at Davidville last summer who had come to the revival, prayed, and walked away without his crutches. Or the time the Taylor woman had called him to her husband's bedside after the doctors had given him up. They'd prayed all night and the next morning he was still alive. He was alive today, well and hearty, tending to his farm.

He hadn't pretended to understand those things; he had shrugged. But the memory of the light in the eyes of those people stayed with him.

He knew now that only a like miracle would save Martha's life.

When he had the strength, Samuel stumbled to the car, swung it out to the road. Alone, he was no match for the mob headed by Tom Matthews and his bloodhounds. He had to find the sheriff who was somewhere back in the hills on one of the countless winding roads.

He had only driven two blocks when a man came running out of a doorway, waving him down.

It was the undertaker, Jeb Tompson. He was bareheaded and his face was white as putty, his eyes glazed and bulging.

He clawed at Samuel's shirt. His teeth were chattering. "He-he…" He pointed toward his funeral parlor and giggled. He clung to Lincoln, trying to get a grip on himself. Finally he chattered: "I was d-driving back from Clinton a few minutes ago. Saw a Model A comin' at me down th' road. I gave it a c-close look because it was just like the car I keep back of the shop. It was dark and went by fast, but I woulda swore it was Elijah Matthews sittin' behind the wheel." He gulped.

"'Course, I told myself I was just imagining things. B-but when I got back, I went into the back of the shop where I had Elijah stretched out on a table. And," his voice went up to a squeak, "he wasn't there!"

Samuel shook the frightened undertaker. "Had you done anything to the body?"

Tompson shivered. "Hadn't touched it. Went over to Clinton for supplies this afternoon right after Tom brought him in."

"Come on." Samuel half lifted the shivering man into the car beside him, turned and headed toward Clinton, five miles away.

THREE and a half hours could be a long time to a man following bloodhounds through tangled brush. It could be an eternity to a man in a car, trying to get back to the woman he loved before an insane mob tore her to pieces.

When Samuel Lincoln finally got back to his cabin with two other men in the car beside him, he saw the flickering glow of a dozen torches around the field. He heard men's voices and a woman's scream. His blood turned to ice water.

He rammed the flivver to a halt, leaped out and stumbled over the broken field. They had Martha up by the cabin on a little mound of earth. The hounds were straining on leashes, baying at her. Tom Matthews was holding the struggling woman while one of the other men threw a rope over a pine tree limb above the hummock.

When Samuel was close enough, he saw her white face in the flickering, smoky, torch light. It was a contorted thing, filled with animal fear. Her eyes were black, her lips twisted.

He got up on the mound beside her, faced the men.

"Hey, it's the preacher again!"

Tom Matthews' angry bellow drowned the other men's voices. "He's no better'n she! He was hiding her here in his cabin. Like I said, they were carryin' on behind Elijah's back, an' him half out of his mind with hard work and worry. They planned out this murder between 'em!"

The crowd of sweating men roared, surged forward.

Samuel Lincoln, lifted his hand. It was a precarious moment; some of the men had shotguns and their fingers were itching.

Samuel knew these men better than they knew themselves. They were simple people; emotion swayed them quicker than reason. When he preached it was in a dramatic, theatrical manner. Sometimes he'd cry out and sometimes his voice would drop to a whisper. Sometimes his voice would break and other times he'd chuckle.

Now he had to preach the best sermon of his career, and he had to do it the right way. One wrong move, a single ill-chosen word and those shotguns would blast out his life and Martha's before he could lay the truth before them.

A simple statement of the truth might only inflame them and they'd kill him before he could back his words with evidence.

He chose the more dramatic way. His voice rung out across the fields and woods like a bell. "You people have blinded yourselves in your sin. You've blinded yourselves to the power of the Lord. He said to his disciples to go out preachin' and baptizin' and healin'. Even raisin' from the dead, if need be."

He pointed down to the edge of the clearing. "Look down yonder, you sinners, and fall on your knees and repent!"

A hush settled over the crowd. Then an unbelieving whisper stirred through them. One of the men dropped his gun and cried out. Tom Matthews' rough hands fell away from his brother's wife. He moved around to the edge of the mound, squinting down to where the torches spread an uncertain light over the clearing. His face turned the color of a dirty white rag. His slack lips shook.

Elijah Matthews was walking slowly through the crowd, followed by Jeb Tompson. He came up between the petrified mob, up to the mound of earth. The torches flickered over his grey face, over the bullet holes in his temples.

"Raised from the dead!" a man breathed and fell to his knees.

Elijah stood there a moment, then pointed a finger at his brother. "This is your evil doing," he whispered hoarsely. "You found me in the barn with the gun in my own hands; you knew I'd shot myself. But you coveted my lands. You've always been a greedy man, Tom Matthews, without enough gumption to work for what you wanted."

"You took and put the gun in the house, carried me to the funeral parlor and roused the town against my wife. With us both dead, the lands would have fallen to you."

Elijah stood there a moment longer, swayed and crumpled to the ground.

His brother, Tom, stared down at him with bulging eyes; gibberish spilled from his slobbering lips. Then he turned and ran for the woods. When he stumbled, he kept going on his hands and knees.

It would have taken a stronger man than he to have faced the dead come back from the grave.

There was a medical explanation for what had happened to Elijah Matthews, Samuel thought. A doctor could have traced the course of the bullet, showing how it missed any of the vital centers of the brain; people had been shot through the head before and lived to tell about it.

Elijah had been knocked unconscious for a while from the shock of the bullet, had came to in Jeb Tompkins' funeral parlor, and wandered out, got in Jeb's old car and driven to Clinton.

In the excitement of finding his body and Tom's stirring up the town against Martha, no one had bothered to see if Elijah was completely dead. He'd certainly looked that way, stretched out white and still with the bullet hole through his head. Jeb Tompkins, who was also the coroner in Millsborough, hadn't planned to examine the body until he returned from Clinton.

That, at least, was the medical explanation for what happened. But Reverend Samuel Lincoln preferred to think it was a miracle that came out of his prayer when he knelt in the dust of the road at Millsborough.

Martha's fingers bit into his arm. "But I *did* shoot him," she whispered through stiff lips. "We were in the barn. He flew into one of his insane rages; he picked up a pitchfork. He'd of killed me, Sam. I did it without thinkin'. I grabbed up the rifle and shot him."

Samuel held her hand. "Quiet, Martha. I know what happened; he told us on the way over here. I reckon he had gone completely insane. Somehow, though, the shock of the bullet cleared his mind. When we told him a lynching mob was after you, headed by his brother, he said the only way to stop them was to say he'd shot himself; it was the truth about Tom's wanting you lynched so's he could get the land."

She looked down at Elijah's still figure. "Is—is he—"

Samuel nodded sadly. "Yes, he's dead now. The strain and the trip over the rough roads finished him. I reckon he really must have loved you a lot before his mind went haywire. The Lord spared him just long enough to save you."

She covered her face. "Oh, Sam," she sobbed.

He comforted her. "You're not to blame, Martha; you had a right to protect yourself from an insane man. Elijah doesn't blame you. Neither does the Lord."

Now, more than ever before, he saw a pattern behind things. “The Lord moveth in strange ways,” he murmured. He turned to the mob, which was sober and frightened now. Faced with something they couldn’t touch or see, they were looking for comfort and reassurance.

“I reckon a brief service wouldn’t be out of place,” he told them. He turned his face to the east where a new moon was creeping above the mountain tops. It shed a pale light over the preacher’s tall, gaunt figure. His voice rang out above the pines in a way it never had before.

“I will lift mine eyes unto the hills.”

There was a singing inside him like the voices of a great Cathedral choir.

Afraid to Live

DOROTHY was behind the wire cage in the parking lot where she worked, totaling up the day's receipts. Dan stood looking at her for a long moment, trying to swallow the big ache in his throat. Then he pushed through the office door.

It was easy to see why Mel Duggard would go for a girl like Dorothy. She had a cloud of blonde hair and nice, wide-open blue eyes. She was fresh and young and her mouth was clean and her eyes still had youthful wonder in them. She had a good figure, too. Mel wouldn't overlook that.

She looked up from her tickets and when she saw it was Dan standing there, her lips drew into a thin line.

"Dorothy."

"Listen, Dan I'm busy. I don't know what you want, but I wish you wouldn't bother me any more."

He wanted to tell her a lot of things. He wanted to tell her he was sorry about the quarrel and maybe it was his fault. He wanted to tell her how empty the apartment was since she moved out and how lonesome he was.

He tried to say all that, but he couldn't get the words out, somehow.

He took his hands out of his pockets and then put them back again. "Dorothy, you-you aren't going out with Mel Duggard, are you?"

He didn't know why he'd asked her that. The words just seemed to come out.

Her eyes got little glints of fire in them. "That's no longer any of your business, Dan Skeels." She went back to counting the tickets.

The trouble was, Dan was a coward.

He'd grown up with a kind of cringing sickness inside him. That's why he hadn't been able to stand up to Mel Duggard. He'd just had to hang around, sick and shaking, and watch Mel take Dorothy away from him. You ought to, he thought, be able to go to a doctor for the kind of sickness that was inside him.

He started walking, a skinny kid with a shock of black hair, big eyes and large bony hands that dangled at the ends of thin wrists. He walked for blocks and finally he went down a flight of sidewalk steps into a damp little cellar honky-tonk where blind Mamber played piano every night.

Mamber was playing *Body and Soul* and it was something to hear, the delicate, haunting music the blind old man wrung out of the rickety upright piano. He played with his head tilted back, smoke from the cigarette in the corner of his mouth drifting past his sightless eyes.

A few couples were swaying out on the tiny concrete floor. One or two were at the bar. Otherwise the place was empty. Dan sat on a chair on the bandstand and listened to Mamber play, letting the music lessen some of the ache inside him.

When he finished that chorus, Mamber snuffed his cigarette out against the scarred piano, turned and smiled. "Hello, Dan."

Dan's fists were so tightly clenched in his pockets, his fingernails were eating into his palms. "Mamber," he asked suddenly, "what makes a fellow a coward inside?"

Mamber nodded slowly. He started playing again and didn't say anything for a long time. "I wondered when you was gonna talk to me about it, Dan. You been fightin' yourself a long time, ain't you, boy?"

"It–it ain't easy. Sayin' it right out like that."

"Takes the beginnin' of a man to admit it, Dan. I always knowed was somthin' eatin' at you. When a man plays good trumpet like you do, it's because he's got somethin' wrong inside him. He ain't tuned up with the world right, somehow. An' he's got to play it out of him or burst wide open."

Mamber tilted his head back and went into *Mood Indigo* softly, with a steady, moving rhythm in his left hand. "You ask me whut makes a man a coward, boy? Well, it's cause something taught him whut fear is when he was a right youngun. He wasn't bo'n afraid. He learned it, from somebody or somethin', back in his chil'hood."

"But what can you do?"

Mamber smiled. "Sometime ain't nothin' you kin do. Most all of us is cowards 'bout something, though we won't admit it. Jes' don't fret, boy. Time comes when you really got somethin' big enough to fight for, the Lord will give you stren'th. Now go home and git your horn. It's time for you to go to work."

Dan walked through the gathering dusk to his two-room flat. Somehow, when Dorothy had been with him, this neighborhood hadn't looked so sordid. He hadn't noticed the yelling kids or the wash hanging between the buildings or the smell of garbage in the alleys.

The two rooms had looked pretty bad at first. But after they brightened the dark woodwork with ivory enamel, put new checkered linoleum in the kitchen and hung pictures on the bedroom wall, it looked a lot better. On hot nights, when Dan wasn't playing, they'd sit out on the fire escape, holding hands and looking at the city. Some time Dan would play his trumpet, softly beside her in the darkness. Dorothy liked music as much as he did.

He went up the back stairs, now, fitted his key in the lock.

MEL DUGGARD was in the bedroom, waiting for him. He was sitting in a chair, propped against the wall, leafing through a magazine. A spiral of smoke curled up from his cigarette, which was burning the edge of the new radio-phonograph combination Dan had given Dorothy for her birthday.

The familiar sickness ran through Dan, making his knees weak, his mouth dry, leaving a pit of nausea in his stomach.

"Hello, kid," Mel grinned. He took a long drag on the cigarette, laid it back so it would burn a new spot on the radio's mahogany cabinet. He looked at it and at Dan and grinned again. Then he stood up. He was a big guy, towering over Dan three or four inches. He wore thick-soled shoes, high-waisted slacks, a loud striped green shirt with an off-color bow-tie and wide suspenders. He had crinkly red hair that seemed to stand straight up in marcelled waves. The girls all went for Mel and his snappy line. The maroon convertible his Pa had given him helped some, too.

"Congratulate me, kid," he chuckled. "I'm about to be a happy bride-groom."

The sickness got worse inside Dan, only now there was a cold hand squeezing his heart, too.

"Ain't you interested who the lucky girl is? Well, I'll tell you. It's Dorothy." He peeled a stick of gum, wadded it into his mouth and grinned at Dan.

"She, she's my wife, Mel," Dan stammered, his heart going like a trip hammer.

Mel shook his head. "Ha-ah. *Was* your wife, kid. She wants a divorce."

Dan blinked. "No," he said.

Mel pursed his lips. "Well now," he sighed. "Dorothy said you might be a little stubborn. She told me I'd have to come around and convince you."

"She was happy with me until you came along," Dan said past the tightness in his throat, blinking rapidly to keep the hot fog out of his eyes.

He thought about the fun they'd had together, furnishing this little flat, saving money for records. How they'd planned to buy a second-hand car, soon's Dan got a job with a bigger band.

"Exactly," Mel was saying. "But you see, I did come along. So now she ain't happy with you any more. She wants to marry me."

"No," Dan said. "She doesn't know what's best for her. She's young and kinda crazy. But she'd be miserable with you. Go away and leave us alone, Mel. Go away."

The grin was spread all over Mel's face now, everywhere except in his eyes. They were small and beady and there was a kind of insane light in them. Like the time Dan remembered back in school when Mel caught a puppy by the tail and stamped the life out of its twisting, squealing body. He started walking toward Dan, grinning like that, and Dan backed up until the wall stopped him. Mel took a handful of Dan's shirt and twisted until the seams popped.

"You gonna divorce her?" he panted in Dan's face.

Dan was so scared his teeth clicked. But he shook his head.

Duggard brought his big hand up and it crashed into Dan's face, again, again, again, and all the time he grinned with the wild light in his eyes.

The room swam before Dan's eyes. He could taste warm blood. He was suddenly a kid in school again, getting one of his weekly beatings from Mel.

"All right," he heard himself sob. "I'll give her a divorce. Please don't hit me any more, Mel!" Duggard had beaten him down to his knees.

Mel gave him a parting kick. "That's just a sample of what you'll get if you change your mind," he panted. He gathered up his loud, plaid sport coat from the bed. As an after-thought, he shoved the radio-phonograph off the table and it hit the floor with a splintering crash. He laughed, going out of the place.

Dan sat on the edge of the bed with his head in his hands. Even after it got dark and the neon sign across the street cast its reddish light into the room, he didn't move. Finally, he got up. He went in the bathroom and washed his bruised face. He examined his lips in the mirror. They were puffy and swollen. But only one corner was cut. He'd be able to work tonight.

He picked up his trumpet. He looked once at the broken radio on the floor. Then he walked out of the room.

He was playing with a five-piece band in a little night-club half way on the other side of town. He walked every night to save money.

It took nearly an hour. As he started down the steps into the night-club, a girl came out of the shadows. She caught his arm. It was Dorothy, her face was white and twisted, her eyes big, dark splotches. Her fingers biting into his wrist were like ice.

"Dan, I'm in a jam." She began crying. She pushed both hands into her hair at her temples and started getting the shakes. In a minute, Dan could see, she would be having hysterics.

He got her down into the stuffy little night-club that hadn't opened for business yet and forced some straight bourbon between her lips. She choked on it, but it brought some of the color back to her face and stopped her from shaking so much.

He had her back in a booth where it was private. Maybe he should have asked her why she had come to him. Maybe he should have been bitter about it and told her to go to Mel, if she was so crazy about him. But he did none of those things.

She was his wife and she was in a jam. So he said, "Tell me."

She swallowed. She was staring straight at the wall, as if hypnotized. "Dan, I—you have to come over to my place right away."

He nodded. "All right, sure." He told the bandleader he'd have to get along minus a trumpet player for a while. Then he and Dorothy took a taxi. She had rented a small apartment in the same neighborhood where Mamber played. They went up the stairs silently. She got out her key but she was shaking so much, Dan had to put it in the lock of the door for her.

She whispered, "It isn't pretty, Dan."

THE door swung inward and Dan looked down at the man lying there. She was right; it wasn't pretty. It never is when a man gets shot in the face. Dan nearly gagged.

You could tell from the looks of the room that Dorothy lived here. Everything was neat and orderly. It was a one-room efficiency affair with a tiny gas range and refrigerator at one end and a single bed in the other. There was a stack of Dorothy's favorite movie magazines on the floor beside the bed and a box of candy. A tiny radio on a table next to the bed was still playing softly.

There was enough left of the dead man's face for Dan to recognize. He was a small, rat-faced man dressed in a loud striped suit. It was Sam Cockerell, a crooked little loan shark who ran a hole-in-the-wall office in this part of town. Musicians called him "Dillinger" Cockerell because of the rates he charged and the strong-arm methods he used to collect. If you owed Sam Cockerell money and didn't pay on time, you might find yourself in some alley, beaten to a pulp. That's why Sam never asked for collateral.

Dan shivered at the thought of Dorothy's getting mixed up with a crook like Cockerell.

"I owed him money," she whispered through stiff lips. "I wanted some new dresses, so I made a loan. It was due today, but I didn't have it and I didn't go to his office. He came up here tonight when I got home from work. He started getting nasty, Dan. I was so terribly scared."

"Dorothy…"

She shook her head. "I know what you're thinking, but I didn't shoot him, Dan. I swear I didn't." Her fists were two icy knots at her sides. She was fighting to keep her voice from rising hysterically.

"He was facing me with his back to the door. He was saying some terrible things. And just then the door opened. Quietly, Dan. He didn't see it. A man was standing there. I couldn't see what he looked like. The hallway was dark and I was frightened. He said one word, 'Sam', just like that. Cockerell turned and the man shot him. Then he stepped back out in the hall and closed the door." She spread her hands over her face. "I never saw a man die before, Dan."

"You haven't any idea who this man was?"

She shook her head. "I tell you it was dark in the hall, Dan. I wouldn't have known if it was you standing there." She started crying softly, hopelessly, "Dan, when the police find out I owed Cockerell money, they'll think I…"

The telephone rang. Dorothy stopped crying, stared at it with wide, dark eyes, as if it were the police calling to say they knew she'd shot Cockerell and were on their way up to arrest her. The whole room seemed to be holding its breath. There was only the soft drip of the kitchen faucet, the radio playing "Cruising Down the River" and the persistent telephone.

She snapped the radio off, picked up the telephone. She said, "Hello" in a small voice and then listened for what seemed an eternity, staring at Dan with wide eyes. Then she whispered, "Yes, yes, all right. Right away." She hung up.

"It was Mel Duggard, Dan. He says he knows about the murder and I should come over to his place right away. He said not to let anybody see me leave the apartment."

Out in the back street, they caught another taxi. They rode in silence to where Mel Duggard lived. His father owned a delicatessen store on the corner. Mel's long maroon convertible was parked in the side street beside the store. Old man Duggard, a widower, lived above the store. Mel had an apartment in an old, frame, three-story house back of the store.

Dan walked beside his wife down the dark side street. They stopped before Mel's house. There was a light on in his downstairs apartment.

Ever since Dorothy had come to him for help tonight, Dan Skeels had had a strange feeling. She had seemed so small and afraid beside him. He had been scared too, probably more than she had ever been, but he hadn't let on. He had acted almost like a man. He thought about what Mamber said. That most people were cowards about something, though they wouldn't admit it. Maybe they were doing what he had done tonight, pretending. Maybe that's what being a man meant. Being scared and sick inside, but not letting it show.

Now that they were in front of Mel's house, though, even the pretense left Dan, he stopped, clenching his fists in his pockets.

Dorothy looked at him. "Aren't, aren't you coming in with me, Dan?"

He ran his tongue over his dry lips. "I—maybe I'd better wait outside, Dorothy."

She stared at him. Then her shoulders skimped. Her eyes became bleak and dead. "For a while I thought..." She choked. "Oh, nothing." She ran up the steps, rang Mel's bell and then went in his apartment.

Dan stood there, hating himself. Hating what he had seen in Dorothy's eyes. Wishing he were dead. He drew a shaking hand across his eyes. Then he slipped up on the front porch of the old building. One of Mel's blinds was only half drawn. He could see into Mel's living room. Duggard was standing there in a silk dressing gown. His red hair seemed to be standing up straighter than ever. He was grinning down at Dorothy.

It was very quiet in this neighborhood. Dan could hear a cat mewing in some alley, the exhaust of a car in the next block. And he could hear Mel's and Dorothy's voices.

Dorothy was saying, "Why did you phone me, Mel Duggard? What do you know about—about Sam Cockerell?"

Duggard grinned at her. "Don't be in such a hurry, baby. We got plenty of time. C'mon, sit down." He tried to put his arm around her, pull her down beside him on the couch. But she wrenched away from him, backed up.

"Tell me what you know about Cockerell."

His grin widened. "I know you're in a bad fix, baby. And you'd better start getting friendly with ol' Mel if you want to get out of it."

Dan didn't get this. Dorothy wasn't acting as if she were in love with Mel. As if she wanted to marry him, the way he'd told Dan when he gave him the beating.

She suddenly gasped. "You killed him, Mel Duggard. You were the man in the hall."

"Now my baby's getting smart," Mel said. "And if you'll get a little smarter, everything will be all right."

"But, why? Why did you do it?"

"Why? Because ol' Mel is smart, honey. He always gets what he wants. One way or the other." He shrugged. "I knew you owed Sam Cockerell money. I knew what kind of a guy he is. I phoned his office today, told him you couldn't pay the debt and you were leaving town early in the morning. If he wanted to collect, he'd better get to your apartment when you got off from work tonight. I followed him. I waited until he was in your room, then I opened the door and shot him. You begin to understand?"

Her face was like chalk. Her shoulders slumped. "I–I think I do."

"The gun I used is the one they keep in your desk down at the parking lot. I found it one day when I came to take you to lunch. You see how bad it looks for you?"

Mel chuckled. He walked over to a writing desk, opened a drawer, took the gun out. He showed it to her, then dropped it in the drawer again and slid it closed. He lit a cigarette. "Now, honey, you say 'yes' to Mel, like I been tryin' to get you to do for the last two months. Then everything will be okay. I'll give you a perfect alibi. I'll tell the cops you were with me, riding, when Sam got shot. I'll throw the gun away. They won't be able to prove a thing without the weapon. Sam had dozens of enemies. They'll think he went up to your place to wait for you and somebody else came in and killed him."

"If—if I *don't* marry you?"

He shrugged and his face got mean and ugly. "I don't like for girls to say no to me, baby. I'll see that the police find this gun, and the I.O.U. that you gave Sam. That's all they'll need. They'll know Sam was killed in your place, that you owed him money. And when they trace the gun and find out it came from your desk at the parking lot, honey, that's all they'll need to send you to the chair!"

He tried to put his arm around her again. "Aw, baby, don't make me do it. I can give you everything. A pretty apartment, a car, clothes."

She shook her head. She seemed dazed. "But I love Dan."

"That sniveling coward."

She closed her eyes. "I—a girl can't live with a man she doesn't respect," she whispered. "But I can't stop loving him, just the same."

"He wants to divorce you," Mel swore. "He told me tonight he was going to start divorce proceedings in the morning."

Dan was beginning to get the whole picture. The whole fantastic scheme sounded like Mel Duggard, all right. Dorothy had probably been a little dazzled by his car and money at first. But she hadn't really cared anything about him. She'd refused his advances. Mel couldn't take that. It would drive an egomaniac like him out of his mind for a girl to refuse him.

Dan walked off the porch and stood on the sidewalk. He knew what he was going to have to do. His thin, pale face was clammy with sweat.

Mamber had said, "Time comes when you really got somethin' big to fight for, the Lord will give you stren'th."

Dan prayed for that strength now. He had something plenty big to fight for, Dorothy's life.

He had thought it all out tonight when he sat on the bed in his apartment after Mel beat him up. He'd thought about what Mamber said, "You ask whut makes a man a coward, boy? Well, it's cause something taught him whut fear is when he was a right young-un. He wasn't bo'n afraid. He learned it from somebody or somethin'."

Dan had thought about that a long time and had finally come up with the answer. He'd dug back into his childhood and he remembered how his Pa had been. A weasely, sniveling man, always afraid. Afraid of losing his job, afraid of getting sick, afraid of his boss. A kid ought to have an old man he can brag about and make his hero. But the spineless, whimpering excuse of a father Dan had only taught him to fear. He'd lost his first fight with Mel in the second grade. After that, Dan hadn't tried any more.

Well, he wasn't going to get over being afraid. As long as he lived, there would be that awful, sick weakness inside him. But he'd never let it show again, to Mel or Dorothy. It was just something he and God would know about.

He opened the front door and walked into Mel's room and his legs were water and cold sweat was gluing his shirt to his thin chest and his stomach was twisted up in a knot. He was so scared he couldn't trust himself to speak. He only stood there, blinking to keep his eyes clear.

Mel's mouth fell open. "What do you want?" he snarled.

Dorothy had whirled as he came in. She was staring at him with a strange mixture of disbelief and hope.

He half stumbled over to the writing desk, fumbled at the drawer where the murder gun was hidden.

"No you don't," Mel swore. He crossed the room in two strides, grabbed Dan's shoulder and whirled him around. His big left hand smashed into Dan's face, sent him crashing against the wall.

Dorothy screamed. Then she ran out.

Dan lashed out with his foot. It caught Mel in the shin. Duggard dropped the paper weight and grabbed at his leg with a hoarse cry. Dan pushed to his feet, bracing his back against the wall. He lashed out with his right fist as hard as he could swing. Pain ran all the way up to his shoulder and he knew he'd broken some knuckles.

Duggard's nose was bleeding in great red spurts. He put his hand over his nose and then took it away and looked at it. "I'll kill you," he gasped, sobbing now with pain and rage. "I killed Sam Cockerell with this gun and now I'll kill you, Dan Skeels. And if I have to, I'll kill that cheap little wife of yours."

For the first time in his life, Dan Skeels got mad. A red haze came down over his eyes and the savage instinct to kill with his bare hands gripped him.

He lurched forward, clutching at Mel Duggard. He scratched and bit and gouged. He didn't know that he had Mel on the floor and was swinging with both hands, beating the red-headed bully's face into bloody pulp while Duggard screamed for mercy.

He didn't know when Dorothy came in with the police, the two patrol officers she'd found cruising in this neighborhood in a squad car. He didn't hear them say, "It's all right, son, you can stop now. We heard Duggard say he killed Sam Cockerell."

He felt them tugging at him, trying to pull him off what was left of Mel Duggard. "Let me hit him once more," he panted.

And he heard his wife, Dorothy Skeels, tell the other policeman proudly, "He's my husband."

Die-Die, Baby

It was like this every night. Me wringing tunes out of Nick's tinny upright while I stared through the foggy smoke, across the tables and the dancers, until finally she appeared in the doorway. Then I'd look down at my fingers that had become sweating ice cubes and swing into *Star Dust,* trying to make it sound as if it were coming from a baby grand, like you can do when your soul's in it.

Tonight I led her across the room with my eyes. I whispered. "Come on, baby."

She picked up her drink at the bar, then moved through the dancers, sipping from the glass while her unfathomable, scared blue eyes flicked around. Her left hand pressed a beaded handbag tightly against her side.

Looking at her was like hearing a hymn in a cool, dark church. "Pretty baby," I said, letting my fingers find their own way over the keys, "when are you going to get smart? Nick Mockert…"

She was dragging at the cocktail and her teeth chattered against the rim. Her eyes dragged from the piano keys to my lips. "Keep playing, Danny. I'm hungry for it."

She leaned over the piano, one rounded white arm pressing it, and stared down at the keys. Every night, while Nick was busy, she'd slip down and drink in the music that way for a few minutes. Sometimes she was lucky and he didn't notice. Sometimes he did notice. Then, maybe, I'd see her next time and she'd have a bruise under an eye or a swollen lip. I fed her the old riverboat rhythms that ran down into my fingers. She lit a cigarette with trembling fingers, put it between my lips. And that was when I saw it.

I stopped playing. "Lonnie Jo!"

Her lips suddenly started shaking. "Danny, please don't look at it. Keep on playing."

She looked like a cold, white candle. She'd tried to cover the long purple blotch on her cheek with powder, but you could see it. And if you looked close, you could see the red marks around her slim throat where heavy fingers had tried to press the life out of her a few minutes before.

I started sweating. Big, cold beads that stood out on my forehead. I sensed something in the stuffy, smoke-filled room. You could feel it closing down like an invisible giant hand.

I twisted sharply, ran my eyes down the crowded bar. There were two of them, shouldering their way in through the main door, big, tuxedoed hoods. I knew 'em. Two of Emmet Whitney's boys, their hands inside their coats.

I looked back of me, at the little side door under the blue, neon-rimmed clock. And I saw another of Whitney's hoods. He was coming in slow, too. His eyes were darting over the room.

I swung back to Lonnie Jo, my stomach a sick twisted knot in my middle, my heart hammering.

"Lonnie."

SHE'D vanished. I stumbled up, spilling my chair back of me. I caught a glimpse of her fighting through the heavy crowd, toward the store rooms. She was still clutching the beaded handbag as if her contract on life were in it.

I went a little crazy. I don't remember getting through the crowd, but by the time I reached the back door, Lonnie Jo had vanished again.

She'd run into the store rooms and probably out the back door, her high heels flying. Nick Mockert's place was down on the water front.

It had been an old warehouse before he remodeled it. The back rooms were small, damp cubicles piled high with old newspapers, overturned tables and chairs, boxes crawling with spiders. Over the muffled noise of the crowd, I could hear the slow lap of water far below.

Knowing Whitney's men were on my heels, I stumbled, cursing frantically, through the deserted rooms. I found Lonnie Jo outside, at the end of the pier.

She was leaning drunkenly against a post, staring down at the oily black water licking at the wharf. The water was a magnet, drawing her swaying, slumping, down to it.

I caught her just before she slipped off the edge. She fought against me and I shook her.

"Talk, baby. Quick, tell Danny what happened. Whitney's boys are coming."

Her face was a white, wrecked thing. I think in that moment she hated me for stopping her. She sobbed once, brokenly, shoved the beaded handbag at me.

"Hide this," she mumbled. "Nick Mockert is upstairs. He's dead. Please hide this good, Danny."

I did the best I could in the moment left me. I dropped it and kicked it across the pier with the toe of my shoe. I felt metal when I kicked and I knew the bag was weighted down with a gun, the gun that killed Nick Mockert.

I dug my fingers into her arms and tried to shake the hysterics out of her, but then Whitney's man came up out of the gloom and shoved a pistol into my ribs.

"I found her," he called back to the others. "Her'n that hopped-up, shrimpy piano player that works for Mockert."

The other two broke through the shadows. One of them started frisking me roughly while the other jerked Lonnie Jo back toward the center of the pier and asked her what she did with the pistol she used on Mockert.

She just sobbed, burying her face in her hands, her brown hair tumbling down.

The one going over me finished. "He's clean. We better take 'em both up to the office. Emmet wants 'em."

I chanced one covert glance backward as the hoods pushed us toward the building. Lonnie Jo's handbag had slid into a pile of old rope. A search would uncover it quickly, I knew.

Upstairs, the carpeted hallway leading to Mockert's office was dark. But there was a splash of light at the end of the corridor. When we approached it, I saw it poured through the splintered door of the dead man's office. Whitney's men had broken in through the locked door.

EMMET WHITNEY was sitting on the corner of the mahogany desk, sipping a finger of straight rye. Nearby, slumped down in an overstuffed chair like a giant, surly toad, was Big Hyatt, Nick Mockert's bodyguard. He was stroking a tiny white kitten with thick fingers, while his small, colorless eyes rested somberly on the sprawled-out body of Nick Mockert at his feet. Whitney kept a gun on him.

"We found her down on the pier," the hood told his boss, shoving Lonnie Jo through the broken door. "Mockert's piano player was with her."

"Get the gun?"

The hood said we hadn't had a thing on us.

Emmet Whitney stood up. He was a tall, spare man in his early fifties. The streak of gray in his hair, the way he dressed, his soft, well-modulated voice typed him a banker or business man. He was a bookie, a successful one and a hard one. Nick Mockert owed him forty grand. I figured he'd come up tonight to collect. Nick didn't have the money, made a play for his gun, and got knocked off. Now Whitney wanted to pin it on Lonnie Jo.

But that didn't explain the busted door. Or Lonnie's running with the gun. Furthermore, she wouldn't have stopped at my piano, if she'd known Whitney's men were after her.

Whitney looked troubled. "Who's the punk?" he asked, nodding my way.

"A hopped-up squirt Mockert keeps around to do odd jobs. Plays piano downstairs. He came back from doing a stretch last year; Mockert hired him. He's on dope and Nick keeps him supplied. Name's Danny Voss."

Lonnie Jo's eyes burned for a second at the hood's short, ugly, but very true biography, then went dull again. Big Hyatt didn't even glance at me. He just stared down at Nick Mockert's body, and stroked the kitten.

Emmet Whitney moved close to me. "Since you worked for Mockert, you knew he owes me forty grand."

I shrugged, trying to keep the fear out of my voice. "Nick never told anybody his business. He didn't have a friend in the world, except Big Hyatt."

Whitney ignored that, continued, "I found out Mockert had a ten-thousand dollar win ticket on Lucky Lady today. She came in at five to one. I drove up with the boys tonight to get my cut. When I get here, Mockert is dead with a forty-five slug in his back."

"Did you call the police?" I mumbled, trying to hold onto my courage. "You're supposed to report things like that."

He slapped me hard, twice, across the mouth. I cowered, and all the courage ran out of me. It wasn't nice to see, but Lonnie Jo looked at it, and in her tired eyes you could see she died a little.

"D-don't," I begged.

"You'll get worse. Start talking. There isn't a cent in this office. Where did Mockert put the fifty grand, and where did the girl hide the gun she plugged him with? I can very easily get a murder-rap shoved in my lap. The cops know I threatened Mockert because of that debt. I want my money, and I want the gun, so I can call the cops and clear this thing up."

I shook my head. "Honest. I don't know anything."

"Why," suggested one of Whitney's men, "don't we just keep the dope away from him for a few hours until his nerves crack. Then he'll talk. Meanwhile we can work on the girl and Mockert's bodyguard."

Whitney thought it might be a good idea,

He turned to Lonnie Jo. She was sobbing.

My fogged mind wouldn't work. My dope-ridden hull of a body was shaking, and my nerves were screaming. First, I centered my eyes on the body in the middle of the room. Nick Mockert was sprawled on his stomach. He'd been shot very neatly between the shoulder blades. His gold key chain with the key to this office had fallen across the floor, half under him, the tip of the key touching the drying pool of blood.

My eyes went to Big Hyatt. He was still seated heavily in the leather chair. He hadn't said anything, and I knew he wouldn't. Whitney had probably found him downstairs, got the drop on him, and brought him up. One thing was certain. Big Hyatt wanted Nick Mockert's murderer more than any one else in the room. And when he found him, there'd be another death.

Big Hyatt was the only man in the world Nick had trusted. He was a burly mass of solid beef. He wore blue serge suits that looked slept in, and he always carried a kitten or a pet mouse or a puppy around with him. He could kill a man without squinting, but he couldn't bear the sight of a hungry kitten. I hadn't heard him speak three full sentences in the year I'd worked for Nick, but when he did mutter something, it sounded like the rumble of the elevated train.

While I was thinking, and Whitney's sharp, incisive threats were whipping Lonnie Jo to pieces, I noticed a scrap of cardboard on the floor near Big Hyatt's chair. I mopped my sweating face with a handkerchief, dropped it. Nobody noticed that I scooped up the cardboard when I bent to retrieve the handkerchief.

In a moment, I got a chance to glance at it. It was half a pawn-ticket, torn down the middle. A serial number was stamped across one end. The letters "Automa" scribbled in blue ink ended at the ragged edge. That could have spelled out "Automatic." The address of the pawn shop was on the back, a place down in the sixties.

Then I began sweating again, because I knew what I was going to have to do. It wasn't going to be easy. I no longer had the guts to do it. Five years ago, maybe.

But I knew a sweet kid was being moused around by a bunch of hungry cats, and I was the only guy in the world who could help her. Because I knew that, and because maybe there was a spark of what I'd once been left in me, I tensed and dove into the unsuspecting hood nearest me.

It was the last thing any of them expected. The way I'd been sniveling, I don't think they'd have been more surprised if Big Hyatt's white kitten had tackled them.

That was why I managed to drive the hood into the desk, twist his gun from him.

Lonnie Jo screamed. Emmet Whitney shot twice, but I flung his man between us, twisted and dove for the door. I blasted a couple of parting shots at the confused bunch. Howling lead thudded into the wall near me, smashed splinters out of the remains of the caved-in door. By then I was in the hall.

I figured Lonnie Jo would be safe. Whitney needed her to take the murder rap. Maybe she *had* finished off Nick Mockert, but I didn't think so. And the scrap of pawn-ticket clenched in my sweating hand should prove it.

Downstairs, in the cold black night, I found Big Hyatt's fast sedan, parked in the alley, dash light burning, key in the ignition lock. I swore with delight, tore the door open.

Footsteps pounded out of the building. Orange flashes ripped the night. A bullet spanged off the hood. A driving weight caught my shoulder, knocked me into the car.

I couldn't seem to use my left hand, but I twisted the key with my right and somehow got the motor roaring.

I felt the warm stickiness down my left arm then, and the burning pain started, and I knew one of Whitney's bullets had found a mark. It had been hours since I'd had any morphine.

Crazy, jumbling memories were packing my mind. A little midwestern town where the air was clean and fresh. Danny Voss going to high school, and country club dances, and church on Sundays. A nice family. People that had been too good. It had been years since I'd thought about those things.

The jerking thoughts stopped when I found the little pawn-shop in a dingy part of the sixties. By now it was ten o'clock, but the little place was still open. The shuffling old fellow kept a file system, and a twenty-dollar bill talked him into looking up the torn stub's serial number. The ticket covered a .38 automatic, which had been redeemed this afternoon by a Saul Wettklo. He gave me Wettklo's address.

I knew Wettklo, a little hunch-backed jockey that used to hang around Nick's place a lot. I think he'd been barred from the tracks for something shady he'd pulled. I hadn't noticed him around lately.

When I crawled out of the car, things went black for a moment. I slid to the running board, my head swimming groggily. Somehow I pushed to my feet, staggered up the flight of concrete steps. In the hall, by the sickly light of a dim ,ten-watt bulb, I saw a pay telephone.

Apparently, I'd lost Whitney's men after leaving Nick's place. Now, though, I was at the end of the trail with pay-dirt in sight. I needed assistance. I tried a long shot, dialed Nick Mockert's office.

The phone buzzed, then I recognized Whitney's cautious "Yeah?" He'd sent his boys after me, but he'd stayed back in the office.

I licked my lips and said, "Whitney, this is Danny Voss. One of your boys clipped me when I was getting into Big Hyatt's sedan. I'm ready to spill the whole thing and give you the gun that killed Nick Mockert. I'm going out fast." Then I gave him Wettklo's address and told him to bring along Lonnie Jo and Big Hyatt or the deal was off.

There was an eternity of silence while Whitney thought. Finally he decided, "I don't see how you could be pulling anything fancy. We'll be there in ten minutes."

Then I started the slow, painful climb up the dingy stairs to Saul Wettklo's room. On the second landing, I stumbled through a pile of empty beer bottles and trash. Somewhere a kid squalled. A couple of flights up, a man and his wife quarreled raucously. I rapped on Wettklo's door, heard him stirring. Then the door cracked open a slit.

Wettklo's face was a sharp, ugly thing, cut by deep scars from an old track fall. His beady black eyes burned with a steady flame of bitterness that matched the leer of his lips.

"You know me, Saul," I told him.

He nodded. "Danny Voss. Nick's piano player." His little eyes were busy taking in my condition.

I gave it to him straight. "Nick's dead, Saul. He was killed an hour and a half ago."

I didn't think it would affect him quite like that. The guy was floored.

I stumbled in and folded in a straight chair, poured a drink from a half-empty pint on the table while Saul went over and collapsed on the edge of the unmade bed.

Numbly, he nodded. "I took the gun along for pertection, Danny. I was up to Nick's tonight. But for God's sakes, Danny, I didn't kill the guy. I don't want Nick dead. That's the last thing I want."

He went on. "I been bleedin' Nick for years, Danny. I fixed a race for him a long time ago. It gave him his start. But the next one I tried for him got me barred from the tracks permanent. I hit the skids an' been livin' off Nick's money ever since. I keep quiet about what I done for him, an' he keeps payin'. Lately, he ain't been comin' through so good.

"But today, I get wind of a fifty-grand win Nick made on Lucky Lady. So I go up to Nick's place. I never know when he'll get fed up and get ideas about having Big Hyatt rub me out. So I carry the heater for pertection.

"Well, Nick's in a good mood. Yeah, he says, he hit on Lucky Lady. He ain't cashed the ticket yet, but he will in the morning, and after he pays off Emmet Whitney, he'll give me a coupla hundred. Then he opens the desk drawer to show me the ticket. Well, Danny, it ain't there. It's been stole!

"Nick goes higher'n a kite. Only this doll of his, Lonnie Jo, has been in his office, he says. He phones down for Big Hyatt to bring up the jane. He's madder'n hell, so I figger I better ease out. I go downstairs for a drink. I wait around till eight-thirty, then go back up. The office door is closed, locked. I knock, but there ain't no sound from inside. Then I hear someone comin' up the steps. I beat it down the back stairs. That's all I know, Danny. So help me."

I knew he was telling the truth. All of a sudden I was awfully tired. I knew now what had happened in Nick Mockert's office.

They said once I could have been a great pianist. But the wrong things happened. A talented kid in a big city, fast crowds, wrong crowds. Now the dream was ashes. And I had turned to ashes inside, *too.* I had done this to Lonnie Jo. Because of me she had gotten tangled up in this. And because of what I'd done, I was ashes inside, bitter, dry.

There was a quick rap at the door.

Saul started up from the bed. "Cops," he gasped. "You dirty…"

I told him to relax. Then I went over and let in Emmet Whitney, two of his boys, Lonnie Jo and Big Hyatt.

LONNIE Jo's face was a tense, white mask.

When she saw the dark stain soaking my left coat sleeve, a ragged sob tore from her lips. She tried to tear loose from Whitney.

"Let's have the gun, Danny," Whitney demanded.

"It's back on the pier where your boys caught us, under a pile of ropes."

The room was quiet. Saul Wettklo was breathing hoarsely. Big Hyatt still had his kitten. It mewed disconsolately. Upstairs, the family brawl was still in progress.

"Lonnie Jo," I went on flatly, "stole Nick Mockert's fifty-thousand dollar win ticket on Lucky Lady out of his desk drawer tonight." She sucked in her breath with a pitiful gasp. "I know why," I continued in a dead tone, "but that isn't important. Nick called her up, then, accused her of it. I guess she lost her head and admitted it. He started choking her."

Whitney interrupted impatiently. "I knew the girl killed him."

I shook my head. I don't know how anyone could be so dead inside and still keep talking. "She didn't kill him. Nick phoned down for Big Hyatt to bring her up." I turned to the huge, surly man. "You're a funny guy, Big Hyatt. You're as cold-blooded as they come. But you can't stand to see helpless things hurt. Nick Mockert must have slapped Lonnie Jo around plenty of times while you sat there and watched. It must have started slow fires burning inside you. Lonnie Jo was good to everybody. She was good to you. She was the only person in the world who treated you like a human being instead of a freak gorilla. She wasn't afraid of you. I guess in a funny way you loved her. Tonight when you saw Nick choking the life out of her, you couldn't stand it any more. You went nuts, Big Hyatt. You pulled your gun and killed Mockert!"

The silence was deafening. Big Hyatt was sweating. His eyes, drawn back under heavy eyebrows, were on fire. He looked like a giant grizzly, cornered, measuring his captors for a way out of the trap. The kitten squalled as Big Hyatt's tremendous left hand unconsciously closed too tightly around it.

"Lonnie couldn't have shot Mockert in the back while he was choking her," I went on. "And there were only two persons in the world who had keys to that office, you and Nick. You locked the door on the way out. You were going to get in your sedan and leave. Lonnie was going to get rid of the gun and disappear."

The ashes had come up in my mouth, drying it. "This—this can't be proved. Big Hyatt. It's just what I figured out. But Lonnie Jo is going to the chair because of it. Do you want that, Big Hyatt?"

I was prepared for this moment. I knew what Big Hyatt would do. As he dove for Whitney's gun, I slammed into Lonnie Jo, tumbling her roughly into the hall. I guess Big Hyatt got the gun, I don't know. They were already shooting before we cleared the room. It could only end one way. There were too many of Whitney's men there. By the time Lonnie Jo and I reached the front door downstairs, it was all over, except you could hear the faint, heart-broken mewing of a kitten.

I drove Lonnie Jo to a hotel, told her I'd be back after I got my arm dressed. But I didn't go back.

The next morning I went to the post office and drew out the long envelope I knew would be in my box. The fifty-thousand-dollar win ticket on Lucky Lady was in the envelope, a tiny note tucked in with it. The note wasn't signed, but I'd know Lonnie Jo's handwriting anywhere. The envelope was postmarked seven p.m., a few minutes after she'd stolen the ticket the night before and mailed it. An hour and a half before Big Hyatt killed Mockert.

The note said: "Please, Danny. There are hospitals that can help people overcome drug habits. Then there will be enough left over for you to go away and start over. Please, for me, Danny."

Well, I cashed the ticket that morning. I put forty-thousand dollars in an envelope and sent it to Emmet Whitney. He had a right to it. I sent Saul Wettklo a couple of hundred. The rest, nearly ten-thousand, I sent to Lonnie Jo. It was her money.

She comes from a little mid western town where the air is clean, too.

She'll go back there when she realizes there is no more hope of finding me. You see, she did it for me. She even married Nick for me, hoping he could help her get me straightened out. But Nick wouldn't bother because he wasn't that kind of a guy. He wouldn't even give her the little money she needed for herself, so she finally became desperate and took the fifty-thousand dollar ticket.

It will hurt her at first, my disappearing. But it will be better for her that way. I don't know where I'll go. They say there are docs that can help guys in my fix. Maybe I'll hit the road and try to find one. Maybe he'll help, and some day I can go back to the little mid-western town and tell Lonnie Jo it all worked out O.K. I know what it would mean to her. You see, Lonnie Jo is my kid sister.

Home for Killers

AFTER I passed Goliad, the road turned to rutted clay. Thickets of blooming huisache, cleared patches blanketed with blue-bonnets, chaparral clumps and now and then a freshly plowed field bordered the road. The wild, rolling Texas countryside spread around me like a giant patchwork quilt tossed out to soak up the spring sunshine.

The bitterness of years past came up into my mouth, as dry and acrid as the powdery white dust that curled around the tires of my canary-hued Buick convertible.

I rested my fingertips on the steering wheel, half closing my eyes. The sunshine was good. I couldn't get enough of it. I wanted it to reach inside and warm the coldness that came to a man who'd been dead inside for a long time.

I swung off the road and down a narrow, barb-wire fringed lane, followed it for a mile, and pulled up at the farm house.

This is it, Joe Jureski. Your home. Remember? But, no, you wouldn't. That was too long ago to remember. A million years ago.

It hadn't changed much. It still needed a coat of paint. The porch roof sagged a little more, the barn leaned a bit more to the right. But the north forty had been broken into rich, moist loam, and the cattle grazing in the pasture were sleek. That would be Tom's doing. He would make a good farmer. It was in his blood, inherited from his father. I was grateful for that.

The sagging house dozed peacefully amidst its fields and cattle. Far up on a distant hill, the old moss-covered Spanish mission, La Bahia, brooded solemnly, like a tired old sentinel guarding the countryside while reminiscing over its bloody past. Two buzzards wheeled in the clear blue sky. Somewhere a windmill creaked and a dog yelped.

She would have liked this, Joe. This warmth and peace and quiet. She'd never seen anything like this. Only gray city canyons and slum apartments and standing behind department store counters. That's why she looked so thin and pale and her eyes were so enormous.

But she's going to die, Joe. Because of you. So she won't get to see anything like this. Never.

I was pounding my fist on the steering wheel, slowly, steadily, when a voice beside the car jerked me back to reality.

"Joe?" the voice murmured hesitantly, incredulously. I stared at the unruly-haired young man in overalls. He ran his wide-eyed gaze from one end of my sparkling pile of chrome and yellow metal to the other, then looked at me again and blinked.

"Tom!" I choked. I got out and hugged the kid, knocking his hoe out of his hand.

He was laughing and crying at the same time and saying my name over and over.

"You've come home from New York!"

I looked at him again. "I don't believe it, kid," I murmured softly, shaking my head. "When I left you were a youngster. Now you're a man. But the place is hardly changed. Looks wonderful to me."

"I've been running the farm, Joe," he told me proudly. "Since Dad…"

I nodded and looked down at my dust-covered imported tan shoes. "I was sorry, kid."

"We—The money you sent, Joe, covered all his funeral expenses. We were so glad. There wasn't any insurance."

"Forget it," I said roughly. I remembered that that had been back when I had the idea you could buy off your conscience. Now I knew differently. *"I* wanted to come for the funeral, Tom. I really did, but I just couldn't make it."

"Sure, Joe. We understood. New York is a long way off."

"Yeah," I said, and the word was like dust in my mouth.

He looked at the car again, admiringly. "You sure done well in New York, Joe. Real well!"

"Where's Ma?"

"In the house. But go easy, Joe. Her heart ain't so good any more."

I went in and the smells and sounds swirled around me like ghosts out of the past. The twang of the patched screen door, fresh bread baking out in the kitchen, a kitten mewing. I moved into the dark parlor and my eyes picked out the plush sofa, the embroidered "Home Sweet Home" motto on the wall, the white blur that was the big seashell I used to hold to my ear.

She was sitting beside a window, looking through the family album at pictures and tokens of other days, her lips moving silently. She looked up, and the lace curtain stirred and swirled around her.

The lines had furrowed deeply now, and her hair was like snow. Her eyes were faded, as if too many tears had washed the blue out of them. Her fingers trembled. "Joe!" she whispered.

I knelt beside her and she murmured something in Polish and cried.

"It's all right, Ma," I said. "I'm home now. To stay."

I was out in the barn, later, when I saw my sister, Pola. Tom had proudly taken me on a tour of inspection, showing me the silos bulging with feed, the sleek cattle, the chickens and the new farm station wagon. Pola, he'd said, was over at our neighbors.

He'd left me for a while and I was standing in the barn, chewing on a bit of straw, running my eyes over the harness and gear which was neatly mended and hung on the wall, when I heard a footstep behind me.

Years of instinctive training spun me around, whipped my hand up to the bulge under my coat. Then cold sweat washed my body and the strength went out of my knees and I clutched at a post.

"Mary," I gasped in a strangled throat. "Mary…"

The pale, dark girl moved through the shadows, up close to me, frowning up at me, and then smiling. "Joe? Joe, don't you know me? Your sister?"

"Pola," I whispered. "Pola, darling!"

In the dark barn, it was no wonder that I had for an instant mistaken her for Mary. She wasn't a little girl any more. She was tall and slender, with wild, Slavic beauty, fully ripened. Her hair was like midnight, skin like fresh cream, a red, wide mouth, huge black eyes; her body was curved and soft and suddenly mature.

"Pola," I said. "You're beautiful!"

She laughed, a little tinkling, silvery sound, and she kissed me. I knew it wasn't the first time a man had told her she was beautiful.

"Who did you mistake me for, Joe? One of your New York cuties?"

I took a cigarette, my fingers shaking. "Yeah," I said, with my mouth full of rags. "Yeah."

"Give me one of your cigarettes, Joe."

I handed her one. "Ma know you smoke?"

She shrugged, pouted a little as she leaned toward the lighted match I held. "A girl grows up some time, Joe. But parents don't think so."

She looked up at me and I noticed for the first time the violet smudges under her eyes, the tight lines around her mouth, the faint haunted shadows in her black eyes. "Joe," she whispered with a strange, sudden intensity. "I'm glad you're back!"

Then she was laughing again. "There's a dance tonight, Joe. A real old-fashioned, Texas country dance. You can see all your old friends. You can drive that nice yellow car and show everybody what a smart, rich brother Pola Jureski has!"

But her voice had little edges in it and the cigarette trembled between her fingers. She reminded me again of the girl in New York who had been afraid, too.

WE all dressed for the dance that night and I felt like a little kid again, washing behind my ears for Saturday night excitement. We took turns using the tin bathtub and Ma heated water on the iron cook stove and brought it in great steaming kettles. Pola and Tom fought over who'd get the bathroom when I was through with it.

In the bedroom, I dressed in a hundred-and-fifty-dollar imported plaid sport coat, a silk shirt, white and tan shoes. I knotted a sporty panel bow tie and looked in the mirror. There was a difference between Tom's lean, ruddy face and mine. Mine had pads of soft flesh and a network of lines from too much rich food and liquor and soft, easy living.

Ma came in and sat on my bed. "So much fine clothes," she said, shaking her head. "So much money. It ain't my Joe. It's like I'm with a stranger."

I sat on the bed, took her frail hands in mine. "Ma, it's Joe. Your Joe, like always. You want to tell me something?"

She plucked at the home-made quilt, then smoothed her hands over her dress and gazed down at them. "It's Pola, Joe."

"Tell me about Pola, Ma. Is there something wrong? She looks worried, frightened."

Ma shook her head. "Too much beauty can be a curse, Joe. This boy she goes with. I don't know. I'm an old woman from a foreign country. I don't understand the ways of these young people. But they stay out so late, almost until morning. This boy doesn't work, but he's always got money." She shivered. "You tell me, Joe. You look at him close and tell me. You're smart, you know about these things. You look at him and tell me I'm a foolish old woman filled with fears for a too-pretty daughter."

She touched my cheek and whispered to me in Polish.

I met Ralph Jessep. Pola introduced us when I went into the parlor. I looked at his quick, shifting eyes, his soft, manicured hands and his clothes that were too casually perfect and listened to his hard, bright talk. I knew why Ma was worried.

He shook hands with me, his eyes narrowing as if he sensed a kind of kinship between us. He was in his late twenties, a good ten years older than Pola. A blond man, fairly tall and well built, he had too much grease on his hair. But he would, I supposed, be considered handsome by a woman. Especially by a kid like Pola who'd lived on a farm and suddenly had grown up and got her eyes full of stardust.

Pola chattered brightly, too brightly. Her cheeks were flushed and her eyes glittered feverishly. But when her fingers brushed my hand, they were like ice.

"We'll see you at the dance, Joe, Tom. And don't you dare forget to dance with your sister!"

"I'll save them all for you, kid," I called after her. But there was a new coldness inside me. I stopped in my bedroom and strapped on the shoulder holster, which I'd first planned to leave in my bag.

Tom was taking the station wagon. He had a date with a girl in town. I kissed Ma and drove to the dance in the yellow convertible.

THERE seemed to be a thousand cars parked around the dancehall. It wasn't much of a town. Just a cotton gin and a general store and a huge, barn-like dance hall at the intersection of several country lanes.

The hall looked as big as an airplane hangar. A round structure with a tin roof, it had great wooden shutters on hinges all the way around that were propped open in summer so it became a cool pavilion. In front, under dangling lights, were the cold beer and soda stands. Here the older men lounged, talking crops and weather over cold beer and hamburgers.

I walked down there and I had a beer with the men who had been my father's neighbors. They remembered me as a teenage youngster, always in trouble at the community school.

When the music started, I bought a ticket and went into the hall. The floor was a great, round circle of polished hardwood, generously sprinkled with powder. The band sat on a raised dais on the far side. Long benches circled the floor behind a railing. Spectators would fill these as the crowd came in. And I knew that by midnight they would be littered with sleeping infants.

I drifted through the dancers and joined the crowd of stags in the center of the floor. The band, a piano, fiddle, guitar, drums, trumpet and clarinet, played the kind of rhythms I hadn't heard in a million years.

Schottisches, polkas, square dances and waltzes.

I couldn't find Pola anywhere among the dancers. The crowd drifted in from the parked cars until the dance floor was jammed with laughing, sweating humanity. I looked at my platinum wristwatch. It was nearly eleven before I saw her.

I followed her around the floor with my eyes until the band played a waltz. Then I cut in on her. "Hello," I smiled. "Remember me?"

Her dark eyes lifted to my face and her lovely red mouth twisted into a smile. "Yes, you're my brother Joe. My big brother who went away to New York and came back with a million dollars. Are you having a good time, Joe?"

I shook her firmly. "Pola, what's the matter? You're shivering."

The smile stayed on her face. It was fixed there. "Yes? I shouldn't be doing that. Should I, Joe? It's so warm." She bit down on a corner of her lip. "Joe, lend me the keys to your car. Just for a few minutes. No, please don't ask me why."

I stood there in the swirling crowd and watched her disappear. Then I cursed myself for many things and I pushed after her. By the time I had worked through the crowd she was gone. I ran down through the parked cars. I heard a motor roaring. I saw the sweep of a long, yellow convertible glittering with chrome bounce over a cattle guard and disappear down the dark road in a cloud of dust.

I ran down the line of parked cars, skinning my legs on fenders and bumpers until I found Tom's station wagon. I breathed a prayer of gratitude when I saw the keys in the ignition lock. I was out of the parking lot in seconds, leaving some dented fenders behind me. Then I was on the road behind Pola, eating her dust. I'd never catch her. That was out of the question. I could only follow her to where she was headed and pray that I didn't arrive too late.

Far behind me, I saw another car pull out of the parking lot. But I didn't think about that. I concentrated on not losing Pola.

When we struck the main highway, she veered to the right and I thought I knew then where she was heading. There was a town of about ten thousand population some twenty miles from here in that direction. On the straight highway, I lost her completely. I knew she was holding the convertible's speedometer near ninety. I tried not to think about that.

I didn't see the yellow car again until I crossed the railroad tracks on the outskirts of the town. I caught it out of the corner of my eye, parked in the shadows of the small, dark depot. I braked to a stop beside it, ran up the wooden stairs to the office.

Pola was sitting there alone, huddled on a bench away from the light.

See how much she looks like Mary, Joe.

"Pola, honey." I sat beside her and I saw the train ticket clutched in her white fingers. Behind his cage, the white-haired old agent stared at us curiously.

She was crying without making a sound. "Please leave me alone, Joe. Go back to the farm with Tom and take care of Ma. Tell her I'll write soon."

I shook my head, holding her icy fingers. "It isn't any good, Pola, running away. You and I, we're alike. We always run. When we're afraid, we run."

"You've got to stay and face it, Pola, or you'll find you really didn't run away from what you were afraid of at all. You just made it worse."

I lit two cigarettes and gave her one. She dragged deeply on it, her cheeks hollowing. Then she let the smoke drift from her lips with a sigh, looking down at the cigarette between her enameled finger tips.

"It's Ralph Jessep, Joe. I didn't know it would be like this. He was so nice at first."

"You afraid of him, or of something you did?"

"Him, Joe. After I'd been going with him a while, I found out he did all sorts of things. He gambles, steals. One night he held up a filling station while I was sitting out in the car. I cried all the way home, I was so scared. I told him I didn't want to see him again, ever. But he won't let me go. He threatens to do all sorts of terrible things to Ma. To Tom. He says he's crazy about me and I've got to marry him. Right away. Tonight."

The cigarette fell from her hand and she dug her long white fingers into her black hair. "I wouldn't care what he did to me, Joe," she sobbed. "But I'm afraid for Ma and Tom. I've got to go away. Far away."

"But you see, baby," I told her, "running wouldn't help. Ralph would find you, or he'd still be here if you came back. You don't solve things that way."

I ground my cigarette out under my heel, loosened the snub-nosed

.38 automatic in my shoulder rig, and went out into the cool night. I thought that I knew now who'd been in the car that pulled out of the parking lot behind me back at the dance.

I lit another cigarette and stood there on the station platform, waiting. After a few minutes a black sedan swung into the depot yard and parked beside the station wagon and my convertible.

I threw the cigarette away, walked down there before Ralph Jessep got out.

I laid my hand on the door beside his shoulder. "Jessep, leave the kid alone. Beat it. She doesn't want to have anything to do with you any more."

To make sure he understood, I jerked the door open and hauled the punk out and slapped him into the cinders. He crawled up, dragging at his hip pocket. He had his gun out before I could get to mine. He swung it across my face and a thousand stars exploded.

Far in the distance, I could hear him running. I dragged myself to my feet, swearing and shaking my head to clear it. My mouth was full of blood and broken teeth.

I brought my gun up and split the night open. He stumbled, turned and fired. A coal raked my side. I doubled with a grunt, then got my balance as I followed him up on the platform. Somewhere in the distant pounding surf that filled my ears, I heard Pola scream.

Desperately, I jogged down to the end of the platform, bent over from the fire in my side. I saw that he had Pola, was dragging her after him by her wrist. I couldn't risk another shot.

He'd jumped from the platform to a string of old freight cars, was running along their tops, forcing Pola to go with him. I could see that he planned to run down to the end until they were lost in darkness, then crawl down to the tracks and double back to the car.

The train Pola had been waiting for was puffing into the yards and its headlight silhouetted Jessep and Pola momentarily. I fired a wild shot over their heads. Jessep twisted to answer. There was one horrible moment when he seemed to hang there, one foot dangling, swinging his arms in the air to regain his balance. I don't know if he or Pola screamed just before he fell. But when I got to Pola, she was still screaming hoarsely, digging her fingers into her hair, looking down where Jessep had fallen to the tracks under the wheels of the puffing passenger train.

I slapped the hysterics out of her, got her down to the cars. I made her drive the station wagon and I followed in my car. I knew that in a few minutes there would be police and questions. I couldn't afford that. They could ask Pola later, after I'd gone.

We left the station wagon at the dance and I drove slowly home in my convertible. Pola cried herself to sleep on my shoulder like a little girl. I lifted her gently and carried her into the house and laid her on her bed. She stirred once, but kept right on sleeping, with her fingers curled beside her cheek on the pillow.

I sat beside her in the darkness, beside the flushed girl in the crumpled, torn evening gown. A moonbeam slanted through the window and caressed her tear-stained cheek.

I thought that Mary would look a lot like this tonight. She would have cried herself to sleep, too. Only there wasn't any big brother to help her out. Mary didn't have anyone. Not anyone.

QUIETLY, I went into my bedroom. I taped up the flesh wound along my ribs, changed my blood-soaked shirt for a clean one. I threw my clothes back in my two suitcases, picked them up and stole through the house.

I paused at Ma's room. I went in for a moment. Just a last look. But as I turned to leave, she whispered, "Are you going without telling me good-bye, Joey?"

"Ma," I said. I sat on the edge of the bed, my eyes stinging with something they hadn't known in years.

She touched my hand. "Now you're my Joey again. Not a stranger any more."

"I'm scared, Ma," I said simply.

"Yes. That's why you came down here. That's why you ran away from New York."

"I'm like Pola," I went on. "When there's trouble, I get scared and run. I don't face it. I don't think. I've always been like that."

She smiled sadly in the darkness.

Outside, the old windmill creaked, a chicken on the roost stirred; down in the huisache a mockingbird sang. I sat there in the dark, quiet, farmhouse and told her the whole story. I knew it would be better for her to know all of it, now.

It hadn't been like I'd told them in my letters. There hadn't been any important job with a fancy office and my name on the door. I'd made money, a lot of it, but not that way. I'd found there were ways you could skirt the edge of the law and make it faster, easier. The numbers racket, and others. I'd had my fingers in a lot of things, none of them clean.

I got caught at last in a mess. It didn't matter about the details. I turned state's evidence and got a five-year suspended sentence. It had been my first offense.

But I was on probation, you see. I had to get a regular job, report every month and be careful who I was seen with.

It went along all right. I was scared.

I didn't want to spend those five years behind bars.

Then one night, two weeks ago, I met Mary. I walked into this bar and I saw her sitting in a booth alone. She was a thin, dark, pretty kid, about Pola's age. Looked a lot like her. I bought her a drink. We started talking, went to some other bars.

I didn't give her my right name. After a few drinks, she started bawling and told me about the trouble she'd had with her husband. A big, tough guy, his favorite pastime was beating her up when he came home from work at night. Tonight, he'd given it to her good. She'd run off.

That should have been my cue to drop her like a hot coal. But what the hell. I liked the kid, and I was lonesome, too. We had some more drinks, started enjoying ourselves. We got in the jam at this bar around midnight. A drunk picked a fight with me. He came at me with a bottle. Without thinking, I pulled my gun, shot him in the arm.

I wasn't supposed to be carrying a gun.

To be caught with it would break my probation. But I knew some of the boys I'd dealt with were sore at me for turning state's evidence and clearing out of the deals we'd been in. I felt a lot safer packing the heater.

If the police picked me up for shooting the drunk in the saloon, they'd throw the five-year suspended sentence at me. They were just waiting for something like this.

So I ditched the girl and ran.

The next morning, I read the papers. Nothing in them about the saloon fight, but the girl was there, her face right on the front page. It seems her husband had been murdered about eleven o'clock last night. The neighbors said they were always fighting. Last night they battled violently. Then things got quiet. The police picked the girl up, wandering around the park early the next morning. They'd charged her with the murder.

She swore that she'd been at a bar with a guy who'd picked her up at the time her husband was killed. She gave them the false name I'd given her. Of course, they couldn't find anyone by that name. None of the bartenders would identify her for certain. They were only human. They weren't sticking their neck out for a dame they weren't sure about.

I was the only one in New York who could prove she hadn't killed her husband. I could give her an alibi. But if I did, I'd have to explain about every place we'd been. The police would check and they'd find out about the tavern shooting. It would be five years for me.

I'd kept telling myself it wasn't my neck. Let the girl get out of the mess herself. I didn't want to do a five-year stretch. I'd seen what that could do to a man. God, I didn't want to do five years.

"But I couldn't run away from Mary, Ma. She followed me right down here. I see her every time I close my eyes. They'll give her the electric chair if I don't go back. She keeps saying that to me."

I kissed Ma. "Now you take care of yourself. I'll be back in five years or so. This time to stay. I promise."

I went out into the cool night and threw my bags in the car. I drew a deep breath, tasting the perfume of wildflowers, freshly turned earth and dew-wet grass. I thought that when I came back. I might be bringing a new wife with me. I thought that Mary would like to live down here where the air was fresh and clean and you didn't have to be afraid.

Five years wouldn't be so long if you had that to look forward to.

Eddie Builds His Mousetrap

It was ironic. All the beautiful dolls Eddie Price had on his string, and a plain little mouse like Ginny Potucek finally hashes him up.

The morning he was going to kill her, she came out of the kitchen, her face flushed and damp from the heat of the stove. She was untying her apron. "Eddie, we're out of bread. I'll have to run down to the grocery store."

"Oh?" Eddie said. Not that he was really surprised, having just tossed their last loaf out in the alley.

He stood in front of the dresser mirror, whistling, buttoning up a clean white shirt. It was easy to see why the dames fell all over Eddie Price. He was six feet of man, adequately spread out around the shoulders and chest. He had lazy, grey eyes that would drift over a girl, caressing her, sending shivers up her spine, and a shy, little-boy grin that twisted her heart. After that, she'd be a fit subject for Freud if she didn't run her fingers through his thick black hair and whisper in his ear.

But he wasn't thinking about dames at the moment. His fingers were all thumbs, knotting his tie, and there was a sick pit of nausea in his stomach. In a few minutes he was going to kill his bride of two months,

Ginny, in a very messy way. He wasn't too enthusiastic about it.

He forced himself to keep standing there, whistling casually until the hall door closed behind Ginny. Then he grabbed up his hat and coat and beat it down the back fire escape to the alley. He'd parked the stolen sedan there a few minutes ago. He scooped up some mud, smeared it over the license plates. Insurance companies could get very nosy and he didn't, therefore, want the car tracked.

He pulled around to the street in front of the building. It wasn't much of a neighborhood. Brownstone tenement buildings huddled like sordid old women. Lines of dripping wash flapped over sour-smelling, garbage-cluttered alleys. Some skinny, ragged kids were playing hop-scotch on the sidewalk. Ginny had paused to watch them. She liked kids, she said.

Eddie slid his damp palms along his trouser legs. The blood was hammering in his temples.

He wished he didn't have to do this. He wished he could have waited six more months. Ginny'd be dead then, a natural death, all nice and legal. He wished Nick hadn't put the bite on him for the money now.

EDDIE had stumbled on the deal in a doctor's office a little over two months ago. He'd gone there for a checkup. There hadn't really been anything wrong with him except an overdose of women, liquor and rich foods. But he'd thought a few vitamins wouldn't do him any harm. He'd overheard this doctor talking with his nurse in the next room about Ginny Potucek.

". . . shame. She's just in her twenties. But there's nothing more we can do."

In a few minutes, the doc and his nurse walked down the hall to the X-ray room. Out of idle curiosity, Eddie wandered into the room they had just left. Her chart was lying on a table. "Ginny Potucek. Age, 23. Typist, Brown and Barnes, law firm. Address, 799 Craig Street." There followed a lot of medical hocus-pocus in nine-syllable words. But enough was in plain English for Eddie to get the drift of things. This kid, Ginny Potucek, had come off with a nasty rap. Some sort of brain tumor. She'd be dead in less than a year from now.

He shivered, lit a cigarette. Then it hit him between the eyes with the force of a sledge hammer. "Ginny Potucek," he breathed, "you just turned into fifty thousand bucks for little Eddie Price."

Yes, the setup that comes once in a lifetime. It was so simple. And the money'd be clean. Everything legal, almost. He'd marry this Ginny Potucek. Then he'd take out life insurance. A husband-and-wife family policy that paid off in the event of either partner's death, to make it look all right. Eddie knew a doctor who would fill out her insurance medical papers without looking too close if Eddie waved enough long green under his nose. He'd sit back for six or eight months, let nature take its course. Then he'd collect the insurance money, and he and his girl, Lou, would head for Florida.

Lou hadn't taken to it with much enthusiasm at first. "Eddie, honey," she'd pouted, "I don't like the idea of you marryin' some dame, even temporarily."

"But think of the money, Lou," Eddie had argued. "You can buy a lot of pretty clothes with fifty grand."

She thought about that and decided maybe it wasn't such a bad idea. Like Eddie, she figured nobody gives anybody anything in this world. The idea is to grab off all you can for yourself.

So Eddie married Ginny Potucek.

Think it was hard? Not for Eddie Price. She was a woman, wasn't she?

Of course, she was different from any of Eddie's other women. He wouldn't have given her a second glance under different circumstances. She had faded blonde hair and large, grave eyes. Her figure was too thin to rate any whistles. Her clothes were neat, but they had come from a bargain basement and had taken a lot of washings and careful mendings.

She hadn't laughed at Eddie's wisecracks at first. It took her a while to understand that he was clowning most of the time. She was a serious, quiet little mouse.

On their first date, Eddie took her to a four-bit movie, bought her a bag of popcorn and a coke, and when they went home, her eyes were lit up like Christmas trees, as if they'd been to the Astor. Lou would cloud up if he didn't blow at least fifty bucks on a date!

He courted her for two weeks and then proposed. He had a bad moment there, when she tried to tell him about her illness. He couldn't let her know that he knew she only had a few months left to live. Because then, when he took out the policy, she might smell a rat, put two and two together and leave him flat.

She was all choked up and mushy. "I–I love you, Eddie" she'd whispered. And it sounded different from the way Lou and the other dames said it. As if she hadn't said it to anyone else before. She made it kind of sacred, like a prayer. Eddie guessed she had it bad.

But then she put her hand over her face and started crying. "But I can't marry you, or anyone. Eddie, there's something you don't know about me. I–I should have told you right at the start."

"Eddie, do something quick," he told himself. "Or the whole thing is washed up!"

He took her in his arms. "Look kid," he said with just the right amount of huskiness in his voice, "there's a dozen things you don't know about me, baby. My old man was a lush. I grew up in pool rooms, graduated from the state reform school. There's other things I'm not going to tell you about. But I'm selfish and I want you. So, let's make a deal. Let's forget the past and let's not think what's ahead. Let's just get married and think about right now."

Eddie should have been an actor in a soap opera. He was sweating when he got through with that speech. It was so good he almost had himself in tears.

But it did the trick. She agreed to marry him. And every time she tried to bring up the subject of her illness, he kissed her and said he didn't want to hear anything about her private life.

Everything went smoothly, the marriage, taking out the insurance policy. She was in such a sentimental fog she hadn't known what she was signing. And Eddie talked fast again.

Then he had to get mixed up in this Nick Specht thing and louse up the whole deal.

The horses hadn't been running right. Eddie had found himself low on cash and up to his neck in IOUs to Nick Specht, the bookie, to the tune of four thousand dollars. You don't owe that much money to a guy like Nick for long and stay healthy.

Nick had made him the proposition about the jewelry store. Eddie was to help Nick loot a jewelry store. Out of his share of the take, Eddie could pay Nick the four thousand. But it hadn't come off right. The police got wised up and surrounded the place after they broke in. Some bullets were tossed around and a young beat cop, Johnny O'Malley, caught one in his heart and died on the spot. Eddie and Nick and one of Nick's boys managed to get out of the mess, but they couldn't take a cent with them. Nick Specht had been identified by one of the policeman and was as hot as you could get. He was holed up in a room somewhere in town. He needed money bad and he'd sent his boys around town, collecting every cent owed him. The way Nick figured, since the jewelry-store deal had fallen through, Eddie still owed him the four thousand. And he wanted it right away.

Eddie couldn't scrape up that kind of money. *Unless Ginny died ahead of schedule.*

So now he sat in the car with his foot poised over the accelerator. Ginny had left the kids now, and she was about to cross the street to the grocery store. She was wearing a freshly starched house dress. Her hand was over her eyes, shielding them from the sun, and Eddie knew she was having one of her headaches. Eddie thought they must get pretty bad. She was always taking pills on the sly and sometimes at night, when she thought Eddie was asleep, she'd get up and walk back and forth in the darkness. But never a whimper out of her. The kid had guts.

Eddie tried to swallow. He scrubbed the sweat out of his eyes with the back of his hand. His shirt was stuck to his back in great damp patches of cold perspiration. His muscles were quivering. Maybe it wouldn't be so hard if he hadn't lived with her for two months. He kept thinking how she looked, darning his socks, or looking up with that eager smile when he came in the apartment, or brushing her teeth in the bathroom. He swore at his own weakness. It was his life or hers. Nick was getting impatient for that money. He pulled his hat down low over his eyes, turned his coat collar up around his ears. Then he jammed the car into low gear with a metallic rasp, tramped the accelerator to the floorboards. The car leaped like a spurred horse. He could see Ginny through a hazy blur. He aimed the car for her back.

He could feel how it would be. The bump when he hit her. He hoped she wouldn't scream or make any noise. He hoped it would be over for her in a hurry.

Everything was going past Eddie's eyes in a blind swirl. He was maybe three feet from the girl when a hoarse cry wrenched from his throat and he yanked the wheel over. He missed her by inches. The fender brushed her skirt. She hadn't been aware of the car behind her. Her scream rang in Eddie's ears as he careened past her. He heard her scream again, behind him. He glanced up in the rear-view mirror and saw her standing there, her fingers pushed up in her hair, sobbing with fright and shock.

Eddie was shaking as though he had the flu and was calling himself every name he could think of for not going through with it. He'd signed his own death-warrant. Nick wasn't a guy to argue.

He ditched the car several blocks away, ran back to the apartment. Wild thoughts of jamming some clothes in a suitcase, getting Lou and leaving town for a while, were racing through his mind. He ducked into the alley back of the apartment house, headed for the fire escape. Then he stopped. For the moment, he wasn't even breathing.

"Hello, Eddie," Bitz Fowler said quietly.

Bitz was leaning against the fire escape, trimming his fingernails with a clipper. He folded the clipper, dropped it in a vest pocket, examined the job he'd done on his nails carefully. Bitz was a quiet, meticulous guy. He was dressed in a conservative grey business suit, white shirt with high collar, dark maroon tie. He had a round, pale, baby-like face with a small red mouth. He looked sensitive, effeminate. He might have been a bank clerk or an artist. Actually, he was a killer, as deadly as they come.

And Nick had sent him after Eddie.

"I thought you'd come back, Eddie," Bitz explained softly, brushing off his trousers as he came away from the fire escape. "I was up at your apartment early this morning, but you weren't in. I thought if I came back and waited around, you'd show up."

Eddie licked his parched lips. For once he couldn't think of a thing to say. His stomach felt as if it had a lump of wet bread dough wadded up in it.

Bitz took his arm. “Don’t try anything, Eddie,” he warned softly, running his left palm over the breast of his coat where it bulged slightly. “You wouldn’t get very far. Now, let’s go have a talk with Nick.”

Nick Specht was holed up in a rooming house in a crummy part of town. The yard was cluttered. The house was weather-beaten, its brown paint peeling off in large flakes. It leered at Eddie as Bitz parked his car out front. They walked up to the house, Bitz holding lightly to Eddie’s arm. Eddie was having trouble with his knees. They had suddenly become water.

Nick was in the parlor of his three-room apartment. He was hunched over a card table in his undershirt, scowling at his solitaire hand. He was a small, dark man with a shiny, bald head. He had blue jowls and tufts of black hair sticking out of his ears and sprouting from the tops of his share shoulders. His dark olive skin was slick with sweat.

“Listen, Nick,” Eddie began blubbering as soon as they got in the room, “you got to give me a few more hours. I’ll have the money for you, sure. Even with interest.”

“Turn it off.” Specht took a frayed cigar out of his mouth, laid it in a saucer. “You sound like a leaky tire. Besides, you don’t owe me any money any more. Bitz didn’t know. He didn’t have to bring you here.”

Eddie didn’t get it. He stood there, looking blank. “Dame come in. Early this morning. Give me the four G’s. Said you sent her with the dough.”

The words were in English, but they didn’t make sense. Eddie ran them over a couple of times, but they still didn’t make sense. Had it been Lou Durkee? But how would she get four thousand dollars, singing in a night club? And anyway, if she got it, she wouldn’t spend it on him.

“It was that little blonde mouse you keep up in your apartment. Says she’s your wife.” Nick grinned, flashing a gold filling. “You’re slipping, Eddie. Maybe you should see an eye doctor ? Or did you win her at a raffle?”

It had been his wife, Ginny!

But how had she learned of his predicament? How had she located

Nick's hideout? And, most of all, where had she gotten that much money?

Nick explained part of it. He'd sent Bitz to their place early that morning, looking for Eddie. He wasn't there, so Bitz thought it might help to throw a scare into Ginny so maybe she'd pass the fright on to Eddie. He'd shown her his gun and said he was looking for Eddie on account of a gambling debt Eddie owed his boss. He had left no doubt that she'd be a widow if the money wasn't paid by that night. It had scared her, all right. White-faced, she'd asked how she could get the money to Nick. Bitz gave her the address of a pool room in Nick's neighborhood. She'd gone down there with the money about ten o'clock that morning. One of Nick's boys was there. He took her to Nick.

But that still didn't explain how she got the money.

Bitz apologized politely for having caused Eddie this unnecessary trip. Eddie wondered a little hysterically if Bitz took his hat off before he shot people.

He grabbed a taxi for Lou's apartment. It was the early part of the afternoon by now. She was just getting up. She looked like a sleepy, tawny-haired Persian cat. Eddie Price could sure pick them. She had milky-white skin, a red splash of a mouth and smoky green eyes. The kind of a dame some guys shoot themselves over.

Lou agreed with Eddie's philosophy: nobody gives anybody anything. She wasn't giving anybody anything, either. She was like an expensive car, yours as long as you kept up the payments.

"Hello, honey," she yawned and wound herself around him.

Eddie peeled her arms from his neck. "Later, baby."

She frowned at him. "What's eatin' you? You're as white as a sheet of paper."

He shook his head. "I–I don't know. Something screwy is going on. I'm going to find out what, now. I just wanted to tell you to stick around the apartment. I may call you in an hour or so and tell you to pack. We may be leaving."

He took a taxi to the apartment. Ginny wasn't there. Playing nursemaid for one of the neighbor's kids again, probably. Why didn't they hire baby sitters?

He pried some ice cubes out of the refrigerator, dug out a bottle of gin. He was shaking so badly that the glass rattled against his teeth when he drank it.

He stood there in the kitchen, feet spread apart, jaws clamped together to keep his teeth from clicking.

There had to be an angle somewhere. Granted that she had somehow grabbed four thousand dollars out of thin air, she still wouldn't be giving that kind of money away. She had to have an angle. Nobody gives anybody anything! Especially not four thousand dollars. Not without having an angle.

Eddie suddenly knew that he was scared. What of, he wasn't yet sure. But he wished he'd never seen Ginny Potucek. He wished he'd never thought up this insurance deal. He wished to hell he could make himself run out of this apartment, not wait for her. But some force was holding him there.

He walked into the other room. It was hot that time of the afternoon. Everywhere you looked you could see Ginny. She'd made curtains for the windows, painted the drainboard, put shelf paper under the dishes. The goldfish bowl by the window, the pot of ivy, the picture on the wall, the embroidered bedspread, all of it was Ginny's doings. She'd made the squalid, two-room flat a home.

He sat on the edge of a chintz-covered chair. He tried to light a cigarette, but his fingers were trembling so, he fumbled around, scratching up half a book of matches before he finally got one going. Just then the buzzer sounded and he jumped, spilling the matches and the lighted cigarette down his shirt front.

He stood in front of the door for half a minute, breathing shakily before he could make his sweating palm turn the knob. He didn't recognize the man standing in the dark hallway. Sort of a young guy with an old face. Prematurely grey hair. "Mr. Price?" he asked.

"Yeah," Eddie gulped. ''What are you selling, friend?"

The man shook his head, a corner of his mouth lifting in a tired smile that slid right off again. "Your wife here?"

When Eddie shook his head, the fellow said, "Well, that might be better. You see, I'm her doctor. I made a call in this neighborhood and since 1 was this close, wanted to stop in and talk to her. But I think it would be better if I talked with you."

Eddie remembered him then. He was the sawbones Eddie'd gone to a couple of months back. The one who was treating Ginny.

Eddie offered to fix him a drink, but he shook his head and sat wearily in a chair. He looked all in. Eddie couldn't figure a guy wanting to be a sawbones in this neighborhood. Downtown, in the right place, with the right patients, it was probably a good racket that paid off. But not around here. Eddie guessed he was just one of those dumb guys that never amounted to anything.

The doc leaned forward, his hands on his knees. "Frankly, Mr. Price, I'm at a loss to understand why she decided against the operation at the last minute this way. This man I was sending her to has had marvelous results with his new method. I feel sure that she would have better than a fifty-fifty chance of complete recovery."

"Wait a minute!" Eddie spilled his drink all over his trousers, but he didn't notice. "What kind of operation?"

The sawbones frowned. "She hadn't told you? Perhaps she wanted to keep it from you. She called me early this morning. Told me to cancel everything. I had even bought the plane tickets. She was to fly to Chicago to this brain specialist some time this week."

Eddie whispered, "This–this operation. It costs a lot of dough?"

"Well, yes. The trip and all. But she told me she had enough money in the bank to cover everything. Several thousand dollars from a small legacy, plus money she'd saved while working. Frankly, I can't understand why she decided against it. Try to talk her into it, won't you? It's her only hope."

Long after the doctor had gone, Eddie sat in the quiet apartment, chain-smoking cigarettes. It got dark and still he sat there, not moving.

And then at last she came in. She snapped on the light and she gasped when she saw him. "Eddie, I didn't know you were home! I've been over with Mrs. Logan across the street. She hasn't been feeling well. I'll start supper right away." She headed for the kitchen.

He caught her arm. "Wait a minute. I want to talk to you."

She gave him the funny, crooked little smile she'd learned since they'd been married. "Yes, Mr. Husband. Have I done something wrong? You going to beat me?" She shook her head. "Eddie, your tie is crooked again."

He pushed her hand aside. "Why did you do it?" he asked in a hoarse croak that wasn't his own voice. "Why did you give Nick the money you needed for your operation? Why did you save my hide? *What was your angle?"*

There wasn't a drop of blood left in Ginny's face. Slowly, two large tears formed in her eyes and trickled down her cheeks. She kept looking up at him that way with her big, wide eyes. "Then you know," she whispered. "Eddie, you're hurting me."

He let go of her shoulders. His hair was glued to his sweating forehead. "Why? What do you want?"

"Want?" she repeated slowly. "Why, I wanted six more months with you, Eddie."

The tears were trickling down her cheeks and she went on talking. His plain little wife, Ginny Potucek. "I guess you don't know what it's like to be lonely, Eddie. All my life I've been lonely. I thought I was going to have to die alone. Then you came along and all of a sudden everything was wonderful. The things we did together. This apartment. Cooking meals for you. I learned how to laugh.

"Then that horrible man came this morning. He said he'd kill you, Eddie. I couldn't stand that, to be alone again. A whole lifetime wouldn't do me any good if you weren't along, Eddie. I'd rather have six more months with you."

The blood was pumping like turbines in Eddie's head. He looked down at her. At plain little Ginny Potucek Price with her faded blonde hair, her big, dark eyes, her pale lips. But she wasn't plain any more. Not to Eddie. There was a glow about her and she was the loveliest doll he'd ever known. More glamorous than Lou and all the other babes put together.

In that moment, Eddie knew the answer to a lot of things. He knew now why he hadn't been able to go through with killing her this morning. He knew why he'd been so scared when he came back to the apartment this afternoon. He'd been afraid of what he was going to find out about himself.

He knew that he, Eddie Price, was in love, too. The way you read about in books and he'd always laughed at. He was in love with his wife, Ginny.

Like she said, it had been wonderful, the few lousy shows they went to and the gin rummy they played in the apartment. More fun than all the night clubs he'd been to. Because maybe he'd been lonely, too, in a different way, before he married Ginny Potucek.

He knew what he was going to have to do now. And he wasn't scared any more. He was going to see that Ginny had her operation and that she got a chance for a better guy than Eddie Price. A guy she really deserved.

"Ginny," he said. Then he kissed her. Eddie guessed that was the closest he'd ever come to praying, that kiss.

Then he walked out of the apartment. He took a cab and gave the driver an address. Fifteen minutes later, he pulled up in front of Nick Specht's hideout. He walked into Nick's room and he wasn't afraid at all.

Nick was still playing solitaire. Bitz was sitting in a rocking chair, reading a newspaper. Nick's mouth dropped open. "What the hell do you want?"

Eddie picked up the telephone and dialed the police. He said carefully, "Get this the first time. There isn't going to be a repeat. You know that jewelry store stickup and the Johnny O'Malley murder? This is Eddie Price talking. I'm the one who shot O'Malley. Nick Specht engineered the stickup. You'll find him hid out at 744 East Water Street, if you hurry."

The two guns roared almost simultaneously. Nick and Bitz were both on their feet, shooting. Neither one missed.

Eddie didn't feel a thing. He just slipped off where it was warm and dark and safe. And, going, he thought it was nice about husband-and-wife family insurance policies. They paid off both ways. And now Ginny could have her operation.

So Eddie Price, who always figured nobody gives anybody anything, gave away his life…

About the Author

Charles Boeckman (often spelled "Charles Beckman, Jr." in story bylines) writes of himself:

I grew up during the Great Depression. We had enough to eat but no extra money for music lessons, nor did we have much for university tuition after high school. My mother did save enough to send me to a local junior college for a one-year business course.

What I got most out of that was advanced typing skills. By the end of the course I could type 100 words a minute without errors on a mechanical typewriter. (No electric typewriters or computers in those days.) My typing skills got me numerous part time jobs while I was learning to write short stories for money.

I also taught myself to play the saxophone and clarinet from fingering charts and listening to records. Music has always been an avocation, adding some income to what I earned writing short stories. I also studied, on my own, music theory and harmony, which enabled me to write arrangements for bands on which I played. Eventually, I had my own band. We played traditional New Orleans jazz. In 1990, I earned a star in the South Texas Music Walk of Fame after 70 years of playing professionally. My music has played a dual role in my life as my avocation and as the backdrop for some of the scenes in my stories. My jazz band still plays at the Texas jazz festival in October

When I was in high school, I made up my mind that when I graduated, I was going to find a profession that would give me the freedom to travel and spend time in all the big cities. I ran across a publication called the *Writer's Digest*. In it, I read that there were magazine publishers who paid money for short fiction stories. That was something my school teachers hadn't told me about.

Before television, people got their entertainment by reading short stories. The newsstands carried a great number of magazines that were published every month. There were many different story categories, such as suspense, western, adventure, romance, and science fiction. There were ten to fifteen stories in each magazine, and they sold for about 10 cents or 15 cents each. They were printed on cheap pulp paper and usually had garish, eye-catching covers. Because of the paper they were printed on, they were called The Pulps.

It was a large market, hungry for stories. They could pay only one cent a word to their writers. One could actually make a pretty good living writing for the pulp market if he or she could turn out a lot of stories quickly. At the same time, there were also the big, slick magazines such as *Saturday Evening Post*, *Colliers*, *Liberty* and others printed on more expensive, slick paper. They paid a lot more for stories but a writer had to be quite good to break into that market.

I started reading pulp stories when I was 10 years old. I mowed lawns to buy the magazines. Fortunately, they were cheap, ten or fifteen cents for a magazine that had ten or fifteen stories.

By the time I graduated from high school in 1938, I had learned enough music to earn money playing at country dance halls on weekends. Those were the days of the big band era, bands like Benny Goodman, Duke Ellington, Count Basie, Artie Shaw and many others. They were on the radio every night and often in short movies.

When I left home in the 1940's, I had $30 in my pocket, a used portable typewriter, and a clarinet and saxophone I'd bought at a pawn shop. I grew up in Texas and had always liked the Gulf coast. So I took the bus to Corpus Christi. The next morning I had found a part time

Charles Boeckman
Musician and pulp author

"A Hot Lick for Doc"
Justice, November 1955

"Speak of the Dead"
Famous Detective, June 1955

job and landed a music job playing with a band on weekends.

My goal was to begin selling stories to the pulp magazine market. I wrote suspense and western stories at night and in my spare time. They all came back with rejection slips.

But then in 1945, I received a very nice letter from the legendary editor, Mike Tilden, who edited *Detective Tales*, a popular suspense magazine by Popular Publications. Mike's letter informed me that he was buying my story, "Strictly Poison," and asked for more. ("Strictly Poison" is the first story in this collection, and Bold Venture publisher Rich Harvey decided to name the anthology after it.)

I had broken into the pulp market! After that, I turned out suspense and western stories and sold all of them. I quit my day job and realized my dream of visiting the big cities, New York, San Francisco, New Orleans. My favorite was Manhattan, where I became friends with many of my editors, such as Jake Jakobsson, who edited *New Detective*, and Harry Widmer, an editor of Popular Publication's westerns. I've already mentioned Mike Tilden.

Television dealt a death blow to the pulps of the 1940's. In the 1950's publishers changed their format to a stapled booklet such as was used by *Alfred Hitchcock's Mystery Magazine*. Some in that category were *Pursuit*, *Justice*,

Malcolm's and others. I had stories in all of them and some of the stories are in this anthology. One of the first in that new format was *Manhunt*.

My story, "I'll Make the Arrest," was in *Manhunt's* first issue, dated January 1953. (Mickey Spillane had the lead novel.) It was picked up by Screen Gems for *Celebrity Playhouse*, a television anthology series broadcast on the NBC network from 1955-1956.

After I began selling stories regularly, I divided my time between Manhattan and Corpus Christi. In New York, I leased a neat apartment a block from the west side of Central Park. In the fall I saw all the Broadway shows, including *My Fair Lady* on opening week with the original cast.

In the early 1950's, several top pulp writers settled in St. Petersburg, Florida. In this group were Day Keene, Talmage Powell, Harry Whittington, Gil Brewer, and others. I spent several weeks with them. One evening a week, we'd gather at Day Keene's home to gossip about editors, writers, and the pulp story writing business in general. It was fun making friends with such well-known writers.

While I was there, Talmage and his wife Mildred took me to a section of Tampa called Ybor City, a settlement of Cuban immigrants. I used that for the background for story you will find in this collection.

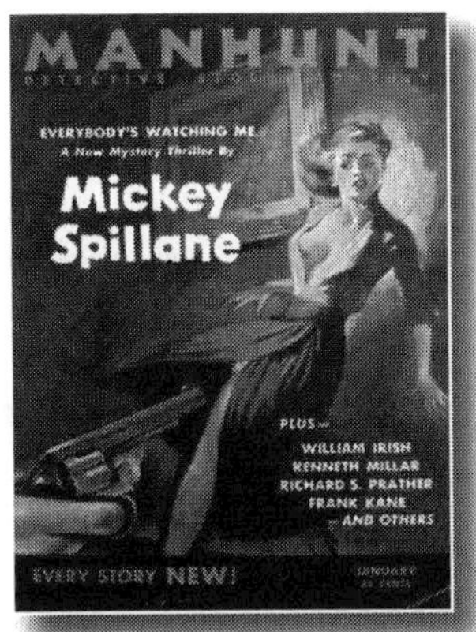

"I'll Make the Arrest"
Manhunt, January 1953.

"Ybor City"
Manhunt, June 1953.

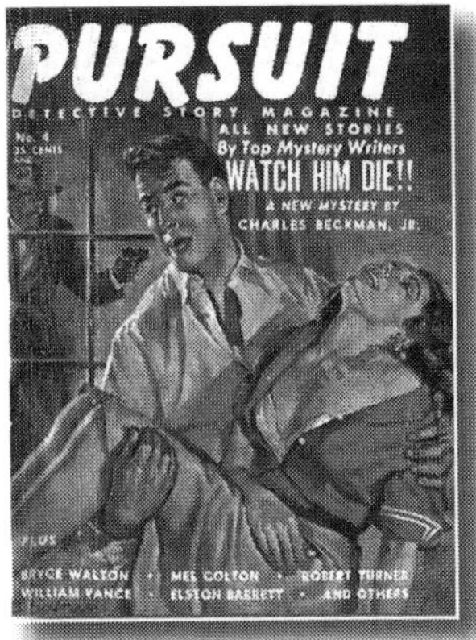

"Watch Him Die"
Pursuit, July 1954.

"Mr. Banjo" was published in *Alfred Hitchcock's Mystery Magazine* and picked for a place in *The Best Detective Stories of The Year*, 1976.

I was a swinging bachelor for quite a few years, and then I met Patti Kennelly, the love of my life. We have been married for 47 years and as much in love as newlyweds.

When we met, Patti was teaching school, but she had an interest in writing. She has a natural talent and, after I gave her a little coaching, she was getting her writing published. Then, Patti and I collaborated on 26 romance novels for Silhouette Publications. After Harlequin took over the Silhouette line, they sold rights to our stories all over the world. Altogether, Harlequin sold some two million copies of our titles.

About 30 years later, after we had the rights to those books returned to us, we sold nine titles to a Japanese publisher for their line of picture books, called Manga.

Who knew that our writing from those long ago days would have a new audience decades later? I surely didn't.

The same is true for pulp stories from the early part of the last century. Although I had made an on-line acquaintance with a well-known writer who collects pulp magazines, I had no idea that an active, loyal fan base existed for any type of short stories, much less for pulps.

Leave it to Patti, my most devoted fan and self-appointed publicity agent, to be wandering around on the Internet some time ago when she decided, on a whim, to key in some variations of the words, "pulp aficionados." What she found astounded her.

There existed an entire subculture of pulp readers and writers who love the genre. She learned that collectors have bookshelves stuffed with those old pulp magazines. They buy, sell, and trade them, and are writing original pulp-style stories just for the fun of it. We made contacts with some of those individuals, and I developed a renewed emotional connection to my writings of yore. So, we decided that it was time to get out all the old, brittle copies of my pulp short stories that I had boxed up decades ago, and do something with them.

Thus, the idea for this anthology was born. We hope that pulp fans will find it, read it, and enjoy it.

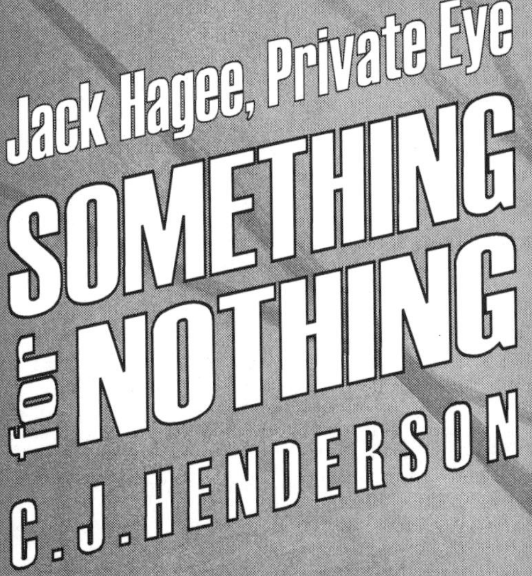
Jack Hagee, Private Eye
SOMETHING
for
NOTHING
C.J. HENDERSON

BOLD
VENTURE
boldventurepress.com

Made in the USA
San Bernardino, CA
25 June 2015